ABOVE AND BEYOND

TWIST OF FATE #4

LUCY LENNOX
SLOANE KENNEDY

Copyright © 2020 by Lucy Lennox & Sloane Kennedy

Cover Images: ©Wander Aguiar

Cover Design: © Cate Ashwood Designs

Copyediting by Courtney Bassett

All rights reserved.

No part of this book may be reproduced in any form or by any electronic or mechanical means, including information storage and retrieval systems, without written permission from the author, except for the use of brief quotations in a book review.

ISBN-13:

9781660839001

ABOVE AND BEYOND

Lucy Lennox

Sloane Kennedy

ACKNOWLEDGMENTS

We would like to thank Claudia, Kylee, Courtney, Victoria, and Lori for their help in bringing Above and Beyond to life.

Also, thank you to Michael Dean who is currently creating the audio version of Above and Beyond.

CHAPTER 1

ZACH

My brother was a dead man.

"Just stop by and check on him, Zach. As a favor to me. It'll take five minutes."

Those were the words Jake had spoken to me shortly after my plane had landed in Missoula, Montana. The *him* in question was the son of my brother's best friend, Xander, and Xander's husband, Bennett. But the five minutes had quickly turned into ten, then fifteen.

A brief glance at my watch was proof that yet another fifteen minutes had gone by.

Which meant I'd been staring at the kid for *half a fucking hour*.

It took everything in me not to yell out of my truck's window and demand that the kid go inside already.

Because maybe then I could finally take my eyes off of him.

I couldn't make sense of how much he'd grown up in just the past couple of years. When I'd first met him, he'd been only fifteen and he'd worn his innocence and sweetness on his sleeve, along with his heart. Back then, I'd wanted to tell him how dangerous a thing that was... how exposed it left him to people, and to men specifically, who'd take pleasure in using his naivety against him for their own gain.

Men like me.

No, I wasn't one of those types who *intentionally* sought to use and to hurt, but I was just as guilty of leaving shattered lives in my wake. Thankfully, I'd learned my lesson pretty young and hadn't since repeated the mistakes of the past. Any girl or guy I got involved with knew the score. Sex was just that—*sex*. And it rarely went beyond one encounter.

I'd also gotten better at knowing if a potential partner could handle my rules.

I knew without a shadow of a doubt that Lucky Reed was one of those people who most definitely wouldn't be able to.

When he'd been fifteen and clearly crushing on me, it hadn't been an issue. I never would've touched any minor and had gone out of my way to discourage sweet little Lucky's undeserved adoration. Problem was, the kid had been persistent and by the time he'd reached eighteen and was a college freshman, my brain had tried to convince me that the teenager was legal and that all bets were off. It had taken an emotionally charged encounter with him one Christmas for me to realize that my iron will to not touch him had taken on some pretty serious chinks.

I physically shook off the memory of the things I'd said to Lucky back then. It wasn't one of my proudest moments. In fact, that night had been a harsh reminder of why I'd pulled away from my friends and family so long ago.

After reuniting with my family in the wake of my brother Jake's reappearance after having been missing for several years, I'd used my run-in with Lucky as an excuse to keep my distance once again. But the teenager had been only part of the reason I'd started finding excuses to stay away from the little town of Haven, Colorado.

My brother and parents had just assumed it was my most recent deployment that had kept me busy during the holidays and special events. They had no way of knowing that I'd intentionally turned down any opportunities to return stateside for visits and that I'd actually finished my most recent tour of duty six months early after damage to my knee had ended my career in the army.

At the mere thought of the incident that had changed everything for me, I felt my chest tighten and my breath shorten.

Not here. Not now.

I closed my eyes and tried to focus my thoughts on something more pleasant than the day I'd nearly lost my life... the day too many of my brothers-in-arms had lost their lives. I told my brain not to go where it usually did when episodes like this started to happen, but as usual, my rampant mind ignored the order and focused on the one person it wasn't supposed to.

You've got this, Zach.

The memory of Lucky's gentle encouragement helped ease some of the pressure in my chest. I let my mind drift back to that moment on the snow-covered hill near my brother's cabin when a still fifteen-year-old Lucky had been teaching me to ski. The rest of the family had been gathered in Jake and Oz's—his now husband—cabin for Thanksgiving.

I'd agreed to the impromptu ski lesson after Lucky had learned that I'd never skied before but had always wanted to try it. It'd been just me and the teenager and the stillness of the trees as heavy flakes of snow had fallen around us. It had been one of the easiest, purest moments of my life. I'd forgotten about needing to keep the teen at arm's length and had simply enjoyed his company. There'd been nothing untoward about the encounter. It had just been two people having fun and living in the moment.

Easy.

As I remembered the end of our lesson and the snowball fight that had broken out between us, my breaths began to come easier. I was leaning back against the seat of the truck but was too tired to move beyond turning my head just enough to see if the object of my memories was still where he'd been when the unexpected episode had begun. I had a habit of losing time when the panic attacks occurred. I knew that was what they were, but I wasn't particularly interested in giving them much thought beyond that. Words like trauma, survivor's guilt and PTSD had been thrown my way countless times by all sorts of medical professionals, but I cut those conversations off at the knees before they could really get going.

Lucky was still sitting on a bench outside the campus's student center. I let my eyes drink him in for a moment and then remembered why I wanted to murder my brother.

The kid before me was no longer that. At twenty, the only way to describe him was absolutely stunning. His baby face had morphed into gorgeous features that included high cheekbones and what looked like the most beautiful set of lips on anyone, man or woman, that I'd ever seen. Granted, I was too far away to see things like his eyes, but I'd memorized those a long time ago. Chocolate brown with flecks of gold and green in them. And long, thick lashes that drew you in and forced you to ponder everything the mirrors to his soul were saying.

The clothes he was wearing were loose-fitting, so I couldn't really make out if he'd grown into his body more in the last couple of years. My dick didn't really seem to care. Nor did it seem to care that the young man before me was practically related to me. Hell, he called my brother *Uncle* Jake. Fortunately, he'd never called me that, but maybe it would've helped if he had.

I shook my head as my cock thickened in my pants. Yeah, no way being called Uncle Zach would have changed anything except to make me feel like even more of a letch the few times I'd allowed myself to fantasize about the teen once he'd become legal.

I silently cursed my brother again as I watched Lucky interact with his friends. He laughed freely with the guys and girls surrounding him and I felt this odd sense of rightness go through me. The last time I'd seen him had been that fateful Christmas Eve after he'd turned eighteen. The memory I'd been left with had been his clear humiliation along with the tears that had slipped down his cheeks as he'd tried to calmly turn and walk away from me after I'd turned down his inexperienced advances. Lucky had let out this god-awful sob right before he'd reached the hallway that led to the back of the hotel his fathers owned, and I'd sworn I'd seen him take off running across the backyard toward his family's house behind the hotel a few moments later.

While I was glad to see him so light and free among his friends today, it didn't lessen the memory of the things I'd said to him, of the things he'd said to me two years ago.

Since Lucky was clearly fine and I could honestly report that back to my brother, I reached for the keys in the ignition with the intent of starting my truck and heading to my hotel. I was just about to turn over the ignition when I glanced one last time in Lucky's direction, hoping to absorb just a little bit more of his happiness so I could tuck it away in my mind in case I'd ever need it in the future. My fingers stilled as my eyes didn't fall on a smiling Lucky. In fact, he was no longer sitting on the bench at all.

I hated that my breath caught in my throat a little as I quickly searched him out. My relief at finding him standing by a tree a few hundred feet from his friends was short-lived though.

Because he was no longer smiling... and he wasn't alone.

I didn't recognize the guy who was with him as one of the friends he'd just been chatting with. He looked to be about the same age as Lucky, but he had a much heavier build and stood a good four or five inches taller. I had no way of hearing what the pair were talking about, but it didn't really matter because, as always, Lucky's expression spoke volumes. He was clearly uncomfortable and had trouble maintaining eye contact with the guy looming over him. The only thing that kept me in my truck was the fact that there were other students in the vicinity. But none of them seemed to notice the way Lucky shrank back against the tree behind him. I supposed that to most people, it looked like nothing more than two friends having a conversation, but Lucky's body language said it all—he wanted to be anywhere but there. And while the guy with him wasn't doing anything outwardly obvious to stake his claim on Lucky, my instincts were telling me that the way he kept leaning in and appearing to keep his voice low at the same time that he crowded Lucky, staking his claim was exactly what he was doing.

I was reaching for the door handle before I could think better of it, but Lucky chose that moment to twist away from the guy. He began hurrying back to his friends, but I kept my gaze on the man who'd been hassling him. I knew that look... whatever conversation had been happening between the two, the asshole clearly wasn't finished having his say.

My eyes shifted back to Lucky as he said his goodbyes to his friends. The smile on his face was as wide as ever, but now it looked forced. None of his friends seemed to notice the newfound tension in his frame.

Lucky gave his friends a wave and then began heading in the opposite direction of the quad where the encounter with the other guy had taken place. Since I couldn't really follow in my truck without drawing attention to myself, I waited a moment before getting out. I figured Lucky was on his way back to his dorm or apartment. The chances of anything happening to him in broad daylight were slim to none, but I didn't give a shit. The guy who'd been hassling Lucky had disappeared, so I wasn't about to let Lucky out of my sight. Once he was safe in his place, then I'd go. I'd send a text to my brother telling him the kid was just fine and then I'd seek out the privacy of my hotel. And if I happened upon a bar on the way, then so be it.

I might not have initially been particularly interested in finding some guy or girl to spend an hour or two with, but things had changed.

I wasn't proud of the fact that after seeing little Lucky Reed, who wasn't so little anymore but still looked just as sweet and innocent and even more untouchable than ever, I needed a drink and a fuck, preferably in that order. It was what it was. I wasn't in the habit of lying to myself and there was no point in starting now. The gorgeous Lucky was still miles out of my reach, but that didn't mean I couldn't find a stand-in to lose myself in for a bit.

A beautiful brown-haired, brown-eyed, not-so-innocent stand-in who knew how the game was played...

I was so caught up in the idea of finding a Lucky look-alike to slake my needs that I lost track of Lucky for several minutes and ended up having to double back a few times in my search for him. I actually blew out a sigh of relief when I finally found him in a small, isolated parking lot. But that relief was short-lived when I saw who Lucky was with. The guy who'd been harassing Lucky only a few minutes earlier was once again in his face but this time he had Lucky pressed up against a small gray sedan. And there was no doubt about his claim of ownership now as he pinned Lucky to the side of the vehicle with his body. If there was a conversation happening, I didn't hear it because all I saw was red and the only sound in my ears was the white noise that usually accompanied me when my body and mind made the shift to predator mode.

In the moments it took me to close the distance between myself and the two young men, I changed my priorities for the rest of the day.

Imparting a meaningful lesson with my fists on the pushy asshole first, then a hard fuck with that stand-in, and finally enough drinks to make me forget all of it.

Especially the young man who was about to see I most definitely wasn't any kind of hero.

CHAPTER 2

LUCKY

One minute I was contemplating throwing a punch at Davis Teasley and the next, someone was doing it for me. It all happened before I could tell the persistent asshole to fuck off, much less draw my arm back the way I itched to.

Suddenly there was a scramble of bodies shoving me even harder against the car. The sounds of fists and grunts drowned out the sound of my gasp as I struggled to catch my breath in the press of larger bodies.

"Stop!" I tried shouting, but I couldn't draw in enough air to yell the word like I wanted to. So instead, I grabbed for the back of the stranger's shirt to pull him off Davis. I might not have liked the asshole, but he didn't necessarily deserve to get jumped in broad daylight by a complete stranger.

When the man took a long enough break from whaling on Davis to glance at me, I gasped again like a melodramatic idiot. Familiar hazel eyes peered at me with an even more familiar sparking temper in them.

Zach.

"What the fuck?" I blurted. "Zach?" My brain scrambled to fit the information into some kind of logical order. What was Jake's brother doing in Montana? And why was he beating up on my...

Ex.

Oh hell. This wasn't good.

"Stop," I said again, only this time I almost growled it. "Get the fuck off him, Zach."

Not surprisingly, Zach didn't release Davis instantly. An almost violent tremor went through me when Zach's flinty eyes hardened even more. He was still holding Davis by the front of his shirt. The younger man's mouth was bleeding and he had a red mark on the side of his face that was most likely going to turn into an ugly bruise. But it was like my ex had disappeared and it was just me and Zach as we stared at each other. It was moments like this that had gotten me into trouble with the gorgeous man so many times in the past. Too many times I'd imagined the looks to be something they weren't. I wasn't going to make that mistake again.

No fucking way.

Zach chose that moment to let his eyes roam the length of my body. My breath caught in my throat, and I was once again transported back to the night I'd bared my soul to yet another man who hadn't wanted me.

"I love you, Zach. I always—"

"Don't. Even if I were interested, I don't fuck around with kids. Go chase someone else for a while... I'm getting sick of you always being right there every time I come out here to hang out with my brother."

The familiar sour taste of bile crawled up the back of my throat as my stomach dropped out. The instinct to flee was as strong now as it had been then, and I longed to tear my eyes from Zach's.

Davis chose that moment to open his fat fucking mouth, which I was oddly grateful for. "Lucky, call the police! I'm being robbed. Don't just stand there. Do something!"

I turned the humiliation I was feeling into something else and threw it at my jackass of an ex. "You're not being robbed. You're being taught a fucking lesson." I wanted to add that Zach was damn good at teaching the kind of lesson you'd never forget, but with Zach's eyes still pinning mine, I was hopelessly ensnared.

Davis shook himself out of Zach's grip and hopped two giant steps away from the angry Army Ranger. "What the fuck? Who the hell are you? Lucky, sweetie, do you know this man?" Davis tried to shift closer to me, his hand extended like he was going to reach for me again, but Zach stepped between us.

The move seemed to unlock my brain.

"Why are you here?" I asked the muscled military man as I stepped around him to move closer to Davis. I had no interest in being anywhere near my ex, but I knew overprotective behavior when I saw it. After all, I'd had years of watching my fathers and uncles chase off potential guys they'd decided hadn't been good enough for me. But having Zach display the same behavior and knowing it was out of loyalty to his brother and my fathers gave me a new sense of courage. "What the hell's wrong with you?" I bit out.

Zach's attention shifted to me and his eyes once again roamed over every inch of me like a goddamned caress. I suppressed a shudder because I did not fucking care. At all. I knew he'd never look at me that way. He was most likely checking me for injury the way he'd been taught to in the service.

"Are you hurt? Did he fucking touch you?" Zach's growly voice washed over me as he once again began scanning my body like he was looking for something.

"None of your goddamned business," I snapped at him because my body was very inconveniently responding to his perusal. "Answer my fucking question."

"Watch your mouth," he bit back. "What would your dads say if they heard that kind of language out of you?"

I stared at him in shock, ignoring what his commanding tone was doing to the lower half of my body. I had no clue what possessed me to do it, but I stepped closer to him and dropped my voice as I said, "Why? Because I'm still just a kid, right?" Zach's eyes flashed with some unnamed emotion as I sneered the word "kid." This time, he was the one to look away and I grabbed onto that like it was the biggest win of my entire life. It was Christmas Eve all over again, but I was no longer some dumb kid declaring his undying love beneath a stupid sprig of mistletoe. I moved until I was practically flush against Zach's body and whispered, "Maybe someone needs to spank me so I learn my lesson... you know, so I respect my *elders*."

I swore I saw Zach's throat struggle to swallow, but I couldn't be sure. I'd hoped the jab at his age would do the same thing to him that him always referring to me as "kid" did to me, but instead of moving away from me, Zach pressed his body closer to mine until there was only the tiniest whisper of space between us.

His warm breath washed over my temple as he dropped his mouth closer to my ear. Butterflies danced in my belly and heat crawled beneath my skin in anticipation. I forgot all about where we were or that even if this man hadn't been straighter than an arrow, he wouldn't have been interested in me.

"Maybe they should," Zach murmured in my ear. Every nerve in my body lit up in response and it was all I could do to bite back a moan as my dick hardened uncomfortably in my pants. Zach's mouth was *right there*... if I moved my head just a little—

"Um, hello?" I heard a familiar voice call out.

Right.

Davis.

Damn.

My body began shaking with thwarted desire as Zach stepped back and then moved around me. "Shut the fuck up, you little shit," he practically snarled. Davis threw his hands up as Zach began moving toward him. I grabbed Zach's arm to stop him because he looked pissed enough to tear Davis limb from limb. Davis worked out religiously in a gym to maintain his killer body, but he was no match for the career military man. I ignored the electricity that fired up my arm as I moved between Davis and Zach again.

"What are you doing here, Zach?" I asked. My anger had dissolved and all I felt was really tired.

"I'm here for a job," Zach responded.

"The Rangers don't have any bases here," I retorted before I could think better of it. "The only military installation is Malmstrom Air Force Base and that's in Great Falls. There's an army corps recruitment center here, but unless you fucked a general's wife or something, I doubt you'd be demoted to pinching students from the university."

Zach's eyebrows had lifted briefly at my comment about fucking a general's wife and I felt my cheeks heat. I could only mentally pray that the man didn't ask how I knew so much about the army's presence in the great state of Montana in the first place. But by the time I was speaking, his expression had shifted and he looked almost... broken.

What the hell?

"Zach," I began when he didn't say anything. I made the mistake of reaching for his hand to get his attention. He jerked back at my touch and his eyes went wild for the briefest of moments. He scanned the area around us like he didn't know where he was.

"Zach," I repeated softly in the hopes of getting his attention back on me. I had no clue what was going on with him, but I'd never seen him so rattled and seemingly confused. When his gaze finally landed on mine, he pulled in a deep breath and I saw some of the tension in his frame leach from his body.

"Different kind of job," was all he said.

My gut was telling me he wasn't going to expound on his comment so I said, "But what are you doing here on campus? Did my fathers ask you to check on me?"

His non-answer was answer enough.

I let out a sigh. I loved my fathers more than anything on the planet, but I couldn't help but be a little hurt that they'd sent someone to check on me. I knew part of it was my fault because I hadn't been going home as often as I had during my first year of college, but I had a good reason for it.

It just wasn't any kind of reason I could tell them about.

I'd hoped that when the twins had arrived, my fathers would be too busy to check up on me as often as they did, but apparently that wasn't happening. Part of me was unreasonably glad about that because as much as Xander and Bennett Reed had treated me like their own son in the years since they'd adopted me, I still occasionally had this fear that they'd find me lacking and finally cut me loose. I'd confessed my feelings to my uncle Aiden once, but he'd reassured me that I was and always would be their kid. He'd said that it didn't matter how far away life took me as I got older… Haven, Colorado would always be my home and my fathers would always be the family that fate had given me. I hadn't been sure whether or not to believe him, but my first year away at school had proven to me that my parents weren't going anywhere. I'd gotten calls and texts on a near daily basis, and I doubted any other student on campus received more care packages than I did.

But admittedly, my fathers had a habit of wanting to protect me just a little too much sometimes, and the arrival of my little brother and sister hadn't diminished that in any kind of way. So it wasn't really a revelation that they'd sent someone to check on me, especially after I'd gone a little more silent than usual. Between keeping my former relationship with Davis a secret, not going home for the past couple of summers and being tight-lipped about *why* I hadn't gone home, I should have been more surprised that it had taken them so long to send a warm body to make sure I was okay. But sending Zach, of all people? As if I needed the older man to see me as a child any more than he already did.

"Tell them I'm okay," I said dismissively. "I can take care of myself," I added over my shoulder as I turned to deal with Davis. The last message had been more for Zach than my fathers.

Davis once again picked the worst timing. "This a friend of your dads? What, they're sending their goons to check up on you or something? Jesus, Lucky, when are you going to grow up? The stupid nickname, your daddies' short leash… do you still need them to change your diapers too?" he snarked. "You better not have told them about me!"

Zach made a move toward Davis. "Or what?" he asked. The barely leashed anger in his voice had my insides going all warm and gooey even if they shouldn't have.

Davis rolled his eyes, but I knew him well enough to know he was doing all he could not to piss himself. He was far too soft to ever be able to hold his own against someone like Zach. The soldier was solid as a damned rock and tough as nails.

"Just go, Davis," I said with a sigh. "I told you it was over and I meant it."

Davis's eyes bore into mine but I barely noticed because Zach was practically pressed against my back. I couldn't help but inhale the combination of masculine sweat and woodsy shampoo coming off Zach's body. So help me, if I let out even a whimper of need, I was going to beat myself silly or find someone to do it for me at the gym.

"It's far from over, Lucky. We're going to fix this," Davis promised.

His empty promises no longer had any impact on me. And something about having Zach at my back reminded me why messing around with Davis had been such a monumental waste of time.

"Maybe fix it with Natalie instead," I suggested with more anger than I'd intended. "Since she's the one carrying your fucking baby."

So maybe I hadn't stayed as calm as I'd hoped. The last thing I needed was for Zach to report back to my dads that I'd made such a big mistake. But the words were out there, and clearly Zach had heard since his entire body went rigid at the word "baby."

"I told you there's no baby," Davis said before taking a breath and pasting on a reptilian smile. "It's all a big misunderstanding. You'll see. I'll text you, babe."

This time there was no verbal warning. Zach merely reached past me to grab Davis, causing the other man to jump back in fright. I bit my tongue against a laugh as I put my arm out to stop Zach from snagging my idiot ex.

"Go, Davis. My arm is getting tired and my daddies' *goon* seems extra irritable today."

As my stupid ex-boyfriend—if you could even call it that since we'd never gotten past me giving Davis furtive hand and blowjobs when my roommate was at work—bolted to his car, more memories of the last time I'd seen Zach pinballed through my brain. The brief taste I'd had of him was as fresh now as it'd been then, and it was all I could do not to pull his arm around my waist and lean back into him. I could practically feel his broad chest supporting me as I tilted my head back in invitation...

The squealing of Davis's tires as his car screeched out of the university parking lot brought me back to the present and I quickly stepped away from Zach and turned around to face him. I was about to lay into him for having intervened in the first place when I saw a familiar figure striding toward us.

"Oh shit," I muttered as I recognized the unleashed fury in my best friend's eyes. Min, or Minna as she was known to everyone else, had clearly seen most, if not all, of what had happened. Her expression of outrage was much like the one she'd worn two years earlier after I'd run to her house to hide out from my parents and uncles after my run-in with Zach on Christmas Eve. I felt like I was right back there in that crowded closet full of my best friend's familiar oversized hoodies and hiking boots, lamenting what a fool I was and what horrible luck I had with men.

Minna raised an eyebrow and glanced at the tall soldier standing next to me, the man I hadn't seen since that humiliating night.

"You going to introduce me to your guard dog?" she asked as she took a step toward us. I wasn't quite sure what she was playing at since she knew exactly who Zach was. They hadn't officially met but she'd been at the Christmas Eve party. She'd even helped me come up with my stupid plan to seduce the older man.

"Minna Pedersen, this is Zach Warner, Jake's brother," I muttered.

Zach held out a hand while sizing up the five-foot-nothing brunette. "You don't look Norwegian."

Min barked out a laugh. "Good catch. Unfortunately, my big brothers got the tall blond genes and I got the shit runty ones from some Hungarian offshoot no one talks about." I watched her expression turn frighteningly calculating before she added the kicker. "But man, you should see my brothers. Gorgeous specimens. At least that's what everyone says. My girlfriends all curse the fact they're both into guys. But not everyone minds that. Right, Lucky?"

I thought of her idiot brothers who were still in high school. She jokingly called them her big brothers only because of their height, but they'd always been a pain in both our asses and dumb as a box of rocks. Between the two of them, they were lucky if they could come up with one brain.

But I played along. I knew better than to contradict her when she was clearly up to something. Whatever it was, there was no chance of it working on Zach.

I made a sound that wasn't exactly an agreement, but it had Zach's eyes narrowing right before he turned them back on me. "Stay away from that prick. I don't know what his deal is, but—"

The way he gave the order like there was never any doubt I'd follow it had me seeing red. I cut him off with, "But it's none of your business? Agreed. M'kay thanks bye." I grabbed Min's elbow and steered her back toward the center of campus with the hopes she'd forgive a little manhandling if I bought her a coffee and her favorite cookie at the Drip.

"Lucky, stop."

Min let out a squeak at the same time my body immediately obeyed the deep command and skidded to a stop. I didn't bother turning around to look at him.

"What?" I forced out through clenched teeth.

He stepped up behind me until I felt the barest hint of stubble against the shell of one ear. I squeezed my eyes closed and prayed to every earth nymph and wood sprite I'd ever called on for safety in the wilderness. *Please don't let me pop a boner. Please don't let me pop a—*

"Stay out of trouble, kid," he said in a low rumble that made me instantly sprout wood. Fucker.

"I'm not a fucking kid," I hissed back, but by the time I got my body under control enough to turn around to make sure he'd heard me, he was already gone.

"Thank god," I muttered, though my words were more to convince Minna I was just fine because I wasn't up for one of her lectures on why falling for gorgeous, older, completely unattainable men was not really a good thing.

But inside, it was another word entirely that kept playing on a loop as I tried to deal with the disappointment that Zach was once again gone from my life.

Damn.

CHAPTER 3

ZACH

"He's fine, Jake," I said tiredly as I reached up from the steering wheel to rub the spot between my eyes that had been pounding like a mother all afternoon. I'd gotten used to the headaches in the past six months, but I still wasn't very good at figuring out how to keep them from turning into full-on migraines. The doctors who'd declared the headaches a side effect of the head injury I'd suffered had told me all the party lines like needing to reduce stress and getting enough sleep to keep the pain manageable, but it was all just a bunch of psychobabble as far as I was concerned. I'd seen countless members of my unit suffer far worse injuries and live with them each and every day.

A little paltry head pain was nothing compared to what many of the men I'd served with and who'd also managed to survive the bloodshed dealt with.

"Is he *fine* like you?" my brother asked softly.

I let out a little sigh. It shouldn't have surprised me that my big brother had his suspicions about me. It also shouldn't have surprised me that Jake wouldn't have been satisfied with my simple text saying Lucky was fine.

I debated how much to say to Jake as I considered my run-in with

Lucky and his boyfriend. My fingers automatically clenched as I remembered the sight of the larger man pinning Lucky against the car. That memory inadvertently led to ones that were nearly as disturbing.

Like how good Lucky had felt pressed up against me.

Or the images that had gone through my head when he'd made the comment about someone needing to spank him.

My body began to react all over again. "Look, I did what you asked and checked on him. He seems okay. Seems to have a lot of friends and he looks…"

"Looks what?" I heard Jake ask but my tongue felt heavy as I remembered how fit Lucky's body had felt beneath his clothing and how vibrant and passionate his eyes had been as he'd stood toe to toe with me.

Beautiful.

"Healthy," I blurted.

"Healthy?" Jake asked in confusion.

I wanted to pound my head against the dashboard. "Yeah, um, he looks like he's getting enough to eat," I added lamely.

Stop talking, Zach. Just. Stop. Talking.

"That's good," Jake responded awkwardly. "But I think his fathers are a bit more concerned about other things."

"What things?" I asked. I closed my eyes and tried to quietly take in a few deep breaths because my headache was getting worse. Why the hell hadn't I just gone back to the hotel like I'd told Tag I was going to? My friend hadn't pushed me into going out for drinks like we'd originally planned, which I'd been grateful for. But instead of calling it a day and crashing in bed until my headache passed, I was exactly where I shouldn't have been.

In front of Lucky's goddamn apartment.

"He's just been… distant," Jake said carefully.

"He's a junior in college. I think part of the job description is to be distant."

I waited for my brother to shoot me a smart-ass comeback, but he remained silent. "What?" I asked. "What aren't you telling me?"

When he didn't respond, I said, "Jake."

"You weren't around to see it, Zach, but Lucky's got these fears..."

"What fears?" I asked. Pain momentarily forgotten, I leaned forward in my seat and wrapped my free hand around the truck's steering wheel.

"After his fathers first got him, he was always afraid of being sent back to his mother. At first, he thought Xander and Bennett would be the ones to change their mind about adopting him. Then after he got settled with them, he'd have nightmares about being given back to his mom and whatever piece of shit boyfriend or pimp she had at the time. He did better for a while but then something happened after he turned eighteen—maybe he thought being a legal adult meant his fathers would kick him out or something, I don't know—anyway, he went through a rough patch. He came home a lot the first year of school but then spent the past two summers working in Yellowstone, only coming home on the big holidays. He's not coming home this summer either. Xander and Bennett are worried that the twins' arrival is bringing back Lucky's fears of being abandoned."

My fingers had tightened considerably on the steering wheel of my truck, but when my brother mentioned something happening to Lucky after he'd turned eighteen, it felt like little daggers were being plunged into my temple.

What if *I'd* been what had happened to Lucky? Since my brother hadn't confronted me about what had happened between me and Lucky on Christmas Eve, I'd assumed the teen hadn't told anyone. But what if my rejection had brought back painful emotions from his past?

The pain in my head began to build to the point that my stomach began to roll.

"Look, Jake, he seemed okay. Really. If I thought you had anything to worry about, I'd tell you." My words were the truth. While the incident with his ex had clearly upset him, Lucky had seemed more angry and annoyed than anything else. And he sure as shit hadn't seemed upset when he'd stood his ground with me.

"Yeah, honey, it's Zach," I heard my brother say. There was a pause and then Jake said, "Zach, hang on, Oz wants to say hi."

Before I could protest, the call switched to a video chat which I had no choice but to answer. I pulled in a breath and tried to steady my expression. The last thing I needed was for my doctor brother to figure out I wasn't feeling my best at the moment.

I reluctantly hit the button to accept the call. My brother-in-law's features filled the camera frame. I usually didn't go for "pretty" men, but there was no denying that Jake had found himself a gorgeous specimen of a man in the model-turned-fashion-designer. But as stunning as Oz was on the outside, his physical looks had nothing on how beautiful he was on the inside. My brother had struck pure gold the moment he'd met the fiery young man on the side of a snow-covered mountain road.

"Zachary, sweetie, I love you like I love Dolce's spring line, but Boo and I have a bone to pick with you." Before I could respond, a face with bug eyes and a head covered in tufts of snow-white fur entered the frame. The ugly little dog's mug had me forgetting my pain for a moment.

"Hey, Oz," I said. "I'm sorry for whatever I did, but can we lay off the close-ups of your girl? Her unique beauty is better appreciated from afar."

The camera shifted back to Oz. He shook his head at me. "Boo's going to make you pay for that next time you visit," he said. "And *I'm* going to make you pay for the sleepless nights you're putting my husband through... and I'm not talking about the good kind of sleepless nights, either."

Guilt went through me at Oz's words. I heard my brother say his husband's name. The image on the phone switched to a shot of the floor, so I used the moment to get control of myself. When the phone was righted, Jake was holding it and he had his husband pressed up against his side on the couch. Boo was curled up on Jake's lap.

"Sorry, Zach," Oz said softly as his sad eyes met mine. I felt like even more of a bastard when my brother leaned over to press a kiss to Oz's temple. It was rare to see my brother-in-law looking so down.

My gaze shifted to Jake and I immediately saw what Oz was talking about. My brother looked like shit. There were dark marks beneath his eyes and he looked like he'd lost some weight. I'd looked like that myself when I'd learned my brother had gone missing years earlier when he'd been a med student.

"It's fine," I choked out as best I could. "I'll... I'll talk to Tag about getting some time off over July fourth or something, okay? It's not that far of a drive to Colorado."

Jake smiled. "We'd like that, Zach."

"Boo, I'll bring you something pretty, okay?" I offered. I saw Oz smile even as the ugly dog in the glittery sweater ignored me.

"She's in a pastel phase," Oz said. "No florals, even though that's the rage this year. Our girl likes setting new trends."

I couldn't help but chuckle. "Got it."

"I guess I should get back to work," Oz said before he reached up to kiss my brother on the mouth. I had to clear my throat when things started to get too heated between the two men. Oz blushed while Jake sent me a look of annoyance. I wanted to remind him that *they'd* called *me*. Oz leaned in to whisper something to my brother before he shifted off the couch... and got on his knees in front of Jake.

"Uh, guys," I began. While PDAs between my big brother and his husband were nothing new, I had to draw a line somewhere.

"Get your mind out of the gutter, baby brother," Jake said as he shifted the camera. "Oz is working."

I laughed out loud when I saw what kind of "work" Oz was doing. He was crouched over a pair of sparkly boots on my brother's feet.

Women's boots.

"I think that's a bit too much heel for you, Jake," I said as I took in the three-inch stiletto heels on the boots.

"Bite me," Jake grunted.

"Actually, I've been trying to convince your brother to show some of my new models how to walk in these," Oz chimed in. "His runway walk is to die for. Although he's only done it for me at night after we—"

My brother's hand appeared in the frame and clapped gently over

Oz's mouth. This time it was Jake whispering something to Oz that had the pretty young man blushing to the roots of his hair.

"Okay, that's my cue," I said because there was no missing the sparks that were flying between the two men. I said my goodbyes but I wasn't even sure if the pair heard me because they were too busy having what sounded like an argument over who would be wearing the boots in the bedroom later.

I tossed the phone into my cupholder and leaned back against the seat as I tried to relax my mind. My head was screaming at me to seek a dark, silent place. I glanced at the door to Lucky's apartment building and then reached for the keys in the ignition. As much as I wanted to keep watch on Lucky's place to make sure his ex didn't show up, I knew at the rate I was going, I wouldn't be able to drive soon. I was just about to start the engine when the apartment door opened and Lucky's familiar form appeared in the doorway. He was talking on his phone.

I automatically scanned our surroundings again to make sure there wasn't anyone waiting for Lucky in the shadows. I'd been sitting at his place for over an hour and had only seen minimal foot traffic. I idly wondered if I'd be able to manage to follow Lucky wherever he was about to go… just long enough to make sure he made it to his destination, of course. Then I'd go crash in my bed for the night.

I willed the pain in my head to ease as I watched Lucky head to his car, which was parked on the opposite side of the street from me. I couldn't see the driver's side of the car from where I was, but there was no mistaking when Lucky paused at the car, then stepped around to the front of it. The car was parked under a streetlamp, so I could see his expression as he stared at the front of the vehicle. He looked… confused. His eyes lifted momentarily, then his whole body seemed to stiffen. I watched as he approached the windshield but I couldn't make out what he was looking at. Lucky didn't move for a good minute. As the seconds ticked past, my concern began to ratchet up. What if Davis had somehow gotten into the car and even now had a gun aimed at Lucky or something?

I kept my eyes on the vehicle as I reached for my gun, which was sitting on the passenger seat. I was out of my truck a second later. I practically ran around the back of Lucky's car in the hopes of getting a bead on anyone inside it. But I couldn't see anyone.

"Where is he?" I barked at Lucky who stood frozen by the driver's side of the car. "Lucky, where is he?" I called again.

This time, Lucky jumped.

"Zach," he said softly. He looked shell-shocked. His eyes fell to the gun in my hand.

"Where is he?" I asked again, this time dropping my voice and stepping closer to him. "Where's Davis?"

He shook his head. "Don't know."

I couldn't make sense of Lucky's reaction. He was clearly upset but there was no anger or fear. I opened my mouth to ask him what was going on when a splash of color caught my attention. I glanced to my right and felt my breath catch in my lungs when I saw bright red standing out against the stark gray of the car's paint.

I stepped around Lucky and to the front of the car to get a better look. I could tell the red color was from spray paint but it took me a moment to understand what I was seeing.

Then I was the one seeing red. "Lucky, who did this?" I asked, ignoring the pain that began to explode in my head as my heart rate went through the roof.

Lucky stood there, frozen.

"Lucky!" I practically yelled as I grabbed his arm.

"I—I don't know!" he responded. His voice dropped several notches. "It was… it was just notes before. I thought someone was just messing around with me."

I looked back at the car and realized that in addition to the ugly word that had been spray-painted on the hood, both headlights had been broken.

"What notes?" I asked even as my vision began to dim. "What notes, Lucky?"

That was as much as I got out before the nausea hit me fast and hard. I closed my eyes but it was too late. Starbursts of light began to flash behind my lids and I lost my balance.

"Zach?"

Lucky's panicked voice was a terrible thing to hear. I tried to tell him I was fine, but I couldn't hold back the bile that crawled up my throat. Humiliation tore through me along with the agonizing pain in my head as I began retching right there in front of Lucky's car.

"Zach, hang on, I'll dial 911," Lucky called. I could feel his warm hand settle on the back of my neck. I managed to shake my head.

"Migraine," I managed to say. "Pills… pills in my truck." I didn't even consider trying to get through the pain without the medication. It was a crutch I'd happily lean on at that point.

"I'll get them," Lucky said quickly, though this time he kept his voice down. I braced my hands on the front of his car to keep myself upright but when I saw the word that was scrawled across the hood, I had no choice but to close my eyes again. But that one word that some asshole had dared to call the young man continued to play on a loop in my head with each repetition of it making the pain in my entire body feel like someone was stabbing me with a hot poker.

Thief.

Thief.

Thief.

It seemed to take hours for Lucky to return to my side. I managed to open my eyes long enough to see him struggling with my prescription bottle. I tried to put my hand over his to calm him, but I couldn't manage it. So I did the one thing I could do and made him a promise I *could* keep.

"I'll find him, Lucky. Won't—won't let him hurt you. Won't let anyone—" I had to stop talking when my body teetered and my knees gave out. But my body didn't hit the road like I expected it to. Lucky had somehow managed to catch me, and despite him being smaller, he was holding me up. I let my head roll against his shoulder.

"Hang on, Zach. You're okay," Lucky repeated several times. I could hear the fear in his voice which reminded me of the promise I'd been trying to make.

"Won't let anyone hurt you… ever hurt you," I managed to say in a rush of air and then I gave up and let the darkness have me.

CHAPTER 4

LUCKY

I was grateful Zach had managed to tell me what was wrong with him, or I might have panicked. As it was, I was fighting off the nausea in my belly as I witnessed the terrible pain Zach was dealing with. Fortunately, my training and certification as a paramedic made it a little easier for me to assess Zach's condition. After a quick check of his vitals, it was clear he didn't need an ER visit, and since he already seemed to know what the problem was and had the appropriate meds for it, what he really needed was a more comfortable place to recover than a gritty street.

I forgot all about my car and focused on Zach as I knelt over him.

"Zach, I need you to wake up for me a bit, okay?" I said. I could hear the shakiness in my own voice but tamped it down as best I could.

Zach mumbled something and lolled his head from side to side. I used my hand to support his neck while I pressed one of his pills to his tongue and gave him a sip from the Coke bottle I'd found in his truck, which had fortunately been unlocked.

Some of the soda dribbled from Zach's mouth but he managed to swallow. I cradled his head against my chest for a moment. "Try to take deep breaths, okay? And keep your eyes closed." I didn't wait for

Zach to respond as I shoved the medicine and soda bottle into my pockets and gently eased Zach up to put him in a firefighter's carry.

"Too heavy," Zach grumbled. "Walk."

Despite the pain he was in, his voice still held that commanding tone. I was half-tempted to carry him anyway just to show him I could, but the fear he'd fight me once I had him over my shoulder had me shifting him next to me in a walk assist with my arm around him and my other hand holding his hand over my own shoulder. We made our way into my apartment building and up to my place.

As soon as I opened the door to the apartment, Min was there.

"What the hell? What's wrong with him?" She hustled over to help me get him past an overflowing bookcase and to the beat-up leather sofa in the living room.

I knew the medicine he'd taken was going to wipe him out for hours, hopefully through the entire night, and he wouldn't spend those hours comfortably on our old sofa.

"My bedroom," I told her, changing direction. As we herded him into my small room and onto the double bed, Zach tried telling us he was fine, but his deathly pallor and tightly closed eyes said differently.

I shot Min a look. "Close the blinds and turn off all the lights. He needs dark and quiet. Migraine."

Her face pinched in concern as she moved to do as I'd asked. Once the room was dark and still and Min had gone to fetch a cool washcloth for his head, I looked down at Zach's face. His eyes weren't open all the way, but they still peered up at me.

"M'okay," he mumbled. I couldn't hold back a snort.

"You're not, but you will be," I promised in a whisper as I knelt on the bed next to him. "Before you drift off, I need to know if you take a preventive migraine med."

His brows furrowed in confusion, and I caught myself before reaching to smooth them apart. I kept my voice low as I continued. "The medicine in your truck is an abortive—a drug to stop one after it starts. Do you take a daily med to prevent them?"

Zach closed his eyes with a brief shake of the head. "Don't like it. Makes me sleepy. Can't fly."

I remembered overhearing him talk to his brother about fixed wing versus helicopters in the army. Even though I wasn't exactly sure what Zach did in the service, I knew he had some kind of flight training.

His face pinched in pain again and I finally allowed myself to reach out and run a cool hand over his warm forehead. As soon as I touched him, his entire body seemed to relax into the bed.

"Let go," I said softly under my breath. Zach's body seemed to tense for a brief moment, then suddenly he turned his head to the side and I felt his fingers touch my leg. It was as if he was making sure I was really there. As soon as I had the thought, I dismissed it. Zach was here for one reason and one reason alone… because my fathers had sent him to check up on me.

Despite that, I found myself massaging his temple with my thumb as I remembered his frantic vow to keep me safe just before he'd passed out. I wondered what kind of fear my dads and Zach's brother, Jake, had put into him when they'd asked him to check up on me. Whatever the reason, it was enough to tell me he wasn't going to rest easy as long as he thought he was still on that mission. The man was a soldier, after all. He thrived on having a purpose.

"I'm safe," I added. "We both are."

Zach's hand came up to cover the fingers I had on his forehead, surprising me with its slight tremor. "Stay."

Just as my heart began to swell and warm at his sweet-as-hell plea, he managed to murmur out the rest of it.

"Safe. Stay inside. Safe."

Fuck me.

Of course he hadn't been asking me to stay and keep him company. He'd been asking me to stay where he could keep track of me. Like a babysitter.

Min came in and saw Zach's hand covering mine and his other hand resting on my leg. I quickly jerked out of his grip and reached for the washcloth she'd brought. The look on her face made it clear I was in for some serious words as soon as I was done playing paramedic.

I turned and placed the cool cloth over his forehead, hoping he wouldn't need ice pack and heat pad therapy. If he did, I'd bet a million dollars he'd throw a fit and storm out, even if he could barely see straight.

But he seemed to doze off just fine, most likely half-numb from the medicine. When I finally joined Min in the kitchen, I noticed her girlfriend was there. The two of them stopped talking abruptly when I entered the room, so there was no doubt who they'd been talking about.

"Hey, Leah," I said, reaching past Min to get the water pitcher from the fridge.

Leah glanced at Min before smiling at me. "Minna says you picked up a stray hottie. Does that have anything to do with what happened to your car downstairs?"

Min didn't give me a chance to answer before poking me in the chest with a stubby finger. "When were you going to tell me about that, huh? What's going on? Did Davis do that?"

The reminder of my car had a lead weight landing directly in my gut.

Leah put a calming hand on Min's shoulder. "Lucky, you need to call the cops. That's serious shit."

I blew out a breath, thinking of Davis and how much he claimed to care about me. Even though he had a girlfriend and had totally lied to my face about everything, the man didn't seem like someone to go psycho with spray paint like that. And so far, his harassment of me had been of the "please give me another chance so we can keep fucking in secret" variety rather than the "die bitch" attitude that vandal seemed to display.

"I don't think it was Davis. I think it was simply the wrong car," I explained. "You know how many students live around here. It could have been someone's jealous girlfriend or boyfriend."

Min's eye-roll was epic. "Yeah, like Davis's jealous girlfriend maybe? Wake up, Lucky. Jesus."

I shook my head as I reached for a glass in the cabinet. "She doesn't know about me. That was the whole point. He's terrified about anyone thinking he's gay. He claimed he kept dating her to keep up appearances to his family and friends because he was scared of coming out. No one in his life knows."

"Then who could it be?" Leah asked. "Have you gotten any other weird messages or threats?"

I focused on pouring the water so I didn't have to make eye contact when I lied. "No. That's why I think it's simply a case of mistaken car identity."

"You still need to call the cops," Min insisted. "Think of the intended victim, Lucky. They need to know."

She was right, but it was too late to report something that wasn't an emergency. I knew firsthand how crazy this time of night could be for first responders, and a spray-painted parked car wasn't 911-worthy.

"Fine, I'll call in the morning. But I'm sure it's nothing." Even as I said the words, I was trying to figure out how I would keep all this from my fathers. The car was in my name but they paid the insurance on it. Not to mention the elephant in the room... or the other room, rather. And it wasn't as much an elephant as it was a big, hunky soldier hell-bent on completing his latest mission... me.

After ignoring the pointed silence that followed, I put the pitcher back in the fridge and made my way to the hall closet to grab my jump bag. As long as Zach was sleeping, he wouldn't notice me taking his temperature and listening to his heart and chest just to be sure there wasn't anything else going on.

When I entered the room, the light from the hallway spilled in enough to show me he was still out. From what I could tell, his color had improved a little, but I still wished I could take his blood pressure without waking him up.

I walked to the foot of the bed to remove his boots and was surprised to feel a thick scar on his calf. Without much light, it was hard to investigate, so I used my hands. The touch was way too intimate, too much like my fantasies of having permission to touch Zach's body the way I really wanted to. I tried desperately to remind myself this was purely medical. I needed to know what his physical situation was so I could properly treat him.

Liar.

My fingers ran up his hairy calf, round with muscle and warm with body heat, until I encountered more scarring.

"What happened to you?" I murmured under my breath.

The last time I'd seen Zach, I'd had the pleasure of inadvertently walking in on him while he'd been getting dressed. It'd been the catalyst for me hatching my plan to finally confess my feelings to the older man. I'd drooled over his gorgeous body for a good fifteen seconds before he'd even realized I was there. And while he'd borne the scars of war on parts of his body, I most definitely would have remembered the damage to his leg that I currently felt.

I silently blamed the medic in me as I stepped out of the room long enough to set my phone's flashlight on the lowest setting. When I returned to the room, I pulled up his pant leg to reveal heavily scarred skin from ankle to knee. The joint itself was covered with both jagged and straight scars. The skin was pink and raw looking—proof that the injury was fresh and probably still healing. Someone with a mangled knee like this wouldn't have been able to fight Davis in the parking lot. Or race over with his gun drawn when he saw me freaking out by the car.

Unless he was a stubborn-assed army soldier.

Had he been in a combat incident? Was this the result of an IED? The marks on his lower leg definitely looked like the result of shrapnel but the knee itself looked like it had sustained more damage. Gunshot maybe? Or maybe it was both gunshot and shrapnel? The surgical scars surrounding Zach's knee were clear enough.

I ran my fingers over the twisted lines, trying to imagine the pain of an injury like this. If his brother had been notified of a combat injury, Jake would have told the rest of us because we'd become a family over the years. Even if Jake had decided to keep it to himself, we would have known something was wrong beyond the regular amount of worrying Jake always did about his brother after he left for his latest deployment. The way we all worried…

Zach shifted in his sleep, pressing his leg further into my touch and letting out a breath. I wanted to stay connected to him, lie next to him and wrap my arms around him to hold him tight and keep the pain away. But I was nothing to him. No one. The child of a friend, that was all.

After taking his vitals as gently as I could, I forced myself to pull away and tuck him under the covers. The one indulgence I allowed myself was to strip his holster, belt, and pants off so he would be more comfortable. If I snuck a peek at the way he looked in tight boxer-briefs, well, it was part and parcel of being a paramedic. No one needed to know. I shoved my equipment back in the bag and kicked it under the bed in case I needed it again when I checked on him in a few hours, but when I walked out to the family room to make a bed out of the old sofa for myself, I saw Min and Leah in the middle of a hot and heavy make-out session there.

I turned back to my room to wait them out, taking a seat on the other side of the small bed from Zach. I didn't dare turn on a light or even use my phone for fear of waking him, so it shouldn't have surprised me that I fell asleep.

What did surprise me was waking up with my face pressed against a warm T-shirt that smelled like heaven and my arm wrapped around a firm body. My leg was thrown over one of Zach's, and if I hadn't woken when I did, I'd probably have been humping his thigh soon enough.

I heard my phone beeping and without thinking, I leaned across Zach to grab it off the nightstand. In my haste to silence it, my fingers hit the switch for the lamp instead. I tried turning it off but managed to jar the entire nightstand instead, causing one of my textbooks to hit the floor with a resounding thud. Before I could even react, a heavy arm was pressed against my throat, pinning me to the mattress. I gasped as my airway was cut off.

"Who are you?" Zach snarled at me. I didn't recognize his voice, and for the first time since I'd met the older man, I was afraid of him. "Where are the others?"

I shook my head because I couldn't draw in enough oxygen to manage any words.

"How many are there?" Zach demanded as he looked frantically around the room. The harshness in his expression was crippling. My heart felt like it was going to pound out of my chest as I realized he wasn't seeing me at all.

"How many?" he shouted.

Fear went through me because I knew his voice had been loud enough to wake Min or Leah or both. I tried to say Zach's name, but his hold on my throat was too tight. Several long seconds passed and when neither Min nor Leah came knocking on the door, I was both relieved and terrified. Relieved because it meant the girls had likely decided to go to Leah's place for the night and terrified because that meant I was completely at Zach's mercy.

And right now, the man above me was not Zach.

Not my Zach, anyway.

He was the war-hardened soldier I'd spent many sleepless nights worrying about in the years since he'd left to serve his country one more time.

"Mac! Teller! Report!" Zach jerked his head to the right as if expecting to see someone standing there. It was further proof of what I'd already suspected.

"Zach," I tried to choke out, but I couldn't get his entire name out.

To my surprise, Zach lifted his arm just a little. My body instinctively sucked in every ounce of oxygen it could.

"How many?" Zach repeated, his voice deadly. "I won't ask you again."

"Zach," I managed to whisper. Tears filled my eyes because the effort just to say his name made my throat burn. But I knew my voice was my only chance at the moment… it was the only way to get Zach to see me and not whatever enemy his brain was trying to convince him was lying beneath him.

"Zach, please…"

Zach was straddling my body and holding one of my arms down with his free hand. I felt his fingers loosen just a tiny bit. I seized the moment and said, "It's me, Lucky. We're—we're friends. Your brother, Jake, knows my dads. You came here to make sure… to make sure I'm safe."

I wasn't sure if it was the last part of my statement or the mention of his brother that seemed to finally penetrate. The weight on my throat eased even more.

"Lucky?" Zach grated, his voice sounding as messed up as my own. His confusion was palpable. I took a risk and reached up to stroke his stubbled cheek.

"It's me," I assured him. "You're okay. We're both okay."

"Lucky?" Zach repeated. His confusion quickly turned to disbelief, then horror. "No!" he shouted, then he was scrambling off of me. I sucked in as much air as I could, but my body refused my commands to sit up. I could only lie there helplessly as Zach kept backing up in the small room until his back hit the wall. I couldn't make out his features, but I didn't have to. Between the way he kept repeating my name over and over and his arms lifting to hold his head as if it were too heavy for his own body, I knew exactly what he was going through.

His horror gave me the strength I needed to move. I rolled off the bed, nearly hitting the floor in the process, but managed to catch myself.

"You're okay, Zach. We're okay."

Zach began shaking his head. I'd never seen him, or anyone for that matter, so distressed. I stumbled to him, not sure I'd actually reach him without falling flat on my face. To my surprise, his hands shot out to wrap around my waist right before I went down.

His body was shaking violently, no doubt from the adrenaline still coursing through his veins. I threw caution to the wind and put my arms around his neck. "It's okay, just take deep breaths for me." When Zach ignored my order, I repeated it and then pulled back enough so he could watch me taking the same breaths with him. The vulnerability in his eyes as he tried to calm his breathing made my heart break into a million pieces. I pulled him against me and began whispering nonsense into his ear, mostly just to reassure him we were both okay. I could feel my own strength returning even as Zach's seemed to fade. His grip on my waist was tight as his warm breath washed over my collarbone.

"Do you remember that night I tried to teach you how to ski?" I asked. "And you broke my ski."

Zach didn't respond at first, but the more I talked about the night I'd well and truly fallen for him, the slower his breathing became and his hold on me eased enough so it no longer felt like he was hanging on to me like I was his lifeline. I talked for a good five minutes about anything and everything related to that night because every moment of it was etched into my brain.

"You broke your own ski," Zach softly interrupted just before I was about to launch into another nonsensical round of conversation.

"You stepped on the tip with yours," I reminded him.

"You shouldn't have put your skis under mine."

"I was trying to keep you from sliding down the hill and landing on your ass!"

He was quiet for a long time before he pulled back, putting some very much unwanted space between us. I could see in his eyes long before he spoke that I was losing him again, only not in the way I'd lost him when he'd pinned me to the bed.

"Maybe falling on my ass would have made me figure things out a lot sooner," he said solemnly.

I bit into my lower lip when Zach's arms loosened. There was no missing his unspoken message. The memory of that perfect night under the stars morphed into that moment when I'd bared my soul to him beneath a piece of mistletoe.

"I love you, Zach."

I pulled free of Zach's hold completely and stepped back. I couldn't stop myself from wrapping my arms around my waist. I mentally cursed myself for trying to mimic Zach's touch and quickly dropped my arms.

"You need to lie back down. You might get dizzy and lose your balance or the migraine could come back—"

"I'm fine," Zach cut in. "I don't need you to take care of me—"

"Yes you fucking do! If I hadn't, your ass would be lying in the street right now." I pointed at the bed. "Lie back down."

It was the exact wrong thing to say to the man because his eyes flared wide before narrowing again. "Make me, kid."

My body seemed to come alive at that moment and I forgot all about the fact that he was my patient and I was supposed to be taking it easy on him. I reached for his arm and yanked, forcing him back onto the bed before he could get over his shock at my move. As soon as he realized what was happening, he wrestled me over until he had me pinned. This time, there was no fear as he held me down, only something... *else*.

Both of our chests heaved with exertion as I still fought to get the upper hand. Zach's shirt had ridden up and the fuzz on his belly had my dick reacting. I sucked in a breath and tried to sink my hips into the mattress so he wouldn't notice.

"What the fuck is going on?" Zach growled. "Why am I in your bed without any fucking clothes on?"

The fact that he was going to conveniently forget about the episode that had triggered him to attack me just pissed me off even more. Since I didn't have the physical strength to match his, I went for another weapon that would hopefully do the trick.

"Tsk, language, Zachary. What would my fathers say if they heard you having such a negative influence on their precious baby boy?"

Fire burned in his eyes, and it made it hard to draw breath. I watched the gears turn in his head.

"You took care of me," he said as if just remembering some of the details. "You... you fucking listened to my heart with a stethoscope and had a..." He peered over the side of the bed where I thought I'd done a better job of hiding my shit. "A giant medical bag? Lucky, what is this?"

My heart dropped. "Nothing. None of your business."

He studied me like I was a bug under a scope. "Tell me," he demanded, his voice dropping to that low, sexy level that would normally have me spilling my guts. It was at that moment that he looked at my neck and sucked in a rush of air. I used his momentary lapse to throw my weight against his as I shifted my body. We wrestled again until he was on his front on the bed and I straddled his ass. His very round, very tight ass.

Fuck.

"You want to share secrets?" I breathed down behind his ear. "You first."

"Get off me," he warned through clenched teeth.

I threw his words back at him, no longer caring if I was poking the beast.

"Make me."

CHAPTER 5

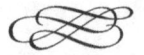

ZACH

It took less than ten seconds and two moves to get him on his back again. But this time around I had to be careful about putting my weight on him, mostly because my cock had decided it'd liked the feel of Lucky straddling my ass just a bit too much. I ended up using my legs to hold his still and then it was just a matter of waiting him out.

As sweet, innocent Lucky threw enough swears at me to fill a garbage can, I tried to process everything that had happened in the time since I'd been running across the street to save Lucky from some unforeseen evil.

The car had been trashed.

That much I remembered.

Lucky had said something about notes…

My brain began to pound inside of my head as I tried to think back to just before I'd blacked out. I gave up on my train of thought and focused on the squirming young man beneath me. Unfortunately, my eyes instantly went to his throat.

The sight of the ugly bruise that was starting to form on his skin made my stomach rumble in protest, and I instantly released Lucky and scrambled backwards. Lucky's tirade ended mid-sentence and he quickly sat up.

I'd attacked him.

My eyes flitted to his throat again. He must have known what I'd been thinking because his fingers drifted up to his neck.

"What happened?" I bit out as I dropped my eyes so I wouldn't have to look at the fucking marks and know I'd put them there.

"I'm okay, Zach. You didn't hurt me."

I nearly laughed. His response was so *Lucky*. The bruises on his throat were already forming yet he was more concerned with reassuring me.

"What happened?" I repeated, this time more softly. I hated showing him any more vulnerability than he'd already been witness to, but I was desperate to know what had happened. "I remember the car and you helped me up here. You… you checked me over." I glanced at the medical bag on the floor and sent Lucky a quick look.

Yeah, we *would* be addressing that later.

"What else do you remember?" Lucky asked. The pitying look he gave me had me getting off the bed. My knee protested the quick move, but I didn't care. No way I could look at him right now.

"You said my name," I admitted. "I thought it was a bad dream—me holding you down like that…" I fell silent as I remembered Lucky's pale features as he'd struggled to breathe.

In *my* hold.

"You were asleep. I only meant to sit on the bed until Min and her girlfriend went to bed and then I was going to move to the sofa, but I guess… I guess I fell asleep. When I woke up, you and I were… we were…" Lucky paused and dropped his eyes. His cheeks filled with color. "I didn't want you to wake up with me… like that."

At that moment, I would have killed to know exactly what he was talking about. I'd had countless fantasies in the past two years about what it would be like to wake up in bed with Lucky.

Now I'd have to live with the nightmare of what I'd done.

"I tried to get to my phone without waking you but I must have jostled you or something because you…"

"Attacked you," I finished for him.

Lucky shook his head. "No, you—you were just confused."

"Confusion doesn't leave bruises, Lucky!" I ground out. I began pacing because if I didn't keep moving, I'd put my fist through the wall like I wanted. The abject terror Lucky must have been feeling—

"Hey," Lucky said as he scrambled out of bed and put himself right in front of me. When he reached for me, presumably to hold me closer to him, I stepped away from him. I hated the sadness that filled his pretty brown eyes but I didn't dare step into him like I wanted. While I wasn't about to physically hurt him, my body was too on edge and the sight of Lucky in his pajamas was too much of a temptation. If I got him flat on his back again, he'd most definitely stay there until I'd tasted every inch of him.

"I promise, Zach, it looks worse than it is," he said somberly as he reached up to touch his throat. "I feel fine. And yeah, I was scared but I knew you wouldn't—"

"Hurt you?" I offered, since that was exactly what I'd done. The guilt of it felt like a lead weight in my belly.

"I just had to make you see me. I knew that once you did..."

I didn't bother completing his statement for him. We both knew there'd been no way for him to know he'd be able to snap me out of the episode.

I wasn't sure how much time had passed before Lucky took a step toward me. "It's PTSD, isn't it?"

I nodded because there was no point in trying to hide it. Hell, I'd practically waved it on a flag in front of him.

"Did it happen during your last deployment?"

I didn't answer that question because I knew what his next one would be. He'd want to know the details of everything that'd happened to me. Nope, not going there.

"Does Uncle Jake know?" Lucky asked.

His use of the title of "uncle" for my brother made me want to laugh at the absurdity of it all. How the hell had I let this happen?

"Does he?" Lucky insisted. He was only feet away. It would be so easy to close the distance between us and take him like I wanted. He'd let me. I was sure of that. Despite what I'd done to him, I knew that if I said his name a certain way or touched him with the softest of caresses, he'd be mine.

For the night or for as long as I wanted.

Familiar words that were from a voice that wasn't anywhere near as sweet as Lucky's repeated themselves for the millionth time in my pounding head.

You're mine, Zach. Even when you say you're not, we both know the truth.

It wasn't until Lucky whispered my name that I snapped out of the past those words had drawn me into.

No.

No fucking way would I let Lucky make the same mistakes as me.

"No," I finally responded before moving back again. My body had a strange habit of drifting closer to Lucky without me even realizing it.

"You should tell him. He's your brother, Zach. He loves you. You don't need to keep secrets from him—"

"Kind of like you're keeping secrets?" I asked as I nudged the edge of his medical bag.

Lucky looked as if I'd physically attacked him again. "That's different."

"How?" I asked. "How is it different?"

I knew his move to cross his arms was meant to show defiance, but I saw something else in his eyes.

Guilt.

A whole shit ton of guilt.

"It's not the same thing because I just took a couple of CPR courses. I took them all the time back home. I don't need to tell my dads about something they already know."

Irritation went through me as I reached down to grab the bag. I began tossing medical equipment onto the bed.

"How many CPR courses hand out stethoscopes to their graduates?" I asked. I looked over the items on the bed. "This looks like a go bag to me. In fact, Jake has one that has a lot of the same things—"

"Fine," Lucky snapped. "I took some advanced courses."

I tossed the empty bag on the bed. "Try again," I responded. I wasn't surprised when Lucky tried to move past me so he could leave the room.

"Move," he growled when I stepped into his path.

"You don't need to keep secrets—" I began to say, mimicking Lucky's earlier words, but he cut me off.

"Fuck you, Zach!"

Lucky shoved me hard, once again reminding me that he was much stronger than he looked. My instincts took over as I grabbed him by the upper arms and walked him backwards until his back hit the wall. I loved how pissed he got whenever I manhandled him, though I had no clue why I liked it so much.

Because it proves he can handle you...

I told my inner voice to put a cork in it and simply waited for Lucky to settle down. The muscles of his biceps filled my hands. His skin felt hot against mine and I wondered if it was always like that or if it was just because he was pissed.

If that were the case, what would it feel like when he was turned on? I cursed the train of my thoughts, especially when I realized I'd once again moved closer to Lucky. There were only inches separating us and at some point, Lucky had stopped fighting me. His breaths were coming in pants and his gorgeous lips were parted enough to let the air pass. I imagined what it would be like to slip my tongue into his hot mouth... then my cock. Would he suck me eagerly or shyly?

I must have made some kind of sound because Lucky's eyes darted from my eyes to my mouth and back again.

"Zach," he breathed.

No... *begged*.

He was begging.

Just like my body was begging me to let go of the tightly held leash I had on it.

Before I knew what I was doing, my thumb was tracing the line of his mouth. Lucky inhaled sharply at the contact. His body squirmed against mine, and I could see that he'd fisted the hand I'd released.

Probably to stop himself from touching me.

I almost told him not to, but some shred of sanity stopped me. But that logic was failing me when it came to my exploration of Lucky's beautiful mouth with my too-rough finger. "Did he kiss you?"

When Lucky didn't answer my question, I growled it again. "Did he?"

"Wh-who?" he managed to get out.

"The asshole in the designer polo shirt."

"Davis?" Lucky asked, clearly confused.

All I managed was a nod. I knew my question was unreasonable because what guy would resist being able to kiss Lucky's perfect mouth, but that didn't keep me from pressing the issue.

My gut clenched when Lucky shook his head. "He wouldn't."

I wanted to punch the fucker all over again, but Lucky's next words stopped me cold.

"Haven't been kissed since one time when I was fifteen. Some guys since then have wanted to, but I wanted…"

Lucky's eyes shimmered with emotion as his voice broke.

"Wanted what?" I asked as my heart jumped in my chest.

"I wanted the next guy to be yo—"

That was all he got out before his phone began beeping loudly. It reminded me of the days when people carried beepers.

Lucky closed his eyes and that was enough to break the spell. I quickly released him and stepped back. My body felt thwarted.

Lucky moved past me to grab his phone off the nightstand. He looked dejected as he stood with his back to me. It only lasted a few seconds because then he reached for the items on the bed and stuffed them into his bag. "I have to go," was all he said.

"Go where?" I asked.

He didn't answer me. I watched as he jerked on a pair of navy pants and some kind of uniform shirt. It wasn't until he pulled a jacket out of his closet that had the word "Paramedic" emblazoned across the back that I realized what secret he'd been hiding from his family.

Lucky wouldn't make eye contact with me as he shrugged the jacket on and then stepped into his shoes. When he headed for the door, I moved in front of him.

"I have to go, Zach. I'm the most junior member of the team, so they only call me when they really need me."

"Why haven't you told your fathers?" I asked. Lucky looked so grown up in his paramedic uniform that I almost didn't recognize him.

"You've been gone a long time," Lucky murmured. "I have the best parents in the world, but there are days when I know they wish they could wrap me in bubble wrap..."

Reality dawned and I remembered my brother's words about Lucky's behavior after I'd left.

Jake had called it a "rough patch."

While being a paramedic wasn't the most dangerous job in the world, it would definitely put him in some precarious situations with drug overdoses, horrific car crashes, and gunshot victims. And from his comment about his dads wanting to wrap him in bubble wrap, my guess was that Lucky knew what their reaction would be if they found out what he was up to. I couldn't imagine Xander and Bennett being anything but proud of their son, but what did I really know? I'd purposefully kept my nose out of any business relating to Lucky from the time I'd realized he'd had feelings for me.

I stepped out of Lucky's way.

"You should rest some more," Lucky murmured as he moved past me.

I ignored the warmth that spread through me at his show of concern despite everything that had happened. "I will," I said.

"Liar," Lucky said with a slight grin. I couldn't help but smile myself. But then reality returned.

"We need to talk about what happened to your car. And the notes," I said.

Lucky paused in the doorway but didn't respond right away. When he did, it was simply to say, "Bye, Zach" and then he was gone.

CHAPTER 6

LUCKY

For three days I tried my best to forget about Zach Warner. Hell, for the past couple of years I'd been doing the same with zero success, so I wasn't sure why I thought things would be any different after our run-in at my apartment. Now I had the memory of his firm, warm body against mine in my bed. I had the scent of his hair on my pillow and the feel of his strong arms around me imprinted forever in my brain.

So maybe it shouldn't have come as a surprise when I found myself shitfaced and desperate that Friday night after the final semester classes had come to a close. My friends had dragged me to Ghetti's for happy hour, and it seemed every other student in a ten-mile radius had the same idea. The place was packed, the music vibrated the floor, and somehow every man in the building reminded me of a certain grumpy Army Ranger I knew.

The thought of Zach was immediately followed by the humiliation of all the things I'd said to him the night I'd cared for him during his migraine. How the hell had I managed to admit to him that I hadn't let a guy kiss me since I'd been a kid because I'd been waiting for him? Why hadn't I just gone ahead and told him I'd only ever given a few guys hand jobs and blow jobs while getting myself off because I knew their hands on my body would only serve to remind me that they weren't Zach's hands? The warmth of the alcohol was replaced by the sting of shame.

"They shouldn't call them Rangers. They should call them grumpy old men," I said out loud to anyone interested.

Min narrowed her eyes at me. "We were talking about Erin's semester abroad in Italy in the fall. How'd you get Rangers from that?"

I glanced at our friend Erin who looked as buzzed as I felt. "You fell in Italy? Are you okay?"

Someone off to my right snort-giggled, but Erin nodded. "Yeah. Totes fine. But I've never been to Italy before."

That was confusing. I looked at Min for clarification, but she simply rolled her eyes. "Never mind," she muttered. "Go dance or something. Work off the beer."

"It's the shots. The shots need to work off," I corrected. "My tongue doesn't feel right. What was that stuff called? What's in an Easy A?" After hearing myself ask the stupid question, I snort-giggled myself. "Determination and hard work, probably. But I mean the shot. The shot called an Easy A. What's in that? It made my tongue feel weird."

Rudy reached over and patted my hand. "Sweet summer child."

I tilted my head at him. "Is that a kind of liquor? I've heard of sweet tea vodka, but I've never had sweet... sweet summer..." A cute guy caught my eye on the dance floor. He'd been in my physics class the year before, and I remembered him flirting with me. Well, I hadn't realized it at the time, but later Min had pointed out the guy had been trying to get my attention all semester. Unfortunately, by the time I'd figured it out, the holiday break had arrived and I'd never run into him again. But there he was.

"There he is," I told everyone. "The physics guy. Remember him, Min? The guy from physics class? He's dancing. Right there." I tried pointing but Min grabbed my arm and pushed it back down.

"No pointing. Trust me on this."

"Maybe I should dance with him," I suggested. "Maybe his name is Rick, but I can't remember. Do you remember, Min? His name? Is it Rick?"

Rudy squinted across at the man. "Oh. Yeah. Been there, done that. His name is Rafe. Super pretty dick. Go for it."

I turned and stared at my friend. "You've… you've seen his *dick*? How? When?"

My friends all exchanged looks across the table before Rudy patted my hand again. "Minna has given you the birds and bees talk, yes? When a baby gay bird meets a well-hung bee from the college football team, the stinger swells until—"

"Stop," Leah said with a laugh. "I thought we agreed not to talk about dicks tonight."

"He's not a dick," I said indignantly, wondering why she'd brought up the subject of Zach. "He's just grumpy. I told you, he's a Ranger. I think that's just how they are sometimes."

Everyone stared at me. "Why does he keep talking about Rangers?" Rudy asked Min out of the corner of his mouth.

I leaned forward to explain. "Because I want to make love to the Rangers." I thought about how that sounded. Slutty. "Not all of them though," I clarified. "Just the one. And not anymore. I don't care about the Rangers anymore. Like, at all. I care about anyone else in here more than that. *Anyone*."

Min shot Leah a look and leaned in to speak over the music at me. "Go. Dance. Now."

As I scrambled up from my chair, I heard Leah say something about someone having it bad and Min responded with something about calling in the Rangers. I turned back to Rudy. "See? I'm not the only one who's talking about the Rangers. Everyone's talking about it. They're Army Rangers. Duh."

And with that, I sauntered off, secure in the knowledge I'd gotten the last word in that conversation. When I bumped into a firm body, I realized my horny radar had led me straight to Pretty Dick Rafe. His face lit up when he recognized me, and he immediately reached for me.

"I didn't call you Pretty Dick Rafe out loud, did I?" I asked over the pounding music. It was good to be sure. I wouldn't have wanted to offend him.

He threw his head back with a laugh. "How much have you had to drink, cutie pie?"

"No, it was the Easy A. I've never had a cutie pie. Is it good? Does it taste like pie? The Easy A tastes like..." I thought about it for a minute. "Hard work and determination."

Rafe leaned in and spoke against my ear. "And Jägermeister, am I right?"

Oh, hell. No wonder my tongue didn't work right. "Shoulda stuck with the pie."

His hands slid down to cup my ass and I sucked in a breath. Even though this was what I wanted, it didn't feel right.

Suck it up. Get over it. Zach is never going to see you as more than a child.

I ran my hands over Rick's chest, noticing the bumps over his pecs and abs that were most likely from his football workouts. Nice enough.

I considered giving him some kind of message that I was interested in more than a dance.

"Come here often?" I asked. As soon as the words replayed in my mind, I winced. No one had ever called me smooth.

His hands squeezed my ass and pulled me tighter against him where I felt the long rod of his erection against my hip. Seemed he *did* come here often.

I snorted at my own joke.

Rick leaned in to sniff my neck. "I'll come here more often now that I know you're here," he murmured into my Adam's apple. "You smell fucking fantastic. What are you wearing?"

I closed my eyes to remember. "Oh! Jeans and my Smoky the Bear T-shirt. And Vans."

The rumble of his laughter vibrated against my chest. That was nice. I kept my eyes closed and allowed myself to enjoy the masculine strength of him, the deep voice and slight scent of sweat. Even the roughness of his stubble against the side of my face was delicious. How could anyone want to be with a woman when they could have this?

I ran my hands up his back, noticing the broad muscles shift under my fingers as he moved to the music. This was nice. Here was a man not afraid to be seen touching me, holding me, flirting with me in public. What was his name again? Rick? Rafe? Raft? Either way, he was sexy and friendly. More than that, he was happy to have me in his arms. And he wasn't talking to me like I was just some dumb kid who didn't know what he wanted.

After leaning my face against his shoulder, I sighed. Who said the earth had to move when all you really wanted was some physical attention? I didn't need a husband. I needed sex. And if I could sex my way out of this obsession with Zach, that'd be great too.

I sighed again.

"What the fuck are you doing?"

The bark startled me out of my reverie, and I blinked my eyes open to see Davis's stormy face over RickRafe's shoulder.

"Uh, dancing?" I said, looking around at all the other people on the dance floor who'd been doing the same. Seemed kinda obvious if he'd just looked around.

Davis seemed to realize he was drawing everyone's attention with his hissy fit. "Come outside. I need to talk to you."

My dance partner's arms tightened around me. "Not happening, asshole," he said with a friendly smile.

That was nice. See? Zach wasn't the only protective man in the world. Other men wanted me. Like... what the hell was his name? Rafe. I was pretty sure it was Rafe.

I decided to back him up. "Yeah," I said. "What he said. Rafe."

Davis's eyes widened. "You're drunk."

I nodded. "Accurate assessment by pro... pro... professional paramedic." That wasn't as easy to say with a numb tongue as it was when my tongue worked better. Maybe he was right.

Davis's face softened. "Lucky, let me take you home."

I thought about how good it had felt when Davis had held me after I'd pleasured him. Admittedly, I'd pictured a certain someone in those moments when Davis's bare skin had been pressed against mine, but despite that, I still desperately wanted to be touched and held. Even if

Davis insisted on keeping me a secret, maybe it was worth it just to feel that miniscule physical attention again.

Rafe cupped my face with his large hands. "Stay with me, cutie pie. I'll get you home safe."

He had pretty brown eyes. But they were missing the green flecks. Why didn't his eyes have green flecks too?

"Some Army Rangers have green-brown eyes," I told him. "It's nice."

His lips curved up in a grin. "That does sound nice. Maybe you want to find those Rangers and invite them home with us tonight?"

I thought about it for a microsecond. "I wish. But they don't like me. They think I'm a kid."

Davis barked again. "Lucky! Outside. *Now*."

How dare he speak to me that way. As if he had rights to me. Nobody bossed me around like that. I didn't take orders from anyone. And if a small voice corrected me and reminded me that I'd be perfectly willing to take orders from one particular someone, well... I ignored that stupid voice. It didn't matter anyway.

Suddenly, I wanted to take a swing at Davis, take out all of my Zach-based frustration on the closeted cheater in front of me. I twisted in Rafe's grip and pulled back my arm, striking out fast and knocking my fist into Davis's upper arm. My aim wasn't so great right now for some reason.

"Get the hell out of here, jackass," I snapped. "Go home to your baby mama."

Davis darted forward like he was going to grab me, but Rafe pulled me away in time and stood between us. His face darkened. "Listen, man. I don't know what the hell is going on here, but Lucky clearly doesn't want to go with you. I suggest you get out of here before making even more of a scene than you already are. Plus, some chick just walked in looking like she wants to blow your shit up."

He flicked his head toward the door where Natalie stood looking exactly as Rafe had described. Murderous. My heart fell into my stomach. While Davis wasn't the best guy in the world, he'd at least seemed to want me, even if it had only been for the briefest of moments.

It was more than *some* people I knew.

"Just go," I murmured to Davis, most likely too quietly to be heard over the noise. I tucked my face into Rafe's shirtfront and closed my eyes, trying to imagine myself in the arms of a certain older man. Rafe's body rocked us to the beat of the music, and I let my buzzy brain turn off enough to simply feel.

At some point, Min came over and tried to pull me away, declaring it was time to go home, but I preferred Rafe's offer of more shots instead. After ignoring Min's hushed reminders in my ear to take it easy, I followed Rafe to the bar. The Easy A went down suuuuuper easy, and after a few more, I was in heaven.

Firm body, pumping bass beat, the scent of sweat and hard liquor mixed with colognes and perfumes. Sporadic colored lights flickered around the dim dance floor, changing the colors behind my eyelids. Rafe's hands explored my body as I continued to try and appreciate the man in my arms instead of the one in my heart.

Live in the moment, Xander had always taught me. *Let go of your fears and lean in.*

That's what I'd do. I was gonna do *that*. I was gonna experience all life had to offer.

So when Rafe pulled back and took my face in his hands again, looking for all the world like he was going to kiss me, I decided not to hold back anymore. My first kiss had been amazing, even if I'd discovered later that the guy who'd given it to me hadn't been. I hadn't wanted to make that same mistake twice, but what was the point? Maybe Zach was right. Maybe it was time to grow up and stop pretending that a kiss meant more than it really did. Why keep waiting for someone special when I could experience it with someone here in the moment? And yeah, Min was right, I wasn't the kind of guy who hooked up with random people... or at all, since I was technically still a virgin. But maybe that was something else that needed to change tonight too...

I closed my eyes, let go of my fears, and leaned in.

CHAPTER 7

ZACH

I'd just returned to the hotel from a late dinner with my buddy Tag to learn more about the flight training program when my phone buzzed with a text from an unknown number.

Come to Ghetti's and deal with this. He's drunk off his ass and won't let me take him home. Says he's getting laid "even if it's not with a Ranger." This is all your fault, so you fucking fix it.

Another text from the same number appeared a second later.

Asshole.

It was followed by a photo of Lucky in the arms of some punk in a club. My stomach clenched in a strange combination of anger and nerves.

I recognized the name Ghetti's as one of the bars near the school where the bartenders probably weren't very picky about fake IDs. It would explain how a twenty-year-old had managed to get blitzed so easily, especially the last week of finals. What was he thinking? And what was Minna thinking, letting him get that drunk? He could get hurt. He could get taken advantage of.

Anger coiled in my gut as I slammed my way back out the door of the hotel room and raced to my truck. All I could picture was that tall stranger leaning down to take Lucky's mouth in his, and it made me see red. If Lucky had waited five years to kiss someone…

*Not someone, **you**,* my inner voice interrupted.

I let out a violent curse. In any case, no matter who Lucky chose to kiss, he sure as hell shouldn't be doing it in some shitty bar when he was too drunk to remember it the next day. His mouth was the kind that should be savored… cherished.

Anger mixed with desire as I threw my truck into gear and hit the gas.

Get a grip, Zach.

I somehow managed to tear my thoughts from Lucky's lips to the task at hand. In the week since Lucky's car had been vandalized and he'd inadvertently mentioned the presence of some notes as well, I'd tried to figure out who was harassing him and why. Despite the promise to myself not to, I'd spent most of the past week following Lucky or sitting outside his apartment to make sure no one tried to mess with him. But I hadn't had the courage to confront him again.

Probably because I was already walking enough of a tightrope as it was. If Lucky's phone hadn't gone off that night when he'd admitted he was waiting for me to kiss him, I would have tasted him for sure. Hell, I likely would have taken him there against the wall.

Then again in the bed.

I would have fucked him in every conceivable place and position and even after all of that, I probably wouldn't have been able to stop.

Lucky had no idea what kind of monster he'd awakened. All his sweetness, his innocence, would have been tainted by what was buried inside of me.

Not to mention the fact that I'd already proven he wasn't physically safe with me.

I'd been plagued with nightmares every night since I'd attacked Lucky after he'd woken me in his bed. In my dreams, reality only returned to me long after it was too late and Lucky's lifeless body was beneath mine. I could still hear the way he'd hoarsely whispered my name as my arm had cut off his oxygen.

Shame crawled through me as I considered what I'd done. Afterwards, I'd tried to call Jake as I'd followed Lucky to work, but I hadn't been brave enough to go through with it. So instead, I'd watched Lucky from afar while trying to convince myself it was only because I was doing a favor for my brother and his friends.

Tonight had been the first night that I'd forced myself not to tail Lucky, and that was only because Tag had insisted we get together so we could go over the ins and outs of my new job. There was no doubt that my friend had really only wanted to see for himself how I was doing since I'd done plenty of search and rescue work in between deployments. I'd been all smiles and laughter throughout the meal but as soon as Tag and his wife and kids had driven off, my entire body had started to shake violently. My intent had been to get back to my hotel room and drink myself stupid, but Minna's text had changed all that.

My thoughts drifted back to Lucky's apparent ex, Davis. Was he the one who'd driven Lucky to go out drinking tonight? I still wasn't convinced Davis hadn't been the one to vandalize Lucky's car. All I'd managed to learn about the kid was that he appeared to be exactly what he was: a spoiled rich kid who thought his shit didn't stink. Davis Teasley was from Castle Pines, Colorado, which was a wealthy country club community south of Denver where his father thrived in real estate investments. There was no hint of trouble in his background, but that didn't mean people couldn't change.

I whipped into an illegal parking space against the curb outside of the bar and made my way inside. The place was packed with college students. I doubted there was even one person remotely close to my age. The noise was deafening and bodies bumped into me everywhere I turned. When I finally found Lucky, he was exactly where he'd been in the photo, trapped in the arms of a muscular jock whose biceps seemed to be stretching the bounds of his T-shirt.

The man's hands were all over Lucky and it was clear Lucky was into it. Just as it seemed the taller man was going to lean in and kiss Lucky, he shook his head and grinned, pulling Lucky off the dance floor toward the back hallway of the bar instead. Apparently, a kiss wasn't what he was after. The jock wanted a back-room hookup instead.

With a guy who was stumbling drunk and in no state of mind to consent.

My guy.

I cursed the wayward thought and whatever mixed wires in my head had forgotten that Lucky wasn't a guy but just a kid who sure as hell wasn't mine. I clenched my fists as Lucky happily followed the man from the room.

No fucking way.

As I strode after them, I vaguely noticed Min's voice calling out to me, but nothing was going to keep me from stopping what was about to happen.

Maybe I should have been thinking about Xander and Bennett, about how they'd flip out if they knew someone was preparing to take advantage of their son, but my head was still in fucked-up, take-no-prisoners mode.

That's my fucking kiss, asshole. Mine.

I ground my teeth hard together and shoved past a couple blocking the doorway. When I got into the dimmer hallway, I saw several small groups of people—young women giggling in a circle while looking at a cell phone, a couple kissing and teasing each other against the wall in front of the men's room, and an older man talking on his phone away from the louder noise of the bar.

But no Lucky.

I slammed open the door to the men's room and saw only strangers at the urinals with both stall doors wide open and empty. When I returned to the hallway, I realized there was a door propped open to the cool evening air past the gaggle of women.

As soon as I stepped outside, I saw the jock palming Lucky's cock through his jeans while Lucky's head was thrown back against the rough brick of the building, exposing the long, pale expanse of his throat to the dim light from a nearby streetlamp. His fingers were wrapped around the guy's wrist, but he wasn't doing anything to try and push the hand away. If anything, he was probably trying to hold it in place as the guy groped him. Lucky's eyes were squeezed closed, and I had a moment's pause about ruining his pleasure. Clearly he was enjoying himself; clearly he wanted to be here in this alley being felt up by some random student.

But in that moment I didn't give a shit about what he wanted. I remembered the slight stumble he'd made when the man had pulled him off the dance floor. I remembered the goofy grin he'd flashed that proved he was probably as drunk as Min had claimed him to be.

"Lucky," I barked, startling both of them. The jock jumped back and looked at me in confusion before glancing back at Lucky. Lucky swiveled his head to face me without taking it off the bricks. His dark hair stood up in a swirl from the move. I thought I saw some unnamed emotion flash in his eyes as he stared at me, but it was gone just like that and the same goofy grin from before returned to his full lips.

"Zachary. What are you doing here?" He turned to the jock. "Zach's here. Isn't he sexy as fuck? Don't tell him though." Lucky's grin dropped and was replaced by a furrowed brow and a frown. "We don't ever want him to think we like him like that even if he makes my stinger swell."

My heart tightened.

The jock's eyes flicked between us again. "Dude, I didn't know he had a boyfriend."

"He doesn't," I admitted just as Lucky said, "I don't."

The man laughed and stepped back from Lucky with his hands up. "Mixed messages, bruh. Drama ain't my thing. I think you're a doll, but I also like my own face, know what I mean?"

Lucky's drunken grin reappeared. "S'okay, Rafe. He's not as mean as he looks. He has teddy bear boxer shorts with little pink hearts on them, but shhhh. He doesn't know I saw them in the laundry."

He whispered that last part and put his finger up to his lips, almost poking himself under the chin in the process. The jock's face softened and he reached out to pull Lucky's hand away before leaning in to kiss him on the cheek. It took all of my self-control not to launch myself at him and yank him back.

When he stepped back from Lucky again, he gestured for me to come closer. "I'm guessing if he knows about your bear trunks, you're close enough for me to trust you to get him home safely?"

Heat flooded my face. I had an explanation for the ridiculous briefs but I wasn't about to explain that to this guy. "Yeah. I'm a family friend."

The guy looked like a puzzle piece snapped into place. "This your Ranger, cutie pie?"

Lucky's forehead creased. "No. He's not my anything. My pain in the ass, maybe. My fucking chaperone, obviously. My..." He sighed as he seemed to lose track of what he was saying.

I overcame my annoyance long enough to reach out a hand to the guy. While I wanted to beat the shit out of him for hooking up with someone too drunk to know what the hell he was doing, it was clear the jock was just as far gone. "Thanks. You need an Uber or something?"

"Nah, gonna go back in and dance more." With a ruffle to Lucky's hair, he was gone.

Lucky narrowed his eyes at me. "Block cocker."

My snort took me by surprise. "I believe the term is cockblocker, and you're in no shape to—"

He held up a hand, cutting me off. "So help me god, if you give me a lecture about consent and alcol... alcol... al*cohol* consumption, I'm going to..." He couldn't come up with the right word, so he just finished with a menacing growl. Or what he probably hoped was a menacing growl.

It was more like an adorable cub growl like a teddy bear would make. I must have laughed or given him some kind of look.

"Don't look at me like that."

"Like what?" I asked, reaching for his hand. He let me take it without resistance, and I led him around the building to where I'd parked the car. I tried like hell not to notice how strong his hand felt in mine. Not delicate or soft, just... *strong*.

"Like I'm a kid, *godsdammmit*." His words slurred together. "I've had sex!" The words were loud enough to get the attention from nearby students partying on the front lawn of a big house. They hooted and hollered their congratulations to him, some lifting up various Solo cups to cheer him on.

Lucky turned his face into my chest with an embarrassed groan. "That wasn't good," he muttered into my shirt.

Before I could stop myself, I tightened my arm around him and held him close, enjoying the brief feel of his body against mine. Just like his hand, his shoulders felt different than I would have guessed. Like they could carry much more weight than I ever would have imagined. And while the skin of his biceps felt hot and silky beneath my fingers, there was no denying the sleek definition of his muscles.

He's off-limits, I reminded myself.

The argument worked for all of fifteen seconds because when I reached my truck and leaned in to open the door for Lucky, he chose that moment to turn into me and press his forehead against my chest. I'd dressed up a bit for my dinner with Tag and his family, so I was wearing a button-up shirt that I'd left open at the throat. The result was that Lucky's lush lips were just centimeters from my bare skin.

I found myself wrapping my arm around Lucky's waist. I told myself it wasn't to keep him where he was but rather to support him in case his knees gave out.

My inner voice called bullshit on me, but I ignored it.

Lucky sighed loudly as he pressed himself more firmly against my body. I nearly came on the spot when his nose pressed against my sternum and he inhaled deeply.

"You smell like the woods," he murmured drowsily. "My favorite place is the woods." His words were still slurred, but his hold on me was strong and the sensation of his fingers curling against my shoulder blades was playing havoc with my emotions.

"Sorry," he said after a moment's pause.

I found myself stroking his hair with my free hand. The noise from the club was spilling onto the streets and there were kids in various stages of drunkenness walking up and down the sidewalk behind us, but we might as well have been the only two people on the planet for all the attention I paid any of the commotion. "What are you sorry for?"

Lucky nuzzled his nose against my chest and this time when he drew in my scent, his lips ended up brushing against my hot skin.

"All of it," he said with a sigh. "Christmas, chasing you away... my stinger always swelling when you're around."

I wasn't sure if it was his use of the term stinger or the dramatic way he said it, like it was the most annoying thing in the world, but I found myself chuckling. I dropped my chin to his head and wrapped both arms around him. "You didn't chase me away, Lucky," I said. It was only a part-truth, but I couldn't tell him why I'd really left. I couldn't tell him that even if he hadn't chased me, I'd been frighteningly close to pursuing him, to claiming him.

To taking advantage of him.

"It was just time for me to move on," I murmured. "It had nothing to do with you," I lied.

He was silent for so long that I actually thought he'd fallen asleep, but then he whispered, "I wish you could like me, Zach. Even just a little. Even if it was like when we first met."

Despite the powerful words, there was little emotion in Lucky's voice as he spoke them. Somehow that was more disturbing than his belief that I didn't like him.

"What do you mean?" I asked. "I like you just fine." I cringed as soon as I heard the patronizing words. I struggled to find the right thing to say, the right way to take back my statement without telling him the truth—that I liked him a lot more than *just fine*—but I couldn't get my voice to work. My throat felt tight while my chest seemed to have a cinderblock sitting in the middle of it. The last time I'd admitted to any kind of feelings toward another person, it had nearly destroyed me. I couldn't... *wouldn't* do it again.

Lucky was so quiet that I once again thought he'd drifted off, hoped for it even, but then he was pushing gently against my chest. There was little fight in him, so it would've been easy enough to hold on to him. I almost did just that because I was reluctant to give up on the press of his body against mine, but then he said, "Please, Zach, I'm going to be sick."

I released him enough that he could turn away from me. He bent over and threw up into the gutter. I kept my hand on his back as best I could as I reached into my truck and grabbed my bottle of water from the console between the front seats. Lucky refused to make eye contact with me after the violent retching ended. There was no mistaking the tears running down his face, though, and while I could've attributed them to the act of vomiting, I couldn't help but wonder if maybe some of those tears were there for an entirely different reason. I handed Lucky the water and tried to avert my eyes so I wouldn't embarrass him as he rinsed out his mouth. My phone buzzed in my pocket. A quick glance at the screen showed a text from Minna.

Where are you? Do you have him?

I kept my answer simple. *Yes. Outside.*

I knew what her response would be long before I got it, and I berated myself for already knowing what I would tell her when her text did come. I didn't even have to think about it, and that was a problem.

A big fucking problem.

I'll be right out to take him home.

My fingers hovered over the keypad as I stole a glance at Lucky. He was leaning back against the side of my truck looking completely worn out. But he refused to make eye contact with me. Instead he was staring off to his right at absolutely nothing.

"Are you ready to go?" I asked him.

He didn't ask where and he didn't ask about Minna or his apartment or anything else. All he did was nod his head. I wanted to believe it was because of his inherent trust in me to watch out for him, but I knew that wasn't it.

He was done. Just *done*. And I had no doubt I was the cause.

I helped Lucky into the truck and got him buckled in. He made no effort to assist me, nor did he acknowledge me in any kind of way. His bleary eyes stared out the windshield. I closed the door and went around to the driver's side of the truck. By the time I climbed into my own seat and got the vehicle started, Lucky's head had lolled to the side and his eyes were shut.

The ding on my phone reminded me of Minna's last message.

I sent Lucky one more glance and told myself the right thing to do would be to send him home with his friend.

That was the *right thing* to do.

But that wasn't what I did.

Instead, I quickly typed a message to Minna and hit send before putting the truck in gear and pulling away from the curb.

Taking him with me. He'll text you in the morning.

CHAPTER 8

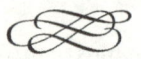

LUCKY

I was never going to drink again.

I remembered telling myself that same thing the last time I'd gotten drunk, which had been closer to the start of the school year. I'd just started seeing a guy who, thankfully, had been very comfortably out of the closet and hadn't looked even a little like Zach. I'd foolishly gotten my hopes up that it was a sign that I'd finally found what my fathers had with each other... or at least the start of it. Unfortunately, the guy hadn't gotten the same message from the universe because I'd caught him fucking his Biology TA the morning after our third date.

The asshole's insistence that none of it would've happened if I'd just loosened up and put out had been a stinging blow, and I'd spent the evening doing shots with my friends at a local bar. Min had tried to cut me off at a certain point, but I'd been too busy trying to silence the voice in my head that had reminded me that yet another man had found me lacking.

That was the night I'd met Davis Teasley. He'd flirted with me in the privacy of the bathroom when no one else had been around and when he'd put my hand on his groin, all I'd been able to think about was losing yet another cute guy because of some childish notion that my soulmate was out there waiting for me. By the time Davis had come all over my hand, I'd felt sick to my stomach. I'd wanted to blame the alcohol but my nausea and my regret had had nothing to do with the booze. It had felt cheap and easy, which was the complete opposite of what my dads had.

I'd figured I'd never see Davis again, but when he'd appeared at my apartment the next day with a bottle of aspirin and some soup, my naïve heart had fallen for all of it. We'd spent the afternoon in my bed and in between the hand jobs and then ultimately the oral sex I'd performed on him, Davis had held me in his arms and told me how amazing I was. I'd once again felt sick to my stomach, but there'd been this warmth in my chest that I hadn't been able to deny. I'd soaked up his praise, and in the following months, I'd eagerly dropped to my knees whenever he'd wanted. I'd convinced myself that the fact that he wouldn't be seen in public with me hadn't been a huge problem... that it was something we'd work through eventually.

The reality was that I just hadn't wanted to give up the feeling of being wanted by someone.

But it had never been about *someone*... it had been about one particular someone.

And that someone hadn't been Davis Teasley.

I wanted to curse the fact that I'd overindulged the night before when I hadn't had so much as even a drink after I'd learned Davis had a girlfriend, and a very pregnant one at that.

No, it had taken only one round with Zach Warner to have me reaching for the very vice I'd so hated when I'd been a kid. My mother and the string of boyfriends she'd kept had made alcohol a regular part of our lives, but it hadn't been until after moving in with Bennett and Xander that I'd realized what role booze had really played during my childhood.

"Never again," I tried to say to myself, but my mouth was too full of cotton. My pounding head and rolling stomach made me sink further into the warmth of my bed instead of seeking out a much-needed glass of water. I reached a hand out to my nightstand to see if I could get to my phone so I could beg Min via text to bring me some water.

It would be well worth the lecture she'd force on me. While Min was all for enjoying some imbibing, she was like a mom on steroids when it came to me drinking too much.

Probably because she knew how much I'd hate myself for it afterwards.

I slapped my hand around on the nightstand but there was no phone. I rolled over to check the other nightstand on the opposite side but encountered dead air instead.

What the hell?

Had I moved my nightstand in the middle of the night? Jesus, how drunk had I been?

I tried to remember the events of the night before. There'd been the drinks with the weird name that I'd downed like candy and there'd been a guy who hadn't had any issue with putting his arms around me on the dance floor but hadn't smelled like the woods. He hadn't been all growly and demanding either. He'd been exactly what I'd been looking for—a casual fling with a guy who wanted me.

I found myself reaching to touch my lips and wondered if I'd finally given up on my kissing moratorium. I tried to close my eyes even more as if that would somehow miraculously bring back all the memories, but there were only bits and pieces. And the only thing I could remember about my lips was touching them against hot, coiled ropes of muscle as I inhaled the sweet scent of...

"Woods," I somehow scratched out.

Oh god.

No, no, no, I silently repeated to myself.

I like you just fine.

"Asshole," I whispered to myself. He liked me just fine. *Just fine.* What a dick. Okay, yeah, I'd stupidly bared part of my soul to him, *again*, but why couldn't he just have kept his mouth shut? Or even just told me the truth? Just fine? Who the fuck said shit like that?

"Here," I heard a rough voice say.

No.

Fucking.

Way.

No, it just wasn't possible. It just wasn't. My luck absolutely, positively, could not be this bad. It just couldn't. My name was Lucky, for Christ's sake. That had to count for something.

But the sound of a water bottle being shaken near my ear said otherwise.

"You're not here," I murmured. "You. Are. Not. Here."

"Drink this or you'll get dehydrated. There's aspirin on the nightstand. The one to your right. The only one."

I thrust out my hand because I knew I was screwed no matter what I did. Maybe I'd actually get lucky and drown while drinking it. The plastic of the bottle felt cold against my skin but my embarrassment was making my blood run hot.

"The cap is already off," Zach said softly.

I wanted to smack him for that. So he could be considerate enough to take the cap off the fucking water bottle, but he couldn't come up with a line that was a little less condescending than *I like you just fine*?

I managed to hold my tongue as I swallowed down a few tugs of water. Once my mouth felt relatively normal, I could taste the sourness of vomit. I groaned when I realized that meant the image of me throwing up next to Zach's truck wasn't just my rampant imagination.

"What's wrong?" Zach asked. I still hadn't opened my eyes but when the bed dipped and a warm, firm palm was pressed against my forehead, I actually jumped.

My eyes popped open and were greeted with the sight of Zach frowning at me. "Nothing," I ground out. "Everything's perfect. Just fucking perfect." I took another sip of water and then glanced around the room. It was clear that it was a motel room. Not particularly cheap looking, but not extravagant either. It was just... blah. There was a green canvas duffel bag sitting on a chair, but that was all I saw. There were no clothes lying about, no personal items like a cell phone or tablet, and no clutter to show that the room had even been occupied.

"Guess I really am a cheap date," I joked, though nothing about the situation felt funny.

Zach, who was dressed in a pair of jeans and a snug black T-shirt that hugged his body perfectly, followed my gaze. "I like to keep things simple," was all he said.

I laughed even though it made my head hurt even more. "Yes, you do," I agreed. "I'm sure my fathers will appreciate you staying under budget."

I made a move to get out of bed, but before I could shift my legs, Zach grabbed my arm and pressed me back against the headboard. His eyes glittered with anger. "For the last time, I'm here for a job. And that job is not you. If I hear you talk about your fathers or yourself like that again—"

"You'll what?" I snapped, my patience with the whole situation coming to an end.

I expected him to threaten me and steeled myself for it. But when the threat came, I was in no way prepared for it. Because Zach chose to lean in until he was practically in my face. I could see every one of the little flecks in his beautiful eyes. With the headboard at my back, I had absolutely no place to go. I wasn't sure that I would've gone anywhere, though, if given the option.

"Don't push this," he growled.

It was the absolute wrong thing to say to me. Zach had no clue that in the years since I'd left home, I'd become an adrenaline junkie. I thrived on danger and challenge, and Zach was both and more. I wanted desperately to know what would happen if I pushed him over the edge. Would it finally get a rise out of him? Not the kind that had happened by accident when he'd had a PTSD episode, but the kind where he let loose the tight hold he had on his self-control.

"Or what? You'll spank me?" I paused for effect and then said, "Careful, I might enjoy being bent over your knee."

If I hadn't been looking into Zach's eyes when I'd spoken, I would've missed it. The emotion was that fleeting. It was pure hunger and raw need. I hadn't been serious about the spanking comment, but just seeing Zach's reaction was like having a lightbulb go on in my head.

First off, there was no denying what that look meant. He *did* want me. Even if he liked me *just fine*, he couldn't deny what his body wanted.

Second, it meant Zach was into men. I'd thought that he'd sent me certain looks as I'd gotten older, but they'd always been so fleeting that I hadn't been sure. After the disastrous Christmas Eve where I'd laid my heart on the line for him, he'd made a comment about me not being his type, so I'd just assumed it had been his way of telling me he wasn't gay or bi.

Third, it was confirmation that I'd been approaching this thing with Zach all wrong. I'd been pursuing him relentlessly, but it hadn't ever occurred to me that maybe he'd want to do the pursuing. But I knew that wasn't quite enough. If I wanted a shot with Zach, I'd have to give him that little extra push. And if I did happen to get him past whatever line he'd drawn in the sand for himself, I had to accept that it would quite likely be another Davis Teasley kind of relationship.

Was I really willing to give up so much of myself again? Even if it would be for the one man I'd spent years pining over? Maybe that was exactly why I needed to do this. Maybe it was the only way to move on and find a nice guy who would treat me the way I needed to be treated, the way I *deserved* to be treated. If I got Zach out of my system, maybe I could finally let someone else in.

Warning bells went off in my head that I was playing with fire, but I didn't care. Even if all I managed to do was send Zach a message that I was no longer the kid he'd left behind, it would be well worth it. I'd already learned that there were more frogs out there than princes. The hopelessly lovesick teenager in me would always see Zach as a prince. Maybe if I did this, my heart would finally understand that he really was nothing more than a frog.

I swore I heard Zach growl beneath his breath, and I was admittedly disappointed when he pushed back from me. He still had his hand on my arm, but his grip had loosened. I knew I'd won this round, though I hadn't really wanted to. Oddly enough, now that I'd thought about being bent over the man's knee and having his big hand coming down on my bare ass, I couldn't *not* think about it.

It was time to poke the bear a bit. I battled back the unsteady feeling in my belly and took another sip of the water, making sure to run my wet tongue over my lips. It was all I could do not to do a victory dance when Zach's eyes dropped to my mouth. He slowly pulled his hand away from my arm and put as much distance between us as he could without actually getting off the bed.

I used the opportunity to slide my legs from beneath the blanket. I could tell I wasn't wearing any pants and while that knowledge would have tempered my behavior a few minutes ago, now I was going to use it to my full advantage. "You know where my cell phone is?" I asked.

"Minna knows you're here," Zach responded.

"I figured. No, I actually want to see if I got calls from anyone else." I threw back the blanket as I spoke. By chance, I'd worn a pair of my sexier underwear. It was a tiny pair of navy briefs that tended to ride up my ass cheeks when I bent over and cupped my dick nice and snugly in the front. I did my best to ignore Zach as I stood up, making sure to give the man a clear view of my backside as I pretended to look for my clothes.

"Who are you expecting a call from?" Zach asked, his voice sharp. I felt like a kid in a candy store. How in the hell had I not realized any of this sooner? Oh yeah, maybe because I'd never considered myself overly attractive, so it hadn't occurred to me that maybe Zach would see me any differently than I did. I was decently muscled from my work, but I was still on the lean side. I just wasn't the kind of guy who would ever be as buff as Zach. And I wasn't tall and skinny and pretty like some of the guys that were so popular at the various gay clubs I'd been to. I considered myself merely average. Who knew that average was just fine with Zach?

"That guy I was with last night…" I began. Then I blanked on his name and realized maybe that wasn't such a bad thing. I sent a silent apology to the guy and said, "Ray or Rick or Rod—" I began.

"Rafe," Zach supplied, but not without irritation.

"Rafe," I repeated. I paused in my pretend searching for my clothes and murmured, "What an exotic name. He was hot, right? I mean, I know you're not into any of that, but if you were, you'd think he was hot, right?" I sent Zach a glance. His face was hard as granite and he had fisted his hands at some point. "I know I'm being shallow, but it's not like I'm looking for my future husband, you know? I just need to get—"

"You said you hadn't been kissed," Zach snapped. His voice was loud in the small room.

"What?" I asked, more to buy myself some time because he'd caught me off guard with the statement.

"You said you hadn't been kissed since you were a kid. That you'd been waiting."

Did he actually seem angry? That didn't make any sense. For him to be angry, he would've had to feel like I was somehow betraying him. But how could you betray someone who didn't want what you were offering?

I shrugged my shoulders and then dropped my fingers to the waistband of my underwear and began fiddling with the material and running a fingertip through the hair leading up to my belly button. "It's not really Rafe's *lips* that I'm particularly interested in," I said. I spied my clothes on a chair in the corner, but took my time working my way over to them. I checked the pocket of my jeans and found my wayward phone. I pretended to look for a message, but since I probably hadn't had a chance to give Rafe my number, I knew there wouldn't be one. And I wasn't particularly disappointed by that fact. Rafe had been hot, and sweet too, but even in my drunken state, his hands on me had still felt wrong. I remembered letting him lead me to the back of the club and then outside. He'd been fondling me through my pants and I'd enjoyed that well enough, but there'd been this voice in my head the entire time reminding me that he wasn't Zach.

That was the voice I needed to silence for good.

I continued with my little experiment by eagerly checking my phone. There were tons of messages from Min, but I didn't bother reading any of them.

"He didn't message you," Zach bit out.

"Tsk, tsk, tsk," I said with a shake of my head. "Have you been invading my privacy?" I asked as I held up my phone. I expected

Zach to be embarrassed, but instead, he stood up and strode toward me. I held my breath as he reached for my phone and then tossed it casually onto the bed. He didn't say or do anything else, so I wasn't sure what to make of the move. I shrugged my shoulders and said, "No matter. He's a regular at the club. I'm sure he'll be there tonight."

"You're not going back there," Zach growled.

I reached for my pants and took my time slowly drawing them on, making sure to turn my body so Zach had a good view of my ass as I worked the fabric up my legs. I left the pants unbuttoned as I grabbed my shirt and toyed with it.

"Are you gonna play chaperone?" I asked. "Because I don't think a guy like Rafe really cares if we have an audience or not. I kind of got that vibe from him. I think he even mentioned something about inviting others to join us—"

That was all I got out before Zach closed his fingers around my throat and walked me backwards until my back hit the closet behind me. His hold on me was gentle, so I knew he wasn't having an episode. But the expression in his eyes was clear as day.

He was pissed. Hell, pissed probably wasn't even the right word. Enraged was better. But it was a quiet rage that left me apprehensive.

"Are you sure you want to do this?" Zach asked softly.

Too softly.

His body was so close to mine that I could feel his reaction to my needling. There was no mistaking the erection that was pressing against his jeans and into me. My intention to mess around with him flew by the wayside as my body went up in flames. I'd never been so turned on in all my life. I didn't know what that made me, but I didn't care either. All that mattered to me was that I was his. Whether it was for a few seconds or a few minutes, I didn't care.

I was his.

"Are *you*?" I managed to ask. His thumb was brushing back and forth over my pulse, so I knew he had to feel how my heart was racing.

He ground his hips into mine. "What does that tell you?" he asked.

"This is what you wanted, right? To prove to yourself, to me, that I can't keep denying that I want you?"

It was the way he asked the question that kept me silent. Not only did he sound angry, but he sounded disappointed. Like *I'd* disappointed him somehow.

"Has it ever occurred to you that there's a reason I've stayed away from you?" he asked bitterly.

I shook my head because it honestly hadn't. Yes, he was friends with my parents and his brother was like an uncle of sorts, but I hadn't seen that as a tipping point. Maybe I'd just assumed that my fathers and his brother would understand. They'd get that I was an adult, that my feelings for Zach were genuine, and that my decision to be with him was just that... *my* decision.

"My parents—"

"It's not about your fucking parents!" he practically yelled. It was the most emotion I'd seen out of him in a long time. He seemed less like a hardened soldier and more like... *a man.*

A broken mystery of a man.

Zach pulled in a breath as if he were trying to get control of himself. He dropped his eyes briefly, and I held my tongue. I sensed I was in completely new territory, one which I was entirely ill-equipped to handle. My fears were confirmed when Zach said, "Look at that bed, Lucky. What do you think will happen there? We'll start by fooling around a little, you get that kiss you want, and then we'll make love and spout some bullshit words to each other? Afterwards, we'll cuddle and talk about our feelings?"

The way he made it sound was ridiculous of course, but even more ridiculous was the fact that maybe I *had* thought it would end up that way. Maybe there would've been some kinky stuff going on which I would have been all-in for, but yes, afterwards, we would've lain in each other's arms and joked about why it had taken so long to end up there.

"Zach," I began, but he shook his head.

"My turn," he bit out. "You want to know what would really happen in that bed? You'd get fucked," Zach growled. "Literally and figuratively. Because I would take you in every way that I want to, my relationship with your parents and my brother be damned. There'd be none of your precious kissing or sweet words. It would be me telling you how I want you and where. It would be me ordering you to take my cock so far down your throat that you wouldn't be able to breathe. You'd have to watch and wait for me to give you the order to take that breath and then we'd start all over again. I'd come before you... maybe once, maybe twice, maybe a dozen times. On your back, on your stomach, on your knees—for as long and as hard and as fast as I want it. And the only time you'd get to say no was when you were ready to walk away." Despite the crudeness of his words, Zach's thumb gently caressed my skin. "Afterwards, that's it. There wouldn't be a repeat and there sure as shit wouldn't be cuddling and words of love or us spending the night asleep in each other's arms. We wouldn't be exchanging phone numbers or sending cute little texts to each other. I wouldn't be making promises of fidelity while we're apart and there wouldn't be any declarations in front of your friends or family."

Every word Zach spoke was delivered with such coldness that it left my insides feeling like ice. All the pleasure in knowing he wanted me was gone. There was no doubt in my mind he meant every word he said. With Davis, there'd been an illusion of contentment, and that had been enough for a while. With a guy like Rafe, there'd be some harmless but mutually beneficial fun. With Zach... I knew he'd slay me. In my gut, I knew I could take anything he dished out physically. But to have him regard me that coolly, to be able to walk away from me so easily...

I shook my head because I knew that was the part I wasn't equipped to deal with.

Zach's hold on my throat disappeared, but only so his hand could slide down to rest in the center of my chest. He almost looked disappointed, but I couldn't understand why. He wanted my body and nothing more. I was a conquest, one of probably many. He could find ten of me in any club who would be more than willing to give him what he wanted, who would thrive on it. I hadn't even answered him, so why did he look so... rejected?

It was a feeling I was all too familiar with. The idea that he could be afflicted with the same insecurities chipped away at the ice inside of me. "Zach—"

"Don't, Lucky," Zach whispered. His eyes were on the hand he had over my heart. "If you care about me like you claimed to two years ago, then don't do this."

I snapped my mouth shut because I *had* been about to do it. I *had* been about to throw caution to the wind and tell him that it didn't matter. That I'd take him no matter how I could get him. His plea for me to be the one to say no meant there was shit going on inside of him that I couldn't even begin to understand. I had a million questions, desperate ones that I hoped would somehow help me make sense of him. But I didn't utter even one of them.

Instead, I did the hardest thing I'd ever had to do and reached up to cover his hand with mine. But I didn't link our fingers like I craved, or pull his hand up to my mouth for a kiss. Instead, I wrapped my fingers around his wrist and gently removed his hand from my chest. "I should go," I somehow managed to croak out. It made me feel like a failure, like I was letting him down, but he just looked relieved.

He didn't try to stop me as I shrugged my shirt on and he didn't move when I brushed past him to grab my phone off the bed. My feet felt like they had lead weights on them as I slipped on my shoes and made my way to the door. I searched for something to say to him, but there were no words. I wanted to stay, and I wanted to go. So I settled for what *he* wanted and walked through the door, not looking back.

Even though that was all I really wanted to do.

CHAPTER 9

ZACH

I'd been at the training center in Glacier National Park for five days. Five days of trying not to think of Lucky heading to his summer job in Yellowstone. With any luck, I wouldn't see the kid again for a long while. When I was done training Tag's airborne search and rescue recruits, I'd squeeze in a quick Colorado visit before Lucky had a chance to take a break from his own summer job, and then I'd be on my way... somewhere... after that.

The fact I didn't yet know what I wanted to do now that I was worthless as a soldier was a sore subject and the very last thing I wanted to think about when I was already in a deep enough pit of self-loathing after turning Lucky away.

It was for the best. He had a bright future ahead of him regardless of which direction he chose, and his leaving Davis behind for the summer hopefully meant whatever stalking behavior had been going on would stay behind in Missoula or travel back to Denver with the richie-rich himself. Either way, I'd forced myself to accept that Yellowstone would be a fairly benign place for Lucky to spend the summer, especially since he'd been there before and presumably had friends already. Although Jake had indicated Lucky was a trail guide for tourists, I couldn't imagine that was true if he had medical training. Worst-case scenario, he was actually working as a paramedic in the park doing nothing more than treating tourists for heat exhaustion, heart attacks, and minor scrapes and sprains. Either way, he'd be safer there than in Missoula.

And more importantly, he'd be safe from me.

It took me the better part of these five days to properly compartmentalize Lucky back into that no-go part of my brain where I kept other things I didn't want to spend much time thinking about. Arriving at Tag's Glacier base of operations helped. Once there, I'd thrown myself into preparing for the advanced alpine search and rescue training I'd been hired to manage by familiarizing myself with the differences between Tag's airborne search and rescue protocol and what we'd used in the military.

The model of the helicopter Tag would be flying was one I was very familiar with, so it didn't take long for me to feel comfortable working with him getting her ready for the course. We'd already completed several test flights in the first few days I'd been there. Not being able to fly the bird myself because of my damned head was frustrating enough, so I vowed to give one hundred and ten percent to the rest of it, including producing the best-trained high mountain airborne SAR specialists possible.

After one final check of the belly band and hoist after our most recent morning flight, I headed back outside to join Tag at a picnic table in the grassy area behind the large hangar. My knee was sore as hell from pushing it too hard on the trail runs I'd been attempting every evening. Despite the injury, I was determined to get back some semblance of normal, and running was part of it. I did my best to hide the pain with a slow and deliberate walk around the side of the building, but I must not have hidden it well enough.

"You okay?" Tag asked as he saw me.

I gritted my teeth and doubled down on ignoring the pain. "Yep. Fine. What's on the menu today?"

Tag's wife, Heather, had been kind enough to send Tag to work each day with a big cooler full of lunch and drinks for us, and I'd already fantasized about sending her a bouquet of flowers if only she'd keep the food coming all summer long.

"Chicken and stuff left over from last night."

Once Tag passed me my share, I dug into the best damned roasted chicken I'd ever tasted. I groaned in appreciation.

"Please tell Heather I want to have her children," I said. "This is fucking amazing, and I know *you* can't cook for shit."

Tag nodded and gestured toward the other items on my plate. "Wait till you get to the ramen noodle salad. That shit's insane."

We ate in silence for a while, thoroughly enjoying the home-cooked food in the late-May sunshine. The weather wasn't very warm, but the sun was enough to lift my dark spirits.

"What about you?" Tag asked after we slowed down.

"What about me?"

"You dating anyone? Got a girl stashed somewhere?"

I didn't answer right away since my mind automatically went to Lucky and the mini reverse striptease he'd done for me in my hotel room the morning after his drunken episode. His intent to make me jealous had worked one hundred and ten percent. Only problem was, he hadn't understood what any of that meant, and a tiny part of me had almost hated him in that moment where I'd had to practically beg him not to push me any further.

I silently berated myself when I realized how quickly my thoughts had gone back to the young man I was so determined to forget. So much for compartmentalizing.

"Or a boy," Tag added with a wink, bringing me back to the present. "Don't much matter to me. Hope you know that. In fact, that reminds me…"

"No," I said finally, cutting off what I knew would be one of Tag's countless offers to set me up with some guy or girl who would be "perfect" for me. "Nobody nowhere, and I like it that way," I added.

"Well, don't let Heather hear you say that unless you're ready to be set up with every damned bachelor and bachelorette in Kalispell." He winked at me and reached for the Ziploc bag of brownies at the end of the table.

I thought of the small town closest to the park. "There can't be more than, what? Three or four of them?" I teased. "No thanks. I'm happier on my own anyway."

Tag narrowed his eyes at me as if he was going to call me on my bullshit. Before he could, I added, "And don't give me that crap about Heather being the one to play matchmaker. I know you're the one who insists on watching that dating show. Heather told me you wrote the host and gave him some tips on how to improve those bogus rose ceremonies."

Tag paused in his chewing and eyed me in all seriousness. "Hey, those people are fighting to find their one true love." It was all I could do not to laugh as he struggled to finish chewing before muttering, "Looks like me and the missus need to have a little talk about discretion."

Since I knew where Tag and Heather's little "talks" always ended up, I changed the subject by saying, "What were you going to say earlier when you said 'that reminds me'?"

"Oh." Tag snapped his fingers. "This kid in the program. I keep meaning to tell you about him. He took the basic hoist class last year and did so well, I encouraged him to take the advanced cliff rescue course this summer."

I glanced up at him. "What do you mean, kid?"

Tag grinned. "He's not really a kid. The man has full SAR experience and medical training like the rest of the students. I only mean he's so young and energetic, he makes me feel old." He chuckled. "But he's a natural on the hoist and is totally fucking steady under pressure. We had this one trip out during the training course where the wind picked up during a longline drill and damned near snapped a rigging plate into one of the trainees' faces just after he'd reached the ground and disconnected the line. The trainee himself froze, but this kid saw it coming and managed to shove the trainee down to the ground just in time."

"Jesus," I muttered, reaching for the brownies. "Lucky trainee."

Tag snorted. "Lucky me since I'm the one paying the liability insurance on this operation. Anyway, another time he noticed a bolt had come loose on the hoist mounting plate. I almost puked right there on the poor kid's shoes. Fired the training manager on the spot. That's why I can't thank you enough for bailing my ass out of a bind this summer. I needed a trainer I could trust."

I blew out a breath. "Fuck, Tag. Remind me to quadruple check those mounting plates. Christ."

His eyes widened. "Right? I still have nightmares about how close we came to a disaster. You should have seen how much money I spent on inspections after that to make sure nothing else had been overlooked."

"Don't blame you." I thought back to how quickly things could go wrong on a rescue mission. "Sometimes all it takes is one wrong move."

He reached over and clamped a hand on my shoulder. "Let's change the subject, or better yet, get back to work. I've got another instructor coming, and you've got mounting brackets to look over two or twelve times." Tag's goofy grin reappeared, telling me our serious talk was over.

"Aye-aye, captain," I said with a mock salute, standing to gather my trash and help clean up.

Tag joined me back in the hangar where he introduced me to a newcomer. The man was attractive and windburned like he'd spent the better part of the winter on the ski slopes.

"Zach, meet Johnny Poole. He's our paramedic and he's also a rope access tech and an excellent spotter. He'll be helping you with prep and rigging, and he'll manage the medical aspects when we get to that stage of the course. Got his start rock climbing as a teen then worked his way up to Alaska where he got his airborne rescue training from the Coast Guard. Johnny, Zach Warner is our lead trainer. Been leading airborne SAR missions since before he got all fancy and became an Army Ranger on us."

I shot Tag the bird before shaking Johnny's hand. "Nice to meet you. Have you done mountain and cliff work on a hoist or longline?"

He nodded and grinned. "Both. And heli-rappelling. Worked at Rainier before coming here. Promise I know my shit. You focus on teaching the newbies what to do, and I'll try not to let you lose any external human cargo. Tag here says it's bad for business."

I shook my head and reminded myself that I trusted Tag. If he'd hired this guy, especially after having trouble with one of last year's employees, he'd made sure the guy was airtight. "Alright, smart-ass. I can see you'll fit in just fine around here. Let me show you the bird."

As soon as I began walking Johnny around the fuselage, pointing out the longline and hoist equipment, he was all business. "Tag said this first group is here for advanced mountain and cliff rescue. I guess that means they're already familiar with the hoist?"

"Yeah. They've all taken basic inland hoist courses and are ready for riskier missions. None of them have worked in flight SAR before, though, so they're all still greenhorns as far as I'm concerned."

"No doubt," he murmured, yanking on one of the mounted hooks before moving to test another one. "You sound like the hardass who trained me. Most meticulous motherfucker I've ever met. Taught me there was no such thing as over-prepared when it came to protecting the lives of the victims and operators."

I liked the sound of that. The man took things as seriously as I did. I met his eyes. "One of my mentors always said that downtime was to be spent either getting more trauma response education or helo maintenance experience so that when shit went down, you could be part of the solution. First thing she ever told me about helicopter rescue was that shit always went down. How you handled it was what separated a successful operator from a dead one."

"Hardcore like mine," he said with a laugh.

I nodded. "We used to joke that she ate carabiners for breakfast, but she knew her shit. Every course she ever taught, she picked the sloppiest tech and booted them right out to teach the rest of us a lesson."

We spent the rest of the afternoon in companionable conversation about search and rescue missions we'd been on and emergencies we'd faced. By the time the workday ended and we'd completed two test flights, I felt comfortable working alongside Johnny and knew Tag had made the right decision in hiring him.

I headed back to the little rental cabin in the woods that Tag had helped me find. It was nice being a few miles away from anyone else at the end of the day, especially after tomorrow when the students would arrive. I knew from experience that training rookies was exhausting since it demanded complete focus and there was no room for fucking up. Being able to escape to my own place at the end of a training day would be critical.

But being alone also meant time to think, which was the last thing I wanted or needed. It was one of the reasons I kept finding myself out on the trails in the evening pushing my knee well past its new limits. After Tag had caught me limping earlier in the day, I knew I needed to abandon any idea of getting back out there tonight. Instead, I christened the cabin's small grill with a fat steak, forced myself to stick to water instead of the beer that would have tasted ten times better, and rounded out the thrilling evening with a long, hot shower.

And if I fantasized about pushing a young, perky-assed paramedic up against the shower wall and fucking his brains out while the hot water beat down on us, well, it was no one's business but my own. But the fantasy followed me from my jerk-off session in the shower into my dreams. It began as purely sexual but then morphed into a crazy combination of flashbacks in which Lucky took the place of one of my teammates. For hours I thrashed around inside my head, screaming for him to get down, take cover, anything to stay alive. But time after time he ignored me, acted as if I wasn't even there, and walked right into danger.

When I woke up gasping and drenched in sweat, I'd never been so relieved to hear my alarm blaring. I returned to the shower in a completely different mood than I'd entered it the night before. It was time to prepare for work, and I needed to get my damned head on straight.

A class full of students were counting on me to lead them through some very dangerous training today, and I needed to focus in order to keep them all safe. I'd be damned if I was going to let my asinine obsession with Lucky Reed fuck with my job.

I whipped up some eggs, made a giant coffee in a travel mug, and hopped in the truck. When I got to the hangar, I felt marginally better. It was going to be a great day. The course was finally beginning and it would help me get my head out of my ass and move on.

Tag met me on the tarmac with a big grin. "Ready to meet the class? It's like Christmas morning in there. Nerves and excitement about what the day will bring. I fucking love this job, man."

I grinned back at him. "Not sure who's more excited, them or you."

He laughed and clapped me on the back as we entered the hangar's single classroom. He was right about the nerves and excitement. The room buzzed with it.

"I'm dying to introduce you to that kid I told you about. It figures he's sitting right up front. C'mon."

We made our way through a group of people chatting and sipping coffee out of paper cups. When we reached the front row of seats, I stopped in my tracks and nearly choked on my own coffee.

"Zach, meet Lucky Reed. Lucky, this is my buddy, Zach. He'll be leading the…"

His voice faded out as the blood roared in my ears. I barely registered the fact that Lucky looked as shocked and horrified as I felt. What the hell was he doing here? He was supposed to be safe down in Yellowstone leading nature walks and educating foolish tourists on the benefits of wearing appropriate footwear on hiking trails and the importance of staying hydrated.

My brain quickly shifted from the picture of a genuinely sincere Lucky chatting happily with a park-goer to him hanging in a harness from a moving helicopter over a sheer mountain rock face with only a length of rope to keep him from plunging hundreds of feet to his death.

"No," I barked. Half the people in the room turned to stare at me. My heart hammered in my chest and I felt like I was having trouble breathing. "No fucking way," I said in a lower voice. My eyes pinned Lucky's as he actually began to stand and reach his hand out to mine like we were meeting for the first time. It didn't even occur to me to take his hand and play into the act. "Lucky, outside. *Now.*"

Lucky's pretty brown eyes went from nervous and unsure to little chips of ice just like that. His entire body stiffened and something in his jaw began to tic as he sat back down in his seat. Not surprisingly, my body reacted accordingly.

"How about no?" he said. "Not only no, but *hell no*. I'm fine where I am."

Tag looked back and forth between us. "Uh, I assume you two already know each other?"

I reached for Lucky's upper arm and pulled him up, leaning in to speak quietly in his ear. "If you think for one minute I'm allowing you inside that helicopter, you're dead fucking wrong. So you can either come outside to talk about it or sit in here and waste your time learning about something you're never going to actually do."

His entire body shook with fury. "Fine," he hissed. "Jackass," he added under his breath.

When we reached the cooler air outside the hangar, I pulled him around the corner and away from view. My brain was whirring in some kind of unproductive spin-cycle in which I stood no chance at putting together a rational argument.

Lucky yanked his arm out of my grip and turned to face me. The morning sunlight washed across his face, pulling warm brown streaks from his hair and setting his eyelashes alight. I realized how much the outdoor living in Colorado had lightened his hair over the years. He was so fucking beautiful, it hurt.

"You're supposed to be in Wyoming," I said like an idiot.

Lucky lifted an eyebrow. "And you're supposed to be a professional."

I clenched my teeth. "Dammit, Lucky, you can't be here." Great, now I was on the verge of whining. Maybe I needed to stomp my foot for good measure.

"But I am," he said calmly. "So unless you can give me an actual reason why I can't participate in your class…"

In desperation, I pulled out the big guns. "Do your dads know you're here?"

Lucky's nostrils flared, and I felt the pinch of regret. "Does Tag know you have PTSD and crippling migraines?"

His question was like a punch to the gut but only because it was a reminder that I hadn't told Tag the extent of my medical issues. I'd started on a migraine prevention medication, and it was on the tip of my tongue to tell Lucky what was truly behind the PTSD episodes when I managed to catch myself and snap my mouth shut before any words could escape.

A cool breeze ruffled Lucky's hair and a bird squawked somewhere in the distance as Lucky and I stared at each other. I heard the sound of metal clanking from another hangar farther down the airfield. Finally, Johnny poked his head around the side of the building.

"Uh, Zach? We're kind of waiting on you to get the ball rolling in here." He noticed Lucky and lit up like a damned Christmas tree. "Oh, hello. Are you in our class?" He reached out a hand to shake. "I'm Johnny—"

"Give us a minute," I snapped. Johnny's eyes widened in surprise.

"Yeah, uh, no problem. See you in there."

When I turned back to Lucky, his eyes were shining with what I could only classify as mischief and his full lips quirked up. "Single?" he asked. "He's cute."

I wondered if Lucky was trained in how to treat a stroke.

CHAPTER 10

LUCKY

I'd never lied to my dads quite this badly before. It was one thing to neglect to tell them about my EMT job at Yellowstone last summer or my paramedic certification this year at school, but it was quite another to tell them I was in Wyoming at Yellowstone while I was secretly in Glacier in northern Montana planning to rappel off a helicopter in flight.

Because of the deception, not to mention the constant thoughts I had about how Zach and I had left things, I carried a low-key nervous stomach all the time. I knew it would be better if I could just tell my parents once and for all what I was doing, but every time I thought I was ready to spill my guts, they'd tell me about Lola's colic or Danny's first tooth or which baby was closer to saying "Dada" or any of the other million adorable things the newest members of the family did and I'd conveniently "forget" to tell them what I was up to. Using the twins as an excuse to keep my secrets to myself was awfully convenient. I knew that. But I was too chickenshit to change it.

So when I'd arrived at the aviation center for my SAR course, my usual nervous stomach had been compounded by the gut-gripping fear that I'd fuck up in the class and my dads would discover my deception via a phone call from a first responder. It was only the slow breathing exercises I'd picked up in counseling that were keeping me from completely freaking out. I knew the exhilaration I'd feel at the end of the day would make these nerves pale in comparison.

I'd taken a seat in the front row and concentrated on breathing until I'd seen Tag walk in. The thrill of finally being able to get started on the training had been instantly obliterated the second I'd noticed the man beside him.

My heart rate had shot through the roof and it had taken everything in me not to start throwing questions at Zach.

Had he had any more migraines or PTSD episodes?

Did he hate me for the stunt I'd pulled when I'd tried to make him jealous in his hotel room?

Did he miss me even the tiniest bit?

But before I'd even been able to greet Zach with polite, professional detachment, he'd begun barking at me again like I was a child.

And there had gone my own professionalism. I had no clue what it was about Zach's arrogant demands that always had me pushing back, because he was one of the only people I ever seemed to do that with, but when he'd threatened to not let me participate in the course, I'd had to give in. I'd followed him outside, frantically trying to come up with a way to convince him to let me stay in the course since I needed this certification and there weren't many programs that offered it. I felt bad about using his PTSD against him, but I'd be damned if I was going to let the controlling asshole keep me from pursuing my dream. If he didn't want me in his life, fine. But then he didn't get to have a say on how that life was going to be lived.

I regretted my desperate attempt to pretend like I was interested in the guy I assumed was our straight pilot the second the man disappeared back into the hangar, but as soon as I returned my eyes to Zach and saw the way he was standing with arms crossed and jaw hard, my mouth opened of its own volition. "Single?" I asked.

"Stay away from him," Zach growled.

"He's cute. I wonder if he has his own place, or—"

"Stay the fuck away from him."

I tilted my head and studied Zach. I was still blown away by the knowledge that he wanted me and even if it made me a bad person, I loved knowing he was jealous. Unlike the last time I'd needled him about being interested in some other guy, there was something lighter in him this time. Yeah, he was pissed, of course, and he looked like he wanted to strangle me, but it was more a throw-his-hands-up-in-frustration kind of thing than the dark, don't-do-this-to-me quality that had driven our last encounter together. It was that knowledge that had me responding with, "I'll make you a deal. You let me stay in the class, and I won't offer the sexy ski bum my ass. Sound fair?"

Zach made a choking sound and sputtered as I turned on my heel and headed back to the classroom without looking back.

I was sure I heard Zach call my name in that no-nonsense tone of his, but I ignored the desire to turn around and spar with him some more, even if it did give me more of a thrill than any adrenaline-charged rescue ever could.

When I took my seat again in the classroom, Tag shot me a questioning look. I returned it with a smile and a thumbs up. Despite Zach's momentary lapse in decorum, I knew the last thing he'd want was to make another scene, especially now that he'd seen I wasn't about to kowtow to him. He could try and humiliate me all he wanted but I'd give back as good as I got. There was no way he was going to physically remove me from this program, and that's what he'd have to do to keep me from it.

I opened my notebook and pulled out a pencil, ready to start the class.

Sure enough, a few minutes later, Zach made his way to the front and began speaking. The only sign of his previous anger at me was the slight tic in his jaw. I remained tense, however, until it was time for our first test flight. There was still the chance he'd refuse me entrance on the helicopter.

But he didn't. He ignored me as if I wasn't even there.

Johnny's charm was on full blast while helping me with my harness, but I noticed he was like that with several other students too. I was pretty sure that it was just his nature rather than any potential attraction he might or might not have toward me. It was fine. I didn't want Johnny. No, I was the idiot more in love with the gruff, asshole training director.

Because I was stupid that way.

It wasn't until we were in the air and climbing over Lake McDonald toward Heavens Peak that Zach finally acknowledged me from the co-pilot's seat.

His voice came over the headset. "Johnny, double-check Lucky's harness."

I blinked up at him, only seeing the back of his head from where I sat. Johnny didn't question anything. He simply checked my harness and confirmed over the air it was good to go.

"You sure?" Zach asked.

Johnny's eyes met mine with a question in them. I shook my head with exasperation.

"Yeah, boss. All good. Why? You have reason to believe—"

"No, no. Just… it's fine," Zach mumbled through the comms.

But when we reached our first landing zone and prepared to load the hook, he did it again. Johnny had started hooking me into the tandem short-haul sling with him since I was closest to the bay doors, but when Zach found out about who was going first, he argued with Johnny.

"Let's start with someone heavier," he suggested. "It'll be easier for Tag on his first run."

Tag's face wrinkled in confusion when he turned around to face the rest of us from the pilot seat. "What the fuck? We're already loading two heavy gear bags in addition to the two of them. Dude, you've seen me drop a half-pound first aid kit on a four-inch cliff edge. I don't have a problem slinging light." He met Zach's eyes for a second before shrugging. "You're the training boss. Whatever floats your boat."

Zach grunted and turned back around, reaching for the heaviest guy in our training class of six. Morrie rolled his eyes. "Ever feel like a fat ass?" he teased the rest of us. The guy was over two hundred fifty pounds of straight-up pro football levels of muscles. As he stood in place while Johnny hooked him in, Morrie continued to joke around, but I could tell he was paying more attention to Zach and Johnny than he let on.

As soon as the tandem pair finally hopped onto the skids and down onto the grass below to review their procedure one more time before takeoff, I turned to the student sitting closest to me. I remembered Luiz from my previous hoist class.

"At least I won't be dead last," I teased. He was very slight despite being a kickboxing and rock climbing instructor at our university gym.

He rolled his eyes and sighed. "Seriously. I should have put some rocks in my pockets before loading up today. If only Amy was taking the class with us, I wouldn't be dead last."

I laughed. Amy had also been in the other hoist course we'd taken from Tag, and the two of us had been paired as partners during several of the training drills. We'd gotten along so well, we'd stayed in touch for a while after the course until Minna and I had run into Amy at a party off campus. Amy had been drunk and had gotten oddly handsy and flirty with me which had been super awkward since she knew I was gay. Min had reminded me that knowing you couldn't have someone didn't necessarily stop you from wanting them.

I glanced up as Zach climbed back into the helicopter.

How true those words were.

I'd kind of avoided Amy after that, mostly because I felt awkward around her. So when I'd discovered she was working as an assistant and equipment manager for Tag this summer, I'd wondered how things between us would be. But when I'd caught her eye in the SAR classroom earlier today and she'd smiled in recognition, I'd been relieved to see it was the familiar smile of a friend rather than the over-anxious smile of someone with a crush. Maybe I'd misinterpreted her behavior that night.

"Why isn't Amy taking the class?" I asked.

Luiz shrugged. "Probably money. She needs to earn it instead of spend it. This shit ain't cheap."

He was right. I'd worked my ass off to save enough for this course, and I'd have to get right back to work when I returned to Missoula in August, too.

We continued to make conversation while Johnny instructed Morrie on the ground and Zach leaned over the pilot's seat to talk to Tag.

Zach had given up on the pretense of bodyweight selection, which meant I was left until dead last. I'd spent the entire afternoon sitting on my hands and pretending to be happy as a clam while inside I seethed. If Zach thought I needed yet another father figure looking out for my best interests, he was dead wrong.

When Johnny reached out a hand to pull me off my seat, I noticed Zach's own hand clench into a gloved fist. Other than that small reaction, he was all business.

Until someone stretched out a leg in front of me at the last minute, and I almost went falling out of the open bay doors.

"Watch it," Zach boomed across the tight space. The student who'd stretched a leg out pulled it back immediately and shot all of us an apology wince, but it didn't keep Zach from glaring at him. "Shit like that gets people killed."

Zach grabbed my hand out of Johnny's grasp and met my eyes for an intense moment before leading me out onto the skids himself and reaching back for the gear bags.

I wasn't sure if my jangling stomach was from nerves or excitement. And was it due to the intensity in Zach's eyes or the anticipation of finally dangling from a helicopter again in the fresh mountain air?

Once Johnny and I were connected to the longline hook and in position, I gave the hand signal to Zach and communicated verbally into the headset inside my helmet. I couldn't believe Zach was actually going to let me do this after acting like such a jackass earlier.

"Wait," Zach blurted, grabbing the front of my harness with his gloved hand and pulling me back onto the skids with him. My heart plummeted as I wondered if this was where I finally lost my chance at participating in this long-awaited advanced SAR course.

My nostrils flared at him, but I kept my mouth shut. This was the moment he needed to decide if we were trainer and trainee or something more than that.

"Go," he barked, shoving me off the skids and onto the lush turf of the meadow. A soft breeze swayed through the early wildflowers, but it wasn't enough to jeopardize our training flights.

I had my answer.

We were nothing more than trainer and trainee. And for the next two weeks of the program, we managed to pretend that was actually true.

CHAPTER 11

ZACH

As I shook out the migraine preventive from the prescription bottle, I realized it had been working. If there was ever a time I should have been getting migraines, it was the past fourteen days of watching Lucky Reed dangle from a helicopter by a long rope over the jagged edges of the Rocky Mountains.

I felt like I hadn't slept in years. Every night when I returned to my little cabin in the woods, I took a long, hot shower in hopes of washing away the day's events. More often than not, those showers turned into angry sessions of stroking myself off to the memory of him standing in front of me in nothing but his underwear, running a teasing finger through his happy trail. His lithe body was tight with muscle and so fucking young. His plump lips teased me all day every day, especially when he bit into the lower one while he was concentrating on something.

I squeezed my eyes closed and swallowed the pill, wishing like hell it could also settle down the part of my brain that was roped off for one overly friendly and hot-as-fuck SAR student.

"Predicting strong winds out of the southeast this afternoon," Tag said, stepping into the tiny bathroom where I'd leaned down to grab another handful of water from the sink faucet. "I think we'd better wrap things up and be back on the ground by one if it's all the same to you."

"You're the boss," I reminded him. "Pilot makes the call."

Tag nodded and headed into the single stall while I left to start class. The students had learned longline rescue, hoist rescue, and rappelling from the helicopter. Today would be the day they were faced with their first case assessment to determine which rescue type was appropriate for the situation. They'd be tasked with rescuing injured climbers with specific medical needs. It meant spending much more time in the air and hovering at the rescue site. If we wanted a chance to get in the air for drills, we needed to review the classroom material and organize our plan quickly.

"Let's get started," I said, striding into the classroom and through the small group of students who'd been gossiping like hens over their morning coffee. "Today we'll be taking turns playing injured rock climber and the rescue paramedic helping them." I handed the short stack of envelopes to the closest student. "Take one and pass it. These have your assignments in them. The first card details which training session you'll play the victim in and what your injuries will be. The second card details which session you'll be the SAR paramedic on the line and what emergency call you're responding to. Take a minute to look your cards over and remember what we talked about yesterday. Not every rescue report is accurate. Sometimes critical information is missing and sometimes they get things wrong, including location, conditions, and status of injuries."

I walked back and forth across the front of the small room. "It's your job to accurately assess, treat, and evacuate the victim based on the reality you find, not the report. When it's your turn to be the SAR tech, we will inform you of the rescue call and leave you at the drop zone to prepare while we fly your victim into position. Use that time wisely the way you would use flight time to prep your jump bag and supplies and plan your mission."

Johnny stood and joined me at the front of the room. "Your helmet will be fixed with a GoPro camera to record the rescue so we can go over it with you afterwards. We know you can handle the mechanical portion of the rescue method, but we don't know if you can handle the challenges of medical treatment on the fly while tethered to a twenty-five-hundred-pound metal bird. We also want to test your ability to determine whether the situation actually requires an airborne rescue or whether the situation would be better handled another way, such as inserting a paramedic into the field, dropping supplies only, or aborting the mission altogether."

I took a sip from my water bottle before taking over. "Can anyone tell me one of the standard questions you should be asking yourself about your airborne rescue mission?"

Several students shot their hands up, and I pointed at Morrie. "Go ahead."

"Is this necessary?"

"Good," I said with a nod. "What else?" I ignored Lucky who sat front and center as usual. "Marcus?"

"Have all hazards been identified and made known?" he asked.

"Yep. Luiz?"

The young man sat up straighter in his chair. "Is there a better way to do it?"

I called on a couple of other students who answered diligently. I had to admit they were a good group.

"Perfect," Johnny said to another student before I could answer. "Lucky? What about you?"

Lucky shot me a look but remained professional the way he had for two straight weeks.

"Should we stop the operation because of weather, communication problems, or conflicting priorities?"

He met my eyes while he said the last part, and I ground my teeth together. "Fine. Alright, let's go."

Half the class moved out to the helicopter where, as usual, everyone took turns giving the equipment final checks alongside Tag while the other half stayed in the classroom to review and critique rescue videos I'd left for them. It was imperative not to have too many people on board when we needed to use larger equipment like the Stokes litter.

Thankfully, Lucky wasn't in the first group, but my short-term relief about it turned around and bit me in the ass. The first group had some problems which pushed us later in the morning than I'd hoped. By the time the second group got up in the air, the wind had started to pick up just a bit and the skies were getting the barest hint of gray.

We got through the first pair's drill easily enough, but then I realized that Lucky had drawn the scenario that required him to rappel from the helicopter to connect to a permanent anchor bolted to one of the faces of Cathedral Peak and pretend to be the victim of a sudden sixty-foot fall and exposure to extreme cold temperatures.

"We should wait," I advised Tag from my position in the co-pilot's seat. We'd left Morrie down in a lower meadow by the lake to prepare for his challenge as we flew Lucky up to his cliffside perch.

Tag glanced at me out of the corner of his eye. "You mean the weather? This isn't bad yet. I think we have until about fourteen hundred before we'll need to be concerned. Morrie and Lucky are the last pairing."

Objectively, I knew he was right. I was being overly cautious, and after that first day's confrontation, I'd promised Lucky that I wouldn't treat him any differently than any other student. We'd agreed to treat each other as if we didn't have a prior relationship of any kind. Just trainer and trainee, that was all.

But inside, my guts were churning and every hair on my body was standing straight up. I had to accept the fact I was worrying for no reason. There would never be a time I could watch Lucky rappel from a moving helicopter onto a sheer rock face and not be scared to death for him.

I had to trust him.

I had to trust the training I'd given him.

When it was time to help him onto the line and out the door of the helicopter, my hands were sweating and my heart felt like I'd run a 10k. I climbed back into the main cabin to triple check all of his harnesses as discreetly as I could. The two other students in the back had helped him prepare for his upcoming acting role, including smearing fake red blood in strategic places and brushing dirty smears of dark makeup to make it look like he'd truly been in a fall. They'd also drawn a fake crack onto his helmet and attached an empty water bottle to a carabiner on his belt. Finally, they clipped on a pair of ripped gloves that left his hands exposed where they'd whitened some of his fingers with more stage makeup. He'd switch out his rappelling gloves for those when he was securely in place.

"I feel like an idiot," he muttered as he stepped close to the open bay door.

"We've been over this," I said more stiffly than I'd intended. "Interpreting visual cues is a big part of rescue."

Lucky met my eyes with a frown. "I know that. I just... never mind." He turned back toward the open door and reached for the handle to ready himself.

I grabbed his upper arm and turned him to face me again. "You double-checked your emergency pack?" I asked, referring to the small pack of supplies strapped to his lower back.

He nodded. "Affirmative."

"If you get cold..." I forced myself to stop talking when Tag's and Johnny's voices came over the comms.

"Ready for rappel in three, two, one..." Johnny said, moving up next to me to help Lucky onto the rope with the rig descender.

And just like that, part of my fucking heart was falling away, into the wide-open air of the Rocky Mountains to try and find a tiny metal bolt on the side of a cliff face that would be his home for the next hour or two.

Tag hovered like a pro while Johnny spotted Lucky down to the bolt. The other two students remained silent while the three of us worked to make sure Lucky was safely clipped into the anchor before releasing from the helicopter's line.

As we flew away, back toward the meadow where Morrie was preparing Lucky's rescue, I watched the tiny orange speck of Lucky's rescue jacket get smaller and smaller against the massive rock face of Cathedral Peak.

If his fathers had any idea what he was doing—under my very own supervision—I'd never see the light of day again.

And I'd fucking deserve it.

CHAPTER 12

LUCKY

Lowering myself down from a helicopter in flight was even more exhilarating than the time I'd gotten up the nerve to skydive last year. I'd learned a long time ago that I was a secret adrenaline junkie, but skydiving had taught me that I preferred something active, something with purpose.

Like the night I'd been one of the first responders to a multi-vehicle auto accident and had spent an hour twisted half-inside a crushed sports car trying to keep a trapped victim from bleeding out. Or the time I'd had to free climb up a steep mountain of boulders in the rain to get to a lost hiker who'd sprained their ankle.

Maybe it was the combination of danger and purpose that gave me a thrill. I wasn't sure what that said about me, but as I hung there from that tiny metal bolt, a thousand feet above the rocky ground below, I felt the familiar rush of adrenaline and intention. Hopefully, my actions today would help someone in the future. It was a crazy sort of win-win situation, and maybe justifying it in my head was silly, but I was actually a little proud of myself for finally feeling such a solid sense of rightness in what I was doing.

I knew what I wanted to be. I could see my future so clearly as a high mountain rescue expert. If only I could say the same thing about my relationship with my grouchy, growly, overprotective trainer.

When the first blast of frigid, misty wind whipped against me, I sucked in a breath and said a silent thanks to high-tech fabric for its ability to keep me both warm and dry while I waited.

But then the second gust flipped me around and pressed me hard into the rock wall, face-first. I heard the thunk of my helmet half a beat after feeling the vibration of my head hitting the rock and my cheek scraping the granite hard enough to bite.

Okay, thank you for helmets too.

I shivered and looked down at my hands, half-exposed from the ripped-up prop gloves.

"Lucky, status check."

Zach's voice over comms was clipped with tension.

"Good to go," I confirmed. There was no way I was going to complain about a little weather at high altitude. It was to be expected in June. Hell, we could still get a snowstorm up here this time of year. A little wet wind was nothing.

A few minutes later, it was Tag's voice in my ear.

"Slight delay, Lucky. Hang tight."

I turned myself back around so I could spot them across the valley on the meadow. The mist had turned to thick fog, obscuring all the helicopter's details. The unnatural red paint of the fuselage was still partially visible through the clouds, but I couldn't see if they'd loaded Morrie in yet or not.

Several more minutes passed. The wind was much more consistent now, swinging me in my rigging enough to cause me to try and find finger holds in the rock to keep still. The temperature felt like it was dropping by degrees every minute and my hands were freezing for real.

I glanced over my shoulder toward the meadow. It was completely obscured now by the fog. If I couldn't see them, there was zero chance they could see me, which meant visibility was too dangerous to fly a helicopter in.

There was no way I was going to ask for an update. I was fine. A little cold, maybe, but fine. Plus, I had my emergency pack if I needed water, food, or first aid. Worst-case scenario, I even had an emergency bivvy bag that would help keep me warm if I had to spend the night up here.

"Lucky, rain incoming," Zach said in the same clipped tone. "Morrie is experiencing sudden severe vomiting. Drill aborted. Put on weather gear. Visibility is fine down here, but not where you are. We're going to run him back to base and then come back for you."

I clenched my teeth in frustration. Morrie and I needed this drill to pass off some of our skills for the course requirements. Colin and Luiz had already completed theirs, so Morrie and I were the only ones left. The poor guy. He'd had some altitude sickness the first few days, but this sounded more like food poisoning or a virus.

Even though I was cold and a little bored, at least I was safe and healthy. It would have been very unpleasant to be the one with severe vomiting while hanging up here.

After so much time of inactivity and without much protection from the wind and rain, I was definitely getting cold. I reached around to the water bottle clipped to my emergency pack and took a few sips. The wet bottle slipped from my grip and clanked against the rock when it fell to the end of its little rope tether. Score one for rock climber ingenuity.

I reached down to fish it back up and took a few more sips before clipping it back to my pack.

My ears were protected by the helicopter helmet I wore, but my nose and cheeks were stinging from exposure. I pulled up my neck gaiter until it was covering the lower half of my face, but I noticed an odd smell. Maybe it was the stage makeup on the ripped gloves? As carefully as I could, I removed the damaged gloves and hooked them into my belt before putting back on the good ones I'd worn to rappel.

At least I wasn't actually a climber who'd fallen and gotten frostbite like my assignment suggested. I spent the next several minutes imagining how much worse it could be until another gust pushed me out from the wall a few inches before pushing me back into it with a smack. I grabbed for the rope with one hand and the rock face with the other to keep from face-planting against it.

Suddenly I felt an odd drop, like someone had just let out an infinitesimal amount of the rope I hung from.

"What the fuck," I whispered, glancing down at the rope and trying to convince my heart rate to calm down.

There, in the brightly colored webbing, was a frayed tear and some odd discoloration.

I stared at it.

A quarter-inch section of the rope had broken open somehow, leaving me dangling by only the remaining half of the braided fibers. That simply... didn't happen. We inspected every inch of rope before every mission, and I knew for a fact this rope had been pristine earlier that day.

"Zach," I called out without thinking. "You still in range?"

"Lucky, what is it?"

"The rope. There's something wrong with the rope." I hated the panicked sound in my voice, but this was unprecedented. We went over our equipment so often, it was ridiculous. There simply couldn't be a worn area of this rope. It was impossible.

"What do you mean wrong? Describe what's happening. Are you safe?"

I fought the urge to cry and beg for help, the desire to appeal to any feelings of protectiveness he might have harbored for me so I could get off that damned rock face and settle safely into the helicopter seat again.

There was only one rope between me and sudden death and it was breaking.

"I..." I gulped and tried not to croak. "I don't know what's wrong. It's discolored... and fraying. Right where I've been holding on to it."

I glanced down at my gloves and noticed a white chalky residue on them. Could the makeup from my hands have been somehow caustic to the rope? Wouldn't it have damaged my skin before damaging the brand-new rope?

Zach's voice was all business. "Okay, listen to me. I want you to clip your harness directly into the anchor bolt. Take the damaged rope out of the equation. Do you understand?"

I glanced up at the bolt a few feet above me on the wet rock face. In order to get my harness up to it, I'd have to climb the damaged rope or climb the slippery rock. If I climbed the damaged rope, I'd be putting more stress on it. If I climbed the rock and slipped, I'd put sudden, massive stress on the compromised rope.

Plus, once I was clipped directly to the bolt, trying to maneuver myself onto the helicopter line would be much more difficult.

"Yes," I said. For some reason, the familiar sound of his voice brought tears to my eyes. Zach wouldn't let anything happen to me. I knew that as well as I knew anything.

He might not have feelings for me, but he was a man of honor, of duty. The last thing in the world he'd want would be to tell our families that something had happened to me.

I reached out for one of the crevices I'd been using for stability against the wind and began to pull myself up the rock face, trying desperately not to imagine slipping and snapping the line before falling to my death on the jagged rocks below. By the time I fought the wind to get my harness even with the bolt, my muscles were shaking and my eyes were watering from the sharp gusts. I clipped myself to the bolt directly and then gathered up the damaged rope to inspect it more closely.

It had the same odd smell I'd noticed earlier, and the damage was definitely in the area where I'd spent the most time holding on to it.

I reached back for the prop gloves and examined them.

"Zach, can you put me on direct comms?" I asked, hoping to block everyone else from hearing me.

"Yeah." There was a pause before he came back on the line. "Tell me you're okay, Lucky."

I nodded stupidly, as if he could see me from miles away through a storm. "I'm clipped directly to the bolt."

"Good. Good." He let out a breath. "We're just waiting for a break in visibility. It's just me, Johnny, and Tag now. Morrie and the others are back at the hangar. We're back on the meadow ready to come as soon as we can."

"There's something on these ripped gloves. I think that's what broke down the rope," I explained. "It's white and chalky. Kind of sticky. It has a weird smell too."

He paused again. "Fuck. Are you sure?"

I looked back down at the gloves hanging from my belt and tried to make sure the GoPro on my helmet had a chance to record the sight just in case the rain washed it all away. "Yeah. Very sure."

"Don't let them touch anything else," he said in a gruff voice.

I clenched my teeth against the desire to snap at him that I wasn't stupid. Instead I said, "Okay."

Another gust of wind pushed me into the rock, bumping my helmet again. I grunted and tried to brace my hands to keep from scraping my face a second time. I could still feel the sting of the first time.

"Lucky!" Zach's voice registered in my ear. "What happened? Sit rep. Fuck. Status check."

I had half a mind to tell him that I knew what a damned sit rep was. But I was trying my hardest to stay calm.

"Wind's picking up," I said. "Rain feels icy now. The rock is slick."

My feet kept slipping off the tiny perches I tried to use as footholds to take some of the pressure off my harness. Every time my feet slipped, I worried about whether or not any of that mysterious substance had gotten onto the webbing of my harness in places I couldn't see. I racked my brain to try and remember what I'd touched while I'd had those gloves on.

The fog had been swirling closer until I could no longer see anything around me but gray air. Sound was muffled strangely and I felt like in some ways I was the only person left on earth, even though I knew better.

I'm scared, I finally thought to myself. *It's okay to be scared.*

I heard Zach's voice muffled and distant as he most likely spoke to Tag about getting the bird in the air. I closed my eyes and tried not to panic. My training had prepared me. I needed to trust my training.

As if he could read my mind, Zach came back over comms and asked, "How's your harness?"

A shudder of fear ripped through me when he voiced the concern out loud. I sucked in a breath. "Fuck," I breathed, trying so hard not to move. I angled my eyes down to inspect my harness for the millionth time, but I still couldn't see all of it. I didn't have eyes in the back of my head or under my ass.

"Lucky! Answer me!"

I let out another sound, watching my breath fog in the cold air. "I… I don't know… I… Zach… it's… I can't see anything…"

"You are fine. Do you hear me? You're okay, Lucky. You're fixed to a permanent bolt with the best equipment money can buy. You have emergency supplies to keep you hydrated and fueled and warm. Here's what I need you to do. Just listen to my voice."

I could hear him barking at Tag to get the bird in the air no matter what, but I was sure Tag was responding with a saner head about it being a suicide mission with this horrible visibility. He was right, too. I could barely see the rock face only a few feet away from me. Wet, dense fog flowed all around me.

When Zach came back to me, he was calm and in control. He walked me through the simple process of taking another sip of my water, fishing out a granola bar from the emergency pack and eating it, and finally he asked if I needed to pee.

"What?" I asked in surprise.

"Go ahead and whip it out. When else will you get a chance to piss on a cathedral?"

"Stop making jokes, asshole. It isn't funny," I snapped. Besides, I didn't need to pee and the idea of whipping out my dick in this freezing rain was not pleasant.

"Hang tight," Zach said quickly.

"Har, har," I said under my breath as I dangled precariously over nothing but low cloud cover.

"We just heard from base. Morrie has appendicitis. They're taking him to Kalispell for surgery," Zach explained.

I knew he was trying to distract me, and I was grateful for it.

"Tough break. Glad you got him down." And I was. As long as I was healthy and safely bolted in, I was still better off than he was.

But it didn't feel that way when I started to shiver.

"Use your bivvy bag," Zach said. "I can hear your teeth chattering."

He still sounded like a bossy know-it-all, but I was so fucking thankful for his voice on the other end of the comms.

"I'm okay," I said. "Want to be ready for you when you get here."

Zach continued trying to pass the time with distracting stories, telling me about the time he and Jake had been sure they'd spotted a crocodile in the river that had run behind their house while they'd lived in a small town in Alaska. Despite my exhaustion, I couldn't help but laugh when Zach told me how he'd tried to make a run for it when he'd been sure the crocodile was coming onshore, but his big brother had tackled him mid-flight so Jake wouldn't be left alone in the inky dark of night when they made their grand discovery. In the end, their big discovery had turned out to be nothing more than large sheets of ice breaking apart and floating downstream.

I closed my eyes and tried to concentrate on the soothing sound of his familiar voice, but within moments, Zach was shouting at me.

"Wake the fuck up! Do you hear me? Wake the fuck up, Lucky Reed, goddammit."

I jerked awake and damned near scared myself shitless, grabbing for the slick rock face and knocking my hip hard into the bolt. "Shit! You scared me to death, asshole! Do you have any idea what it's like to wake up like that?"

My heart almost hammered out of my chest, but I noticed the visibility had cleared a little bit. I could see the barest hint of the red helicopter paint across the valley through the mist.

Within minutes, it moved.

"Incoming," Zach said. "Prepare for short-haul rescue."

"The longline?" I asked stupidly. We'd drilled those rescues countless times over the past two weeks. Someone would hook into the stationary longline in the meadow to be hauled to a rescue site rather than rappelling out of the helicopter. It was safer in many cases. It was also used when the victim couldn't help the ascent into the helicopter. "I can ascend," I told him. "Just drop a line when you get here."

"Forget it," he said. "I'm already on the hook."

Zach was coming to get me. I closed my eyes and breathed out.

CHAPTER 13

ZACH

Four hours.

Lucky had been hanging from that sheer cliff face for four hours while fate kept me from being able to get to him.

It didn't sound like much, but with every damned second that had passed, I'd felt more and more pressure squeeze around my heart until my brain and body didn't even seem to work right together anymore.

"It's not your fault," Tag said for the millionth time over my headset. He thought this was simply my own guilt over stranding a trainee in the middle of a drill. As if Lucky was nothing more than one of my students. "You know as well as I do that weather happens, man. Especially up here."

"I know that," I said. "Just get us there."

I hadn't told him about the degradation of the line Lucky had been hanging from or the mysterious substance on the rope. It would only serve as a distraction, and until Lucky was back safely on the ground, we couldn't afford any distractions.

Tag's approach was careful and deliberate as usual, but it seemed to go in slow motion. When I finally got close enough to lock eyes with Lucky, I wanted to shout with joy.

And then I noticed the blood. He was covered in blood, there was a crack in his helmet, and...

He tilted his head at me in confusion, and suddenly I remembered it was fake blood, a fake crack in the helmet.

Fuck, I was losing it.

I flashed him the "okay" gesture with my fingers which he repeated immediately.

And finally, finally, I had my hands on him.

"C'mere," I grunted, clasping his wrist and ignoring the slight tremor of fear still in my voice. "You okay?"

He was pale and shivering, but I thought it might be more from fear than the actual temperature.

"M'okay," he murmured, reaching out for me with both hands and one leg.

I worked quickly to connect his harness to the longline, taking a moment to inspect the harness webbing for any weaknesses. I'd brought an extra just in case we needed it, but it looked like his was still in good shape. As my hands ran around the webbing along his upper thighs and between his legs to make sure, I heard him suck in a breath.

Do not lose focus, I warned myself. *Remain professional, asshole. Get the job done.*

It wasn't easy. But since I knew from firsthand experience that loss of focus during a rescue often proved fatal, I did what I had to do to get him connected to the hook and untethered from the rock face.

When Lucky finally came away from the rock, he clung to me, and as much as I hated to admit it, I clung to him just as hard.

I never wanted to let him go.

I whispered words of reassurance so softly, I wasn't even sure he heard them. The flight back to the meadow went by in a blink, and suddenly we were standing on firm ground. Even once I disconnected us from the line, Lucky held tightly to me until I pulled back enough to grab his chin and peer into his eyes to make sure he was still all right.

He gave me a weak smile. "Thanks for the ride." He cleared his throat. "It was a good experience. I learned a lot." It was clear Lucky's intent was to pack away his earlier emotion and return to our ridiculous roles of trainer and trainee.

That wasn't happening.

But before I could inform him of the change of situation, Tag's voice came through my helmet. "More weather coming. Load up and let's get the hell out of here."

After that, it was all business. We disconnected the line, stowed equipment, and loaded up for the flight back to the hangar. Johnny took the time in flight to make sure Lucky was in good health and didn't have any first aid needs.

It turned out that some of the blood on his face was real. He'd scraped his cheek against the rock somehow, resulting in two thick parallel scratches along one cheekbone. I clenched my hands into fists to keep from running a finger along his cheek to make sure that was the worst of it.

It wasn't until the helicopter's wheels touched the ground that I felt like I was able to take my first real breath. As Lucky prepared to disembark, I found myself reaching for his arm. "Go wait in my truck while I help Tag and Johnny with post-rescue stuff. I'll take you to the hospital to get checked out."

"Hospital? I don't need to—"

"Yes you damn well do," I yelled. The chopper's rotors had slowed enough that yelling was no longer necessary but I was doing it just the same. Lucky's back stiffened as his lips pulled into a tight frown. It almost felt like he was... disappointed in me. But he didn't respond. He just turned his back on me and climbed out of the helicopter. Within a minute, Tag was ordering me to do the same thing.

"I'm fine," I told him.

"You're distracted!" Tag snapped at me. "How many times do you need to prep that same rope?" I looked down and sure enough, in my hands was a bright orange rope that I'd been winding and unwinding over and over again. I opened my mouth to tell Tag I was okay when his eyes met mine. "Go," he said more softly this time. "Make sure he's okay," he added with a jerk of his head in the direction Lucky had gone. If I hadn't been so desperate to take him up on the offer, I would have spent more time obsessing over how much Tag understood about my relationship with Lucky versus him believing I was just a trainer worried about one of his students.

I snagged the rope Lucky had been using and stuffed it into my duffel bag, then searched for Lucky's gloves so I could examine them more closely for the chalky substance Lucky had been talking about. I gave up the search for the gloves after just a few seconds and hurriedly made my way to my truck. What was left of my control pretty much snapped when I saw the empty cab.

"Son of a bitch," I bit out. I threw my duffel into the back seat and then threw the vehicle into gear. I caught up to Lucky within minutes. He was walking down the access road that led to the bunkhouse he shared with several of his classmates. I drove past him and then jerked the vehicle onto the shoulder and got out.

"I told you to wait—" I began as Lucky neared the truck.

"And I told you I was fine. Clean the wax out of your ears, old man," Lucky snapped as he strode past me like I wasn't even there.

His open defiance did nothing to settle my nerves... at least not in a good way. The adrenaline that had been coursing through my veins shifted gears and headed right for my cock instead. "Get. In. The. Truck," I somehow managed to get out.

"Fuck—" Lucky began, but he went silent when I snagged his arm and bodily dragged him to the vehicle. I practically shoved him into the passenger seat. My hands were shaking violently as I slammed the door shut. Thankfully, Lucky didn't try to get out of the truck when I went around it to climb into the driver's seat.

Since Lucky didn't open his mouth again in the truck, I used the short drive back to his place to try and get control of myself, but all I could see was Lucky hanging precariously from that damn rope. I'd seen the fraying he'd been talking about for myself. There'd been just a handful of remaining fibers keeping him in the air. If the weather had prevented us from getting back to Lucky, the chances that the line would have given out were more than likely. The sound of Lucky's screams as he plummeted to his death were deafening in my head.

The truck rattled to a stop when I slammed on the brakes as we reached the lot for Lucky's bunkhouse.

"This is over!" I growled as I stared out the windshield. Visions of Lucky's slim form jerking as the rope gave out danced before my eyes. I knew it was an illusion but as far as my brain was concerned, at that very moment I was sitting helplessly in that worthless helicopter watching Lucky die over and over again.

I wrapped my fingers around the steering wheel and gripped until I was sure I'd snap the thing off. To his credit, Lucky remained silent.

"Stay here while I get a change of clothes for you, then I'll take you to the hospital."

I had my fingers on the handle when Lucky let out this ragged little laugh. There wasn't even a speck of humor in it. I cast him a glance and saw that he was clutching his duffel to his chest. "There are exactly two people in this world who have the right to order me around and you know what, Zach? You're not one of them. Stay the hell away from me!"

I managed to grab Lucky's arm before he could escape the truck. "Tonight, hospital. Tomorrow you're on the first flight back to Colorado."

"Yeah, let's just see how that works out," Lucky said snidely as he snatched his arm from my grip with surprising force. While I doubted his fury matched mine, I couldn't deny how pissed he looked... and how much that fact turned me on.

I was forced to release Lucky to keep him from hurting himself but I didn't hesitate to get out and follow him into the bunkhouse. He slammed the bunkhouse door in my face but I managed to catch it before it hit my nose. The flooring creaked as I strode after him through the empty building. I could only assume the other students were out celebrating their first simulated missions or checking on Morrie in the hospital. Either way, it was just Lucky and me, so I didn't have to try and mask any of my rage.

I caught up to Lucky enough that when he tried to slam his bedroom door in my face I was able to catch it. He chose that moment to turn on me with all his guns blazing. "You're right, Zach, *this...*"—he looked pointedly at me, then himself—"*is* over! Get the fuck out of here! Now!"

If he had quietly ordered me to leave, I might have actually done it, even if it was just so we could both cool off. But something in the way that he was looking at me, as if the conversation really was over—that this thing between us really was over—severed whatever control I'd desperately been hanging on to as I'd listened to the fear in his voice as he'd told me about the fraying rope and the worsening weather conditions.

The loss of control was like a valve being opened on a steam pipe. Instead of walking back out the door, I slammed it shut instead, ignoring Lucky's gasp of surprise. I strode toward him, seizing on his moment of uncertainty, and reached for him at the same time that he took a step back. He let out a little cry, but I wasn't sure if it was one of fear or shock or maybe even relief.

I was too busy taking what was mine. What I'd been denied for far too long.

Whatever sound Lucky had been in the process of making became muted as I crashed my mouth down on his. I expected him to resist my kiss in some way, but there was only the slightest of hesitations and then this sweet little whimper bubbled up from his throat. That sound was all the encouragement I needed. I wrapped my arm around his waist to pull him flush against my body as I slid my tongue into his mouth. The taste of him was a thousand times sweeter than any fantasy I'd ever had. His tongue was tentative as it greeted mine but all that did was remind me that I was only the second man to ever get a taste of him. I threaded my fingers through his thick hair and dragged his head back, breaking our kiss. At some point, Lucky had put his hands on my upper arms, but I hadn't even noticed until that moment. His eyes were dark and heavy with need, and his full lips were glistening.

Lucky looked at me with such trust that I found myself getting lost in his eyes. I once again leaned down and fitted my mouth to his, but this time I resisted the urge to consume him and took my time exploring the softness of his lips.

Lucky's fingers bit into my skin as I toyed with his mouth. I swore I heard him whisper my name between the soft kisses I was pressing to his trembling lips. Warning bells were going off in my head that the young man before me was too innocent, too sweet for any of this, but my body and my brain were no longer working in unison. I ignored my brain's efforts to remind me of things like Lucky's youth and the fact that he was the son of my brother's best friends. All that mattered here in this moment was that he was mine.

He was finally *mine*.

My intent had been to take my time savoring Lucky's mouth, but Lucky clearly had a different goal in mind. His right hand curled around the back of my head so I was the one suddenly being held in place. I could have easily maintained control of what was happening, but the idea of Lucky taking what he wanted from me was almost as exciting as the prospect of knowing I was finally going to have him.

Lucky's moves were still inexperienced as his tongue dipped into my mouth, but his excitement was obvious. I could feel the outline of his cock pressing against me. The little moans and whimpers escaping him between hungry kisses was like adding gasoline to an already explosive fire. I gave Lucky a few more seconds of control, but when his free hand came up to grip the back of my neck, something inside of me snapped and I forgot all about my intent to savor the young man who'd unknowingly tormented me for so long.

I walked Lucky backwards as I ate at his mouth. He let out a little groan when his back hit the wall, but I had a feeling one thing had nothing to do with the other because Lucky's tongue eagerly met mine as his hands roamed up and down my back. I tried to regain control of myself, but it was like trying to stop the tide. As I continued to feed on Lucky's amazing mouth, I slid my hands down his back and over his pert ass. My hips began pumping against his in the hopes of finding the release my cock was desperately craving.

I probably could have easily come just by rubbing up against the eager young man in my arms, but now that I'd finally given myself permission to have him, there was no way I was going to settle for anything less than being inside his gorgeous body when I came. The need for him crawled beneath my skin like a living thing. I might have managed to utter some kind of apology to Lucky as I tore my mouth free from his and turned him around to face the wall. I should've at least promised him that despite this round being hard and fast, I'd still make it worth it for him, but my tongue felt too thick for my mouth and my brain was now focused on finding some relief for my body. I pressed myself against Lucky's back so I could keep my mouth on his hot skin as I fumbled to get his pants undone. Lucky was panting as heavily as I was. His eyes were closed and he had both hands pressed flat against the wall.

"Stay just like that," I managed to somehow say.

I wasn't sure Lucky was even aware enough to hear me, but when he nodded a moment later, all he did was drive my excitement even higher. I suspected I'd have to break one of my rules and stay longer than just one round of fucking.

Once I got Lucky's button free and his zipper lowered, I used both my hands to push down his pants and underwear at the same time. I snagged a condom and packet of lube in record time from my wallet before shoving my own pants down enough to free my dick. Lucky jumped when I slathered some of the lube over his hole. I tried not to notice how incredibly tight he was in case just the thought of it pushed me over the edge. I leaned in and nipped at his ear before running my lips down his neck. His pulse was racing.

"First time's going to be fast," I admitted. I sucked on Lucky's skin hard, leaving my mark on him before adding, "Don't worry, I'll take care of you." At my words, Lucky shifted his head so he could look at me. His now open eyes were full of an emotion that I couldn't quite make sense of.

"Promise?" he whispered as his eyes held mine.

Those warning bells that had been going off from the moment I'd kissed Lucky were clanging loudly now, but I did my best to silence them. Surely, Lucky knew I was talking about his release... that I'd take care of his release.

I didn't have time to dwell on the question because Lucky chose that moment to push his ass back against my cock. He twisted his hips so it was like he was trying to get me off with his ass. It felt so good that I leaned against Lucky and, on impulse, placed my hands over his on the wall as I gave him what he wanted. The feeling of my dick sliding up and down his crease was the most perfect kind of torture.

But it did nothing to bring down my need.

My fingers were shaking badly when I pulled back enough to get the condom on and put the remaining lube over my hungry shaft. As soon as I was finished, I pressed up against Lucky again and searched out his entrance. Not surprisingly, Lucky tensed up when I began pushing my finger into him. "So tight," I muttered as I tilted his head so I could kiss him on the mouth. He moaned and whimpered into my mouth as I pushed my finger in and out of him. Between the sounds he was making and the way his inner muscles were gripping my finger, I had no hope of holding out any longer. I removed my finger from his body and grabbed my dick and placed it against his hole. I forced myself to keep my moves slow as I began to push into him. There was absolutely no give in his body as I tried to get past the outer muscle. Sweat was dripping down my brow as I fought the need to just shove inside of him. I knew some guys liked it that way, but I didn't know enough about Lucky yet to risk potentially hurting him.

"Let me in, sweetheart," I murmured as I slid my hand beneath Lucky's shirt and caressed his chest. I pushed my hips forward again, but there was absolutely no change in how Lucky's body was fighting the intrusion. Frustration started to get the better of me and the next time I told Lucky to let me in, it came out as more of a growling order than a gentle request. I couldn't figure out what the hell was going on. Lucky had clearly wanted this just moments ago, but now his body was acting like... like...

A horrible weight began to settle in my belly, and I immediately stopped my forward movement. "Lucky," I began, unable to keep the anger at myself from my voice.

"I'm trying, Zach! I don't know how! I don't know how..." Lucky's last words were accompanied by a guttural sob. His eyes were squeezed shut and there were tears dripping down his flushed cheeks.

I instantly felt sick to my stomach as I realized what he was saying without actually saying it. I immediately pulled my body back to put some space between us, being careful to slowly pull what little of my cock I'd managed to get into him back out. Lucky pressed his forehead against the wall. His soft sobs were like someone thrusting a knife into my chest. He kept repeating the same words over and over so quietly that it was a miracle I heard them at all.

I'm sorry.

"You said you'd had sex before," I said stupidly. "At the club. I remember." How in the hell had I missed out on the fact that Lucky was a virgin? His body had been sending me that message from the moment I'd put my finger inside of him, but I hadn't wanted to listen. What the hell had I done?

I turned the anger I had at myself on Lucky. "So what? You were just lying to me when you said that—"

"I didn't lie. Not exactly," Lucky mumbled. He'd put his arm beneath his forehead.

"Then what the hell—"

I heard Lucky's voice enough to know that he was interrupting me, but I couldn't make out what he was saying. I grabbed his free arm and forced him to turn around. "What?" I snapped. The idea that I'd been about to fuck Lucky against the wall with virtually no prep and he'd been willing to keep quiet about the whole thing was threatening to make me violently ill.

"Blow jobs!" Lucky practically yelled. "I know how to give blow jobs!"

I didn't even know how to respond to that. Luckily, I didn't have to because Lucky continued on his own.

"None of the guys I've been with wanted more than that. I... I guess I didn't either."

It wasn't just the words he said, but the way he said them, that had my insides calming a bit.

"I want it with you, Zach. I swear I do. I thought... I thought if I could just relax... I'm sorry. I just wanted it to be you so bad." Lucky dropped his eyes and whispered, "I just wanted it to be you."

There were so many emotions running through me at Lucky's

quiet admission that I didn't know what to do with most of them. I was beyond pissed that he would have risked letting me inadvertently hurt him, but I couldn't deny that if I'd known the truth, I never would've touched him. As it was, I knew I just needed to get the hell out of there.

Remembering my state of undress, I reached down to pull the condom off my dick and tugged up my pants. I could hear Lucky doing the same and when I snuck a glance at him, he was leaning back against the wall, his head hung and his fingers slowly working to do up the zipper and button on his jeans.

I glanced around the room and spied a garbage can. I tossed the condom into it before heading to the door. I knew I was supposed to speak some words to him that would get us both past this moment, but I didn't know what the hell they were. There was no way to laugh off the incident because nothing about it was funny. And there was no way to completely escape him unless I quit my job or convinced Lucky to quit the program. I'd already seen more than enough proof that he was determined to see this through.

That meant I would be the one who needed to make a decision about how to move forward.

The fact was that this had all only happened because I'd followed Lucky to his room. I'd been the one to put us in the situation by being alone with him. There was no reason that needed to happen again. I would just need to be more careful.

I had my hand on the doorknob when I happened to glance Lucky's way. He'd turned himself so his back was to the door. He was still leaning against the wall for support, only now he was doing it with his shoulder instead of his back. The pressure in my chest tightened as I studied his frame. He was hunched in on himself, and from where I stood, it appeared that he was shaking. I suspected he was trying to hold himself together until I left.

That's two, asshole. Good job.

I wanted to ignore the voice in my head, but it was absolutely right. That was twice now that I'd trampled all over Lucky's feelings when he'd been at his most vulnerable. After humiliating and hurting him when he'd been only eighteen and baring his soul to me, I'd been certain it would be the first and last time. But here we were at yet another pivotal moment in his life, and I was once again leaving him with wounds that would eventually scar over.

Scars he'd have to learn to carry much like I'd had to.

I wanted to rant and rave at Lucky and ask him why he'd done this, why he'd put us in this position. More importantly, I wanted to know why he kept putting me on a pedestal I didn't deserve.

I wanted him to see the truth about me, but did I want it like this? Did I really want to be like the cold-hearted bastard who'd used me when I hadn't been much older than Lucky? Who'd held so much power over me that I'd become a shell of the young man I'd once been?

Even as I considered the thought, I opened the door because my body was still ready to flee. Running was easier. It always had been.

It would be this time too.

But even as my mind had the thought, it refused to command my feet to move and I just hung there between the quiet of Lucky's room and the loudness of the outside world that I had to work so hard to hide in.

One step forward.

That was all.

One step.

CHAPTER 14

LUCKY

I was every bit the kid Zach had always accused me of being. I didn't know how else to explain my behavior other than foolish and childish. I'd wanted Zach so badly I hadn't even considered the consequences of not being completely up front with him. I had no idea what had possessed me to believe that I could somehow fake my way through having sex for the first time. Maybe if Zach hadn't been such an observant person, the outcome would've been entirely different, but chances were I'd be wallowing in my room and crying for an entirely different reason. And not once had I even thought to consider how Zach would feel about the entire thing. Maybe some guys wouldn't have had a problem with being duped into having sex with a virgin, but Zach was not just "some guy." The guilt he would've carried if he'd believed that he'd physically hurt me in any kind of way would've been immeasurable.

I knew that much about him, at least.

As soon as I heard the door snick shut, I let go of the nearly painful sound I'd been holding in from the moment Zach had realized the truth. While it felt good to finally let my emotions out, the walls were thin and the last thing I wanted was for any of my bunkmates to hear me and come check on me. So I turned around with the intention of grabbing my bathroom supplies from the closet by the door so I could retreat to the shower and hope the water would muffle the sounds of my sobs, but the second I did, I ran directly into a broad chest that I'd come to recognize all too well.

I was horrified at the possibility that Zach had heard me completely lose it after I'd thought he'd left, but before I could say anything or try to even come up with an explanation, Zach's hand curled around the back of my neck and then his mouth was once again on mine.

Shock reverberated through me for several long seconds as Zach hungrily kissed me. By the time the fog of confusion lifted away, Zach's big body had me crowded against the wall once again. I finally managed to kiss him back, but inside I was waiting for the other shoe to drop.

Was this some kind of strange goodbye kiss? Or worse, was it a pity kiss because he felt sorry for me?

I tried to pull back enough so I could ask him any one of those questions, but my brain refused to listen to the command and I didn't blame it. The things Zach's mouth was doing to mine had to be illegal. I felt consumed—completely owned. And I had no desire to change that.

I felt practically boneless by the time Zach broke off the kiss. While I gulped down some much-needed air, Zach's mouth was trailing a path along my throat. At some point, I'd curled my fingers into the front of his shirt, probably so I could hang on to him in case he tried to walk away again. One of Zach's hands was at the small of my back while the other was pressed against the wall above my shoulder, kind of like he was trying to brace himself. Most of his body was flush with mine except for his hips. I desperately wanted to know if his erection had returned because while mine had faltered when he'd first started breaching me, my cock was very happy about his return.

Once I caught my breath, I ended up holding it all over again as I waited for whatever Zach was going to say. And I knew he would say something—he had to. Maybe all this was just some way for him to end things on a positive note before we went our separate ways.

Maybe his goal was to make sure we could still have some kind of working relationship. I didn't know what was coming, but I just wanted it over with. If he'd intended this kiss to be some kind of closure for our relationship, he hadn't really succeeded. If anything, I'd mourn the loss of him even more now because this was the Zach I'd fallen in love with so long ago. This was the Zach I'd wanted to know in every possible way.

Zach's mouth returned to mine. He kissed me slowly, almost lovingly. The hand he had braced above my shoulder moved down to seek out one of my own hands. He linked our fingers and then lifted our joined hands and pressed them back against the wall. His thumb moved back and forth over the base of mine, much like his mouth was doing to my tongue.

When he broke the kiss, he kept our hands joined and he continued that hypnotic move with his thumb. I forced myself to keep still as Zach nuzzled a spot just below my ear. My entire body felt alive, even more than when he'd kissed me earlier. Before I realized what I was doing, I moved my free hand up and settled it on the back of his neck. I expected him to protest or to move away from the contact, but he remained where he was. I tried not to read too much into it, him standing there like that and holding me and letting me hold him in return, but my wayward mind was already trying to come up with reasons for why any of this was happening.

"Be sure this time, Lucky," Zach whispered. His lips skimmed the shell of my ear, but he didn't attempt to kiss me again and he didn't try to move away. I knew in my gut what he was telling me, but I was afraid to believe that I was getting another chance with him. I wanted to know what it all meant, but I had the sense not to ask him that. And instead of obsessing over all the different possible reasons that he was here with me, I focused on just that one little fact.

He.

Is.

Here.

I slid my fingers over the soft skin just below where his hair ended.

"I'm sure, Zach. I've never been more sure of anything in my entire life," I admitted.

He hung there for the longest time, his face still buried against me. I thought I felt him shudder when I told him I was ready, but I couldn't be sure. When his mouth finally sought out mine again, I could feel tears pricking the backs of my eyes. I managed to keep them at bay and threw myself into kissing him back.

Unlike the majority of his earlier kisses, this one was slow and deep and patient. His tongue curled against mine in certain ways and when I mimicked the act, he let out a whisper of a groan. It went on like that, him teaching me and me figuring out what he liked best. I couldn't say how long we just made out like a couple of kids discovering each other for the first time, but I did know that nothing felt more right in that moment.

It wasn't just Zach's mouth I had the pleasure of exploring. His big hands had moved down to my back and beneath my shirt. The rough pads of his fingers sent delicious slivers of sensation along my nerve endings. That was all it took for my dick to roar fully back to life. In no time, I was desperately rubbing my groin against his. I was glad to feel he was hard too.

"Off," Zach growled as he tugged at the hem of my shirt. He helped me work it off my body but before the fabric had even cleared my hands, his mouth latched on to one of my nipples.

"Zach, oh god!" was the best I could come up with. While he tortured the little nub of flesh, his hands explored any place they could reach. My back, my belly, and most importantly my ass. He gripped my backside firmly and held me in place as he rubbed himself against me. I felt like the top of my head was going to blow off. The sensations were overwhelming and we'd barely even gotten started.

Zach's mouth returned to mine, and I hungrily took control of the kiss. His fingers snuck beneath the back of my waistband and began rubbing up and down the top of my crease. My kisses grew more frantic as my body began to spin out of control.

"Put your legs around me," Zach demanded suddenly as he removed his fingers from my pants and his hands gripped my ass firmly. I barely had a second to comprehend what he was asking me to do when he lifted me up. I instinctively wrapped myself around him, with both my legs and arms. His mouth returned to mine, so I wasn't able to protest the fact he was carrying my entire weight on his overstressed knee. Fortunately, he didn't have to take me far because he deposited me on my bed and then followed me down. I actually did cry out when his weight landed on mine. I'd imagined it a million times, his big body covering my smaller one, but none of my fantasies had done it justice.

Something in the sounds I made must have alerted Zach because he drew back and looked at me. But he didn't say anything. In fact, all he did was take his hand and smooth it over my hair as he stared at me. Then he dropped his mouth again and started all over with the long, slow kisses that I felt in my toes. His hands caressed my upper body and within minutes I was tearing at his shirt because I desperately needed to feel his skin beneath my fingers.

Zach lifted up long enough to reach behind his head and pull his shirt off. Seeing him straddling me as he revealed his broad chest was like watching a work of art being unveiled. I'd seen Zach shirtless a few times when I'd been younger, but seeing his body and knowing that it was, for the moment anyway, mine was entirely different. His muscles were taut and his tanned skin glistened. He didn't have a lot of body hair but the treasure trail that disappeared into his pants had my erection reaching a whole new level. My fingers ached to touch him, so before he'd even finished removing the shirt, I reached out my hand to see if the hairs running from his abdomen southward were as soft as they looked. Zach actually stilled when I put my fingers on him, and I quickly jerked them back.

His eyes lifted to meet mine and he held my gaze as he removed the shirt entirely. I heard it rustle a bit as it fell to the floor and then it was forgotten because Zach was reaching for my hand. He put it back in exactly the spot it had been and then covered it with his own.

I took the move as permission and began exploring the planes and curves of his body. Zach's hand stayed on mine, but he didn't guide my moves at all, and at one point, he actually closed his eyes and seemed to just relish my touch. The sense of power that came over me, knowing that I brought him pleasure, was almost too much to take. The kid in me was afraid to take the leap but the man in me reveled in the opportunity to give Zach the chance to lose himself for a while. I wanted more than anything to chase away whatever demons haunted him, even if it was just for a short time.

I used one hand to leverage myself up off the bed. Zach accommodated me and shifted back a little so I could sit up. I wrapped my arms around his back, marveling at how hot and tight his skin was. I stroked his shoulder blades along the length of his spine as I sucked in a breath and closed my mouth around one of his nipples like he'd done to mine. All the awkwardness I felt went up in smoke when Zach moaned and then threaded his fingers through my hair as if to hold me in place. I had nothing to go on but instinct and the memory of what Zach had done to me, so I did my best to mimic it. I wasn't sure how I was doing until a breath of a whisper reached my ears.

"Lucky," Zach murmured. I almost didn't recognize his voice. It was a mixture of soft and hard. Of relief and need.

His fingers tightened in my hair and he pulled my head back so he could lean down and kiss me. This time his kisses were desperate and needy, almost frantic.

I loved it.

I loved every second of it.

I didn't even regret that my exploration session had ended when he lowered me down to the bed and took back the control he'd so generously given me. I was still able to use my hands to explore him as my mouth worked frantically to keep up with his. I could feel a few raised patches of skin along his rib cage and on his back, but I couldn't tell what had caused the old injuries. I would have noticed them years earlier when I'd seen him shirtless, so I knew they had to be new. Maybe from when he'd been redeployed. If we'd been a real couple, I would've softly asked him about them. But we weren't a couple and I knew if I voiced my concern about them, it would bring what was happening between us to a screeching halt.

I had no clue how long Zach and I kissed for, but when he shifted off my body, I actually cried out, "Zach, no, don't stop!" I grabbed his arms hard in the hopes that I could somehow convince him not to end this. He paused and then leaned over me and brushed a soft kiss over my mouth.

"I'm not going anywhere, baby," Zach whispered. He kissed me deeply and then, instead of climbing off of me, he proceeded to kiss his way down my body. I still found myself holding on to him for as long as I could but when he did climb off of me, I sucked in a breath and forced myself to release him. I watched him with apprehension as he stood alongside the bed. But he didn't turn and walk away. No, he bent over and put his hands on my hips and then he gently pulled my body to the edge of the bed. I thought that meant he wanted me to stand, but when I tried, he flattened his palm over my chest. I got the silent message and stayed where I was. With him looming over me, I should've been nervous or scared, but nothing about Zach frightened me beyond him walking away. I knew that no matter what happened between us, he'd never physically hurt me.

Zach's hands caressed my belly for a second and then his fingers nimbly began working on the button and zipper of my pants. A bout of unease went through me as he began pulling them and my underwear down, but when he told me to lift up, I did so. I also made myself keep my eyes open, even though I was afraid of seeing his reaction.

What if I was too skinny for him? I was well muscled, but I was still a small guy. The things that worked for me in my job weren't necessarily things he might find attractive in a lover. I tried to ignore the insecurity that washed through me as he removed my clothing and I lay before him entirely naked. I watched him as he watched me, but his expression was unreadable.

It felt like hours passed before Zach suddenly leaned down and covered my body again with his. "So beautiful," he breathed in right before he kissed me deeply. The position we were in was somewhat awkward with me lying at the edge of the mattress, but I did my best to wrap myself around him. His mouth trailed down my neck, then down my body. I held my breath as he reached my groin but let it out when he bypassed my erection and kissed my thigh instead. His mouth moved all the way down my leg, even to my toes. I couldn't resist laughing when his mouth pressed kisses against the sole of my foot.

Zach looked up at me. "Ticklish?" he asked with a small smile.

I nodded, sure my cheeks were about to go up in flames, they felt so hot. The most gorgeous man on the planet was making love to me and here I was laughing because my feet were ticklish. I expected him to move on from there, but something lit up in his eyes and all of a sudden his mouth was on my foot again, but he kept looking at me. Then he began torturing me with even lighter kisses in the one spot that I couldn't control my reaction to.

"Zach," I laughed as I tried to twist away from him. It quickly turned into a wrestling match that left me laughing like a crazy man. It was like all the tension and fear that I'd been holding in chose to leave my body in the form of the giggles. I covered my eyes with my hands and murmured, "Sorry."

Zach was suddenly over me again and when he removed my hands from my eyes, I nearly gasped. He was smiling widely, to the point that I could actually see his teeth. I couldn't even recall the last time I'd seen him smile... *really* smile. Hell, he wasn't even smiling, he was grinning. And his eyes... they were alight with something so soft and beautiful that I was completely overcome.

God, I loved him.

Despite everything, I loved him still and probably even more.

I found myself reaching for his cheek, maybe so I could see if the dimples I thought I was seeing were really there or not. As I caressed him, Zach's smile faded but the softness in his eyes didn't and when he pressed a kiss to my palm, I knew I hadn't screwed things up by getting lost in that perfect moment.

"I guess you'll just have to find my ticklish spots," Zach said with another one of those sweet, small smiles.

"Promise?" I asked before I could think better of it. I could see it was the wrong thing to say when some of the light went out of his eyes. I kicked myself for my stupidity. Before Zach could say anything or pull away, I dragged him down for a kiss. I put everything into that kiss in the hopes of keeping him there. It was only when he started kissing me back that I felt any measure of relief.

Things moved more quickly after that, for which I was grateful because I needed that haze of pleasure to keep me from saying more stupid shit that would ruin the moment. When Zach kissed his way down my body again, he settled on the floor between my legs. It wasn't really clear to me what was happening until his pointer finger ran the length of my hard dick. Electricity fired up my spine as I let out a little gasp. Before I could even fully recover, something hot and wet swept over the tip of my cock. I opened my eyes because at some point they'd closed without me even realizing it.

All I saw at first was Zach's hair. But then he deliberately lifted his head so I could see his eyes. He put his hand around my shaft to hold my flesh in the position that he wanted and then he bent his head and flicked his tongue over the tip of my crown again. I rested my body on my elbows so I could watch him, but once again my eyes slid shut as I reveled in the pleasure that raced through my blood. I'd given head enough to know that it brought a man pleasure, but never in a million years would I have guessed that it was like this. Now it made sense why Davis had been satisfied with just oral sex.

Zach licked me a few more times and then he took my crown into his mouth.

"Oh fuck," I cried, arching my back. It felt so good that I wasn't capable of saying anything else. In fact, when he sucked on me a few more times, I gave up on trying to hold myself up so I could watch and crashed back onto the bed. I'd never actually let myself fantasize about Zach doing this to me because I'd just assumed he wouldn't want to. Even if I had fantasized about it, the reality couldn't compare to anything I could have ever come up with on my own. I'd masturbated plenty of times, but my own hand certainly didn't measure up to Zach's talented mouth. By the time Zach's nose was pressed against my groin and my dick was firmly buried down his throat, I was nothing but one big exposed nerve directly connected to Zach's mouth. He controlled every aspect of my body with just the flick of his tongue and the gentleness of his mouth.

I fisted my hands in the bedding as Zach began to bob his head up and down on me. I lost all sense of time and reality. My only goal was to come. But it didn't happen. Zach just kept driving me higher and higher and as soon as I'd get close, he'd back off and move on to another part of my body. When the raging desire calmed just a little, he'd start all over again. By the time I was begging him with incoherent sobs for relief, I hadn't even realized what his plan was. But there was no missing his probing finger at my entrance. The move had some of my senses returning, but admittedly, it was difficult to focus on his finger when his mouth was going to town on my dick.

I had no clue how long Zach worked my hole with his gentle touch, but when the tip of his finger began to breach me, instead of fearing it, I welcomed it because I suddenly felt too empty. It hadn't been like that when Zach had been trying to put himself inside me during our first encounter. That time, my body had locked up so tight that I'd been unable to focus on anything but the pain. But now when my muscles gave way and Zach's digit penetrated me, it didn't hurt. It felt strange, yes, but it didn't hurt.

I gave over to Zach completely in that moment because I realized everything that he was doing was for me. My pleasure was all that mattered to him. Even if his end goal was to fuck me, it was clear he wanted me to enjoy the experience too.

Yeah, I was definitely a goner for Zach Warner.

Zach took his time letting my body adjust to his finger. When he began to slide it in and out of me, I was stunned by how good it felt. He was still using his mouth on my dick, but only to make sure I couldn't focus for too long on any one thing. When he added a second finger, there was a coolness that came along with it and I assumed it was lube. I knew I should probably ask him if he had another condom, but the truth was I didn't care. I knew I should, but my trust in Zach was implicit. He'd take care of me and that was what I needed more in this moment than anything I'd ever needed in my entire life.

The torment of Zach's mouth and fingers had my body strung up tight, so when he released my cock and moved over me so he could kiss me, all while keeping his fingers inside me, I smashed my mouth against his so I could show him what his torment had been doing to me. He let me kiss him like I wanted, and when I finally pulled back so I could take in a breath, I swore I saw him smile again. But it didn't last. Instead, his free hand came up to caress my temple and he pressed soft kisses to the corners of my mouth. "You still want this, sweetheart?" he asked. "I can make you come like this, with my mouth and my hand."

If someone had told me that Zach Warner would be offering to pleasure me in return for nothing at all, I would have called them insane. Up until that moment, it had never even occurred to me that my pleasure was all Zach was thinking about. I almost made the mistake of blurting right then and there that I loved him, but luckily something in my head kept the words where they belonged… inside.

"Want you," I began to say, but then I had to pause so I could get control of my emotions because those damn tears were back and threatening to fall. "Want all of you, Zach," I somehow managed to get out. "Please."

He didn't respond with words, but the way he kissed me was answer enough and the relief of knowing this would continue was like a mini orgasm all in itself. Zach took his time working me back up, but just when I was ready to blow, he eased off and pulled his fingers free of my body. One of his arms went around my back and then he was gently moving me on the bed so my head was on the pillow. I was physically exhausted but still tense with need, so all I could do was lie there and watch Zach as he prepared himself. His moves were deliberate as he removed the rest of his clothing and donned a condom that he'd pulled from his wallet. It made me nervous that he could be so cool and relaxed, but then I saw the tremble in his fingers as he worked the latex down his hard shaft.

When he climbed onto the bed, I expected him to turn me over so he could take me from behind. But to my surprise, he lay down on top of me, his body settling between my legs. When he kissed me, it was passionate, hungry. Lube was getting all over my own dick and belly, but I most certainly didn't care. I kissed Zach back with newfound confidence that I didn't really know the origin of.

Zach's hand reached between our bodies so he could position his crown at my opening. He broke the kiss and murmured, "Bear down on me, okay?"

I nodded and curled my hands around his upper arms.

I did as he said but there was no denying that it did hurt when he started to push into me. But unlike the first time, my body didn't seem to resist the intrusion as much and while it burned, it wasn't the same level of pain I'd experienced the first go around.

"Breathe," Zach urged. He peppered my mouth with tiny kisses. In between, he told me what to do and when, and he praised me with the sweetest of words as he pushed deeper inside. He only went about halfway in before slowly pulling back out just a little. The move shot a tingle of excitement up my spine because it didn't hurt. The pressure was intense but something about that little glide had my faltering dick returning to attention.

Zach continued to move in and out of me slowly, going deeper each time. He reminded me to breathe at the same time that his hand began moving along my side. When he was finally all the way inside of me and I felt his balls pressed up against my ass, I wanted to die of happiness right there on the spot. I knew there was much more to come, but just knowing that I'd been able to do this and do it with Zach was a life-altering event in itself. No matter what happened after tonight, I'd always get to say Zach had been my first. That my first time had been with a man I loved. There were so many people who didn't get to have that kind of memory.

Zach continued to love on my body with his hands and on my mouth with his lips. I quickly became an active participant again. When I began kissing Zach back, he shifted his weight until he covered my body completely. His hand moved beneath my ass so he could lift my hips. That slid him deeper inside of me, and I gasped at the sensation.

Zach began to glide in and out of me in slow, long, smooth strokes. The friction with each powerful thrust tightened the coil of need in my belly and made the pressure in my balls almost unbearable. There were no more words spoken between us, but somehow it didn't matter. I saw everything I needed to in Zach's eyes and in the way he held me, and I wanted to believe that he could see the same in me.

As Zach's plunges began to grow harder and faster and the only sounds in the room were of skin slapping against skin and our labored breathing, I wrapped my legs around his hips so he'd have better leverage. His hand moved between our bodies to grip my dick. He matched the pumps of his hand to his thrusts into my body, and all I could do was hang on for the ride. We were drenched in sweat as we each chased our orgasms. I lost the ability to think or speak, so I just clung to Zach and trusted him to take us where we needed to go. I couldn't say how many more times he pounded into me or how many more kisses he stole as he stroked my cock, but when I reached the edge of that cliff, I found my voice again.

"Zach, please," I begged. "Please! I need to come!"

"Come for me, sweetheart," Zach said softly against my mouth, but there was demand there too and that was ultimately what sent me over. I cried out as light and dark mingled behind my closed eyelids and something exploded deep inside of me. The tight coil that had been building and building snapped, and then I was falling and rising and falling over and over again. I dug my fingers into Zach's back as I rode out the endless waves of pleasure that consumed me. Zach was practically slamming into me, and I knew that had to be prolonging my own release. His mouth was buried against my neck so when he came, I both heard and felt his scream of pleasure. His dick throbbed inside of me as he tried to go deeper and deeper. He held me so tight I could barely breathe, but I didn't care one little bit. If I died in that moment, I'd die a happy man.

I took in every sound Zach made as his orgasm consumed him. The only thing missing was the feel of his essence inside of me, and I wondered if there was any way I'd be able to talk him out of using the condom the next time we made love. I pressed kisses along his cheek as my own orgasm eased and Zach rode out his. When his body relaxed, he turned and sought out my mouth, kissing me as hungrily as he had when we'd first started making love. But there was something strangely more desperate in his kiss.

Unfortunately, I didn't have much time to consider it because he pulled his mouth away before reaching down between our bodies. As he gently slid his dick free of me, I felt both satisfaction and a strange sense of loss that didn't really make sense to me. I figured I'd have time to process it as well as every other emotion I had gone through once we were settled under the covers and Zach's arms were around me.

I curled onto my side when Zach got up so he could dispose of the condom. I watched him move around the room and figured he was looking for something to drink or something to clean me off with. I didn't really care about the semen on my belly or it mixing with my sheets. As far as I was concerned, it was a badge of honor.

I felt all loose and smiley as I snuggled against my pillow. I was about to ask Zach what he was looking for when I saw him snatch his pants off the floor and begin putting them on.

Okay, maybe he liked to sleep in them.

A tingle of fear raced down my spine as I watched him button up his pants. He didn't look at me. When he grabbed his shirt and pulled it on, then sat down on the edge of my bed so he could stamp his foot into his boot, the bottom of my belly fell out and I knew what was about to happen.

I just couldn't fucking believe it.

With every step that Zach got closer to being fully dressed, I told myself there was an explanation. My mind went into overdrive making up excuses like maybe he was just getting dressed so he could go to his place to get some things, or to go get us some food, or make a run to the bathroom. Maybe he just wanted us to spend the night at his place since there would be more privacy.

But my heart knew the truth. Strange that it would figure things out before my mind.

The whole thing ended like it had begun. He was there one moment and gone the next. As he walked out of the room, he didn't look back at me, didn't ask if I was okay, didn't even say he'd see me tomorrow. He just walked through the door and closed it behind him and that was that.

Just like making love to him had changed something inside me forever, him walking away from me without a word did too. I expected tears but there was nothing but a strange numbness that came over me. It was nothing like the weirdness I'd felt after giving Davis head, though.

This was worse.

So much worse.

Everything inside me threatened to shut down except for the one thing that was hurting the most.

My heart.

It had decided now was a good time to relive every single word, every single touch in graphic detail as I curled up on my side and stared at that stupid fucking door.

I wanted to tell the foolish organ not to bother because I already knew the answer to why Zach had left. It was the same reason he'd stayed away from me so long in the first place. It was the same reason so many people in my life had walked away.

It was time to get on board with the truth.

I wasn't enough.

Once again, I just wasn't enough.

CHAPTER 15

ZACH

Zach... Zach, please...

"Zach!"

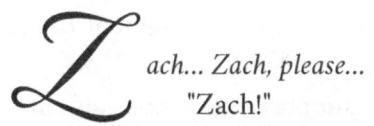

I jolted at the sound of my name being called in a voice which most definitely *wasn't* the same voice that had softly whispered into my ear over and over again the night before. Lucky had the most husky way of saying my name when he was begging me to let him come...

"Zach!"

This time, the frustrated voice pulled me from my thoughts and as the fog cleared from my muddled mind, I remembered where I was. My eyes locked with Tag's. He was standing at the back of the room, his expression one of confusion and concern. The dozen or so expressions of the students sitting in front of him were mainly just of confusion.

"So, yeah, that's..." I began, but then let my voice drop off as I once again shifted my gaze to Lucky's seat.

Lucky's *empty* seat.

Tag interrupted. "So I think what everyone can take from this discussion is that even if you're feeling just a little bit off, you need to remember that the lives of your teammates and the rescues are in your hands. The only time you should be getting on that rope is when you are one hundred percent on. Now, why don't we take a short break and then we'll move on to today's lesson?" His voice was steady and even as he excused the students. All I could do was stand there numbly as the room cleared.

"Hey, you okay?" Tag asked as he approached me. It was probably the tenth time he'd asked me that since I'd arrived at the hangar that morning.

I once again lied and said, "Yeah, I'm fine."

The truth was that I was anything but fine. I forced myself to tear my eyes from Lucky's seat and went around the desk to the whiteboard and began jotting down some of the points that we'd be discussing today.

"You sure?" Tag said. "Because you seem a little distracted."

I almost laughed at that. Distracted was the understatement of the decade. I was so much more than *distracted*.

I made some kind of sound that was supposed to pass as affirmation. Fortunately, Tag didn't push me with any more questions.

"Morrie called me from the hospital this morning. They're releasing him today. He should be cleared to resume his training by the end of the week."

"Uh-huh," I murmured.

"Not sure about Lucky, though," Tag said from behind me.

"What do you mean?" I asked. I managed to keep my attention on the board in front of me, but my ears were entirely focused on Tag.

"Guess I misjudged that kid. I thought he had what it took."

My grip tightened on the marker in my hand as I slowly turned around. Tag was toying with one of the ropes we used for demonstration purposes in the classroom. "What are you talking about?" I asked with barely leashed anger.

Tag shrugged and said, "Lucky... I mean, I get that yesterday freaked him out, but for him to decide to just call it quits without even discussing it with me is a bit of a disappointment."

"Quits?" I practically shouted. "He quit? He's leaving the program?"

"You'd think he could've had his chickenshit moment early enough that I could offer his spot to someone else, but I guess it's better to know now what a coward he is than when he's in the field for real."

I was on Tag before I even realized what I was doing. My hands curled around the front of his shirt and then my face was in his. "That kid has got more guts than you and I combined!" I snapped. "If I ever hear you talking about him like that again, you and I are going to have a serious problem, friendship or no friendship."

I shoved Tag hard and then hurried past him. The door to the classroom seemed like it was miles away.

Lucky is leaving.

No, he wasn't even just leaving. He was giving up on his entire dream because of me. Because I was a worthless piece of shit who'd taken the precious gift Lucky had given me and shit all over it.

The memory of how I'd walked out on Lucky without even a word hit me all over again. My stomach lurched violently, and it was all I could do not to lean over and just start puking all over Tag's floor.

What have I done?

Over the years, I'd had more anonymous hookups than I could count, but I knew for a fact that I hadn't ever walked out on any one of those men or women as callously as I'd walked out on Lucky. Hell, even if I hadn't known my date's name, I'd still had enough manners to bid them farewell or tell them I had a good time or whatever. I'd treated Lucky no better than if I'd paid him for his services. Christ, there had even been a few times where I *had* paid someone for sex and I'd *still* managed to be a decent human being around them.

But Lucky...

It felt like little shards of glass were being pressed into my chest one by one as I remembered the way he'd watched me expectantly from the bed after I'd pulled out of him and gotten up. I'd pretended not to notice, of course, but I'd been deeply aware of every expression, every sound he'd made as understanding had dawned while I'd gotten my clothes back on. And *still* I'd walked out like he was nothing... like what had happened between us was nothing.

When it had, in fact, been everything.

"Zach, wait," I heard Tag call, but it wasn't until I was halfway out the door that he grabbed my arm to stop me.

"Let go," I snarled as I rounded on my friend. Tag threw his hands up in supplication.

"He's not leaving," Tag blurted before I could say anything else. "Lucky is okay... he's not leaving, Zach."

My relief was palpable, so much so that I found myself reaching out to brace myself against the doorjamb.

"I just said all that shit about him to get a reaction out of you," Tag added.

It took me a moment to process his words. "What the fuck, Tag?"

"Do you have any idea how often you tell people you're fine?" Tag interjected. The raw anger in his voice caught me off guard and effectively silenced me. Tag ran his fingers through his hair and blew out a breath. "God, I fucking hate that word. *Fine!* Do you want to know when the last time was that you told me you were fine and I actually believed you?" Tag snapped. "It was when you left for basic training and I told you not to get yourself killed. You were so goddamn excited to enlist... it was like you'd finally found that thing you'd been looking for your entire life. Next time I saw you, you were about to be deployed. I didn't even recognize you. But you said you were fine. Every leave after that I watched more and more of you disappear and still you'd tell me you're fucking fine. Your brother goes missing for years and guess what... oh yeah, Zach's fine. Then Jake comes back and for once I believe that you might actually be fine and then you up and reenlist. The military spits you back out even more unrecognizable than ever but don't worry, you're *fine*. And now there's this kid... this kid you clearly have some kind of history with because one second you're ignoring him, the next you're coming down on him for nothing. Fast-forward to yesterday, and I'm watching one of the coolest heads I know completely lose it. So do me a fucking favor, Zach. Have enough respect for me to not tell me you're goddamn fine!"

Tag's unexpected tirade left me standing on the edge of a cliff, though I had no idea how I'd gotten there. How had my friend seen all the things I'd worked so very hard to hide? And if he'd noticed, did that mean Jake had too? And what about my parents? Had they fallen for my *"Zach's fine"* routine or had they known it was all bullshit too?

"I called Lucky this morning to check up on him," Tag said softly after a moment. "He wanted to come to class, but I told him to take some time for himself. Guess what word he used when I asked him if he was sure he was okay," Tag said with a harsh laugh.

I didn't answer Tag because I knew he wasn't expecting a response. When I did manage to find my voice, it was only to ask, "How did he sound?"

It was Tag's turn not to answer and that in itself was answer enough.

"I fucked up," I somehow managed to say. I felt hot and cold all over. Exposing any kind of vulnerability, whether it was to a friend or enemy, felt like I was exposing my throat for the deathblow. "I fucked up," I repeated more firmly. The words were for me as much as they were for Tag. I couldn't bring myself to look at my friend. I was afraid of what I would see in his eyes.

I sensed rather than saw his approach. I couldn't help but flinch when he settled his hand on my shoulder.

"Then fix it," was all Tag said and then he left the room. I desperately wanted to do what I'd done the night before after I'd left Lucky. But going back to my cabin and drinking myself into a stupor wasn't really an option.

I wasn't sure how long I stood in the doorway but when the students started filing back into the room, I blindly made my way back to the front of the class. I kept my hands busy by slowly writing things on the whiteboard that weren't necessary. When the chatter had died down, I forced myself to turn around. I avoided eye contact with Tag because I was afraid of the disappointment I'd see in his expression. He said to just fix things, but it wasn't that simple.

Nothing about being with Lucky was simple. But at the same time, there had been this strange sense of rightness when I'd held him in my arms. He'd fit me so perfectly, like his body had been made for mine and mine for his. His trust… *that* had been what had done me in. He'd trusted me to take care of him without even asking. And in those minutes after I'd come and I'd lain in his embrace, I'd trusted him too.

For the first time in a long time, *I'd* felt taken care of.

Tag cleared his throat at the back of the room, reminding me of where I was. I opened my mouth to speak but at that exact moment, the door to the classroom swung in and the object of my thoughts stood there in the doorway.

Pain exploded in my chest at the sight of Lucky. On the one hand, I was relieved that he hadn't left. Tag had admitted that he'd made that part up, but somewhere in the back of my mind I'd accepted that it was a real possibility. On the other hand, the sight of Lucky threatened to do me in. The scrapes on his cheek were scabbing over, but there was a new patch of raw skin under his jawline that looked suspiciously like beard burn. I scratched some fingers through my overgrown whiskers and continued assessing him. He was pale, and dark circles marred the soft skin under his eyes. I suspected he'd had as little sleep as I had. Even with the space between us, his eyes looked red, and I could only assume it was from the tears he'd shed after I'd walked out on him.

"Sorry," Lucky mumbled. His eyes met mine for the briefest of moments before he dropped them and entered the room. Many of the students got up so they could go to Lucky and give him a hug. I couldn't really hear anything Lucky was saying in response to all the praise and support he was receiving from his classmates, but it was clear that the small smiles he gave people were forced. There was an irrational part of me that wanted to ask the other students if they couldn't see for themselves that he was far from okay. I wanted him to tell them the truth about what an asshole I was.

White noise took over my brain as I watched Tag go to Lucky and give him a brief hug. I couldn't hear the conversation they were having, but I knew Tag had a lot more to say to Lucky than his classmates did.

I used every minute of the distraction Lucky's entrance had provided to try and pull myself together. The only way I was able to even conduct the class was to not look at Lucky even once. By the time I was done with the session, I had no clue what I'd said, but since Tag hadn't been forced to intervene, I figured I'd managed to pull it off.

I waited for that inevitable moment when Lucky would come up and confront me, but it didn't happen. Not in the classroom and not later in the day during the hands-on training portion. When it came time for me to check Lucky's harness and the lines that would secure him, I'd imagined all the different ways he'd go off on me. But he didn't say a thing other than to acknowledge my instructions with a simple nod of his head. I wasn't sure he was really even seeing me because his eyes just looked... *dead*.

He also failed to interact with his classmates on any kind of meaningful level and when the session ended, instead of hanging out at the hangar to get some hands-on practice, Lucky murmured an excuse about being tired, and then he was gone. After calling it a night myself, I returned to my cabin and started in on the alcohol. By the third shot, I'd found enough courage to text Lucky the half-assed question, *You okay?*

Not surprisingly, I didn't get a response. The fifth shot gave me enough confidence to dial Lucky's number but my call went straight to voicemail. As the hours passed and my attempts to contact Lucky continued to fail, I lost myself in more and more alcohol. The bottle was close to empty by the time sleep claimed me. By morning, I was left with the headache from hell but fortunately it was Sunday, and there was no training scheduled.

One glance at my phone showed not even a single response from Lucky. I hated that my mind went to the image of his phone sitting on the nightstand of some guy he'd met the night before while blowing off some steam. The idea of some random jackass putting his hands all over Lucky's gorgeous skin had me wanting to reach for the bottle all over again. I settled for taking a long shower and unpacking my bag. The sight of the frayed rope that had nearly cost Lucky his life had me stilling. It took several long beats to catch my breath as I considered how few strands of rope there'd been keeping Lucky from falling to his death. Once I felt a little more levelheaded, I reached for my phone and dialed Jake's number.

"Zach," Jake said in surprise. "How's it going up there? I see you're having some weather."

"Yeah. Just glad it's not snow. Listen, didn't you tell me one time you had a lab test a mysterious substance one of your patients found on a baby bottle or something?" I knew I at least owed my brother some questions about how he and Oz were doing, but my impatience to determine what had caused the nearly disastrous accident was at the forefront of my mind.

There was a pause while Jake presumably tried to remember what I was talking about. It had been a long time ago.

"Oh right. No, it was an unlabeled bottle of something that a child had gotten into in their grandparents' garage. When the kid ended up in the hospital, the parents suspected it was due to ingesting the mysterious substance, so we needed to know what it was to help us determine whether or not there were any long-term effects. Why? Is someone in your program sick?"

If he knew the real reason I was asking, he'd flip his fucking lid and show up here in Glacier with a troop of angry uncles demanding justice for the adopted nephew they all considered blood. Right after they went off on whoever was responsible for the stuff getting all over the rope, they'd be coming after me for defiling their sweet, innocent little Lucky.

And rightfully so.

"No one is sick. We just found a mysterious corrosive substance on one of our ropes and wondered if there was a way to have it tested to determine where it came from," I murmured. God, Jake was going to hate me for what I'd done to Lucky. My big brother had warned me that Lucky had struggled after I'd rejected him two years earlier, and I'd gone and done the same damn thing but a thousand times worse.

"Sure. There are several labs that can do that kind of testing. I'll email you a list." Jake paused to talk to someone else, presumably Oz, before coming back to me. "Anything else? You still planning on coming to see us soon?"

I ran my fingers through my hair. "Yeah. We'll be done here in another week or two, depending on the weather. Then I can come down."

I hated myself for the lie, but I wasn't about to explain to my big brother why I was reneging on my promise to come for a visit.

"Great, I've got a special brew in the works for you."

I found myself half smiling. My brother had a strange obsession with making his own beer. When we were kids, he'd absolutely refused to even have a sip of alcohol before he'd turned twenty-one, but once he'd hit that legal age, he'd become a beer aficionado. I, on the other hand, was happy as long as my beer was wet and cold.

"How are things going up there?" Jake asked hesitantly.

"Fi—" I began to say before Tag's words about me always saying I was fine cut me off at the knees. I searched for something else to say, but everything I could come up with sounded like another version of the "I'm fine" response.

"It's beautiful up here, Jake. We should... we should maybe plan to climb here sometime," I said softly. I knew it would never happen because I couldn't risk being around my big brother for that amount of time and still keep my secrets from him, but even just the thought of having that kind of time with Jake made something inside of me twist painfully.

"I'd like that, Zach," Jake responded. He hesitated a moment and added, "Lucky's fathers are planning this family hiking thing for when he comes home... maybe you can join us for that since you guys will be here at the same time."

"Maybe," I hedged. "How... how's Lucky doing?" I asked. "He's in Yellowstone, right?" I pinched the bridge of my nose for bringing up the obvious lie. What was I doing?

"Yeah. He's been... quiet," Jake responded. "But I'm sure he'll snap out of it when he's back home."

I was pretty certain he wouldn't... especially if I was anywhere nearby. It was another reason to turn tail and run from this whole thing the second I was able to.

"Hey, um, I've gotta go," I said.

"Alright. You sure you're okay, Zach?" Jake asked.

"Yeah, I'm fi—" I began, then stopped suddenly. Fuck, who was I kidding? I pulled in a breath and said, "I'm fine, Jake." I could practically hear his disappointment when he finished saying his goodbyes, but I couldn't find it in myself to say anything else.

So what if "fine" was my new normal? It had gotten me this far, hadn't it? And Lucky... he'd get over what had happened between us. He was young and had a good family and friends to watch out for him. He'd find himself a nice guy who knew how to treat him right and he'd go back to being the sweet young man who was so much more than "fine." This whole thing with me would be nothing more than a brief regret in an otherwise perfect life. In two weeks, we'd go our separate ways for good.

Two weeks...hell, with the way I'd treated him, Lucky would be completely over me in two days if he wasn't already.

CHAPTER 16

LUCKY

"Like I said, Lucky, don't let it get you down. Any one of us could have made the mistake." My classmate, Luiz, patted me on the back and sent me a smile before adding, "I'll see you later, okay? My parents are driving in from Seattle, so I have to play tour guide."

"Yeah, sure. And thanks." While I appreciated Luiz's words of encouragement, I knew that not everybody would have made the same mistake I had. Tying a monkey's fist knot was something Xander had taught me the very first year I'd gone to live with him and Bennett. Under normal circumstances, I could've touched the nylon blindfolded and known the knot was wrong, but nothing about the last two days had been normal. So I'd thrown the monkey's fist and watched in horror as the entire thing untied itself into a puddle of rope on the ground instead of winging across the river the way it was meant to.

In search and rescue situations, every rope toss could be the difference between life and death, and I'd fucked it up.

Even if my mistake hadn't had potentially life-threatening consequences, the fact that it had been Zach who'd witnessed it was just icing on the shit show of a cake that was my life. I would've liked to have blamed the error on my lack of sleep, but the reality was that I'd been so frazzled about being around Zach and having him actually speak to me that I hadn't even given the knot itself much thought. I'd spent so much of the last two days just trying to avoid any kind of interaction with Zach that I'd gotten sloppy and had merely tied the wrong kind of knot. Not surprisingly, Zach had used the opportunity to lay into me. Before I'd made the monumental mistake of sleeping with the man, I'd let similar encounters just roll off my back, but I could safely say I was no longer immune to Zach's criticism.

Not that I had been before, but somehow it had been easier to accept it. Now it just felt like insult added to injury.

I heard someone call my name from behind me but instead of turning to see who it was, I quickened my pace. I was tired of all the invites I was getting to join my well-meaning classmates for coffee or parties. They clearly knew something was up with me, but I'd been selling them all the same story—that I'd just been feeling a bit under the weather.

As far as I was concerned, the night with Zach had never happened. No, it wasn't that simple to forget about the whole thing, but I sure as hell didn't want to go telling anyone about it. Even Min didn't know the truth. As far as everybody else was concerned, I was just having a bad few days and needed some time to myself. There was no reason for them to know that I'd become numb to the world around me.

Instead of exiting the building through the regular door, I made my way to the side entrance where I wouldn't have to deal with anyone else. I was just reaching my hand out to push the door open when strong fingers closed around my upper arm and drew me back. "Lucky, wait."

Even if I hadn't recognized his voice, my body knew his touch. How it could have memorized the weight of his fingers or the feel of his skin after just one night together was beyond my understanding, but it was yet another thing I had to figure out how to forget. I automatically yanked my arm from his grip. The old me had always been looking for a reason to get Zach to touch me, but now that was the very last thing I wanted.

I had the satisfaction of watching Zach's eyes darken with an unfamiliar emotion as he pulled his hand back. The numbness that had been keeping me company was replaced with a stark pain exploding inside of my chest. "Don't touch me," I hissed. I didn't recognize my own voice.

Zach took a step back, clearly startled by my reaction. I didn't blame him. I hadn't been expecting it either.

"Lucky, I just wanted to—"

"What? What did you want, Zach?" I asked bitterly. "How about I save us both some time here. No, I'm not going to tell anyone," I said as I ticked up one of my fingers. "Yes, I will be more careful next time and not make such foolish mistakes in class that force you to actually speak to me," I continued as I ticked up another finger. "Yes, I agree we should pretend the whole thing never happened and just try to stay out of each other's way," I finished as I held up a third finger.

"That wasn't what I wanted to talk to you about," Zach murmured. For the first time that I could ever remember, he seemed unsure of himself. If I hadn't known better, I would've thought our roles had reversed and I was the confident one while he was the insecure mess.

"Then what?" I snapped impatiently. "What do you want?"

Zach was silent for a beat and then he shook his head. "You're not eating."

"What?" I asked, caught off guard by his observation.

"You haven't been joining your friends for lunch. I thought maybe you were going back to your room, but I saw you today sitting by yourself at the lake—"

"And what? You thought I was pining for you?" I asked. I couldn't help the bitterness that went through me. "Okay, Zach, let's pretend I was. What was your plan? Were you gonna give me some words of wisdom about how I should grow up and that what happened between us was just sex and that you warned me all about your stupid rules? Well, don't trouble yourself. If I was a kid before, I'm definitely not one anymore. No more stars in my eyes, no more dreams of saving myself for that right guy. If anything, I should be thanking you. You've opened up a whole new world for me by helping me get rid of that pesky V card."

I didn't wait to see what Zach thought of my little tirade. Since my numbness had abandoned me completely, the tears I'd managed to run from for so long were threatening to finally fall. And there was just no way in hell I would cry in front of this man.

I made a move to push through the door again when Zach's hand shot out. Instead of grabbing me, he held the door so I couldn't open it.

"Let go," I demanded.

"You haven't returned any of my calls or answered my texts. You haven't been home the last two nights."

A painful laugh bubbled up in my throat. But I didn't recognize the sound that ultimately came out. I dropped my hand from the door and took several steps back. "Is this just some kind of game for you?" I asked. I put out my hands and said, "What card am I supposed to play now, Zach? Because I have no fucking clue. I can't be touched by your supposed concern because I know you don't give a shit about me. And you sure as hell can't be jealous about where I'm spending my evenings after you walked out on me. So what do you want?"

"I just wanted to make sure you were okay," Zach murmured.

All I could do was stare at him as I played his words over and over in my head. "Wow," I said softly. "Someone really did a number on you, didn't they?" Just like that, my anger began to dissolve. I'd attributed Zach's behavior to something I'd done wrong, but the more he stood before me, completely incapable of connecting with me on any normal level, I realized his behavior had very little to do with me at all. Zach shifted uncomfortably but didn't respond in any other kind of way.

"You know what," I murmured. "I'm fine, Zach. You and me... we're fine," I said tiredly. Despite the strange revelation I'd come to, it didn't change the way my heart ached for him. Maybe if I hadn't had those few glimpses of the man he'd once been, I could've just passed him off as another selfish asshole who deserved whatever he got. But those smiles he'd gifted me with during the lighter moments of our lovemaking were burned into my brain.

Fucked, Lucky. You guys fucked.

I found myself nodding to the voice in my head.

"See you later," I murmured. I reached for the door, fully expecting Zach to stop me, but he didn't make a move toward me this time and I stupidly found myself feeling rejected all over again.

"His name was Mitch."

The words were spoken so softly, I almost didn't hear them. For a brief moment, I thought Zach and I were no longer alone in the side corridor because I barely recognized the uneven voice that spoke the words. I froze in place, my hand still on the door handle, as I waited to see what would happen next.

"Mitchell Dorsey. But everyone called him Mitch. Not me, though. He wanted me to call him with whatever title he had at the time. Or Sir. He always liked Sir the best."

I eased my weight off the door so it wouldn't inadvertently open and just held on to the handle itself. I was afraid to look at Zach because my gut was telling me this was some big moment for him... for us.

"I was just out of college when I met him. I'd always had this dream of becoming an Army Ranger but my parents really wanted me to go to college. So I did both. I went to college first, and then I enlisted in the army the day after graduation. I started basic training and met Mitch the very first day. He oversaw all of the new recruits. I used to fantasize that he'd seen something special in me that first day when he welcomed all of us, but I eventually figured it out," Zach said. His eyes were on some spot on the opposite wall.

"Figured what out?" I inserted carefully.

"He'd seen me flirting with one of my fellow recruits in the bar the night before and knew I at least swung both ways. I found out later he'd also seen me get shoved away from the guy in disgust, so he figured he could take advantage of the situation."

"How?" I asked.

Zach sighed. "By offering me a safe haven, making me feel like he was the one person there who'd always be in my corner. He seemed to recognize my lack of confidence, my eagerness to please. So he played on all those things. Within a week of arriving at boot camp, he was calling me into his office to commend me for all my hard work. Then he started talking about how fit I was becoming and how that would benefit me..." Zach began drumming his fingers on his thigh. I suspected he didn't even realize he was doing it. "I was so stupid," he said with an ugly laugh. "I actually thought he really was impressed with me and for once I felt..."

Zach's voice fell off as he dropped his eyes to his feet. "He was my first."

I found it suddenly hard to swallow as I stepped away from the door. Even if I could have spoken, I wouldn't have known what to say.

"I didn't really even have time to consider what was happening. He was older than me, handsome, smart, and I respected the hell out of him, so I let him do whatever he wanted. It was over fast. I can't say I really enjoyed it or anything, but afterwards when he started talking to me about stuff like I was his equal..." Zach shook his head. "Like I said, he knew what strings to pull."

"What happened? Did you tell anyone what he did?" I asked. While I knew nothing about the military, I figured it wasn't exactly okay for commanding officers to seduce their subordinates.

Zach shook his head again. "I foolishly thought one thing didn't have to do with the other. I knew I couldn't tell anyone we were dating"—Zach let out a harsh laugh—"I actually thought that's what we were doing..." He paused and added, "I compartmentalized things. I was a regular guy training to become an Army Ranger, and I was also a guy who happened to be sleeping with a man who had the kind of military career I could only dream of. I think part of me hoped his success would rub off on me, or maybe his connections would ultimately benefit me too. But more than that, I really thought he was the one for me, that it was the real deal."

"So what happened?" I asked. I was beyond stunned that he was sharing as much as he was and was terrified of doing or saying something to mess it up.

"The relationship went on for five years."

I gasped at that but if Zach noticed, he didn't remark on it.

"Five fucking years before I learned the truth."

"What truth?"

"He was simply using me for sex." Zach's fingers began tapping more quickly on his thigh. "Mitch was married. He even had kids my age."

If the information shocked me, I could only imagine how it'd felt to Zach at the time. "How did he keep it a secret from you for that long?"

"When he was assigned to Fort Benning, his family stayed behind in Fort Bragg since he was so close to retirement. He'd simply drive home from time to time to visit them. He told me he was visiting his parents who lived in North Carolina, and they didn't know he was gay. That's why I could never come with him. And I accepted that, because on base... well, he was possessive of me and my time. So much so that he'd actively discouraged me from applying to Ranger School since the deployments would take me away from him too much."

"But didn't you always want to be a Ranger?" I carefully asked. "That's what Jake told me."

He ran his hand through his short hair. "Yes, but he made me feel wanted. Important. I trusted his advice. I truly believed he loved me and we were going to build a life together. I listened to every word he said as if it were a decree from God himself. He told me over and over again how lucky we were to have each other so we could stay closeted and still have a fulfilling sex life in the military. He'd served before and during Don't Ask, Don't Tell, so he was adamant about keeping closeted for the sake of both our careers. So I overlooked some of his questionable behavior and the things he wanted from me. I just thought it was a normal part of relationships."

"I don't understand," I admitted. He glanced at me, and I flinched at the pain I saw in his eyes.

"He got off on controlling me, in and out of bed. The things he said were meant to feed into all of my worst insecurities. Sex was always about him… he didn't just push my boundaries, he went right past them. I always had the right to say no, but if I did, I wasn't saying no to whatever sex act he wanted, I was saying no to the entire relationship."

"You would have lost him," I murmured. I felt sick to my stomach and found myself leaning back against the wall.

"He'd become the only thing in my life that mattered. I'd lost touch with my family and friends, especially after Jake disappeared, and I'd put applying to become a Ranger on hold like he'd asked. But then when I found out he was married, I tried to break it off. He threatened to ruin my career. And truth be told, part of me hadn't wanted to end it. I'd come to believe that he was the only reason I was no longer boring little mediocre Zach Warner who had no hopes of following in his big brother's footsteps."

"I don't believe that," I said with a firm shake of my head. "You could never be any of those things. Your brother is a great man, but you, Zach, you're…"

Zach chose that moment to look at me, and all the words that had been on the tip of my tongue got stuck there. He looked so damn sad that I was sure I could feel his pain in my own chest. Zach held my gaze for a few more beats before dropping his eyes again.

"My entire life felt like a lie but I didn't know how to escape it. I was certain that the success I'd found in my career was only because Mitch had pulled strings or put in a good word for me. I couldn't imagine anyone wanting me the way Mitch did, so I convinced myself it had to be love. I convinced myself that Mitch's wife was a terrible woman and he'd only stayed with her because of societal pressure and their kids. When he talked down to me it was because I wasn't smart enough to understand something. When I'd walk in on him flirting with some young cadet, it was because I couldn't keep him satisfied." Zach blew out a breath and fell silent for a long time.

A really long time.

His fingers had stopped moving but there was no missing the tic in his jaw. That had me keeping my mouth shut and my feet planted where they were. My gut was telling me that he was struggling with old emotions he'd thought long ago buried. I could see the exact moment he got control of himself because he pulled in a deep breath and stood up a little straighter.

"It took a long time for me to wake up. But wanting out and getting out were two very different things. The more I pulled away from Mitch, the more he held on. He convinced me he could ruin my entire career with just one phone call, and I knew he'd do it. He didn't like to lose."

"What did you do?" I asked. My fists were clenched as I imagined what I'd do to the faceless Mitch if I could just get my hands on him.

"I stayed. I lived by his rules for way too long. I knew by then I'd never really loved him... I'd loved the *idea* of him. I'd loved finding someone who'd known what I'd needed—"

"He didn't," I cut in before I could think better of it.

Zach paused to look at me. As big and imposing as he was, he looked so damn broken. I would have given anything in that moment to push into his arms and just hold on to him for dear life.

"He didn't know what you needed," I said more softly.

Zach held my gaze for a moment, then nodded in agreement. "When I finally found the guts to end it for real, he tried exactly what he'd threatened... to end my career. By then, I'd discovered I hadn't been the only young recruit he'd done this to. And with that knowledge, I made sure he wasn't in any position to screw me over."

"How?" I asked.

"Mitch was in the process of getting a divorce from his wife of forty-some years... since he'd come from money, they'd signed a prenup, I guess. So she stood to walk away with next to nothing. I told Mitch that if he didn't retire, I'd be his wife's star witness in their divorce trial. He couldn't forget my name fast enough. A little birdie may or may not have anonymously called his wife to tell her all about her future ex's predilection for pursuing recruits under his command. Given how many guys he took advantage of over the years, she had plenty of ammunition against him and ended up walking away with a pretty nice settlement."

"Good," I said under my breath but Zach must have heard me

because he smiled briefly. I found myself getting lost in that smile of his all over again until it suddenly hit me why he was telling me all of this.

"You're not like him!" I blurted. I was in his space a second later. "You don't use people like that—"

Zach silenced me by putting a finger to my lips. I forced myself to grit my teeth together so I wouldn't open my mouth again. Zach's finger drifted along my lip for a second, then over the curve of my jaw.

"I wanted you from the moment I saw you, Lucky. Thankfully, I'm not so far gone that I'd ever dream of laying my hands on a teenager, but I'm not a saint either."

I nodded in understanding. He'd wanted me, but he hadn't wanted to be *with* me.

"It took me a long time after Mitch to be with another man. I ended up dating primarily women for a while. When I did hook up with a guy for the first time after Mitch, I took control from the start. Everything was on my terms. And I loved it. So I did it again, and again... with men *and* with women. I made sure my partners got what they wanted, but I also made sure they understood I was only interested in sex." Zach paused and ran his finger down my throat. I shivered in response.

"I know you desperately want to believe I'm not like him, Lucky," Zach said softly. "But the truth is, I'm *exactly* like him."

I began shaking my head. "No... no, you came back after I told you the truth about not having been with a guy before. You came back and you were slow and patient and loving—"

"And that's why I walked out as soon as it was over," Zach interrupted.

"That doesn't make sense," I said in frustration because I could tell by the tone of his voice that nothing between us had changed.

"I wanted to be your first and I wanted it to be a good memory for you," Zach explained.

Unlike the memory of his own first time. I kept the words to myself, though, because I knew he wasn't telling me all of this so we could discuss it.

"It was," I choked out. "It was perfect."

To my surprise, Zach drew me into his arms and held me tight. "It was," he admitted. We clung to each other for a moment before he put some space between us. "I shouldn't have walked out on you like I did. I don't regret anything else we did that night. But that moment... it made me wish things could be different. That *I* could be different."

"But you can—"

Zach brushed his mouth over mine in the softest of kisses. I began to cry because I knew what it was.

"No, Zach, not like this. Don't say goodbye like this. I can do better. I can be what you need—"

This time I was the one to cut myself off as I heard my own words. Hadn't Zach just ripped his own guts open to show me how easy it had been for him to twist around who he was to become what Mitch had needed... all because he'd believed he'd loved the controlling bastard?

I shook my head. "I don't mean like that. Not like what that asshole did to you."

"Lucky, look at me," Zach said. "Please," he added when I refused to look up. When I did, his expression looked pained and I realized this had probably been the exact conversation he'd wanted to avoid after we'd had sex.

"I can't be what you want... what you *deserve*. There's not one damn thing about you that needs changing. It's me. After what I went through, I'm... I'm broken. I can't trust like that anymore, and you deserve someone who can give their whole self to you. Someone who isn't jaded and fucked up. But I want you to know, I *need* you to know, I look at that night between us as my first time in a lot of ways too. I know that doesn't make sense—"

"It does," I said as I tried to blink back the tears. I wanted to triumph in the fact that all those little things that I thought I'd seen in him while we'd been making love hadn't been just an act, but my heart was too busy fracturing into a hundred million little pieces. And I wanted to assure him that I loved him, broken or not. But I wasn't going to talk him into something he clearly didn't want.

Zach carefully extricated himself from my hold. "I'll talk to Tag about bringing someone else in for the last couple of weeks of training. I know a couple of guys who might be able to help out—"

"No," I interjected. "No, I want to learn from you."

"Lucky," Zach began, but I shook my head and took a few more steps back.

"Zach, we're practically family, so we need to figure out how to get along. If I... if I promise to keep my hands to myself from now on, can we maybe just be... friends?"

"Friends?" Zach asked suspiciously.

"Yeah. It's that thing that they made this whole successful sitcom about back in your day—"

Zach actually took a swipe at me. I jumped back and grinned.

"Uh-uh, hands to yourself," I reminded him. "So what do you say?"

"Friends?" Zach asked, his voice clearly unsure.

I nodded, then stuck out my hand. "Friends," I said firmly because at that point I was going to take as much of Zach Warner as I could get.

"Friends," Zach agreed, then he was shaking my hand. I managed to keep my expression neutral but inside my brain, the same phrase kept repeating on a loop.

Oh, Lucky, what have you done?

CHAPTER 17

ZACH

"I'm not sure about a 5K with my knee," I admitted, avoiding Lucky's eyes. It wasn't easy admitting my weaknesses to anyone, much less him, but there was no way I could run three miles on paved roads. It was hard enough running on the softer ground of the trails near my cabin, and even then, I was only up to a couple of miles on a good day.

"You're not listening," he said with a grin. The afternoon sunshine sent greedy fingers all the way across the open hangar to paint warm stripes across his face as he handed me equipment from our last airborne drill. It had been three days since our new friendship agreement, and Lucky was helping me clean up from a half-day of training. The day had been cut short when a fire in the park had required Tag's help ferrying firefighters and equipment to the site. He and Johnny had dropped the rest of us off before winging away to help with the emergency response.

Lucky continued. "The Running Rabbit 5K is just the name of the event that this whole festival centers around. I'm not saying I want to actually do the race, but when Nimrod puts on this famous race, they also have the Goat Lick Music and Arts Festival."

I stowed the last of the gear in the metal locker at the back of the hangar and turned back toward him. "You're making this all up. Who's Nimrod?"

Lucky flapped his arms in frustration. "God, you're such a man."

I couldn't help but laugh. It felt so good to be back on steady ground with him. "Explain, please."

"Are you seriously not listening to a word I'm saying? Nimrod is the name of the town. It's just past Goat Lick Overlook and west of Running Rabbit peak. The combination of names is what ended up drawing people to the area a few years ago. Once they had a cult following for this hometown event, it like… boomed. Now all of these hot musicians and artists go to it which draws in more and more people."

One of the things that attracted people to Lucky was his wide-open enthusiasm for life. I'd noticed it many times over the years, and especially as I'd spent more time with him during this course. People were drawn to him. His entire being seemed to bounce and brighten when he was sharing something he was passionate about. Just today, I'd overheard him telling one of the other students about an emergency call at school where two students had been found in a bizarre cycling accident. One of the mangled bikes had wound up twisted around the sign for a pub called The Peddler.

He'd flashed a big grin when he'd said, "The wheels ended up framing the bottom part of the two letter d's. So they just left it there. And now it's part of the sign. Totally meta, right? And now both cyclists get free drinks whenever they go in. They're like local celebrities there."

By the time he'd finished telling the story, everyone around him had congregated over to hear it. That was what it was like being in his presence.

It had reminded me of the time I'd been with my brother and Lucky's family at a cookout and I'd seen Lucky off to one side of the backyard showing a little boy some tricks Lucky's dog, Bear, could do. As Lucky progressed through Bear's repertoire, every other kid and half the adults had wandered over to watch the animated teenager command the goofy dog with nothing but his voice and hand gestures.

"I'll go," I said suddenly. Because of course I wasn't going to let him down. I knew if I didn't agree to go with him to the festival, he'd most likely still go by himself. And I didn't want him to be alone. More than that, I didn't want him to go by himself and meet someone else there. Someone new, someone *better*.

Which, of course, was stupid since we were just friends.

Just friends, I reminded myself. *Because that's all you're capable of.*

I cleared my throat. Maybe I needed a buffer there to keep me from being tempted to become more than friends. Again.

"Hey, so… do you want to invite anyone else? Maybe we could make it a group thing?" I offered.

He frowned and looked around. "Everyone's gone. They went to Kalispell for the rodeo. Dude, where have you been?"

I shook my head, remembering. "No, yes. I remember now. You said you didn't want to go because you're not a horse person." I finished wiring the broken locker closed and then tossed the pliers into the toolbox with a clank. "Which is bullshit, by the way. Jake told me about your love affair with a certain mare named Crumpet."

As I leaned down to close up the toolbox, I realized he hadn't answered. I glanced up at him and found him staring at me with a knowing smirk. "You give a shit," he accused. His eyes sparkled at me and his cheeks pinked. "Admit it. You *do* listen and you remember stuff about me."

I rolled my eyes and looked back down at the toolbox. "Whatever. It doesn't explain why you didn't go to the rodeo with everyone else."

There was another pause which caused me to look back up at him again.

"I just…" He shrugged. "I don't know. Ever since my rope broke, I feel like everyone's watching me… like they're waiting for me to break down or something. And I can't stop thinking about that rope and the way it started to fray… It's stupid, I know."

I stood and walked over to him, placing a hand on his shoulder. He'd put some of my own fears into words, and I kicked myself for not thinking to discuss this with him earlier.

"You think someone messed with the rope on purpose?" I asked softly.

Lucky shrugged. "No, I don't know. Probably not. But it was still scary as fuck, not gonna lie. And I guess I just wanted a break from the group for a little while." He looked into my eyes. "You don't have to come with me if you don't want to. I'll be fine on my own."

"I'll go with you," I said, making his entire face light up. He did a little hop and fist pump move before beginning his usual chatter about everything.

I hid my smile in the collar of my shirt as I leaned down to grab the toolbox to lock it in the classroom before leaving.

"You have everything you need?" I asked. Lucky was in the middle of describing the fair food and craft beer he hoped I'd sneak him at the festival.

He followed me to the classroom. "Yeah, just need my backpack so I don't have to come all the way back here later."

I thought about how spread out everything was in this area. The bunkhouse where the students were staying was a mile to the south whereas the cabin I was staying at was on the way to Nimrod.

"You can always stay at my place if we get back late," I offered without thinking. As soon as the words were out of my mouth, I wanted to call them back. Me and Lucky under the same roof? In a place where there'd be no chance of interruption? Visions of lowering myself over Lucky's body in front of the fireplace began to flash in my mind. Or I could just bend him over the kitchen table... no one would hear his screams of pleasure.

I chanced a glance at Lucky who'd frozen in the act of picking up his backpack. "Um. No, that's okay. I'd... I'd rather sleep at the bunkhouse if it's all the same to you."

I should have been relieved but strangely enough, his rejection stung in a way that I didn't expect.

I shrugged. "Sure, that's fine. Let's get going." After making sure everything was stowed and locked, I led Lucky to my truck.

The silence was a little awkward, so I found myself desperate to get us past it. "Do you have any recent pictures of the twins?" I asked, hopping in and pulling on my seat belt.

Bingo. His entire face lit up as he reached into his pocket for his phone.

"Absolutely. Xander just sent me some this morning. Oz made them these little lion and tiger outfits, and they're amazing. Look," he said with a big grin, holding out his phone. My hand brushed the warm skin of his as I took the phone from him. I did my best to ignore the memory of his bare skin on mine that flashed through me at the touch.

Two chubby-cheeked faces peered out from fuzzy hoodies. I laughed. "My brother-in-law does good work, but that's awfully different from what he sends down the runway in Milan."

"Right? I told Xander Oz ought to consider a kids' line sometime. How fun are these? I can just see some celebrity parading their baby around in it on TMZ or something."

He continued to catch me up on news from home, ignoring the elephant in the truck of his deception toward his dads of where he was this summer. My guilt over not telling them had subsided at some point, mostly because I'd determined that with me there to look after him, he was at least better off than alone.

As we drove farther away from the airport and through the natural vistas of the park, I felt the stress of the past couple of weeks melt away. Spending time with Lucky was easy. He was always happily chatting about something and I was content to ride the pleasant wave of his steady company and learn what made him tick.

It was a relief to have the old Lucky back again. He was once again the sweet, exuberant young man he'd been when I'd first met him, but somewhere in the back of my mind I'd stopped seeing him as a kid. He was beyond intelligent, resourceful, brave, patient and giving. While there was always a measure of competitiveness in SAR programs to be the top student, Lucky was the type of guy who wanted all of his classmates to succeed. And while he and I hadn't talked any more about our night together or the things I'd told him about my past, he'd thrown himself into his vow to make a friendship between us work. It was a level of forgiveness I didn't deserve, but he'd gifted me with it anyway. Admittedly, the whole friends thing wasn't easy for me, especially since I hadn't had many friends growing up besides Tag and my brother, but Lucky didn't seem at all bothered by hesitations. Yes, there was always this underlying "thing" between us when we were together, but Lucky had kept his word to keep his hands to himself.

Which kind of sucked sometimes.

Like now when my fingers itched to settle on his thigh.

I shook myself free of the thought and focused on the twists and turns of the road before us. When we got close to the turnoff to West Glacier, Lucky made a funny sound in his throat. I glanced over and saw him looking longingly across me out the left window. "Why do you look like a kid who's passing by a candy store?" I asked.

He blushed and looked forward again. "Nothing. Well, I've always wanted to hike Lake McDonald, that's all. After flying over it so much and seeing it from the air."

I glanced over at the turn for the famous lake. "Why don't we? It's only about seven miles along the western shore. Couple of hours, maybe. Then it's only thirty more minutes to the festival. We'd be there by four. Doesn't it go into the evening?"

All it took was him glancing innocently down at my knee for me to jerk the wheel to the left and turn onto Going-to-the-Sun Road.

"What are you doing?" he asked, clutching the handle on the door.

"We're going for a hike. I may not be able to handle a 5K run, but I can handle a damned nature walk."

I expected him to argue with me or take back his enthusiasm for the prospect, but he didn't. Instead, he hooted in celebration and sat forward as if trying to catch a glimpse of the lake as soon as it came into view. A few minutes later, we were parked at the Fish Creek Campground and hopping out of the truck.

Lucky stretched and turned his head up to the sun, revealing a strip of tanned skin on his lower belly above the waistband of his gray hiking pants. The barest sliver of red briefs also peeked out above the waistband for just a second, but it was enough to heat my blood. I closed my eyes and shook my head.

Fuck. We'd been over this and over this. Friends. Friends only.

I cleared my throat. "It's pretty flat. Should be okay in running shoes, but let's fill our water bottles before we head out."

He leaned into the footwell of the truck to grab his bottle and I watched his shirt fall forward over his back, this time revealing the peek of red underwear just below the twin dimples of his lower back. The swell of his ass in the nylon hiking pants made my palms itch. I clenched my fingers into fists.

I busied myself grabbing my own water bottle and a couple of protein bars out of a bag in the back. I shoved the bars into a cargo pocket in my pants and led the way to the restrooms to fill up our bottles.

When we finally got onto the trail, the bright sun was shining on the clear water of the large lake and the sky was an impossible blue with giant fluffy clouds moving slowly over the peaks in the distance.

"God, this place is amazing," Lucky said in a reverent voice. "I could totally live here year-round."

"It'd be cold as fuck," I warned with a chuckle.

He shrugged and kept walking ahead. His steps were practically silent on the smooth dirt of the narrow path. "I like the cold. But more than that… I like the hush of fresh snow and that feeling of solitude that comes in wild places in the dead of winter."

I looked over at him in surprise. "I would have thought you'd miss the social stuff. If you lived in a place like this, you'd go stir crazy, wouldn't you?"

He shook his head and smiled, throwing his arms out to the sides and spinning around like Maria from *The Sound of Music*. "Hell no. As long as I have an internet connection, I always have friends with me. Look at this place. It's gorgeous. If I lived someplace like this, I could be social for a while in a cozy cabin by the fire and then head out on a winter adventure. Snowshoeing, skiing, ice climbing… you name it, I want to do it. As long as I have good gear..." He shrugged again. "I'm happy."

I pictured Lucky hanging from an icy crevasse by nothing but a single ice axe, and shivered. "Jesus," I muttered. "Tag's going to have to rescue you one day."

"Nah, I'm safe. I love an adrenaline rush, but I don't have a death wish."

That was good to hear, although I wasn't sure how he defined the difference between the two.

I pointed to a little cluster of yellow wildflowers hidden under the edge of a nearby rock. "Sagebrush buttercup," I murmured before continuing on. "What do you want to do after graduation?"

"This," Lucky said immediately. "I mean, not admiring wildflowers, although I'd like to do that too," he said with a grin. "But I'd like to do alpine search and rescue. Hopefully I can find a job here in the Rockies, but if not, they're always hiring in other areas. Alaska, the Cascades. Even the Grand Canyon has need of rope and rigging paramedics."

"I thought you wanted to become a doctor, like Jake?" I asked as we continued walking. I remembered clearly how he would ask my brother question after question when he was younger.

"I did. Until he hired me part time to help in the clinic. I was bored to tears. I realized very quickly I can't stand to be inside all the time. I had more fun working for my dads' outdoor adventure program. At least then I could be in the wilderness."

I leaned down to grasp a particularly good skipping rock and slung it out into the still water. It hopped across the surface, setting off ripples along the way. "Why not stay home and take over their program?"

Lucky searched for his own rock to skip and then stepped even closer to the water's edge and sank into a squat before whisking it out across the lake.

He paused before he made his admission.

"I need the rush." He glanced up at me as if to judge my reaction. "Hanging on to that rock the other day scared the shit out of me,

Zach. But I have to admit, it made me feel alive. Situations like that remind you how fragile life is, you know?"

I thought back to some of my missions. I'd had the exact same feeling. Part of the reason I'd pursued search and rescue in the first place was that same visceral reminder of how close we are to being lost, how immovable nature was and how small we are in comparison.

"I know exactly what you mean. I remember coming back stateside after a search and rescue mission overseas. There'd been a landslide, and I was part of a US military team sent in to help with airborne SAR." I watched Lucky step over some rocks embedded in the trail and stop to point them out to me wordlessly so they wouldn't trip me up. "Thanks. We spent hour after hour pulling people out, trying to rescue as many people as we could before the expected rains started again and destabilized the area even more. It was literally a life and death race against time. I remember my heart pounding in my chest, my palms sweating on the stick, the steady cadence of the spotter's voice in my ear, and the unexpected shaking hands of my co-pilot."

We stopped to watch two hawks dip down over the water before flying away.

When Lucky started on the trail again, I continued my story. "Our crew saved over a hundred people that day. But we lost seven before we could get them to safety. A total of two thousand people died or went missing in that natural disaster. And I'll never forget walking off the airplane in the Atlanta airport and looking around at all of the happy, clean, healthy Americans jetting off to business meetings, visits to grandma's house, fancy vacations, and wherever else, just... like nothing would ever touch them. Like there hadn't just been this incredible natural disaster that had wiped out entire towns and ruined so many people's lives forever."

Lucky turned to face me with wide eyes. "Exactly. It's like tunnel vision. Like... you're going through something the rest of the world has no idea about. And they're sitting at home in their comfy recliner watching a football game or whatever while you're doing chest compressions trying to keep a little girl from becoming an orphan."

Our eyes met for a few beats while the unfamiliar feeling of connection drove hooks into me. Was this what it felt like to be understood? To open up and share feelings?

Lucky's nervous chuckle broke through the thick air between us. "Wow. I don't think I've ever heard you talk so much in one go. Someone must have slipped you a Red Bull or something."

And just like that, the connection was gone again.

CHAPTER 18

LUCKY

As we walked around the lake, we talked about how the SAR course was going, how quickly Morrie had bounced back from his appendicitis, and how each of the other students was coming along with their skills. Finally, Zach brought up my dads again.

"I think they'd be proud of you, Lucky," he said in a soft voice. "You're really good at this."

I looked up from where I'd been focused on the path ahead of me. Zach's eyes were trained across the lake, but I could tell he was tuned in to my reaction.

"Thank you. I..." I swallowed. "I want to tell them. I'm just... I guess I'm afraid they'll forbid me from doing such dangerous work. I can't stand disappointing them. I'm not sure I'd be able to go against their wishes if they asked me to give up alpine rescue."

Zach turned to face me. Crinkles of confusion marred his forehead. "Why would they ask you to give it up if you love it?"

I looked at him with a flat expression. He sighed. "I know. They worry. And rightly so. If you were my k—"

I clapped a hand over his mouth. "If you were getting ready to say 'kid,' I'm going to have to kick you in the nuts right now."

Zach's eyes danced as I pulled my hand away. "Alright. But I can understand why they'd worry. That doesn't mean it should keep you from following your dream. Every parent worries. Why would you let that stop you?"

As we got to the end of the long lake, Zach stepped off the trail and led us through a few trees to the rocky scree on the bank of the lake. We sat down next to the water's edge.

I picked up a twig and began twirling it through my fingers. "I never want to disappoint them or make them…" I sighed and looked out at the water again. "Make them regret taking me in."

Silence descended between us, but it wasn't awkward. I relished the quiet because it meant he was thinking over my words rather than jumping to the expected platitude about my fathers never regretting me.

Zach pulled his knees up and rested his arms on them. "Tell me about your life before Bennett and Xander."

It was an unexpected question, but not an unfamiliar one. Everyone wanted to find out my story as soon as they met my two dads, neither of whom were old enough to be my biological father. Usually, I kept it fairly vague and basic, like a Spark Notes version of a classic novel, when in reality it was a gothic slog, like *Great Expectations* or something. But this was Zach, and Zach was practically family.

"I would have thought you'd heard about this from Jake already," I said, drawing figures in the gray rocky silt with my stick. For some reason, the idea of telling Zach about my childhood made me sick to my stomach. The last thing I wanted was for him to look down on me with pity like so many people often did, even when I told the watered-down version.

He shrugged. "I mean, I know you're from New York and your mom had some problems. And there was a boyfriend involved in kicking you out."

I almost laughed when he referred to my mother as having had "problems."

Remember, watered-down version, Lucky, my inner voice told me.

I shrugged and said, "Yeah, that's pretty much it. She couldn't take care of me, so I bounced around foster care for a bit and then I met Bennett and he reunited with Xander and I got my happily ever after." I flashed Zach a fake smile.

His expression was impossible to read... until he frowned. "You're the expert on this whole friends thing, so tell me, does it include lying and glossing over the facts?"

I blew out a breath. Damn too-observant Army Ranger.

"Fine," I muttered as I began drawing circles in the ground with the stick. I focused on making the most perfect circles I could as I said, "My mom was a prostitute who figured hooking up with her pimp would be a good idea. Said pimp didn't want her kid eating into his profits, so he made sure he didn't."

"He kicked you out," Zach said softly.

I nodded.

"And your mom?"

"She chased after me when I left," I murmured. "I actually thought she was coming after me to tell me she'd chosen me."

"What happened?" Zach asked quietly. I thought I felt his palm smooth over my back for a moment, but I wasn't sure.

"She just wanted her key back," I responded. "You want to know why she named me Lucky?" I blurted before I could stop myself.

Zach didn't respond but I hadn't really expected him to. My lungs felt strained and my throat closed up as I said, "She said I was lucky that she hadn't realized she was pregnant earlier because by the time she did, it was too late to get rid of me."

I could practically hear Zach's disapproval but before he could shower me with pity, I said, "It wasn't all bad. She was young when she had me. No diploma or anything. So when my dad left early on, she was on her own with a baby. She did her best, I guess. Got a job cleaning hotel rooms and stuff. Sometimes she'd take on extra jobs cleaning those tourist boats in the harbor."

My fingers continued to pull the twig through the sand. "And when I was old enough, I'd help too. Well, as much as I could. Sometimes we lived with other folks in an apartment, sometimes we squatted in empty buildings or houses. I guess I was around ten when I realized she was using."

I took a breath. "The drugs meant she couldn't hold a job, so then there'd be strings of boyfriends, or guys I thought were boyfriends. Jerry started hanging around all the time and he hated me. He was mean as hell too, but only when she wasn't around. I didn't dare tell her since he brought us food and stuff. It was hard to focus on school. I started feeling like I should help us out by getting a job or something. But I didn't even get the chance. Jerry kicked me out and that was that. I had no money, no relatives, no place to go. No one wanted me."

I shrugged my shoulders like I didn't really care. "That's when I met Bennett. He found me eating out of a dumpster and offered to buy me dinner. I figured he wanted the same thing all the other guys did when they offered to buy me food or get me a motel room for the night. I never accepted any of those offers, of course, but something about Bennett was different. He felt safer somehow."

I thought I heard Zach draw in a sharp breath but I didn't look at him. I didn't want to see the look of disgust in his eyes. "I ate so much at that little diner he took me to that I was sure I was going to puke. I waited for him to tell me I owed him, but instead we just sat in that diner all night talking. When it was morning, he bought me breakfast. He convinced me to let him help me get into a good foster situation."

"How did you end up living with Bennett and Xander?"

I hesitated, then merely said, "There are a lot of good foster homes out there... and a lot of bad ones."

Since I had no desire to tell Zach any of the details about the bad foster care situations I'd been in, I didn't say anything else.

"Bennett's a good guy," Zach said. "So is Xander."

I smiled, thinking of the two men and how goofy they were with me and each other. "Yeah. The best. I think about my life today compared to what it would have been without them. At best, I'd be bussing tables or sweeping floors. At worst, I would have ended up just like my mom. But look at me now. I'm a certified flight paramedic. Even if I didn't get the advanced alpine SAR certifications, I'd still be able to find good employment and benefits anywhere in the country with the education I already have. I'm one year away from my college degree. I have friends and family who love me. A home in Colorado waiting for me. A new sister and brother." I laughed and shook my head. "Hell, even the clothes I'm wearing right now are a dream come true compared to the life I had in the city."

I kicked the heels of my running shoes together. "These puppies probably cost more than my mom used to pay in rent."

I'd meant it as a joke, but Zach reached out and squeezed my forearm. "You're an amazing man, Lucky Reed. Your fathers are so damn proud of you already and they'll be even more so when you're ready to tell them about the path you've chosen for yourself."

The reminder that I had been and still was lying to my fathers was like a punch to the gut. I knew what Zach was telling me without actually saying it. "I'll tell them when I go home for the Fourth. I'll tell them everything." I hesitated as my eyes roamed up and down Zach's gorgeous body. I could still feel the weight of it as he pressed me into the mattress…

"Okay, not *everything*," I amended with a grin.

Zach chuckled.

The man actually chuckled.

"I appreciate that. I've seen some scary shit in my time, but no training in the world could prepare me for the Lucky Reed Protection Detail. My brother's scary-ass little dog alone would have me running for the hills."

I felt all warm and gooey inside as Zach joked with me. I hadn't thought about the consequences of inadvertently bringing up the fact that we'd had sex, but Zach hadn't gone all dark and broody like I would have thought.

I met Zach's eyes and tried not to see more in them than friendship.

"Thank you," I said softly. I hoped he knew that I was thanking him for so much more than just listening to the crappy story that was my past. I had my answer when Zach nodded briefly and then reached out to brush his finger over my cheek for the quickest of seconds.

We let the silence fall again. Birds swooped down over the water and fat bees buzzed in a nearby flower. The sun dappled through the trees at our backs to set off faint shadows on the water in front of us.

"They rescued you," Zach said at last. "Xander and Bennett."

I glanced back up at him, not quite sure what his point was. "Yes."

He barked out a laugh, jolting me into a half-jump where I sat. "You're dedicating your life to rescuing others."

It was a connection I'd made before, albeit reluctantly. "And, what? That's a bad thing? What's your point?" I asked, trying not to feel like he was laughing at me.

"I'm a search and rescue specialist too. I joined the Rangers and asked for special SAR training in addition to flight training."

I looked at him in confusion. "Yeah, so?"

He turned to look at me, his green-brown eyes meeting mine with their usual intensity. "I searched for Jake and never found him. After that, I made it my life's mission to search for people, Lucky."

I finally made the connection. "You're saying we're a product of our own experiences. I'm not sure that's such a big surprise."

And, honestly, it made me feel a little stupid. As if I was somehow working out my childhood issues with some kind of misplaced rescue complex.

"No," he said, still holding on to my arm. "It shouldn't be, maybe, but it is to me. I never realized what drove me to it until I made the connection with your situation. I'm laughing at myself, not you."

Zach laughed again and leaned back on the pebbled shore, crossing his hands behind his head. "I actually think that's a good thing, Lucky. It means we have a personal connection to this work. We know the value of never giving up on saving someone." He looked over at me and I lay down next to him so I didn't have to crane my neck. "It means we're exactly where we should be, doing the work we're meant to do."

Zach's words were softer and his eyes carried a familiar affection I'd seen him give Jake before when praising him on his medical work. I let out a breath. "Yeah. That explains why it feels so right."

"But that's also the reason you need to tell them," he said gently.

I looked up at the rich blue of the sky and traced the crisscross pattern of fading white contrails. This same sky had been my loyal companion since I'd moved west with Xander and Bennett. I'd spent countless hours in the cool green grass of our yard, looking up into the vast expanse and thinking about everything from the meaning of life to the reason Levi Katz wouldn't flirt back with me in AP calculus class even though everyone knew he was into guys.

The morning we'd gotten the news the gestational carrier was having twins, the three of us had raced outside and danced under the same sky in our pajamas. The evening I'd gotten my acceptance letter to the University of Montana, we'd walked Bear in the thick snow and gazed up at the clear pinpoints of stars blazing across the winter night sky.

Even my very first kiss, with a boy named Calvin on our backpacking trip, had happened here in the Rockies, with the steady blue of the clear western sky overhead.

"I love it here," I said. "I never want to leave the Rockies. It's like… the sky is huge and it makes me feel small. But at the same time, it…" I let out a chuckle. "It makes me feel powerful. Energized. I know that sounds weird."

The corner of Zach's lip curled up. "Not weird. I know what you mean. I can't imagine being stuck in an office all day when you could be outside in this instead."

"Exactly."

We continued looking up at the afternoon sky for several more minutes before getting up and dusting ourselves off.

"You going to split a funnel cake with me?" Zach asked as we stepped back on the trail to lead us back to the truck.

"Only if you'll buy my underaged ass a beer," I said with a raised eyebrow.

He shook his head and *tskd*. "I guess it's the least I owe you after leaving you hanging from Cathedral Peak the other day."

I grinned at him. "Damned straight."

CHAPTER 19

ZACH

We were almost all the way back to Lucky's bunkhouse after the Goat Whatever Festival when we got the call that the fire had spread to an unexpected area due to a wind shift.

"There's a scout group penned in and we need additional help pulling them out of there. The other crews are dangerously past their flying time limits," Tag said over the handsfree speakers in the truck. He sounded exhausted. "Are you okay to fly?"

I thought about how long it had been since I'd been plagued by migraines and realized I'd had three solid weeks without them, thanks to the new medicine. Thankfully, Lucky and I had only split one craft beer at the festival and it had been hours ago. We'd filled up on fair food too much to stomach any more than that.

"Absolutely. What do you need?"

As he talked me through what he needed me to do, Lucky waved us on toward the hangar. I gave him a questioning look to make sure he was up for joining me, and he responded with an expression that said, "Don't be an idiot."

I needed someone else with me in the helicopter, and he was more than qualified for the rescue, not to mention how important it would be to have a paramedic on board if any of the children needed medical care.

It wasn't until we were loaded up and taking off that I realized Lucky would be the one on the line.

"Do you have your emergency pack?" I asked.

"Yes."

I ground my back teeth together as I steered us toward the smoke in the distance. "Do you have a spare harness on your belt?"

I felt Lucky shift next to me, but I kept my eyes on the horizon. "Yes."

My mind rolled through every possible scenario. "Wait. I mean one for you. Not just for the rescues."

There was a pause before his hand landed on my arm. "Yes. I'm ready."

"Remember, if anything comes up and you need to abort—"

He squeezed my arm. "Zach. I've got this. You need to trust me."

He was right. Lucky wasn't Tag's star pupil for nothing. He was a natural on the line, and at this point he probably had more longline training than some of the newer firefighters who'd been doing this work all day.

I coordinated with Tag over the radio and prepared to set down in a clearing he'd directed us to. Once we were down, Lucky scrambled out to begin preparing the line while I continued to communicate with Tag about the rescue. There wasn't a spare spotter, so I was going to have to rely on Lucky's verbal commands to guide me.

Within minutes, we were back in the air, only this time Lucky hung from the line in the dark night sky below as we made our way closer to the fire.

Thankfully, the area where the campers were was large enough that they'd been able to stay safely away from the fire so far. The firefighter crews had already dropped personnel and supplies with the group to help them avoid danger until all of them could be rescued. Because the only option for rescue was using the longline, it was a tedious process of pulling out one or two campers at a time.

We were able to make quick work of it, alternating trips with the other helicopter still actively rescuing members of the same group. Lucky was as steady as could be. His calm, professional voice over the headset assured me that he was handling the challenge even better than I'd hoped.

He was in his element.

And the kids adored him, clinging to him on the line and then letting him distract them from their fear as he told them various jokes and riddles until he untethered them in the drop zone.

By the time we'd collected the last of the scouts and watched the old school bus drive away with the rescued group, Lucky's eyes were shining out of a face covered in soot and dirt.

Johnny and Tag clapped him on the back and praised him up and down before heading off to the other chopper for their final flight back to the hangar. Lucky and I spent some time silently disengaging the main and auxiliary load lines from the belly band. Since we'd been the last crew in the air, we were the last ones in the clearing near Lake Ellen Wilson that had been used as a staging area for loading the longline. The barest sliver of pink sunrise could be seen at the top edge of Lincoln Peak and the cool night air reminded me that the month of June didn't mean warm temperatures at this high altitude.

"You hungry?" I asked, stowing some of the harnesses that littered the ground nearby. "One of the fire crews gave me a couple of sub sandwiches."

Lucky leaned back and stretched. "Yeah. That'd be good. Last thing we ate was that godawful empanada at the festival. Even my mother made better empanadas than that, and her family hadn't seen a drop of Mexican soil in two generations by the time I came along."

I reached into the cabin and grabbed the paper bag with the subs. "That's where your family is from?"

Lucky shrugged. "My mom's side anyway. My dad was a Jersey boy. From everything I heard, I'm pretty sure his people evolved directly from expressways and strip malls. What about you?"

He took the sandwich I offered and bit into it with a grateful groan.

"We're originally from Wisconsin but we moved around a lot

when we were kids. Our dad was an engineer and our mom was a professor. We grew up mostly in Alaska and the Pacific Northwest, so we had a lot of exposure to the outdoors."

I led us down toward the water so Lucky could see the turquoise water up close. The glacial silt that gave the water such an unusual color made it a rare sight.

"What made you want to become an Army Ranger?" Lucky asked when we found a place to sit at the water's edge. I prepared to give him the standard answer about wanting to serve my country, but when my eyes met his, the words wouldn't come. Even worse, the things I did want to say were exactly the ones I shouldn't.

I'd already bared my soul to Lucky once when I'd told him about Mitch. It would be way too easy to give him even more of me... more that wasn't exactly friend-appropriate information. Hell, even Tag didn't know any of the shit I'd told Lucky about Mitch.

But when I opened my mouth to give Lucky the standard, safe answer, it wasn't at all what came out.

CHAPTER 20

LUCKY

I hadn't been sure my questions had been appropriate friend-zone territory, especially after what he'd told me about his experience with boot camp and the asshole who'd taken advantage of him, but to my surprise, he didn't hesitate to answer.

"Not sure if there was any one thing that did it for me. I remember talking to this old guy who used to live next door to us in Seattle when I was in my early teens. He served in Vietnam and would tell me all about the different battles he'd been in. The sacrifices he and his brothers-in-arms made for our country..." Zach shook his head briefly. "I just knew that was what I wanted... no, needed to do. It wasn't that I was eager to go around shooting the enemy... it was knowing that I could protect people like my brother and my parents that made me want to serve. I'd never been a great student or athlete or anything like that and I had no hope of living up to Jake's greatness, but I knew I could keep him and others safe from all the evil that's aimed at us..."

Zach paused and glanced at me. He smiled slightly and said, "Sorry, that's probably more than you wanted to know."

I wasn't sure how I'd managed to keep my jaw off the floor because I hadn't been expecting such an in-depth response. Zach was, after all, the king of one-word answers. Or at least, I'd always thought he'd been.

"No, no," I fumbled as I hurriedly swallowed the food in my mouth. "I think it's amazing. And yeah, your brother is a great man, but why isn't it okay for you to be too?"

Zach looked at me in confusion.

"You always talk about Jake like you need to live up to him or something. Like what you've done with your life is somehow less important than what he's done. You're just like him, Zach. You're saving lives. You're making sure families get to go home to each other every night even though you don't get to go home to yours. Even now, you're still doing it," I explained. "I don't know why you left the army, but you're smart enough and determined enough to get any job you want. Or you could start your own business. Hell, you could probably just go find some quiet cabin in the woods and spend your days fishing. But despite the things that happened to you over there,"—I pointed toward the east as if that would be enough to indicate the area of the world Zach had spent most of his army days in—"you're here, still saving people. How many lives did you save today? I know your brother, and I've listened to your parents tell enough stories about you to know that they're proud of you, Zach. So fucking proud."

Zach hadn't taken even a single bite of his food once I'd started talking. He was staring straight ahead, making me wonder if I'd gone too far. I took a big bite of my sandwich, even though I didn't really want it anymore. What if I'd just screwed everything up? I shifted my gaze from Zach and stared at the ground beneath my feet. Why the hell couldn't I just learn to keep my mouth shut?

"Losing Jake for all those years nearly killed my parents," Zach said softly. I felt the pressure in my chest grow exponentially and it was all I could do to not spit out the food in my mouth. "My dad had two heart attacks in the years after Jake disappeared, and my mom had to see a therapist for everything from anxiety to depression. And all I could do was sit and watch it happen. We wanted to believe he was alive but as year after year went by…"

"You lost hope," I offered.

Zach nodded. "I swore I'd find him. Even if it was just his... his body, I swore I'd bring him home. And then one day I finally got the lead I needed and there he was. We were a family again. My parents, they came alive. And I... I finally felt like things in my life were once again where they were supposed to be. But after a while I got restless. It was like part of me was... was..."

"Missing," I supplied. Zach glanced at me, looking almost surprised.

"Yeah," he agreed. He turned his head again so he could stare off at whatever spot had him so entranced. "Jake and my folks understood when I re-enlisted. For a while everything was good. But then my team got called up for this rescue mission and things went sideways. Bad intel and an ambush there was no escaping led to a downed Black Hawk and the loss of most of my team."

I knew it was against the rules, but I didn't care. I reached for Zach's hand and laced our fingers together. "Is that what caused the PTSD?" I asked.

Zach shook his head. "Surprisingly, no. I've been on countless choppers since that day and haven't once had an episode."

He was so quiet after that that I didn't expect him to continue. But from the way he was clinging to my hand, I knew he wasn't done confronting the past in his head.

"You don't have to tell me," I said softly. "I'm right here, Zach. For as long as it takes."

I wasn't sure if he heard me or not because he didn't move or say anything. My muscles were cramping from having sat in the same position for so long, but I didn't dare move even an inch.

"I can still see their faces," Zach finally choked out after several long minutes.

"Whose?" I asked.

"Kaminski, Teller, Mac..." he responded.

I held my breath but when Zach turned his face away so I couldn't see it even in profile, I knew he was done. I lifted his hand to my mouth and brushed a soft kiss over his knuckles. I knew it was a move that fell way outside the friend zone, but I didn't care. It was the only way I could think of to tell Zach that I got it. Even if he never told me another thing about whatever had happened to him in that godforsaken place, I got it.

We sat in silence for a few more minutes, our meal forgotten. When Zach finally rose to his feet, he held on to my hand long enough to pull me to my feet. He looked at the sandwich but like me, his appetite had clearly waned. We both put what was left of our food into the plastic baggies and then turned to head toward the chopper. We'd taken only a few steps when a familiar, frightening smell assailed my nostrils.

Smoke.

CHAPTER 21

ZACH

"What the hell?" Lucky said, clutching my arm. "Do you smell that? Is that—"

"We need to move!" I barked before Lucky could even finish his question. I immediately began the steep climb up the ridge. "We need to get back to the helicopter!"

Fortunately, Lucky didn't argue with me. He simply grabbed my hand when I extended it to him and threw himself into focusing on the rocky ground ahead of us. As plumes of black smoke began to drift over the top of the hill, I wanted to kick myself for my stupidity. I'd been so caught up in baring my soul to Lucky as I'd recounted the past that I hadn't noticed the winds shifting. But that was exactly what they'd done and now the fire that had been safely off in the distance was bearing down on us.

Fast.

My lungs burned from the acrid smoke as I fought to climb the steep trail that had seemed so easy going down.

When we finally reached the bird, it was covered in thick smoke and hot to the touch. Sweat poured down my back under my clothes and the glow from the flames lit up the early morning sky in an eerie and unexpected way.

Lucky looked over at me with wide eyes. "I thought we were thousands of feet from the perimeter of the fire. How the hell did it get here so fast? We were downwind of it!"

"The winds changed," I yelled over the roar and crackle of the incoming flames. "I shouldn't have let us take so much time to eat. Fuck!" I covered my hand with the edge of my jacket and reached for the door to pull myself in. The heat and smoke were heavier than I could have imagined and I cursed myself for putting Lucky, of all people, in jeopardy.

As soon as I landed in the pilot's seat, I reached for the power switch to turn on the instruments. "Lucky, I need you to grab your emergency pack and anything else you can think of in case we need to bail," I said while flipping on the mains and fuel pump, preparing to prime the engine.

"Got it," he said. The tone of his voice was steady and firm. The man knew how to handle an emergency.

I blew out a breath. "Give me a status on the location of the fire."

While he moved through the main cabin to look out the window, I tried calling in on the radio. There was nothing but static so I changed channels, looking for any open channel to inform anyone of our precarious situation.

"Nearest flames are ten feet to the north-northwest," Lucky said before moving behind me. "I can get the on-board extinguisher."

I almost laughed picturing Lucky trying to fight a goddamned wildfire with a tiny helicopter fire extinguisher. "No, buckle in. We're out of here."

While he climbed into the co-pilot's seat, I tried cranking the engine, but nothing happened.

Lucky leaned over at an awkward angle to keep an eye out the window on his side where the flames were getting closer. I tried cranking the engine again and again, but it wouldn't turn over.

"Fuck," I shouted, banging my fist on the door. "The smoke's too thick for the oxygen intake anyway. We have to go."

Within seconds, Lucky was out of the helicopter, never once arguing with me or second-guessing my commands. I raced around the side of the chopper and grabbed his free hand to lead him away from the fire. He clutched the handheld radio in his other hand and had his emergency pack clipped around his waist and resting on his lower back.

Lucky made a frantic yelping sound as a lone tree near the chopper went up in flames in an instant. Flames hissed behind us as the dry grasses where we'd been taking off and landing all night ignited.

"Jesus," I shouted. "Go, go!!" I practically dragged Lucky behind me as we raced to clear the aircraft. All I could think about was the nearly full fuel tank from the refill we'd gone back for only a few hours before.

"Run," I yelled, tripping over loose rock and trying desperately to figure out the safest direction to go in that wouldn't put us in more danger. The fire was above us, the frigid lake was below us, and the only option was to try and flee across the loose rock near the water's edge. "Over there," I said, throwing our joined hands in the direction of the pass on the north end of the lake. It was less forested and a little higher than the south end, which meant less likely to burn. Either way, we'd be trapped by the flames if we couldn't get away from the water.

The roar of the fire resounded in my ears as we bolted toward the top end of the lake. My knee screamed in pain every time the loose rock under our feet shifted. I tried to mentally time out how many minutes we had before the flames reached the helicopter's gas tank but between trying to hang on to Lucky and dodge the terrain, it was useless.

Lucky's palm slipped in mine from the sweat between us and it was almost impossible not to feel the burn of the smoke rushing into our lungs with each gasping breath. I chanced a glance over my shoulder and saw the entire back half of the helicopter completely engulfed in flames. "We need to get to the pass!" I shouted to Lucky. "The boulders!" I added even as my lungs protested the extra use of oxygen. I wasn't sure if Lucky heard me or not, but his grip on my hand remained tight, and that was all I needed.

That and more time to get clear of the bird as the fire above us consumed it.

But time wasn't on our side and when I heard the telltale blast just seconds later, my only thought was the man next to me, and the realization that I potentially only had milliseconds left with him. Even as my instincts took over and I launched my body at his, my mind went blissfully clear, and all I could see and hear and feel was Lucky. His infectious grin, his gentle touch, his unflappable kindness, his soft laughter…

And then there was nothing.

CHAPTER 22

LUCKY

One second I was running for everything I was worth with Zach by my side, the next I was landing hard on a bed of rocks that cut into my exposed skin. Before I could even contemplate what had happened beyond being on my feet one moment and on my belly the next, a heavy weight landed on my back, knocking the breath from my oxygen-starved lungs. I tried to call to Zach to make sure he was still okay, but even if I could have found the air I needed to make a sound, the deafening blast that rocked the hill behind me muted the world around me. My addled brain managed to put together the fact that the helicopter had just exploded, but that was all I could manage to string together.

The pure strength of the rush of hot air that followed just milliseconds later was proof that I wouldn't have managed to stay on my feet anyway. As it was, I had no clue how, despite the force of the blast, I didn't feel my body being pelted with all the debris raining down around me. At most, there were a few small stones hitting parts of my extremities and nothing more.

Maybe I'd made it to the boulders after all. When Zach had pointed at them and yelled to head toward them, I hadn't even considered why. I'd just put every ounce of strength into keeping up with the man beside me...

Zach.

Holy fuck, where was Zach?

Please, God, let him have made it to the boulders. Let him have made it to the boulders...

I knew before I even finished the silent prayer that he hadn't. Just like I knew the heavy weight pressing me into the hard earth as rocks, ash, and embers blanketed the ground around me wasn't the result of the blast knocking me off my feet but Zach's body instead.

"Zach," I croaked. I immediately began coughing as my body fought to expel the smoke and dust from my lungs. "Zach," I managed to say a little more loudly. My ears were ringing, so even if Zach heard me, I wouldn't have been able to make out his response.

My throat burned as I continued to try and suck in enough clean air so I could get my body moving. "Zach!" I screamed as loudly as I could but there was no movement above me. No reassuring touch, no whispered words in my ear that everything was okay.

No, I whispered to myself in denial.

I struggled to pull my right hand from beneath the crush of our bodies as my left hand reached behind me to touch Zach in any place I could reach. "Zach!" I screamed as tears pricked the back of my eyes.

Nothing.

Nothing but the roar of the fire as tree after tree behind us was consumed like they were nothing more than kindling.

It took every ounce of energy I had to pull my right hand free. My head hurt like a motherfucker but it had nothing on the pain in my chest.

The asshole was fine. He was *fine*! No way on God's green earth was he going to do this to me.

My rage actually gave me the strength I needed to work my arm free. Once I had use of both my hands, I managed to get the leverage I needed to push my body up. It seemed to take forever to carefully ease Zach's prone form off me.

And I spent every second of that time cursing the man.

"You are not doing this to me, do you hear me?!" Tears clogged my throat as I scrambled to move to Zach's side. I should have been relieved to see that he didn't have even a single mark on his beautiful face, but I wasn't.

Because he was still.

Too still.

"Zach…" I whispered. I was too afraid to touch him. Even with the heat of the flames bearing down on us with frightening speed, I couldn't move. Because moving meant knowing for sure if he was gone.

And he couldn't be gone.

He just *couldn't.*

It was Zach's voice that ultimately tore me from my stupor. Not his actual voice, just the memory of it.

Airway. Breathing. Circulation.

I could do this… I could do this because Zach *needed* me to do it. I pulled in a breath, ignoring the sting of pain that accompanied it, and leaned forward to listen for breath sounds since I didn't have a stethoscope. My fingers were shaking when I placed them against his neck to check for a pulse.

Nothing.

Just… nothing.

I let out a ragged sob that consumed my entire body. It was so violent that I almost didn't feel the little flutter beneath my fingertips. A second later it happened again. And again.

With every beat of Zach's heart, I let out a whimper that sounded like a scream in my head. It was only after a good five beats that my instincts finally kicked in and the paramedic side of me fully took over.

"Zach!" I called over the roar of the fire. My hands flew over his body to assess him for injuries. They came to an abrupt stop when my fingers encountered something warm and wet. I steeled myself to accept the sight of Zach's blood on my fingers, but there was really no preparing for it. I'd been witness to some of the grisliest of scenes during my time as a paramedic, but this was so very different.

It was Zach.

My Zach.

Thankfully, my paralysis didn't last long and my training once again kicked in. There was a large laceration along his thigh that was oozing blood at a rapid rate. My hands automatically went for Zach's belt. It took just seconds to get it off him and wrapped around his leg as a tourniquet.

"Zach!" I called over and over as I worked because I could hear and feel the fire getting closer. I was afraid to actually look behind me to see how close it really was. But it didn't matter because a flash of orange leapt into my periphery.

The fire... not only was it catching up to us from behind, it was racing down the mountain where it was encountering even more vegetation to fuel it. At the rate it was going, our escape route to the south would be cut off if we didn't move soon.

No south meant no lodge or lake.

And no help for Zach.

"Zach!" I shouted as I secured the belt as tightly as I could. I leaned over Zach's prone body and began shaking him hard. When he didn't respond, I reached down to roll Zach so I could pull him up into a fireman's carry. I managed to get him into position, but the second I tried to lift him, something in my knee gave out and it was all I could do to catch Zach's weight as I hit the ground. I cried out as pain shot up my leg, stealing my breath.

Sweat coursed down my brow as I tried a second time, then a third to lift him, but to no avail. While I could tell my leg wasn't broken, something had twisted in my knee, probably when Zach had thrown himself on top of me to protect me from the blast.

"You bastard! Wake up!" I screamed at Zach. My rational thought was completely gone. "Why? Why did you have to do that?" I shouted as tears began coursing down my cheeks. Zach had to have known what he was doing when he'd thrown himself on top of me. In shielding me, he'd exposed more of himself to the blast. Hell, he must have known it was coming but instead of throwing himself to the ground, he'd given up precious seconds to protect me instead.

"Zach!" I called again as I grabbed his shirt to once again try to rouse him. When he didn't wake, I scrambled to my feet and put my hands beneath his arms in the hopes I could drag him. But between his dead weight, my messed-up knee, and the rocky terrain, I had no hope of outrunning the flames. I dropped to my knees next to him and just stared at him. He had blood on his face now, but I knew it was from me transferring it to him with all my attempts to wake him. The smoke started to grow thicker, making it harder to breathe.

But that wasn't why I dropped my head to his chest. It wasn't why I whispered his name and clung to him as the world around us became darker and darker as it lost itself to the flames.

I silently apologized to my fathers as I considered what this would do to them, but I was where I needed to be. I had to believe they'd get that somehow. I rested my ear against Zach's chest and tried to listen to the beating of his heart. I couldn't hear it above the fire, of course, but when I pressed my fingers against his throat, it was easy enough to imagine the steady beat and soon it was all I heard.

"I love you," I murmured. The smoke stung my eyes and clogged my throat as a strange sense of peace overcame me. I imagined we were lying in Zach's bed, the softness of it cradling our tired bodies. We weren't doing anything other than lying together, fully clothed, after a long day. No words were spoken. Just him stroking my hair with one hand while the other rested on my waist. Warm sunlight flooded the large room whose walls were covered in pictures of our families and friends. Our gear was stashed in one corner, ready to go for those frenzied moments when someone needed our help again. But until then, it was just us.

Just us.

Lucky.

Hmmm? That was apparently the best I could do when it came to conversation.

Lucky.

I smiled to myself as strong fingers intertwined with mine. Leave it to Zach to never fail to get my attention.

Lucky, wake up, my love. It's time to go.

I nodded in agreement but didn't move. One more minute. I just needed one more—

Zach's grip on my fingers lost their gentleness as he called my name again. This time, there was no softness in his voice, though. No endearments, either. His voice was harsh and thick and then he was coughing, gagging even.

The realization ripped me out of the dreamlike state I'd fallen into. It was just in time for me to hear Zach grate out my name again.

For real.

"Zach?" I shouted in disbelief as I scrambled upright. The smoke was so thick it was hard to make out all of his features. "Zach!" I croaked. His beautiful eyes fluttered open.

"Gggg…ggg—" he began before he was overcome with a coughing fit. My hands flew into action. I searched out my emergency pack and found the extra bottle of water I kept in it. I reached down to rip a couple of pieces of fabric from my shirt, doused them liberally with water and placed one over Zach's mouth and the other over my own.

"Zach, can you get up? We have to go! The fire is moving down the mountain. It's going to cut off our access to the trail leading back to the lodge!"

Zach shook his head, then took the fabric from his mouth and tried to add it to what I already had pressed to my own.

"Go," he sputtered before he started coughing again.

"Yes, we need to go!" I agreed. "Keep this on!" I said as I pressed the fabric back to his mouth. As long as we stayed low, the smoke wasn't quite as thick but I knew it would just be a matter of time before that wasn't the case.

"Go!" Zach ground out again, this time his voice a little more clear. He once again thrust the makeshift mask against my mouth. "You have to go," he growled. "Before it's too late."

You?

What the fuck was he talking about?

"Lucky, go!" he shouted and then he was shoving at me with one hand.

I actually looked down the ridge, then behind me as if the answer I was seeking was somewhere in the orange-red flames that were peeking through the cloud of smoke.

Did he really think I was going to leave him there just so I could save myself? When he pushed me again and literally ordered me to go, I was done.

Finally.

Fucking.

Done.

I leaned over him and pinned his arms to the ground so he couldn't keep trying to shove me away. "You listen to me, you selfish son of a bitch," I snapped. "You want me off this mountain, you're damn well going to have to get me off it yourself, do you hear me? Because I. Am. Not. Leaving. You!"

I released his arms and grabbed his face. "You want to play hero, Army Man? Fine, you do that. But you're going to be right next to me when I call my fathers to tell them I'm okay. And then you're going to tell your brother that you're coming home. Do you hear me, Zach? We are going home. *Together or not at all!*"

I loved the anger that sparked to life in his eyes. It brought my own body back to life. Zach hesitated for a microsecond before he nodded his head in agreement. I had no doubt that if he'd had the time, he would have ripped me a new one. Once we got to safety, I'd happily let him. But no way in hell would he be getting the last word.

I wasn't gentle as I did my best to bodily lift Zach to his feet. Despite the noise around us, I could hear every grunt of pain as he bore his own weight on his injured leg. The only silver lining was that the injury was on the same leg as his bad knee. I put my arm around him to support him and wasn't surprised when he did the same to me. My own knee screamed in protest, but the adrenaline pumping through my veins was a powerful thing. So was the memory of that perfect moment imagining myself lying in Zach's arms in our bed.

I didn't care how unrealistic it was. It was that image above anything else that sustained me as I took a step, then another.

Zach and I were going home, fire or no fire.

I would make sure of it.

CHAPTER 23

ZACH

Fear drove me. Fear for myself but mostly fear for Lucky. I wanted to rage at him for not taking the chance to run when he'd had it. Even now as we slowly made our way to the trail that led down the mountain, I knew there was no way we'd beat the fire. Our only saving grace was that the winds seemed to have slowed a small amount, keeping the fire at our backs from overtaking us. But looking south, I could see the flames were within a few hundred yards of the trail that we'd need to use to get down to the lake and safety.

If I'd had full use of my body, we probably could've made it. But between the pain searing up and down my leg and the pounding in my head, the best I could do was a pathetic little hobble. Even that was reliant on Lucky to keep me upright.

"Lucky—" I began but not surprisingly, he cut me off.

"Shut up and keep moving," he growled. I'd never heard him like that. I'd seen his strength and confidence over the past several weeks, but a tiny part of me had still considered him a kid playing an adult's game. But there was nothing childish about the man next to me.

I didn't remember anything about the blast after the helicopter had exploded. One minute I'd been throwing myself at Lucky and the next minute I'd found *him* lying on top of *me*. I'd worried that I'd somehow not managed to protect him with my body, but when I'd called his name and he'd looked at me with those beautiful brown eyes of his, I'd known he was okay. Not much else had made sense. Then he'd mentioned the fire cutting off our retreat and I'd known there would be no way I could make it to safety. I'd wanted so badly for him to leave me so he could save himself, but admittedly, there was a tiny part of me that was relieved to not have to face this terror alone. It was like Lucky had once said, we understood that death was always at our door but none of us actually relished it.

"We're not going to make it in time," Lucky yelled above the roar of the fire. "We need to head north, up the pass."

I knew he was right but the idea of trying to make our way up increasingly impassable terrain seemed like an impossible thing. "The warming hut," I managed to get out. The small stone structure just over the pass would offer us protection from the cold weather we'd likely encounter the higher we got. Since the winds were blowing south and the vegetation became sparser at the top of the pass, we had a good chance of outrunning the flames.

Lucky made a grunting sound and quickly turned us so we were headed north. My lungs felt like they were going to explode while at the same time my head felt light, but I continued to push forward. Every step Lucky took, I took one as well. I lost track of time, but it seemed at least an hour later before Lucky slowed our pace. I was leaning on him more heavily now, though there was nothing I could do about it. I felt dizzy and sick to my stomach and prayed I wouldn't lose the contents of my stomach right there on the trail.

"I think it's safe to stop," I heard Lucky say, but I couldn't find the energy to open my eyes. I wanted to argue and tell him that we needed to keep moving so we could reach the warming hut before night fell and the temperature dropped dramatically, but no words would come. When Lucky helped me to sit, the pain in my leg ripped me from the near slumber I was falling into.

"Sorry, sorry," Lucky murmured as he helped me prop my back

against a tree. I forced my eyes open only to see Lucky looking stricken as he examined my leg. "You're losing too much blood," he whispered. The fear and helplessness I heard in his voice had me reaching my hand out to him.

"Come," I said softly, though my voice didn't really sound like my own. We'd inhaled a lot of smoke, but fortunately we'd reached an elevation where the air was cleaner.

"No," Lucky responded. "I have to stop the bleeding." His voice was frantic and high-pitched as his fingers hovered over what looked like a pretty good leg wound. Surprisingly, it didn't really hurt much, but I supposed that was probably due to how cold I was. It wasn't a good sign. But seeing Lucky so distressed made my chest hurt.

"Lucky," I breathed. He looked up at me and paused, then something shifted in his gaze and he moved so he was sitting next to me. When I put my arm around him, he leaned into me and wrapped his arm around my chest. There was a long beat of silence, but when I dropped a kiss to his head and whispered, "It's okay, sweetheart," Lucky let out a muffled sob. It was followed by another and another. I felt his tears soak through my shirt.

"I thought you were gone," he said as his fingers curled into my side. "I thought I'd lost you."

"Never," I said without thinking. I skimmed my fingers over the back of his neck. I hated that it took so much of my energy to provide such little comfort. "Gotta keep moving," I managed to say even as sleep tried to claim me.

"Here," I heard Lucky say and then something cool and wet was being pressed against my lips. I had no clue where Lucky had gotten a water bottle from, but I didn't care either. I took several long sips in the hopes that the liquid would ease the burn in my throat.

I managed to keep myself from drinking the entire contents of the bottle. I opened my eyes and lifted my hand so I could push the bottle toward Lucky. "You," I said.

Lucky shook his head and said, "I'm fine."

"Drink," I insisted. "Please," I added in the hopes it would prevent me from having to fight with Lucky about taking the drink. I had no doubt he was trying to conserve our water and would put himself at risk to do so.

His eyes met mine and then he slowly took a small sip of the water. He returned the bottle to his backpack, which I'd only just noticed. "Radio?" I asked hopefully.

Lucky dropped his eyes and shook his head. "I dropped it." He paused and then added, "I'm so sorry, Zach, I dropped it. If I'd just put it in my bag instead of holding on to it—"

I managed to put out my hand and grabbed his chin. I held it firmly as I said, "We are alive because of you, Lucky." I refused to release him until his eyes met mine and even then I held on to him longer than I probably should have. His face was covered in scrapes and dirt, probably from me pushing him to the ground and landing on top of him. I found myself reaching to touch one of the larger cuts, but Lucky grabbed my hand and held it in his.

"They don't hurt," he said softly. It shouldn't have surprised me that he knew what I was focused on. We hung there for another moment and then Lucky climbed to his feet. I didn't miss the fact that he was careful not to put too much weight on one leg. He leaned down to help me stand. The pain returned all at once as soon as I was upright, and I was forced to lean heavily on Lucky as my head spun.

"I've got you," Lucky said softly as his strong arms went around me. I could've easily stood there like that for hours, but I knew that although we'd outrun the fire, we now had another aspect of Mother Nature to worry about.

The elements.

Already the wind was howling and Lucky and I were both underdressed for the cooler weather. I wasn't sure what supplies Lucky had in his backpack, but I knew they'd be pretty limited since neither of us had planned for anything like this. The warming hut would at least give us a chance to get out of the wind. The temperature at this altitude would undoubtedly drop below freezing before sunrise, and we'd need to figure out a way to keep from freezing to death until someone came for us. With that in mind, I forced myself to bear most of my weight so Lucky and I could continue up the pass. It was slow going and I had to take several breaks, but just as night began to fall around us, the small stone structure came into view and for the first time since I'd smelled the smoke, I felt a measure of relief.

I heard Lucky calling out in the hopes of attracting the attention of any other hikers who were using the warming hut for the night, but there was no response. When we reached the stone building, it was dark and cold. Once inside, Lucky helped me sit and then began fussing over me. Within minutes I had a thermal mylar blanket thrown over my body and Lucky had given me more of the water. Pain and exhaustion consumed me as I watched him move quickly around the space, presumably looking for any kind of supplies previous hikers might have left behind. I actually heard him let out a cry of frustration when there was nothing to be found.

I tried to climb to my feet so I could help him figure out the next steps, but before I could rise, Lucky was there, his small hand easily keeping me where I was. "Stay still, Zach. You're still bleeding, and I don't want it to get worse."

"Can help," was all I managed to get out. I wondered why I couldn't form a complete sentence.

"I've got this. Trust me, okay?" Lucky said. His eyes met mine and I quickly nodded. I *did* trust him and would've told him so if I could've found the energy. I let him ease me back to the ground. He placed something soft beneath my head, but I wasn't sure what it was. As Lucky moved around the warming hut, he began talking aimlessly about what he was doing and that we would be okay. I suspected his words were meant to comfort himself as well as me. I wanted nothing more than to take him in my arms and promise we would both be okay, but I was too tired to do even that. I tried to keep my eyes open, but they refused my order.

I was awoken by a gentle hand on my face. "Zach, I need to clean and bandage your wound. I'm sorry, but it's probably going to hurt."

Poor Lucky seemed so distressed at the prospect, but I couldn't reassure him that I'd been through much worse than what was about to happen. I gave him a nod and let him roll me so he could have better access to my leg.

"I, um, have to take off your pants," Lucky said. I found myself smiling at his hesitation.

"Go for it," I responded.

If the process of trying to get my pants off hadn't been so painful for me, I would have enjoyed having Lucky undress me. It was all I could do not to respond when he removed the tourniquet and pressed gauze to the wound. Lucky worked quickly and efficiently to clean and bandage the area, but I could see the worry in his eyes. There was no missing the tremble in his fingers as he secured the bandage around my thigh. I reached my hand down to cover his in the hopes that I could send him the reassurance he needed. He stilled and stared at our hands. I could see silent tears slipping down his cheeks.

"Lucky," I said softly. He lifted his eyes to mine.

"I can't stop it. The bleeding, it's slower now but it won't stop. I don't know how to make it stop." His concern for me was heartbreaking, and I wished with every fiber of my being that I could take away his pain. It was proof that even though I'd treated him so terribly after our night together, he still cared about me. No matter how many times I told him I wasn't worth it, it hadn't changed anything.

"Come here, baby," I whispered. I opened the blanket so he could join me beneath it.

"No, I have to get a fire started and then see if I can find some food because I only have one protein bar, and we're almost out of water—"

"Lucky, come here," I said more firmly this time. The demand in my voice had him freezing in place. He looked at me longingly and it was the first time I'd seen any sign of relief in his expression. This time, he didn't argue as he moved to join me underneath the blanket. He was careful not to jostle my leg as he settled down next to me. He was stiff and tense as he lay flat on his back next to me, refusing to make eye contact. As tired as I was, I still managed to pull him against me and wrap my arms around him. The move seemed to release something for him because he buried his nose against my neck and clung to me as if I were the only thing keeping him afloat in a turbulent river.

His body felt cold against mine, but the blanket and my own body did their job and soon the violent tremors that had consumed Lucky's small frame eased. I gave in to my own exhaustion and finally closed my eyes.

CHAPTER 24

LUCKY

*I*f I'd been fully asleep, it would've been a disaster in the making. As it was, my fear for Zach, along with the cold wind and rain that was seeping through the broken-out windows of the warming hut as a thunderstorm passed overhead, was keeping me from finding any kind of peace in slumber. The fact that I was pressed up against Zach's body helped considerably because I was immediately aware of it when he began to whimper and moan. I was in the process of getting ready to shake him awake from whatever nightmare he was experiencing when I heard him whisper, "Teller, check your six." Right after he said the words, Zach let out a harsh yell and his hands began to jerk at his sides.

I quickly released him and scrambled away from his jerking body because I knew what was happening. Zach was in the midst of another PTSD episode. I stood there helplessly watching Zach's body thrash like he was fighting off some unknown attacker. I wanted to intervene but knew if he got his hands on me, even in his weakened state, he could potentially hurt me. If that happened, there was no way to get off this mountain alive. Not to mention the guilt he'd feel.

"Zach," I called, keeping my voice as even as I could.

Zach's eyes were open as he scrambled to his knees. His hand was fisted like he was holding something in it, but nothing was there. His eyes flew wildly around the darkened warming hut, but I couldn't make out his expression. I moved quickly and quietly to get my phone out of my pocket. While the thing was useless because there was no reception this high up, I'd purposely kept it on me so I'd easily have access to light to check Zach's wound throughout the night.

I fumbled to turn the flashlight app on but didn't shine it in Zach's eyes. Instead, I shined it in my own direction in the hopes that he would see me and not whatever thing or person he was fighting.

He tried to jump to his feet, but his legs wouldn't hold his weight. Instead, he crawled backwards until his back hit the wall. He held his hand out in front of him again, so I could only assume whatever he thought he was holding was some kind of weapon.

"Zach, sweetheart, it's me, Lucky." I kept my voice low and even despite the fact that I was terrified. There was now enough light in the room to see that Zach's injury was bleeding again.

"Kaminski, status check!" he yelled as he managed to climb to his feet. He put one hand up by his mouth. I assumed he was adjusting whatever imagined communication device he thought he had on him.

"Zach, you're safe. We're both safe. We're in the warming hut in Glacier."

There was another flash of light followed quickly by a boom of thunder. Zach grabbed at his head and closed his eyes. He continued to call out commands, most of which I didn't understand. After several long beats, he began lashing out at something that only he could see. Each time the thunder and lightning rocked the warming hut, the process started all over again. It was all I could do to keep my voice even and steady as I called to Zach. Not once did I attempt to approach him.

It was several minutes before I finally saw any kind of reaction and that was only because the timing between the lightning and the thunder grew longer. Every time the lightning flashed through the warming hut, I began telling Zach that he was okay and that it was thunder that would follow. Then I would talk about familiar things like his brother and Oz and their ugly little dog, Boo. I'd tell Zach stories about my fathers and the twins and my uncles, Aidan and Ash. All that mattered was that I kept talking. It seemed to take forever before Zach calmed and would only flinch or jerk when the thunder rattled the night sky. I'd been careful with the light on my phone throughout the episode because I hadn't wanted to contribute to the event.

It wasn't until the thunderstorm that had rolled through so quickly was rumbling off in the distance that Zach finally seemed to come back to himself. He fell back against the wall behind him and began to shake violently. I saw his hand open up as if he were dropping whatever weapon he'd been using during the imagined attack. I approached him slowly, making sure to use his name a lot and to tell him he was okay. It wasn't until he let out a hoarse, "Lucky?" that I increased my pace and hurried to his side. I reached him just as his leg gave out.

It took effort, but I was able to get him back to the middle of the room and to the little makeshift bed I'd made with our jackets. Since Zach had been standing by the broken window, his shirt was soaked through. I quickly stripped it off and then got him beneath the blanket before turning my attention to his injury.

"Did-did I hurt you?" Zach choked out as the tremors in his body became more violent. I knew they were both a result of him coming down from the adrenaline rush as well as the chill that had overtaken his body.

"No," I said quickly. I propped my phone against the backpack that Zach was using as a pillow so he could see me and I could see him. I still wasn't one hundred percent sure of exactly what had triggered his PTSD, but I suspected the dark had a lot to do with it. And since the storm hadn't completely moved off, I wasn't taking any chances.

Zach fell silent after I reassured him again that he hadn't hurt me. I used the time to work to clean up his wound and redress it. It had started bleeding again, but it didn't take too long to slow it back down. Even with the mylar blanket, Zach was still shivering, so I quickly stripped off my own clothes and crawled beneath the thin blanket with him. When I pulled him into my arms, he didn't protest at all. He wrapped himself around me, though I warned him not to move his leg. He pressed his face against my shoulder and just stayed there like that. I stroked his hair and pressed soft kisses against his temple until his body relaxed and the chill seemed to dissipate. He was so quiet I thought maybe he'd fallen back asleep, but then he pulled away from me and rolled onto his back. I felt the loss in so many ways.

I busied myself with trying to check his vitals, but when I put my fingers to his wrist to check his pulse, he surprised me by twining his fingers with mine and pulling my hand up to his chest. He was staring at the ceiling.

I shifted my body so I could rest my head on my hand as I leaned over him. His other hand was covering mine where it was resting against his chest, so I took the opportunity to just rub circles into his skin in the hopes of soothing him. "It's the storms, isn't it?" I asked. "The lightning and thunder triggered an episode."

"Among other things," Zach murmured. I thought back to the night in my room when he'd attacked me. I thought it had been the physical contact, but in fact, it had been the light that I'd inadvertently turned on when I'd been reaching across his body. In the process, a book had fallen off my nightstand. "Not just thunderstorms," I said as understanding dawned. "It's the combination of sudden light and loud sounds."

Zach was quiet for a moment, then let out a harsh laugh. "I sleep with the lights on in the hopes of preventing it from happening again. Some hero," he drawled. "You think they give out medals to guys who come back from that hellhole and are too afraid to sleep in the dark?"

"Will you tell me about it?" I asked.

Zach let out a soft sigh, but at the same time he began running his thumb up and down the back of my hand. "I fucked up," he said. "I fucked up and three good men are dead."

It was on the tip of my tongue to tell him I didn't believe any of that, but I managed to keep my mouth shut. I had no doubt that if he'd told anyone the story already, they'd responded with the typical argument that whatever had happened wasn't his fault or that he couldn't have known what would happen. Zach didn't need to hear any of that from me. He needed to talk, and I needed to listen.

"Tell me what happened," I urged.

"We were sent in to rescue some journalist who'd been taken hostage. There'd been a lot of stories on the news about American citizens being captured and beheaded. That shit doesn't make for good TV, if you know what I mean. The kid who'd been kidnapped was the son of a senator. Didn't matter that he'd gone willingly into the lion's den in the hopes of being the first journalist to snag an interview with the very terrorists we'd been fighting for years. Our orders were to go in and get him, no matter what the cost. I knew as soon as we landed outside the city he was being held in that the intel we'd been given was wrong. It was just a gut feeling, but I knew in my heart it was a setup. I tried to pull the plug on the mission, but the orders came from higher up. Doesn't matter if you're Army or Navy or whatever, in the military the only thing that keeps you alive is the rules and you follow them to a T." Zach fell silent for several long beats, but he continued to toy with my hand.

"They broke us into smaller teams to clear the buildings surrounding the one the kid was supposedly being held in. It was just me and three other guys sweeping the building. There should've been at least a dozen of us clearing it. Everything inside of me was screaming at me not to go in. Kaminski, Teller, Mac, they followed me without question because that was their job. Just like it was my job to follow the orders of the guy above me. I ignored all the warnings in my head and proceeded. I had dozens of chances to turn us around and get us out of there, but I had my orders."

Zach practically spat the word "orders." I could feel his heart pounding beneath my hand. I rested my head on his shoulder and sidled up close to him in the hopes that feeling my body next to his would bring him some comfort.

"Intel had said it was just a small group of rebels holding the journalist and that they had limited weaponry. But it was all bullshit. They had the tech needed to jam our comms so we couldn't call for backup. All I remember is being outside this room, this nothing room, and wanting to just turn around and get out of there. But we went in, sweeping it like we were supposed to, even though the comms were down. There was no electricity in the building, so it was pitch dark. We were using our night vision goggles to see. One second there was nothing but silence, then there was this boom and flash of light. It blinded us because of the night vision tech we were using. Kaminski and Teller got the worst of it because the flash bang was detonated between the two of them. I turned around just in time to see an insurgent run his knife across Kaminski's throat. I gave the order to retreat, but it was too late. The assailants didn't use guns because they didn't want to alert any of our team members. They cut up Teller too. I didn't see what happened to Mac but I saw his face..." Zach's voice dropped off.

"What happened to you?" I asked. My heart was in my throat as I envisioned Zach and his team fighting off their attackers.

"I got jumped from behind, but I managed to keep the guy from gutting me too. He managed to stab me a few times, but not enough to take me down. I was still struggling from the results of the flash bang, but I knew enough to let my instincts take over. The guy and I fought but he came out the loser. I tried to get him to tell me how many others there were, but he died before I could find out. Then the ones who killed my guys came after me, but I was able to fight them off too. During the struggle with the last of them, we both ended up falling down a flight of stairs. That was how I fucked up my knee. Luckily, the other guy broke his neck. I lay there at the bottom of the stairs with just my knife for protection as I slowly bled out. The rest of my team found me that way and I was airlifted back to base. Kaminski, Teller, and Mac weren't so fortunate."

"And you blame yourself for what happened to them," I said, more to keep him talking than anything else. As badly as I wanted to tell him it wasn't his fault, I knew that would just make him angry. The reality was that he *did* blame himself and only he could change that perception.

"Kaminski had just gotten married and had a baby on the way, Mac was a father of five, and Teller was the sole support for his two younger sisters after they'd lost their parents in a car crash the year before. Yeah, it was my fucking fault because I had more than one chance to get them out of there."

"What would've happened to you if you'd gone against orders?" I asked.

Zach shrugged. "Disciplinary action. I probably would have been demoted, maybe dishonorably discharged."

"You said it was a setup," I said softly. "If those men wanted to make an example of you and your team, would they have even let you get out of there?" Zach glanced at me, clearly confused by the question. "If they were using the journalist to bring in American soldiers, whether it was to kill you or take you hostage, don't you think they would've had every escape route planned? So even if you'd changed course, isn't there a chance it wouldn't have done any good?"

Zach shifted his eyes away and stared back at the ceiling. There was a tic in his jaw and instead of rubbing my hand with his finger, he started tapping it. "I don't know," he finally said after several minutes.

"Would you have died in their place, Zach?"

He jerked his head in a nodding motion just once. I didn't continue because I could already see the wheels in Zach's mind turning. Instead, I laid my head on his chest and just held on to him as best I could. It was a long time before his body relaxed and the tapping on my hand stopped and returned to a gentle, rhythmic caress. My own body began to release much of the tension that had been there from the moment I'd woken up to Zach's whimpers.

Rain beat against the roof of the warming hut. I'd hoped to find some dry wood when we'd first gotten to the warming hut, but between Zach's injury and the turning weather, there hadn't been time. Now the wood would be too wet to make a fire. While the mylar blanket was keeping us from freezing to death, it was far from keeping us warm. I'd spent the evening trying to be so brave for Zach that he wouldn't have to worry about anything but resting, but as one hour had passed into another and then another, my worst fears had started to come to light. It was one of the reasons I'd still been awake when Zach had started to succumb to the nightmare that had evolved into a full-blown panic attack.

"Zach," I whispered. On the one hand, I didn't want to wake him if he'd fallen asleep, but on the other, I was terrified about what to do next. I'd had plenty of training for events like this, but I'd always had a certain amount of resources available to me. The helicopter had gone up so quickly that I literally hadn't had time to do anything but grab a few vital items.

Zach's free hand moved to my back so his fingers were running up and down the length of my spine. Although we were both nearly completely naked, there was nothing sexual in the move and I didn't take it as such. It was meant to comfort, and that was exactly what it did.

"I only have enough food to last us a few hours. I've got the tablets to clean the water, but if the fire changes direction again and we have to head farther north—"

"Then that's what we'll do," Zach said firmly. "We'll figure it out, Lucky. You made me a promise, remember?"

"What promise?" I asked.

"You said I could play the army hero. I intend to hold you to that promise." I could hear the smile in Zach's voice. It was so unexpected that I found myself shifting so I could rest my head on my folded hands and look him in the eye while still keeping myself plastered across his upper body. His eyes, though exhausted and pained, also held a certain mischievousness to them.

"Deal," I said. He hadn't spoken any magic words that automatically fixed everything, but knowing he was right there with me and that we would figure this out together was exactly what I'd needed to hear.

"Tag will figure out where we went," Zach said. "It might take him a little time, especially if he and the team are doing more rescues as the fire spreads, but he's going to figure it out. We just need to hang on until then. This rain will hopefully put a dent in the fire spreading, but if we do have to head farther up the pass, we'll figure out how to make it happen. We're getting off this mountain, Lucky."

The tightness in my chest eased considerably after that, but it moved to a whole new part of my body as Zach continued to caress my face. I sent silent warnings to my cock not to react because that was the absolute last thing I needed, but Zach seemed oblivious to what his touch was doing. I knew it wouldn't be long before Zach *did* feel the results of his gentle caresses, though.

"I should go check—" I began to say as I tried to pull away from Zach, but he shocked me into silence when he suddenly shifted our bodies so he was lying on top of me. We were both still wearing our underwear, but we might as well have been naked because I could feel the heat of his dick through the thin fabric. I was panting as if I'd just finished running a marathon. Zach hovered over me, his eyes dark with some unnamed emotion. I instinctively put my hands on his sides, but that was the only move I made. Zach hung over me with one hand resting against my throat. His thumb moved up along my jawline, then over my cheek. I no longer cared that my erection was impossible to hide. All I wanted was for Zach to lean down and take what was his.

What had always been his.

And always would be.

His stare was dark and intense but I couldn't tell what he was thinking. I didn't even want to consider looking away. I wanted him to know exactly where I stood and that I was exactly where I was supposed to be. I felt like my body was already changing to accommodate his, but it was met only with frustration when Zach levered off of me and then lay down by my side. "Sleep," he said softly. "I'll stay awake for a while so you don't need to worry about me hurting you."

It was on the tip of my tongue to tell him that I knew he'd never hurt me, but my heart kept me from voicing the words because it knew different. Zach had the ability to hurt me without even trying. He could crush me with just one word or slay me with a look. Just like he could own me with a kiss or a touch.

Despite all my fears of what would happen if help didn't come, lying in Zach's arms made it easy to fall asleep. I tried to set an internal clock to go off so I could check Zach's wound, but the next time my tired eyes opened, it was because Zach was gently shaking me. Sunlight filtered into the warming hut and the howling wind had died down. "Lucky, sweetheart, wake up. They're here. They found us."

"What?" I asked groggily as I tried to burrow deeper into Zach's body. His skin was finally warm instead of cool, but not overly so, which meant he hadn't spiked a fever. It was *that* fact that had me opening my eyes. I sat up and immediately began searching out Zach's wound. I sighed in relief because there was no new blood staining the bandage.

"Thank god," I said softly. I turned to see Zach watching me with what I could only classify as a hungry look. I'd sat up so quickly that the mylar blanket had slipped off my body, giving Zach a full view of my nakedness. There was no hiding the desire in his eyes. The need to claim him was so fierce in that moment that I found myself leaning over him. His only choice was to lie flat or use his arms to continue to brace himself.

I was happy with either.

So happy, in fact, that I actually carefully straddled his lap before I could even consider what I was doing. I heard his sharply indrawn breath as my ass brushed his hard cock, but he did nothing to stop me as I closed the distance between his mouth and mine. My heart was racing in my chest as I contemplated what I was about to do. But there were no warning bells going off in my head that it was a bad idea or that I'd just end up getting hurt in the end again. No, this time all I could think about was how close I'd come to never being able to taste him again. I wasn't going to squander this opportunity for anything in the world.

Or so I thought.

Because just as my lips were about to brush over his, I heard a loud voice shouting outside the hut.

Tag's voice.

And he was calling our names.

Help had finally come.

"I can walk," I insisted to Min as the nurse parked my wheelchair just outside the hospital doors. My friend leaned over me and got right in my face.

"Lucky Reed, if you move from this chair while I go and get the car, I swear on God's green earth I'm going to tell your parents about the time we mistook their okra plant for pot and tried smoking up their garden."

Whose bright idea had it been to list her as my emergency contact anyway?

Good thing you did or two very angry men would be here right now instead, I reminded myself. I shuddered at the realization of just how much worse this situation could have been. My parents deserved an explanation, but it was all I could do to handle my own stuff at the moment.

I threw up my hands to show I had no plans of going anywhere. Min smiled in satisfaction and sauntered off to get her car. The second she was out of sight, I sent her a silent apology and got up out of the chair. The nurse had already returned inside, so there was no one there to chastise me. It didn't take me long to reach my destination, the second floor of the small hospital just outside the park.

I needed to see him one time, then I'd be good to go.

It had been less than twelve hours since we'd been rescued from the warming hut, but it'd been the longest twelve hours of my life because I hadn't seen Zach even once in that time. With Zach's injuries being more severe than mine, he'd been taken aboard the first rescue helicopter. There'd been no room for me since there'd already been a couple of other hikers on the chopper heading to the hospital. They too had been caught off guard by the fire and while they'd escaped it, they'd both suffered from burns and smoke inhalation.

My own rescue had come a mere hour later. I'd only had to be treated in the ER for a sprained knee and dehydration. No one had told me anything about Zach until Tag had come to the ER to see me. He'd explained that Zach was undergoing multiple tests to check for any internal injuries and he was also receiving blood and fluids to make up for what he'd lost. While I was being released, Zach would be spending the night for observation. I'd asked Tag multiple times what room Zach was in, but the older man had kept putting me off with statements about Zach being in some other department undergoing tests. It hadn't taken me long to figure out why he'd been so vague about Zach's location.

Zach didn't want to see me.

Even though Tag hadn't confirmed my statement when I'd confronted him with it, it hadn't taken a genius to know what he *wasn't* saying. I'd been sure that I'd die right there on the spot because another rejection from Zach had been the very last thing I'd expected, but as the hours had dragged on, my brain had started to play tricks on me. I was certain there had to be some misunderstanding because I couldn't fathom how a man who'd nearly died trying to protect me would tell his buddy not to let me see him. We'd been through more things together in the past twenty-four hours than most people went through in a lifetime. For him to reject me yet again just wasn't possible.

It just wasn't.

That's what I kept telling myself as I slowly began searching the hospital for Zach. It was such a tiny facility that it didn't take long to find him. Especially since I could hear both his and Tag's voices as I neared the room. I stationed myself near the open door but made sure to stay out of sight. I certainly didn't want an audience when I confronted Zach about him not wanting to see me.

"So what? You're just not going to call him? You're not going to explain to your own brother what happened?" Tag said. He sounded pissed.

"There's no point in him knowing. I feel fine and there's no lasting damage. The doctor says my knee will be back to normal in a day or two and I can get the stitches out in a couple weeks." Zach sounded different. Not angry and gruff like he often did when he was irritated. He sounded... *off*.

"The kid's been asking about you," Tag said after several moments.

"He's not a kid," Zach returned. Since I was pretty sure they were talking about me, I almost found myself smiling at Zach's defense of my age. Until he said, "Did you tell him what I told you to?"

There was no verbal response, but when Zach said, "Good," I assumed Tag had answered in some visual way.

"You ever going to tell me what is going on between you and the ki—Lucky?" Tag asked. This time it was Zach's turn not to respond out loud. It was so frustrating that I just wanted to march into the room and demand the man talk to me.

"Doc still cleared you to come home tomorrow?" was Tag's next question.

"Yeah."

"Well, I don't care what he says, I don't want to see you back at that hangar for at least a week."

There was a long beat of silence that had my insides twisting into a painful knot. The Zach I knew would have argued with Tag about taking that much time off. The fact that he was remaining quiet couldn't be good.

Tag must've sensed the same thing because he said, "No. Come on, man, don't do this."

"I told you this thing was only going to be temporary," Zach said. "Johnny can finish the last little bit of training and oversee the final exercises."

"I don't give a shit about you leaving the program!" Tag snapped.

I leaned back against the wall, not listening to Tag going off on Zach. I didn't really care what his arguments were because I knew they wouldn't make a difference. The thing I'd heard in Zach's voice was determination and right now, he was determined to leave. And I knew in my heart that was exactly what he'd do. I didn't know why or when or how, but I'd lost Zach all over again.

Pain lanced through my chest. I found myself putting a hand over my heart as if that would somehow prevent it from shattering into a million little pieces. I'd really thought this time would be different... that he'd come home with me and we'd somehow figure out how to make things work. That stupid vision I'd had in my head as I'd lain across his body waiting for the smoke and flames to take us had been a feasible thing in my mind. And afterwards as we'd been lying in each other's arms in the warming hut, I'd thought we'd gotten past all the things keeping us apart.

But nothing had changed. Not for Zach, anyway.

I stumbled away from the room, ignoring a nurse as she asked me if I was okay. Everything seemed to go dark and there was only a roaring in my ears that matched the sound of the fire that had tried to take my life less than a day earlier. It wasn't until I felt hands on my upper arms and someone calling my name that I snapped out of my daze.

"Zach?" I asked, hoping against hope he'd somehow discovered me and chased after me. That he was going to explain that it was all a big misunderstanding and that he wasn't going anywhere and we would be together forever.

But it was Min who responded. She asked me repeatedly if I was okay, and I must've told her I was because shortly after that, she was leading me to her car and taking me back to the motel room Leah had arranged for us. Both women took perverse pleasure in mothering me, so when we got to the room, she put me into one of the beds and lay with me for a long time, murmuring promises that everything would be okay.

I didn't tell her that I knew it wouldn't be because Zach was leaving again. Just like he'd left two years earlier. I'd recovered from that, but barely. I had no idea how I'd be able to deal with losing him a second time.

Thankfully, sleep kept me in its tight grip for a good twenty-four hours. But when Min gently shook me awake and insisted I eat something, all I felt was this raw, inescapable pain. Even being around my best friend hurt too much. When I told her I was ready to go back to the bunkhouse, not surprisingly, she vehemently objected. But in the end, she gave up the fight and finally agreed.

As much as I wanted to turn down the offer of a ride, I knew Min would pitch a fit if I told her I was okay with walking on my bad knee. In truth, the pain had dissipated considerably and while it still hurt, it had nothing on the agony I was going through on the inside.

As soon as Min dropped me off, I went in the bunkhouse only long enough to pack my meager belongings into the singular duffel bag I had brought with me. I knew running home was the cowardly thing to do, but I didn't care. Nothing mattered to me anymore. Somehow my SAR dream had morphed into something entirely different. A *different* that included Zach. Now that he was leaving, I didn't know how to live the dream I'd once had. All I knew was that I needed to go somewhere where I could just be me again.

My fathers would be beyond happy to have me home, even though they had no idea what I'd been through or even where I'd been. It was time to come clean, but more than that, I needed to see them. Sleep in my own bed. Pet Bear and hope to hell returning to Haven would anchor me somehow. Maybe it was a childish thing to do, to run home to lick my wounds, but I didn't care. I just wanted the hurt inside to ease enough that I could breathe again.

The bunkhouse was empty, so nobody saw me leaving. I'd send Tag a message once I was on the road. I didn't have the heart to say my goodbyes to any of my friends since I felt like I was letting all of them down in some way by not being the happy-go-lucky guy I was supposed to be.

I began the drive to the highway, but the farther my car took me from the bunkhouse and the hangar, the more my chest hurt. I found myself driving in a different direction from the road to Kalispell and Helena. It was like my mind was on autopilot. I knew where I was supposed to go, of course, but I had no clue why I insisted on torturing myself. I just kept going in the opposite direction of home, and before I knew it, I was stopping at the edge of a clearing and staring across the road at the familiar truck parked in front of a small but meticulously maintained cabin. The back of the truck was open but empty except for a small cardboard box.

I stepped out and stared at the box as if it somehow held the key to the scene in front of me.

I wasn't sure how long I'd been standing there when the sound of the cabin door opening made my heart jump into my throat. I held my breath as I watched Zach walk from the cabin to the truck and toss a large bag in the back. I'd expected him to already be gone and had only made my way to the cabin in the hope of finding some strange sense of closure. But seeing Zach was pure torture.

He looked perfect. Besides the slight limp in his leg, he looked completely healthy. He was wearing a pair of jeans and a light green shirt with the long sleeves rolled up to reveal his strong forearms.

Zach slammed the truck shut but instead of going around it and getting in, he returned to the cabin. I ordered my feet to turn around and get back in the car, but my limbs refused to move. They suddenly felt too heavy for my own body.

I had no doubt that this was *the* moment.

The moment he was actually leaving. If I'd waited only five more minutes, I would've missed him.

I told myself to turn around so I would be the one choosing to walk away, but again, my body was no longer under my own control. All I could do was stare at the front door of the cabin.

I wanted to go to him but I also wanted to try and protect my heart, even though deep down I knew it was far too late for that. I'd been in love with Zach in some form or another since I was fifteen years old. If I'd thought my love for him had dwindled even a little over the years, I'd been proven wrong time and time again from the moment he'd come back into my life.

I loved him still, and that meant I couldn't be the one to walk away. I needed *him* to do it. I needed him to come out of the cabin, see me and then get in that truck and drive away without looking back. If he did anything else, it would just let that little spark of hope inside me continue to burn. And I needed that hope to die. I needed to learn to love him from afar and I needed his help to do it.

I forced myself to wait, but the longer that front door remained closed, the faster my resolve started to falter.

Tears of frustration stung the backs of my eyes. All I had to do was turn and walk away. I could slink home to lick my wounds like I had when I was eighteen, and then I'd find a way to move on with my life, leaving Zach behind to become a distant memory. Maybe I'd eventually meet a nice guy who wouldn't insist on keeping me a secret and who thought I was worth more than just a meaningless hookup. And when Zach and I did cross paths again at some family function, there would no longer be the endless ache in my chest.

I just have to turn and walk away...

My feet felt like cement blocks as I forced myself to turn my back on the cabin, but when it came time to take that first step forward, the air in my lungs fled and it was all I could do to remain standing.

I wanted easy.

I wanted safe.

I really did.

But I wanted Zach more.

I didn't care if it was for five minutes or five hours or five years, I just wanted *him*.

I found myself turning around so I was once again facing the cabin, but this time there were no weights holding me in place. I took a step forward, then another and another. I knew the chances that he'd turn me away were high, but that didn't slow my pace. I didn't run to his door just like I didn't falter. It wasn't anger or frustration or even hope that drove me on.

I was back on that mountain, my body pressed to Zach's as I waited for the fire to claim us. I was where I needed to be.

I did my best to steel myself for Zach's reaction, whatever it might be, as I climbed the few steps up onto the porch. I was in the process of fisting my hand so I could knock on the door as soon as I reached it, but the move was wholly unnecessary.

Because the second my feet touched the porch's landing, the cabin door opened and Zach was there.

Right *there*.

I expected surprise or shock or anger or... *something*. But Zach merely stood in the doorway and stared at me. A couple of weeks ago, that stare would have sent me running but I didn't even slow my steps until I was standing before him, a mere foot or two separating us.

I couldn't read his expression but everything from the stiffness of his body to the hardness of his jaw was warning me to run... to grab at this last chance to save myself. But I didn't move. I didn't even consider it.

Not until his hand reached out to grasp my upper arm. Then I *was* moving.

Into the darkness of his cabin and then finally into the circle of his arms.

Where I belonged.

CHAPTER 25

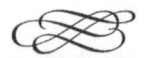

ZACH

I didn't even manage to fully close the door before my mouth crashed down on Lucky's. It had felt like time had been going backwards as I'd watched Lucky approach the cabin. I'd spied him by pure chance through the window as I'd gone in search of my truck keys. The mere sight of him had stirred up so many emotions that I hadn't been able to move or even breathe at first.

Then he'd turned his back on the cabin and something inside of me had died. I'd nearly gone after him. But the same thing that had kept me from checking on him after our rescue had caused me to grip the keys in my hand hard enough to leave marks that would likely turn to bruises in the next day or two.

When he'd turned back to face the cabin, my soul had crumbled because I'd known what it would mean.

For him.

For me.

For us.

I was going to end up hurting him again. It was as inevitable as rain falling from the sky. And I was powerless to stop it.

By the time I opened the door, I'd already run through all the scenarios in my head of what I wanted to do to him.

But none of them were what he'd come here for, because I still wasn't the man he needed me to be. I was a selfish son-of-a-bitch, and I wanted to take what, in that moment, felt like mine.

Lucky whimpered as I consumed him. I tried to remind myself that he was new to kissing, but I had no hope of slowing down. Not when I'd come so close to losing him.

I used my foot to kick the door shut and then I pushed Lucky up against the unforgiving wood. I wasn't gentle about it. Just like I wasn't gentle about yanking at the fastenings in his jeans. I expected Lucky to protest the rough treatment, but to my surprise, his hands joined mine and he was the one to actually push his jeans and underwear down.

And his mouth never once left mine.

In fact, he'd quickly caught up and was returning every one of my kisses.

My body felt like it was on fire and my dick was so hard it bordered on painful. As much as I wanted to savor Lucky's gorgeous body, I knew it wasn't going to happen.

Not this first time, anyway.

Lucky was the one to break the kiss but only so he could look down as he ripped at my belt, then the button of my jeans. I used the momentary distraction to get a condom and packet of lube from my wallet. Lucky's eyes were luminous as his gaze lifted to take in the sight of the condom. His lips were plump and damp from my kisses. I found myself leaning down to cover them again. Lucky slid his arms to my back and clung to me as I controlled every aspect of what my mouth was doing to his. By the time I broke the kiss so I could focus on getting my dick freed, Lucky was leaning heavily against the door.

I didn't bother telling Lucky that it was going to be a rough, hard fuck because I could tell he already knew it. The fact that his slim cock was almost a deep throbbing red and he was leaking copious amounts of pre-cum from the head told me that he was more than ready for whatever I had to give him.

My fingers shook slightly as I rolled the condom down the length of my shaft. When I went to rip the packet of lube open, Lucky wordlessly turned around and presented his shapely ass to me. He pressed his hands flat against the back of the door at the same time that he looked over his shoulder at me, then my cock. His submission nearly made me come on the spot, and it was all I could do to get the lube slathered onto my throbbing dick. I put more lube on my finger and then pressed my body against Lucky's as I searched out his hole.

I kissed him hungrily as I pushed my finger inside of him. He moaned but didn't hesitate to bear down on the digit. My plan had been to go slow with the prep since he was still so new to sex but when Lucky began to hungrily fuck my finger, what little patience I had left was obliterated. I shoved my finger as deep inside of him as I could.

"Zach!" Lucky cried out. The fact that he chose my name as the first word spoken between us had me grunting in response and then I slammed my mouth down on his. Lucky moaned under the dual onslaught of my kiss and my finger. When I slipped a second finger inside of him and rubbed them both over his prostate, Lucky screamed and bucked forward. He ripped his mouth from mine and looked down his body. I couldn't resist looking over his shoulder so I too could watch as jet after jet of semen shot from the head of his dick and hit the door. I kept finger-fucking him through the orgasm until his knees finally gave out. I used my free arm to support him as I eased my fingers from his body.

Lucky was gasping for air as his body shook violently from the aftershocks of his release. I reached my hand around his body and fisted his dick gently. He cried out at the contact and covered my hand with his but he didn't try to stop me from softly stroking him. After a few pulls on his cock, I lifted my hand to his mouth.

"Taste yourself," I demanded. I didn't press my hand to his lips, preferring instead to see what he decided to do. He lifted his own hand so he could maneuver mine. He licked my entire palm without pausing, groaning at the taste.

My entire body jerked in response, both from the perfection of his mouth as he tasted himself on my skin and because he'd done it with no hesitation. His lack of inhibition left me reeling and I couldn't help but replace my hand with my lips. Lucky groaned as I explored the lushness of his mouth. I could taste his essence on his tongue. It was like pouring gasoline on an already raging fire.

"Put your hands on the door," I snapped as I grabbed Lucky's hips and pulled them back. Lucky instantly did as I said, fully exposing his ass to me. I used my hands to split him open. His hole glistened with the lube I'd pushed into him. Despite the fact that I'd used enough of the sticky liquid, I couldn't stop myself from dribbling some of my own saliva over his opening. Lucky moaned in response.

"Hold yourself open," I ordered. Lucky quickly removed his hands from the door and did as I said. I stroked my cock a few times as I used my left hand to rub his entrance. I toyed with Lucky's opening long enough to get him squirming and whimpering, then I guided my crown to his hole and began pushing inside of him.

I didn't go slow or easy but I didn't just ram into him either. Once the tip of my dick was inside of Lucky, I moved his hands back to the door and then settled my hands on his hips as I pressed forward. When my balls brushed up against his ass, I held there for a moment. I wasn't sure what possessed me to do it, but I found myself leaning over Lucky's back and pressing a kiss to his shoulder.

Only then did I give myself permission to move.

I tried to remind myself that it was only Lucky's second time but with his body fisting my dick like a second skin, all rational thought flew out the window. My smooth, heavy thrusts quickly became more frantic as Lucky's inner muscles caressed my cock. Lucky grunted every time I shoved into him and he clamped down on me every time I began to pull out. Between his body's responses and the sounds he was making, it didn't take much for me to begin ramming into him. My fingers bit into his hips hard enough that I knew there would be bruises the following day.

Sweat slid down my forehead as I fucked Lucky hard enough to make him lock his arms so he wouldn't be slammed into the door.

"Harder, Zach," Lucky bit out. His skin was hot and damp and the air around us was filled with the smells of sweat and sex. I did as Lucky asked and pounded into him without mercy. The sounds Lucky made after that had to have been illegal. The pressure in my balls grew with every thrust into Lucky's willing body. I reached one hand around my young lover and found what I'd already suspected.

He was hard again.

"Stroke yourself," I barked as I transferred both my hands to Lucky's shoulders. Lucky's hand flew to his dick and he frantically began to fuck his own hand. The control I'd spent so many years mastering chose that moment to fail me, but I didn't care. The only things I cared about were coming and getting the young man beneath me off again.

"Zach?!" Lucky called. I could hear the fear in his voice and I knew what it meant. The orgasm that was building inside of him was greater than the one he'd already experienced and he was afraid of it.

I dropped my weight to Lucky's back and wrapped my arms around his waist. I moved one hand to his cock and took over stroking him. "Let go, baby," I said softly even as I ruthlessly fucked into him. I nipped the shell of his ear. I felt one of Lucky's hands reach behind us so he could grab my hip. I imagined the picture we made, wrapped around each other like we were.

It took only a few more thrusts and a repeated command to let go to send Lucky over. He screamed as his body locked up. His inner muscles clamped down on me, triggering my own release. I wrapped my free hand around Lucky's throat as I shoved into him over and over. Lucky tilted his head back and arched as he shot his load all over the door as well as my hand. I growled in his ear when my hot cum began filling the condom. I was sure I heard Lucky call my name more than once as the orgasm held him in its merciless grip.

It could have been minutes or hours before my body started to come down from the high. I sagged against Lucky, pushing his body against the door. He was shaking hard and, like me, was struggling to catch his breath. It wasn't until my skin began to feel chilled that I realized I needed to pull out of Lucky so I could remove the condom. But when I made a move to step back, Lucky cried out, "No, Zach, please don't leave me again! Please!"

I froze in place as Lucky pressed his forehead against the door. He kept repeating the same phrase over and over in the softest of whimpers.

Don't go.

I thought back to the first time we'd fucked and how I'd callously walked out on him. I'd explained my reasons to him later, but clearly my explanation had done nothing to heal the wounds I'd inflicted with my cruelty.

"Lucky—" I began, but he shook his head violently.

"No, Zach, please. I… I can follow all the other rules but I need to—to make one too."

He was so upset that it was hard to understand him, so I leaned against his back and pressed kisses against his neck. "Shhhh, take a deep breath for me."

Lucky quieted enough to do as I said. I used the time to carefully pull free of Lucky's body without putting any distance between us. I reached between us so I could pull the condom off but ended up tossing it to the floor since I didn't dare leave Lucky long enough to dispose of it properly.

I turned Lucky around so we could have this particular conversation face to face. "You weren't going to say goodbye, were you?" he asked before I could say anything.

I sighed. "No," I admitted.

"Is it that easy for you?" Lucky whispered. His voice was downtrodden, and he couldn't look me in the eye. It was a stark change from only minutes earlier when he'd been giving in to my every demand without hesitation.

"Is what easy for me?"

Lucky didn't respond right away. When he did, he looked me straight in the eye. "Leaving me."

I knew what I should have said… what answer would be the one that would drive him away for good. But I couldn't make the lie pass my lips. Frustration consumed me as I stepped away from him and yanked my pants up. The pain in my leg was a good distraction, but it wasn't enough.

"Easy?" I grated out as I moved to the opposite side of the entryway. I pounded my fist against the wall a few times but all it did was feed into my anger. "Nothing about any of this has been easy, Lucky!" I snapped.

"Then why the hell do you keep doing it?" he asked. "I thought—I thought we were going to die on that mountain! I was so scared that I was going to lose you and then they came for us and I thought things would finally be different—"

"I never promised you anything," I interjected.

Lucky's face fell so fast that it was like I'd punched him or something.

"No... no, you didn't," he conceded. Lucky seemed to finally realize he was still half naked. He slowly pulled his pants up and fastened them. Then, just like that, he turned and reached for the doorknob. "Goodbye, Zach."

I was moving before I realized it. I slapped my hand against the door and slammed it shut a split second after he opened it. "I told you I couldn't give you what you wanted, Lucky," I bit out.

Lucky stared at the door. "You never asked," he whispered.

"What?"

"You never asked, Zach. You never asked what *I* wanted."

"I didn't need to. You made it clear two years—" I began to say.

"Two years ago I was a lovesick kid making a fool of myself. You're not the only one who changed since then, Zach," Lucky snapped. "But you didn't even give me a chance to prove that I could... that I could..."

"Could what?" I asked impatiently.

"Be what you wanted," he murmured. He tried to open the door again, so I covered his hand with mine.

"I don't want you to be what I want. I want you to be who you are. Because that guy—"

"Don't," Lucky cut in. "Don't tell me I'm perfect or amazing or whatever. What we just did... *that* was perfect. *That* was amazing." Lucky removed his hand from the door and moved closer to me. Before he could say anything, there was a knock at the door, startling us both.

"Zach, it's me," I heard Tag call from the other side.

I glanced at Lucky but he seemed to be in no rush to leave the room. "Why don't you go up to my room and get cleaned up?" I suggested. "Then I'll take you back to the bunkhouse."

Lucky opened his mouth, presumably to argue with me, but then Tag knocked again.

"Lucky, please," I murmured as I pinched the bridge of my nose. The last thing I needed was Tag getting involved in this thing with Lucky. He was already riding me hard about leaving the program without any kind of explanation. The last thing I wanted was for him to blame Lucky in any kind of way.

Lucky left the room without a word. I waited until I was sure he was out of sight before opening the door.

"Hey," Tag said.

"Hey," I responded before motioning for him to come inside.

"Do you know where Lucky is? I have some news I want to share with him before he hears it from someplace else, but I can't find him. One of the guys from the bunkhouse said they saw him leaving with a packed bag."

I stilled at that. "What?"

Tag threw up his hands. "First you, now my best student. I don't fucking get it."

"He's here, Tag," I said. I hadn't had any clue that Lucky had been planning on leaving the program, but he and I were certainly going to have that discussion before we went our separate ways.

Tag's head swung around, then he looked around the room. "He's here?" he asked.

"What's the news?"

"What is he doing here, Zach?" Tag asked sharply.

"You know what he's doing here. Now what's the news?"

"Are you fucking kidding me? That's what all of this has been about? You and him—"

His incredulity irritated me for some reason. Like the idea of there being something between me and Lucky was so far-fetched.

"What did you want to tell him?" I repeated.

Tag sighed before running his fingers through his hair. "You know that girl, Amy Williams?"

"The one who helps maintain the equipment and assists with the classes?"

Tag nodded. "She was in the program last year but didn't graduate. She had good technical skills but she couldn't apply them in the field. Before I could tell her that SAR just wasn't for her, her parents died in a car accident. When she asked this past spring if she could take the course again, I told her I'd think about it. I felt sorry for her, so I told her she could reapply."

I nodded in understanding. While Tag would never risk putting someone in the field who wasn't prepared for it, I knew he was a softie at heart and wouldn't have wanted to dash Amy's hopes completely.

"What does any of that have to do with Lucky?" I asked.

"I usually only take seniors but I made an exception for Lucky because of his natural talent. He got the *last* spot in the program," Tag said.

My whole body went tight as I realized what Tag was getting at. "She's the one who's been stalking him. Sending him notes and vandalizing his car. And the rope—" I was moving toward the door before I even realized what I was doing.

Tag grabbed me. "She's admitted to all of it, Zach. She came to me this afternoon and told me the truth... that she thought Lucky had somehow stolen her spot in the program. She said the rope was an accident. She didn't know we were doing the simulations that day. She used a corrosive substance from a flare on the gloves to damage the rope but she used more than she intended—"

"Even if we hadn't been doing simulations, he still would have gotten hurt," I practically yelled. "Where is she—"

"She's at the police station giving her statement. I've talked to her aunt, Zach. Amy's been having a lot of mental issues this past year. It's not an excuse, but I don't believe she truly intended to harm him... just scare him."

I was on the verge of losing it as I remembered how Lucky had been hanging precariously off the side of a mountain. "He was hanging by a handful of threads, Tag! He—"

"Zach," Lucky called softly. I turned and saw him standing on the steps about halfway down the stairs. He looked to be in the same condition as when I'd asked him to leave the room, so I doubted he'd showered. Which meant he'd probably heard everything Tag had said. I fell silent because I knew Lucky didn't want me losing my shit over any of this.

"What's going to happen to her?" Lucky asked.

"She'll be charged with several crimes including some kind of attempted homicide charge. Her lawyer will likely go for a mental incapacitation defense. For what it's worth, Lucky, she did seem pretty upset."

Lucky nodded. "She was always nice to me up until this past year. I can't even imagine what losing her parents must have done to her."

Tag nodded, then looked between me and Lucky. I could tell he had a million questions, but fortunately he kept them to himself and quickly said his goodbyes before leaving the house.

Lucky sat down on the stairs and folded his hands. He seemed pale and shaken but that was the extent of it.

"He said you packed a bag," I said after several moments.

Lucky nodded. "I was taking a page from your playbook. Only I was running toward home, not away from it."

I sighed and leaned against a wall across from the stairs. "Tell me what you want, Lucky," I murmured.

"I want you to come home to Colorado with me after we finish the program," he said. "And I want to be with you as much as possible here and there."

I opened my mouth to protest when Lucky added, "On your terms."

I wasn't sure I'd heard him right but then Lucky rose and slowly approached me. "Rule one is that you can fuck me any way you want for as long as you want. There won't be sweet words or declarations. Is that about right?"

I nodded my head. Hearing him repeat my own words back to me made me feel sick.

"And no one can know about us."

I nodded again.

"You're in control, you call the shots, but in bed only. And when it's over, it's over, right?"

"Yeah," I responded, feeling off-balance.

"Yes to all of that," Lucky said. "But I have a rule too."

Lucky's finger trailed down the center of my chest. "No matter what, you have to say goodbye to me. Whether you're leaving me after we've fucked or you're leaving for good, you have to kiss me goodbye. No disappearing."

His request was a relatively reasonable one which only served to piss me off because he deserved so much more. "You won't be able to handle it," I said.

Lucky tilted his head as he began toying with the collar of my shirt.

"Maybe not. But you're a good teacher, Zach," Lucky said softly right before he slid his hand down my body and skimmed it over my hardening cock. "Even if I only get a few lessons under my belt, it will be worth it."

I wasn't sure what he meant by that particular statement, but I was already too distracted to care. It was idiotic to even consider his offer, especially the part about returning to Colorado and maintaining a physical relationship, but admittedly I needed the time to work him out of my system. At most, it would only be a few weeks and then I'd be moving on to a new place and a new job.

Three weeks to get my need for Lucky Reed out of my blood and released back into the world to find someone better than me, someone healthy and whole.

It would be more than enough time, I silently reassured myself even as I leaned in to capture Lucky's mouth.

As Lucky's tongue dueled with mine and he pressed his sweet young body against me, a fleeting thought passed through my mind before I sent it scampering.

Three weeks, my rules... so why do I feel like I'm coming out the loser?

CHAPTER 26

LUCKY

Tag's insistence on taking a full week off was reversed when Zach bounced back as quickly as he did. Within two days, we were both functional enough to make it back to class to complete the final requirements. That part, I could handle. When I went to class, Zach was my instructor the way he always had been. It was the hours outside of class that I struggled with. All Zach seemed to want to do was feed me and repeatedly ask me questions about how my knee was feeling.

Not that I minded his show of concern. I didn't. But being around the hot, muscled Army Ranger without any sex, or at the very least making out, was enough to set me on fire with want.

"Um…" I began, approaching him as he walked to his truck that first afternoon after wrapping up for the day.

Zach turned to me with a crinkle of concern between his brows. "You okay?"

Not really. I wanted to touch his naked body with every bare inch of my own, but I wasn't quite sure if that was allowed.

Or how to ask.

"Well…" I said stupidly. We stared at each other for a minute before I cleared my throat and tried again. "Um, so like… can we… or maybe..." I scratched the back of my neck and looked around, hoping like hell some better words could be found in the scraggly trees on the edge of the parking area.

"Lucky, spit it out. What's going on? Is your knee bothering—"

"I wanna get naked with you," I said all at once on an exhale. I blinked at the trees several times in a row before glancing at him out of the corner of my eye.

He was grinning.

"Don't laugh at me," I bit out. "I don't know how to do this, or what... or what the rules are."

Zach crossed his arms and leaned his hip back against his truck. His teasing grin was not attractive. Much.

My neck still itched. Hell, everything itched. I felt like I was crawling out of my skin with want. I hadn't touched him sexually in two whole days after he'd insisted on downtime to rest and recover.

Well, I was plenty rested and beyond recovered. Now I wanted sex. As much of it as I could get before he pulled his expected disappearing act on me. If he suggested watching another damned movie or taking a slow stroll outside to "stretch our legs," I was going to lose my mind.

"Rules?" Zach asked. "Rules about what?" His question was spoken in a lazy drawl which only made me itchier. Why did he have to be so damned sexy all the freaking time?

"You know what," I snapped. "Sex. The sex. Our sex." My hands flapped like dying fish between us in an effort to show him... what "us" meant, maybe? I was pretty sure I was sweating now. In weird places. "Sex," I said again for clarification.

Zach's face lit up in laughter.

My face heated, and my heart, which was already thundering with nerves, roared in my ears. No wonder I'd never had sex before if this was how incredibly bad at it I was.

"Gotta go," I muttered, spinning on my heel and marching off in the direction of not Zach. It turned out to be the back of the hangar that was a solid wall with no door. I stopped and turned again to keep from walking into the side of a damned building.

"Stop," Zach said with a laugh. "Come here."

"Never mind," I called over my shoulder. "It's fine."

"Baby," he said in a low voice. The sound of it washed through me like a drug, making my entire body suddenly feel loose and warm. I closed my eyes and soaked it in. "Come. Here."

I turned around slowly and looked at him. The intensity in his gaze sucked all the air from my lungs. Too much heart rate, too little oxygen. *Airway, Breathing, Circulation,* I thought stupidly. Was it possible to need medical attention for an overdose of unslaked lust?

My feet took me to him without conscious thought, but before I could press my nose into his sternum the way I wanted, he growled another command.

"Get in the truck."

I imagined there might have been a cartoon cloud of dust behind me at the rate I dove around and threw myself into the passenger seat. I didn't even mind his faint chuckle because I assumed there was naked Zach in my near future, and that was all I cared about in the moment.

I clasped my hands together in my lap to keep from reaching for him while he drove the short distance to his cabin. The silence in the cab of the truck was heavy with unspoken promises of what was to come. My pants were way too tight, and I had to press my clasped hands down on my hard-on a few times to keep from whimpering.

Zach seemed completely unaffected which almost had me fooled until he practically pulled into the parking area by his cabin on two wheels and shot out of the truck like he'd been ejected from a fighter jet. Within seconds, he'd yanked me from the truck and thrown me over his shoulder before striding confidently toward the cabin door.

"Oh god," I breathed. *It's happening*, I thought. *Finally.*

Zach's hand came down on my ass, making me squeak.

"You've been driving me crazy for two straight days," he grumbled. "Parading around in nothing but tight briefs and rubbing yourself all over me on the couch while we watch TV."

Rubbing all over him? I'd barely touched him as I'd sat stiffly next to him... and when he'd taken me back to the bunkhouse each night, he'd kept his promise to kiss me goodbye but it had been nothing more than a stiff peck on the mouth and a grunted goodbye.

"Then why didn't you do something about it?" I asked and was rewarded with another slap on my ass.

"Because I needed to know you were sure—"

"I'm sure," I said loudly. "Do you think I parade around in my tightest briefs just to watch movies with my buddies?"

I felt his head shake as he grunted in frustration. My heart sang in triumph.

He was affected. By me.

"So I guess I didn't need to go out and buy an even tighter pair of undies?" I asked, grinning like a fool. A fool who was going to get lucky.

Another spank landed hard on my ass. My blood thrummed straight to my cock. I reached down and grabbed the rounded globes of Zach's butt through his pants and squeezed before spanking him back.

He sucked in a breath of surprise, bypassing the living area and heading straight up the narrow loft stairs. "That's not how this works, sweetheart. You're the one who gets the spankings. Not me."

He threw me down on the bed and began pulling at my shoes. I watched him for a few seconds before realizing if I stripped some of my own clothes off, it would speed up the process. Within moments, I was naked on the bed, stroking myself while Zach stared at me with hungry eyes.

"Hurry," I said, not really meaning to say it out loud. A silly giggle almost escaped my throat when Zach looked up at me with wild eyes from where he'd been working his pants down over his hard cock.

I slapped my hand over my mouth which seemed to turn Zach's frown of concentration into a slight smile. As soon as he was blessedly naked, he stalked toward me like a sexy panther or something.

"Open your legs for me."

I silently reminded myself not to swallow my tongue. My legs bent and moved apart automatically as if anything Zach said was law.

He climbed onto the foot of the bed and began kissing one of my ankles, slowly moving his way up the inside of my calf to my knee and then my inner thigh. The noises coming out of my throat were humiliating, but I didn't care. As long as he kept his mouth on my skin, nothing else mattered.

Zach's nose landed in the crease between my leg and my sac and ran up my body until his mouth latched on to one of my nipples and sucked hard. I grabbed his head with a shout and pulled my legs around his back, locking my ankles together as if scared he might float away.

His eyes glanced up at mine, searing me with the heat in their depths. I felt like time stood still for a few heartbeats until his lips widened into a grin and my poor nipple felt the cool air of the room again.

"You said something earlier about the sex," he said.

I didn't have nearly enough brain cells to figure out how to respond. "Huh?"

"Sex. The sex. Our sex... *sex*." The teasing twinkle in his eyes reminded me of my stupid babbling earlier in the parking lot.

"Shut up." I would have pushed him away if I hadn't wanted him right where he was. "Less talking, more doing."

Zach leaned up to kiss me, and I was surprised by the tenderness of his lips on mine. The frenetic pace of the lead-up was gone, and the sweet, gentle attention he paid my mouth was more like a slow dance.

I ran my hands up his arms to his shoulders and around the back of his neck in hopes it would keep him from pulling away. But by the time he even let me take a breath, all thoughts of Zach leaving me were gone and my body was a heap of putty begging for him to mold it into whatever shape he wanted.

My skin was cool where his openmouthed kisses had left trails all over. My cock pulsed and my brain skittered around in all directions, unable to settle on what exactly I wanted him to do next.

"Turn over," he finally said, pulling on my hip when I took too long to process his words. As soon as I landed on my stomach on the crisp sheets, I grabbed handfuls of them and arched my ass back at him in desperation.

"Please," I moaned into the edge of the pillow.

His hand came down on my ass hard, forcing a surprised gasp out of me. The swat only made my dick harder, and I humped into the bed for friction.

"God, this ass," Zach muttered under his breath. "I've spent hours thinking about watching your naked ass jiggle under my touch." He grabbed each of my cheeks and squeezed, kneading and separating them so boldly, it brought embarrassed heat to my face.

He spanked me again, once on each cheek. The smacks were hard enough that I wondered if my pale skin sported a red handprint in the shape of Zach's large palm. I hoped to god he'd left his mark on me.

"Please," I whispered again.

He leaned over me until the stubble near his lips scraped against the shell of my ear. "You like it when I spank you?" Zach's voice was so deep, it sent shudders through my whole body.

"Oh god." My brain was like static and my balls tightened to the point of serious discomfort. I needed to come. I was ready to beg him for it.

"Answer me."

I closed my eyes and surrendered the last scrap of pride or protection or whatever it was called. All this time, I hadn't wanted to appear weak or young or needy around him any more than I already did. But it was truth-telling time, and this was my truth.

"Yes," I breathed. "I like it when you take control of me."

Now it was his turn to shudder. I felt his groan vibrate against my back and into my ear. The words must have ignited something in him because within seconds he was all over me, nipping and biting at my neck, my shoulders, and my spine, all while his calloused fingers probed my ass with slick lube. His lips and teeth distracted me from the bite and pull of his fingers, until the sensations were too much and from too many directions all at once.

Somehow, he knew that I was about to lose it. He turned me onto my side and lay down behind me as if suddenly we were no longer having sex, but spooning.

"Okay?" he asked, holding one arm tightly across my chest as the other moved between us. Finally, finally, I felt the blunt press of his dick against my hole.

My breath whooshed out in relief and I wanted to cry. Every nerve ending in my skin was tweaked and vibrating, ready for the release his movements promised. He stretched me even more than his fingers had, and I tried my best to breathe and relax for him. His murmured words of encouragement heated the back of my neck.

"Zach," I said, as if he was somehow able to figure out what I meant.

"Shh. I have you." He finally thrust the rest of the way in until I felt the tickle of his pubic hair against the skin of my ass. His hand came around to hold my hip until he reached further around to grab my dick.

There was no telling how much time it took for his thrusts into me and his tight pulls on my cock to render me practically comatose, but I vaguely remembered the feel of his hot cum landing on my lower back and the rough, broken sound of my name echoing off the cabin walls before I orgasmed myself into what I could only classify as a dazed stupor. I felt Zach's warm breath against my back as he pressed soft kisses along my spine and shoulders. It wasn't until he leaned over my shoulder and captured my mouth in a soft kiss that my body went from languid and satisfied to tense and uncertain.

Right... the goodbye kiss.

I could feel tears prick the backs of my eyes as Zach's heat disappeared from my back and he dropped down on the bed behind me. I forced myself to quietly sit up. Shadows fell across the room as I looked around for my clothes. I moved slowly so I wouldn't risk disturbing Zach in any kind of way. He might not have wanted me in his bed for the night but he was gallant enough that he'd offer me a ride home.

And tonight, I really needed to walk. It would help me get my emotions in check before I got home to the bunkhouse and my cold, too-empty bed.

My silent escape was looking good until a light in the corner of the room came on. At first I thought Zach had turned it on, but one glance at it showed it was on a timer.

Because Zach didn't want to risk falling asleep in the dark...

The reminder of Zach's fear of the dark broke my heart, and I cast a glance back at him. To my surprise, he was sitting up in bed watching me. His expression was unreadable.

"Sorry," I murmured awkwardly as I pulled my pants up. The coolness of the semen on my belly made me cringe, but I managed to keep my expression neutral. "Didn't mean to wake you."

Zach's mouth hardened imperceptibly. I couldn't figure out what was causing his obvious anger. Was I not moving fast enough?

I hurriedly went in search of my shirt.

"Don't worry about it," Zach bit out, then he was getting out of bed. If his irritation hadn't been so obvious, I would have gladly ogled his ass as he started yanking on his own pants. "I'll take you home," he snapped.

"No, it's okay. I can walk. I'm sure you're tired," I sputtered.

How the hell had things gone from fun and easy to so messed up in the span of a few minutes?

"Honestly, Zach—"

"Honesty?" Zach repeated angrily. "Right," he sniped. He snatched his shirt off the floor.

"What is that supposed to mean?" I asked in confusion.

"It means if you have a problem with who I am, then man up and say so."

It was the craziest form of whiplash I'd ever experienced. "Your rules—" I began, but Zach cut me off.

"It's a little bit of fucking light," he snarled as he shot the lamp in the corner a glance. "If it bothered you so much, you should have just said something instead of pretending—"

"Pretending what?" I practically yelled, because I finally got what had him so upset. I balled my shirt in my hands but instead of stalking around the bed, I climbed up onto it and walked across it. The position put me above him when he turned around to face me. "I don't give a fuck about the light, you asshole," I snapped. "If you think for even a second I somehow see you as 'less' because you need a little bit of light to sleep with then you don't know a goddamn thing about me!"

I threw my shirt at him, but of course it did nothing but hit his chest and fall quietly to the floor. "I think you are the bravest, strongest, kindest man—" I started to say, then let out a whoosh of air when my legs were pulled out from under me. I landed with a thud on the bed and then Zach was on top of me, his mouth capturing mine.

I was still pissed, of course, but the second Zach's tongue slid over mine, I forgot the reason why. Within seconds, I was moaning and bucking beneath him. When he ripped his mouth from mine, I could barely breathe.

"Stay the night with me," Zach said softly, his eyes holding mine. "If the light is on, I won't hurt you…"

I shook my head in disbelief. Was that truly what he thought I'd been worried about?

"Your rule—" I began, but he cut me off with another hard kiss.

"Stay," he repeated. The insecurity in his voice had my breath catching. When he'd told me his rules, he'd been clear about this particular one… there'd be no cuddling or sleeping in each other's arms—

I couldn't help but glance in the direction of the lamp. What if… what if that particular rule had nothing to do with the act of sleeping in someone else's arms at all? What if there was more to it than that? What if it was a mere act of preserving his own dignity? He'd immediately accused me of having a problem with the light being on all night. Hell, he'd even made an angry joke about being awarded a medal because he was afraid of the dark. And if one rule was in question, what about all of the others? I felt Zach tense in my arms and knew it was because I'd taken too long to respond.

I dragged his head back down and covered his mouth with mine. I kissed him until I felt his body relax on top of mine. "Are you going to bring me breakfast in bed in the morning?" I asked with a grin.

Zach relaxed again. "Doubtful," he said.

"Ok, how about whoever can still walk in the morning has to make breakfast?"

Zach arched a brow. "Seems counterintuitive but fine, it's a deal."

I shifted my weight so I could push Zach onto his back. I nipped at his mouth. "Loser also gets to eat their breakfast off the other person's naked body," I added.

Zach laughed. He was once again relaxed like he'd been when he'd carried me into the house. I reached between our bodies and palmed Zach's cock through his pants. "I should warn you that I'm a terrible cook," I said.

Zach folded his arms behind his head. "Is that so?" he asked. He didn't move as I made my way down his body, placing soft kisses as I went. "So you want me to throw this thing?" he asked. He gasped on the last syllables because I chose that moment to lick my way down his treasure trail.

"I'll make it worth your while," I murmured as I worked the button free on his jeans. I had to carefully ease the zipper down because Zach's dick was quickly responding to my touch.

Zach's eyes had gone dark with lust and all the humor had fled from his expression as he lifted his head so he could watch me. "So do we have a deal?" I asked as I nuzzled his groin. His dick was still trapped in the confines of his jeans.

"Lucky," Zach growled.

I purposefully ran my tongue over my lips. "Is that a yes?" I asked.

"Yes! Yes, damn it," Zach barked. I smiled to myself because I was pretty certain Zach no longer had any clue what our deal was.

Come to think of it, neither did I. Not that it mattered because no matter what, I was coming out the winner because I was exactly where I was supposed to be.

In Zach's bed.

CHAPTER 27

ZACH

We spent the final three days of the program half-dead from sleep deprivation. As soon as I thought I'd worn Lucky's ass out in my bed late at night, he'd wake me up in the wee hours of the morning with a simple touch and it would start the cycle all over again.

I couldn't get enough. Hell, there was no such thing as enough of Lucky Reed. His slender perfect body, his full pink lips, his thoughtfulness and kindness whenever I experienced any kind of pain or discomfort having to do with old and new injuries alike. He was King Arthur and I was the damned sword in the stone. Somehow, I came alive in his hands in a way I never had before. It wasn't something I even noticed until Tag pulled me aside on the last day of classes.

"I take back what I said at the hospital," Tag said with a shit-eating grin.

I tried to figure out what he was referring to. "What did you say?"

He narrowed his eyes at me, trying to figure out if I was pulling his leg or not. But I truly didn't remember much about that day. I'd been on pain meds and more concerned with keeping Lucky away than anything else. I'd known if I'd let him into my hospital room while my defenses were down, I would have said things I never would have been able to take back or even want to.

"To stop keeping yourself so goddamned closed off and give the ki—Lucky—a real chance."

I opened my mouth in shock, but Tag laughed before I could sputter out a *what the fuck*.

"Don't give me that bullshit denial. Any idiot can see you look at him like a lovesick puppy. Hell, Zach, I think it's fucking great. Finally. It's about time you let someone in. I hope it works out for you, buddy. I really do. He's a good man."

I stared at my friend like he'd just stepped off an alien spaceship.

"What the fuck are you talking about?"

He lowered his voice. "If you're going to stand there and tell me you're not sleeping with Lucky Reed, I'm going to punch your lying ass in the face."

I looked around to make sure no one could hear us. "That's not what I mean. You're talking about us like we're... like we're..."

As I stuttered, Tag's eyes narrowed to angry slits. "Don't do this," he hissed. "Don't ruin the best fucking thing that's happened to you in... I don't know how long."

The breath seemed to leave my lungs all at once until I was even more of a stuttering mess than before. "We're not—" I tried again, but Tag held up a hand.

"I said don't," he repeated. "Just do me a favor, okay? Think this through before you fuck it up. Will you promise me that?"

I felt my nostrils flare with all of the denials I needed to spew. But Tag was one of the rare people in my life who'd truly stuck with me through thick and thin. He deserved better than my bullshit. Besides, it wasn't like I was admitting to having certain feelings for Lucky.

Because I didn't.

Okay, sure, maybe things in bed with him weren't like they'd been with all my other hookups but that was still all he was.

Even as I thought the words, I started shaking my head. I heard Tag growl and remembered what he'd been talking about. "Fine," I bit out as I nodded, and suddenly, the anger left his face and he was all cheery smiles again.

"Great!" he said, pounding me on the back. "Good man. Now let's go give these folks their certificates for a job well done."

During the informal completion ceremony, Lucky beamed with pride and cheered for each of his teammates as their names were called. When it was his turn, I couldn't help but flash him a wink as he walked to the front to collect his certificate and paperwork. His cheeks turned light pink and his dark lashes swept down over the tops of his cheeks. I thought about how I was the lucky one. How even within a few hours I would have the chance to touch every millimeter of that smooth skin and kiss those very same pink cheeks.

Watching him mingle with and congratulate the other students reminded me how well-liked he was by his peers. Lucky had always drawn people to him, and I remembered Oz describing him one time like Haven, Colorado's "Snow White." When I'd asked what he'd meant, Oz had said, "Everyone loves him, even the woodland creatures." He'd laughed that tinkling laugh of his before continuing. "One time I swear to god I saw him talking to the birds in the trees. He's nice to everyone. Walk around Haven with him for one hour and you'll see. Everyone comes out of the stores to say hi to him. He's helped, like, everyone with their stuff, volunteering and whatnot."

Oz was right. Lucky cared more about helping others than even reaching his own goals. I'd seen that over and over again during the course of the training. And the very nature of SAR work required a caring, diligent person in the first place. No wonder Tag had raved about him from the first day.

The reminder that I was taking advantage not only of Lucky's innocence but of his kindness too made me feel sick to my stomach. But I knew I wasn't going to be able to give him up just yet. I needed more time to work him out of my system. One of these days I'd wake up with him in my arms and that familiar need to run again would surface. When it did, I'd do my best to let Lucky down gently...

After the ceremony, followed by a big lunch Tag's wife provided, we made our way back to my cabin. Lucky had already packed up his things at the bunkhouse the night before and stowed them in his car before spending the night in my bed.

As we entered the cabin, I noticed Lucky biting his bottom lip.

"What's wrong?" I asked, reaching for his hand to pull him closer. I sat on the back of the couch and pulled him between my legs so I could put my arms around him. Lucky's hands made their way into my hair and began idly stroking my scalp.

"I'm nervous about telling my dads."

I reached up and pulled his poor bottom lip out with my thumb before caressing it. "About the alpine SAR work or about the fire?"

His eyes widened. "I'm not telling them about the fire. Are you nuts?"

I couldn't help but laugh. "They'll see you made it through practically unscathed. They'll be fine."

"You're insane. That will give them even more reason to forbid me from pursuing SAR work as a career."

I stood up and moved us around until we were sittings sideways on the cushions, Lucky between my legs with his back to my front and our legs stretched out along the length of the couch.

"Lucky, you're twenty years old." I tried not to think about the number of years of life experience that separated us. When I'd dared mention our age gap in the past, it'd only pissed him off and stressed me out. "You have one year of school left before striking out on your own. There comes a point where you need to decide who's in charge of your life and how you want your story to play out."

Before he could interject, I continued. "Don't get me wrong. I think keeping your parents' wishes in mind is important. Respect and love for them is always going to color your decisions and your life. But they also love and respect *you*. And sometimes that means having to give you the space to follow your own dreams."

Lucky shifted around until he was lying on his side so he could look up at me. "Will you come with me?" he asked softly. "When I talk to them?"

I blew out a breath and ran my hands up under his shirt to the smooth warmth of his skin. Touching him was grounding. It made me feel more in control of myself and less chaotic.

"They can't know—"

"I know that," he snapped. "They can't know about us. That's not what I'm talking about, and you know it. Come as my fucking friend, Zach. Nothing more."

I closed my eyes and leaned my head back against the arm of the couch. I hated being the cause of his disappointment.

"Yes. I'll come with you. But only as silent support, okay?"

I opened my eyes when I felt the touch of his hand on my face. His warm eyes were filled with gratitude. "You? Silent? How is that possible when you're such a chatty guy?"

I pinched his side. "Smart-ass," I grumbled. "Just for that, you owe me a blow job."

Lucky's eyes went from grateful to lustful in half a second. "Say it ain't so," he teased. "You're so mean, forcing me to do something so awful." He moved down my body, rucking up my shirt with his hand in the process. "But I guess I'll take one for the team. If you insist."

I felt the strange bubbly lightness I'd been noticing more and more these past few days. It was a feeling I associated with being around Lucky. It was something I wanted more of. I couldn't get enough.

"Brat," I muttered, running my hands through his hair and down to cup his cheeks. He looked up at me with a grin.

"Want me to call you Daddy?"

The sound of my laughter surprised even me. Lucky's grin got even wider. "I'll take that as a no."

"Damned right, it's a no," I said, gazing down at him with a smile. God, he was gorgeous.

I watched as he proceeded to tease me, taking his sweet time unbuttoning my pants and pressing his own hard length against my leg. By the time he got my dick out, I was tense and panting, trying not to pull his hair and shove his face in my crotch. I wasn't sure I'd ever been so close to begging before.

"Lucky," I growled.

"Mmm?" he hummed, looking up at me with a sweet blink. Those puppy eyes didn't fool me. He was driving me crazy on purpose.

My dick jumped, grazing the side of his chin. I groaned and squeezed my eyes closed, counting to ten in Spanish in an attempt to distract myself from the need to throw him down face-first and fuck him hard into the couch.

His tongue danced on my shaft as he hummed. "I know what you're thinking," he said between licks.

"Mpfh."

He took my cock into the blessed wet heat of his mouth and sucked hard for several moments before pulling off.

"You're thinking of my tight ass and how you want to fuck it."

"Gnnnh." I was having trouble breathing. My fingers tightened in his hair.

Lucky sucked the crown before trying to deep-throat me again. He gagged which only made me harder.

"Fuck," I breathed. "Fuck. Lucky, *Jesus*. Again."

He met and held my eyes as he licked my dick all over and swallowed it again. I couldn't hold back any longer. I held his head and pumped into his throat once, twice, until I was roaring out my release and his fingernails were digging into my sides.

When I finally released him, tears were streaming down his face, but his reddened, wet lips were wide in happy satisfaction. He looked so damned proud of himself, all I wanted to do was reward him.

I lurched up and pushed him down on his back, practically ripping off his pants to get to his dick. As soon as I had it in my hand, I began licking it, sucking it, coating it in spit and jacking it, until all I could hear were his whimpers and gasps. I swallowed him as deeply as I could and cradled his balls in my hand until I felt the warm tang of his release on my tongue and heard his muffled groans.

I looked up to see him biting his arm, eyes wide in surprise and pupils blown in pleasure.

He was the most beautiful man I'd ever seen. And for the moment, he was all mine.

My chest squeezed in a confusing vise. How the hell was I ever supposed to let him go?

As we lay there trying to catch our breath, with my head resting on his hip and his hands stroking through my hair again, I realized I'd never have the strength to walk away on my own.

I was going to have to come clean to my brother.

And hope like hell he didn't beat the shit out of me.

⁓

The following morning I followed Lucky to Missoula to drop his car off. He'd ride to Haven with me and then ride back with Minna who'd be coming home a week later to visit her own family.

The twelve hours we spent in the truck together went by in a blink. Lucky told me funny stories from his time as an adventure leader for his dads' camp programs and harrowing ones from his time as an EMT, then a paramedic. I told him more about my time in the army, including stories about the guys on my team I'd lost. I had no clue how he managed to get the information out of me because talking about Kaminski, Teller, and Mac was something I just didn't do. But somehow telling Lucky about the good times I'd had with my brothers-in-arms was like a strange balm of sorts.

I also told him about childhood adventures I'd gotten up to with Jake and Tag, and how much fun we'd had.

By the time we crossed into Colorado, Lucky was snoring softly with his head in my lap. I ran my fingers through his soft hair. He was so damned young. The skin on his face was still smooth and unblemished, despite the hours he'd spent in the sun, the same hours that had lightened his hair and built out his frame in the time since I'd last seen him in Haven.

That Christmas seemed so long ago now, but the heartbroken look on his face was never going to leave me. The knowledge that I was going to hurt him all over again like that sickened me.

I was saved from the disheartening direction of my thoughts when the phone rang through the truck speakers.

"Yeah," I answered quietly, despite knowing the hands-free would wake Lucky up.

"Hey, man," Jake said. "I was calling to see if it was okay if we put you up at Xander and Bennett's lodge. The cabin at our place is still under renovation. We were hoping to have it done in time for your visit, but—"

I cut him off. "Yeah, that's fine. Of course. I have Lucky, so I'm heading there first anyway."

There was a pause. "You have Lucky? With you in the car?"

I winced as I realized everyone was still under the belief that Lucky had been in Yellowstone, not in Glacier with me. "Yeah, uh..." I scrambled to think of a way to explain myself when Lucky's groggy voice chimed in.

"Hey, Jake. It's a long story, okay? Don't tell my dads. I'll explain when I get there." He sat up and stretched, running fingers into his hair and looking out the windshield to see where we were. "Should be there in about an hour or so, I think," he added.

Jake gave an awkward reminder to be safe and ended the call. I glanced over at Lucky.

"I'm proud of you."

He turned to me, eyes wide. "What for?"

"Telling the truth to your family even when it's hard."

I glanced back at the road, but turned back toward Lucky when he didn't respond. He was pensive.

"Zach... you know you have some truths to tell too."

I focused back on the road ahead. "Mpfh."

Lucky reached over and ran warm fingertips up the back of my neck into my short hair. "Will you at least consider it? Everything you said about my fathers loving me and supporting me is true for you and Jake too. You know that."

I grunted again, unwilling to turn this around to me. The idea of coming clean to Jake about how I'd failed the men who'd depended on me to keep them alive wasn't going to happen. I couldn't have my brother looking at me with that mix of pity and disappointment. And if he ever found out about my relationship with Mitch... no fucking way.

"Just think about it," he said softly before turning to face out his window. "Life's too short for painful secrets and holding back."

Silence fell between us for the rest of the ride into Haven and down the quiet side street to his parents' large property. The familiar wooden lodge dominated the scene with its wide front porch and hanging flower baskets overflowing with summer color. The late setting sun gave the entire picture a warm glow that seemed to have a similar effect on Lucky's mood.

As soon as we pulled past the lodge and parked by the family home behind it, Lucky was out of the truck and jogging to the open front door where I could see movement inside. Someone must have noticed him coming, because Bennett came rushing out with a giant smile on his face and gathered Lucky into a strong hug, practically lifting his feet off the ground.

When Xander joined them on the porch with a baby on his hip, the happiness on his face was unmistakable. I stepped out of the truck and stayed back to watch from afar, letting the family have their time to reconnect. As soon as they noticed me, the questions would begin.

And then the lightness in Lucky's face would fall away again, and I would be reminded of the fact that I was one of the many secrets Lucky was keeping from the people he loved. But unlike with his SAR certification, there would be no coming clean about me.

Lucky chose that moment to glance my way and, despite making sure neither of his fathers were watching when he did it, it was like a punch to the gut. Not because I knew there was no way in hell we were going to be able to pull this off, but because of another truth I'd been denying from the moment I'd crossed that line and kissed Lucky.

This wasn't a hookup for him. No matter how many times he'd insisted that he'd be able to walk away from this thing with his heart intact, that one look was proof that it was too late for that.

Far too late.

CHAPTER 28

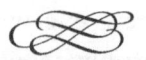

LUCKY

I took little Danny out of Xander's arms and held him against my chest, dropping a kiss on his fuzzy, light hair. "Hey, beautiful boy," I cooed. "Miss big brother?"

My dads both watched me with goofy grins, but before I had a chance to ask why the baby was awake so late, Bennett noticed Zach standing next to his truck.

"Hey man," Bennett said, stepping down the stairs into the yard and reaching out a hand to shake. "What are you doing here? I mean, Jake told us you were coming, but…" He looked between me and Zach, seeming to realize that's how I'd gotten here.

Zach's eyes glanced to me before looking back at Bennett. "I was in Montana on business, so I gave Lucky a ride home since I was heading south anyway. My brother said you wouldn't mind putting me up for a few nights. Hope it's not a bother?"

Bennett shook his hand and grinned at him. "Of course not. Happy to have you. You can help us celebrate having everyone back together again. You know how much we love an excuse to light up the grill and eat outside. Come on in. I'll let Jake and Oz know you made it safely."

Zach met my eyes over Bennett's head before nodding and grabbing our bags out of the back of the truck. I was already coming up with ways to sneak into Zach's room in the lodge each night. The idea of having him so close and not being able to sleep up against him made me restless.

I turned toward the lodge, fully expecting to lead Zach to one of the guest rooms we kept set aside for friends and family who were visiting. But Xander stopped me with a hand on my shoulder.

"Show Zach to your room upstairs in the house."

I stared at him. "What do you mean? I thought Zach was staying in the lodge."

Bennett walked up and took Danny from me, rocking him against his shoulder. "The lodge is full-up and we gave the spare room to Ash and Aiden. Nick is using the other spare room. He's helping with the campers this summer. I thought we told you that. You don't mind sleeping on the couch in the den, right?"

My dream of sneaking into Zach's room evaporated in a desperate poof. I couldn't even enjoy the fact that now he'd be under the same roof as me because it wasn't like I could risk having sex with my boyfriend in my fathers' house.

Boyfriend?

Damn it, I needed to be careful even thinking stuff like that. If I'd called Zach that to his face, he would have high-tailed it out of Haven so fast there'd be skid marks.

"But..." How could I possibly argue this without sounding like a pain in the ass? I couldn't. "Um, okay. Zach, come on. Let me show you where everything is."

We headed toward the house I'd called home for the last five years. I was dimly aware of Zach thanking my fathers and following me, but he didn't say anything even once we entered the house, leaving me to worry about what he thought about all this. I pretty much kissed my newly found sex life goodbye as I trudged up the stairs. When I got to the room at the end of the second-floor hallway, I turned on the bedside table lamp, revealing framed posters and photographs of Everest, Fuji, and Rainier. A forested trail in Yosemite among the redwoods, and a bald eagle's nest in the Cascades. These sights were as familiar to me as the silly knitted pillow Min had made me one summer in a crafts workshop or the purple-ribbon medal I'd won for a mock search and rescue challenge when I was a senior in high school. The idea of Zach seeing the things from my childhood unnerved me. He was already struggling to see me as an adult. What would spending the night around all these trinkets and treasures do to our already tenuous relationship?

"Sheets should be clean," I said, pointing stupidly at the double bed as if he didn't know what or where sheets were. "The bathroom is just through there," I said, nodding at the only other door in the room.

I heard the snick of the bedroom door closing and felt Zach's strong arms move around my front. "What's wrong?" he asked softly.

I turned around and buried my face in his neck, inhaling the familiar combination of woods and man. "I was hoping to sneak into your room tonight like a naughty teenager," I admitted. "Instead, I'm being cockblocked by my dads."

His hands cupped my face and pulled me back so he could meet my eyes. "You need to catch up on sleep anyway. Hell, we both do. You've worn me out, naughty teenager."

I pinched him for the tease and then leaned in for a quick peck. "Fine. I'll see you at dinner," I said.

"Actually, I told your dads I'd be driving up to see Jake and Oz tonight. I'll probably be back late."

My heart fell. God, was he already starting the process of pulling away? I wanted to remind him about his promise not to leave without kissing me goodbye but before I could say anything, he was kissing me softly.

I barely managed to catch the strangled sob from escaping my throat. "Zach?" I whispered as I gripped his arms. Not surprisingly, he seemed to know what was going on with me because he put his arms around me and held me tight.

"It's okay, sweetheart, I'll be back. I promise."

He brushed a kiss over my temple and held on to me until I was the one who finally stepped back. I turned my back on him so I could discreetly wipe at my face. "Say hi to Jake and Oz for me. I'll see you tomorrow, I guess. Text me if you need anything, okay?" I forced myself to turn back around and smile.

Zach looked at me for a beat with a knowing, affectionate expression. My heart kicked up a notch. When he leaned in to kiss me again, it was soft and sweet, unexpected.

I pulled away quickly and mumbled something that probably made no sense. Within moments, I was racing down the hallway.

Lust, I could handle. Sex, I could handle. But affection? Gentle sweetness?

I blew out a heavy breath. How was I supposed to let him go after all this? I'd made him promise me that he'd always kiss me goodbye but now I was regretting it because every time his lips brushed over mine, I obsessed over it being the last time. I'd thought I'd be better off with memories of Zach to sustain me, but I wasn't so sure I could do it. And the second Zach sensed my true feelings, he'd walk away for sure.

Instead of heading downstairs right away, I slipped into an upstairs bathroom and splashed some cold water on my face. I heard Zach leave the house and it was all I could do not rush back to the bedroom to see if his bag was still there. I gave myself another minute to collect myself and then went downstairs. I found Xander and Bennett in the kitchen sharing a bottle of white wine. Clean baby bottles were lined up neatly on a drying rack by the sink and there were colorful burp cloths here and there around the tidy room, replacing our old boring black kitchen towels. Our dog, Bear, scrambled up from his spot by the open window and threw himself at me.

"Hey, big guy," I said, squatting to give him plenty of attention. "You been watching over everyone for me?" His dark fur was thick between my fingers as I scratched his back and sides.

"How did you hook up with Zach?" Bennett asked.

I glanced up at him, my heart skipping a beat before I realized he'd only meant hook up as in catching a ride from him.

"It's a long story. Can I tell you in the morning? I'm kind of beat."

Xander turned his chair around, leaning forward and resting his elbows on his knees. His eyes pinned me in place like only a father's could. "Does this story also explain why you have stitches in your forehead and a healing bruise on your cheek?"

Shit. I'd brought a baseball cap to wear for this exact reason, but then forgot to put it on before I got out of the truck.

"Yes." I swallowed. "And I promise I'll tell you everything, but I just…"

Bennett and Xander exchanged a look before Bennett smiled at me. "Get up to bed. You're on baby duty at first light and those two aren't going to go easy on you."

I blew out a breath in relief. "Got it. G'night." I stood and kissed each of them on the cheek, hugging Xander back when he stood and gripped me tightly.

"We're super happy to have you home, Lucky," he admitted in a tight voice. "Missed you like crazy. I hope you know we love you, no matter what."

I nodded, unable to speak. I did know that, which was why I felt like even more of an ass for keeping secrets from them. But I couldn't do this late at night after being on the road all day. I turned and headed to the den, calling Bear to join me before closing us both in.

I dropped my duffel and pulled off my clothes, sliding between the sheets of the already made up pull-out bed at long last. The smell of my dads' laundry detergent and the stripe of moonlight cutting across the foot of my bed reminded me I was home.

But it didn't feel the same and I wasn't sure why. I loved my family more than anything in the world, and the town of Haven had become a paradise of sorts over the years. I'd expected college to take me away for a few years, but the plan had always been to come back home. Whether it was helping my dads run the family business or settling into some "safe" career, I'd always accepted that Haven was where I belonged. But between the training these past few weeks and my relationship with Zach, something had started to change. I was doomed to fail on both fronts because SAR work was just too dangerous, and I wasn't sure I could put my fathers through that. And the Zach thing…. well, I refused to even let myself imagine that things had changed when it came to my relationship with him. He'd been sweet and gentle and the sex was off the charts, but he'd never once mentioned pursuing something real.

I sighed and turned over on the bed so I could get more comfortable. I was greeted by a wet lick from Bear who was taking up a good chunk of the small bed.

"Not exactly the goodnight kiss I was hoping for, but I'll take it, buddy," I whispered to the dog. As I let my eyes drift shut, I thought about the home I'd left three years earlier to go find myself and wondered what I'd see when I looked in the mirror in the morning. Would it be yet another version of me I still didn't recognize or would I finally get to see the real me?

Morning came way too soon. Sure enough, it was a baby's cry that startled me awake, and I was the first one in to grab the troublemaker. The morning went by in a flash of diaper changes, feeding and bathing the twins, and putting off telling my fathers the truth about what I'd been up to the past month. Fortunately, Bennett was too busy dealing with lodge business and the babies to confront me about it, and Xander had gotten called away to deal with some kind of emergency in town. That would have made me beyond happy except for one glaring problem.

Zach hadn't come home. He'd sent me a text before I'd managed to have a complete and total meltdown, but it had only said that he'd decided to spend the night on Jake and Oz's couch and he'd see me tomorrow. It was nearing lunchtime and he still hadn't shown up. There'd been no additional calls or texts to ease my mind, and it was all I could do to keep myself from driving up to Jake and Oz's place to confront the man. I'd finally broken down and checked Zach's room, or my room, rather, and his bag had still been there. I hadn't gone so far as to search through it to see if he'd taken any of his toiletries or much-needed medicine with him, but at the rate I was going, I'd be doing that soon.

I decided to keep busy by taking the twins for a nature walk of sorts. The "walk" wasn't more than me putting the twins in their stroller and following the path around the lake just behind the lodge, but I used the time to point out every interesting rock, tree, and flower we came across. The babies didn't seem overly impressed because they fell asleep within minutes, leaving me once again to my thoughts.

Which wasn't a good place to be because between checking my phone every five seconds for texts and flashing glances in the direction of the lodge's parking lot in the hopes of spying a familiar dark blue truck, I hadn't made it more than a few hundred feet during the hour that followed. I finally settled for sitting down at one of the many picnic benches surrounding the lake.

I was in the process of trying to come up with a super casual where-the-hell-are-you text to Zach when I heard someone let out a vicious curse.

I looked up and spied my uncle Aiden walking toward me. He was swatting at the air around him.

"Fuckers are as big as the cabs back home," he muttered. "Oh, damn, sorry," he said as he spied me. "Trying to find a place that has decent reception." He held his phone up in the air as if that would somehow give him more bars.

I chuckled and said, "Didn't Ash make a rule that you guys need to unplug when you come out for a visit?"

Aiden grunted. "He had the staff take the landline out," he explained. "Only reason I got this back"—he held up the cell phone—"was my unique skills of persuasion." Aiden winked at me. I laughed because I knew exactly what Aiden was good at when he needed to persuade his hubby to give in on something.

"Tender ears here, Uncle Aiden," I reminded him.

"Pffft, you're old enough to know all about the birds and the bees. Or bees and bees in our case. Or maybe it's birds and birds." Aiden waved his hand dismissively.

"I meant these ears," I clarified as I pointed at the stroller.

"Oh right," Aiden said, then he was looking around, probably for one or both of my fathers. I stood when he reached me and happily went when he pulled me into his arms.

"If it isn't my favorite fake Trekkie. How are you?"

"Good," I murmured against his shoulder. "I've missed you," I admitted. Of all my uncles, I'd always felt a certain closeness to Aiden. Maybe because he'd known me as long as Bennett had, but it probably had more to do with Aiden being that one person who always made me feel like it was okay to be me. He knew about what my life had been like growing up with my mom and even though he'd come from a completely different world, I felt like he'd somehow gotten it anyway. Like he knew what it was like to always be in search of that missing piece of yourself. Of course, he'd found that piece and more with Ash, but he still understood that despite the amazing life I'd had, my pieces hadn't all fallen into place yet.

"Missed you too, buddy," Aiden said. He held me for several beats, then released me enough so he could look me over. I couldn't help but squirm a little. I'd made sure that none of the marks Zach's stubble had left on me over the past several days could be seen, but at that moment I could practically feel them all over me. God, the man's mouth was so damn talented—

"So you finally cashed in the V card, huh? Good for you," Aiden said as he gave me a hearty slap on my back before stepping past me to pretend to coo over the babies.

"There's no way you could know that!" I exclaimed as I turned around.

Aiden glanced over his shoulder and winked. "Oh little one, I have so many things to teach you," he said. "First lesson, when you're going to deny something, actually deny it. Lesson two, don't get distracted by whatever lovely thoughts your man has put into your head because you're like my Ash... you light up like a Christmas tree." Aiden pointed at my cheeks and I made the mistake of reaching up to feel them. Aiden laughed at me, and I realized I'd failed lesson one all over again.

"Jerk," I bit out before I flopped down on the picnic table bench.

Aiden sat next to me instead of across from me. He bumped my shoulder playfully. "So spill," he said. "Who was the lucky guy? Get it? *Lucky.*"

I rolled my eyes at him. "How does Ash put up with you?"

Aiden glanced at the lodge, and I couldn't help but smile at the far-off, wistful look he got. Okay, so maybe I did have a tell. Seemed like all the men around me had them when it came to their partners.

Except Zach wasn't my partner.

I dropped my eyes and checked my phone again.

"So it's like that," Aiden said softly, gently. I glanced at him and saw that all the humor had fled his expression. I didn't bother trying to deny it. Instead, I leaned into him when he put his arm around me.

"He doesn't want me," I admitted. "I mean, he does, but he doesn't."

Aiden sighed. "Yeah," he murmured. Like Zach, Aiden had been the kind of guy who'd favored hookups over real relationships. But I'd seen Aiden around Ash when they'd first met. From day one, he'd wanted more with Ash. It wasn't that way with me and Zach. If anything, he'd been trying to escape me from day one.

"He's an amazing man, Uncle Aiden. I don't want you to think that he isn't. I'm the one who pursued him. Sometimes I think maybe I pushed him too hard—"

"Guys who don't want to get pushed don't, Lucky. It's in their DNA. Is he... is he good to you?"

"He's perfect," I whispered. "I just... I don't know how to enjoy it while I have it, you know?"

I felt Aiden drop his head on top of mine. "Don't settle, Lucky. If you want this guy and you believe he's truly worthy of you, then you push until it feels like your fucking arms are going to fall off, do you hear me? Trust me when I say guys like that get too comfortable because it feels like the only thing that's safe in our lives. It takes someone to knock us on our ass to make us realize that being down for the count doesn't mean we're out of the fight."

I didn't point out to Aiden that he'd begun talking in first person.

Aiden gave me another squeeze. "And you, my boy, are worth getting up for. Each and every time."

I nodded and was about to thank him when my phone began to beep. One text message after another started lighting up the screen. Joy exploded in my chest when I saw that they were from Zach. I went to open the first one but more and more continued to come in. There were almost a dozen in all.

I scrolled through the notifications and smiled when I saw phrases like, "messages not getting through" and "fucking bad reception."

"Never be too afraid to push," Aiden said softly. I knew he could see the message notifications, but I hadn't put Zach's name in the contact information, so only a phone number was showing up.

Aiden stood up but when he said, "Oh hey, Zach," I froze. I turned slowly and saw Zach standing less than twenty feet from us.

And he did not look happy.

He managed to put a smile on his face as Aiden approached him and shook his hand. I wondered if Aiden noticed how stiff Zach was. If he did, he didn't show it.

The men made small talk as I climbed to my feet. My tongue felt like it was in knots and all I really wanted to do was throw myself into Zach's arms. When Zach's gaze shifted to me, I managed to say, "You're back."

"I'm back," he said stiffly.

I didn't miss the way Aiden was looking between me and Zach. I knew I needed to keep my cool.

"Aiden and I were just catching up," I said.

"Yeah, I saw," Zach said. His eyes shifted back to Aiden. "How's the husband?" he asked.

Understanding dawned as Zach practically stood toe to toe with Aiden. I was so shocked at first, I couldn't move.

"Currently passed out in our bed," Aiden said snidely. "Figured it was a good time to catch up with old friends." Then the man actually returned to my side and put his arm around me.

"Right," Zach snapped, then he turned on his heel.

"Are you ready to go, Zach?" I called as I stepped away from Aiden and hurried to Zach. I knew I wasn't allowed to touch him in public, so I got as close to him as I could considering our location and said, "Yeah, you wanted to go to the swimming hole, right? The one I told you about? You said you'd never been behind a waterfall and you really wanted to see it…"

I knew I was blabbering, but I was desperate for Zach to hear me.

"Yeah, right," Zach said. He was still clearly angry but he hadn't walked off, so that was something.

"Okay," I said in relief. "Let's go then," I added quickly.

"Lucky, sweetie, are you forgetting something?" Aiden called.

"No," I barked. I'd absolutely murder the man if he tried to stop me. Chances were he'd already figured out Zach was the guy I'd been talking about. Aiden smiled when I snapped at him, then motioned to the stroller next to him.

"Oh crap," I said. I turned to Zach and added, "Oh man, I'm sorry, I'm babysitting. I can't—"

"You two kids go on and have fun," Aiden interjected. He waved us off as he sat down on the picnic bench. "Uncle Aiden has some life lessons to teach the young'uns."

"Are you sure?" I asked. "I could—"

"Lucky, darling, don't *push* me on this," Aiden said as he side-eyed me.

I snapped my mouth shut and hurriedly grabbed Zach's arm to lead him away.

CHAPTER 29

ZACH

After Aiden turned around, I realized I'd been irrationally angry over... Lucky spending time with his *uncle*.

In addition to the fact that I shouldn't have been angry over Lucky spending time with *anyone*, I was especially embarrassed that I'd actually felt jealous of a man who was essentially Lucky's family. Something was seriously wrong with me. I had no business being jealous of anyone when it came to the young man leading me back to my truck. Jealousy was for lovers, boyfriends; it wasn't for fuck buddies or sex tutors or whatever the fuck we were.

Before I could get too riled up about my stupid mistake, Lucky gestured me toward the house.

"Where are we going?"

Lucky bounced his eyebrows at me. "My room."

I groaned. "Not a good idea. We'll get caught."

He shook his head. "Not true. Xander is gone and Bennett's too busy with work stuff to notice. He's at the lodge. We'll have the house to ourselves."

As soon as we entered the house, my brother-in-law popped his head out of the kitchen. "Oh thank god, come taste this. I think I've accidentally poisoned everyone," Oz said.

Lucky froze and the three of us stared awkwardly at each other for a beat.

"Uh," Lucky blurted. "We can't. There's… a…" He glanced at me in panic.

"Cat," I said stupidly, eyeing one of the baby's burp cloths with cartoon animals on it.

Lucky nodded slowly before turning back to Oz. "Yes. There is a cat. Who… needs to be returned to his home. Down the street."

Oz's eyes flicked back and forth between us. "You know, if you didn't want to be poisoned, you could have just said that. There's no need to lie about it." He turned back to the stove with a huff.

Lucky turned to me with big eyes that clearly said, "Do something."

"So, uh…" I began. "We're just gonna go and…"

Oz flapped his hand over his shoulder. "Whatever. Like I care. I should have had the gourmet grocery store make this shit for me," he muttered. "No one would have ever known."

We made our way through the house and back out the front door.

"What now?" I asked. "Where the hell are we going to get a cat?"

I waited till Lucky looked back at me in confusion before shooting him a wink. His face relaxed into a grin. "Smart-ass," he said, turning back around and heading for the tree line behind the house.

Once he stepped into the trees, he stopped mid-stride and screamed. "Aiiiii! Jesus fuck! Aunt Lolly, god!"

He turned around and smashed his face into my neck, pressing his eyeballs into my skin as if to unsee something.

I glanced over him and saw several naked older folks doing some kind of stretches.

The ringleader was a woman with lovely long white hair. "Lucky, don't be a prude. There's no better way to start a day than with a naked sun salutation. You should try it." She walked closer and I instinctively backed up a step, pulling Lucky with me so he wouldn't fall over.

"We can't," he called.

"Why not? Because you're scared of being nude in nature?" she teased.

"No! In fact, we're, uh, we're going skinny dipping! Same thing, really." He swallowed and stood up, turning only partway so he still wasn't really looking at her. "So we have to go. Sorry to… peep and run, or whatever, but we don't want to, ah, be late."

Another old lady called out, "WHAT DID HE SAY?" at top volume, but Lucky ignored her.

He yanked me back toward the house. I threw a wave over my shoulder in an effort to soften the rapid exit.

"Take us with you!" she called out.

"Pretend like you didn't hear her," Lucky whispered.

As soon as we made our way back around the house, we almost ran Aiden right over.

The attractive man lifted an eyebrow at us. "I thought you were going to the swimming hole."

Lucky threw up his hands in frustration. "We are! We are. Jesus. Why is it anyone's business? Can't a guy just get some… *swimming* action without it being everyone's freaking business?"

He dragged me to my truck, shoved me in the driver's side door, and jumped in the passenger seat.

"Drive."

I glanced over at him. "Where are we going?"

He covered his face with his hands and groaned. "The fucking swimming hole, apparently. Take a left."

As we drove, I could feel Lucky's eyes on me. "What?" I finally asked.

"You were jealous," he said. I could practically hear the grin in his voice. "Earlier. With Aiden."

"Of you and your *uncle*?" I asked, injecting as much disbelief into my tone as I could.

"You didn't remember he was my uncle until after you started talking. Up until then, you looked like you wanted to murder him."

I kept silent, hoping Lucky would drop the whole thing, but then he was settling his hand on my thigh. "It was pretty hot," he said softly.

Lucky's nimble fingers began caressing me through my pants. His hand got frustratingly close to my hard-on but never quite landed.

"Lucky," I growled.

"Yes?" the young man said next to me in all innocence.

"Keep that up and we're not going to make it to that swimming hole."

I glanced at Lucky. His eyes had glazed over and he was licking his lips. "And that's supposed to be a threat how, exactly?"

I found myself laughing. I reached down to grab his wayward hand and lifted it so I could press a kiss to the back of his knuckles. When I was done, I held on to his hand but did so over the console so I wouldn't be too tempted to scrap the whole swimming hole idea and take Lucky in the back seat of my truck.

Lucky sighed and asked, "How was dinner with Jake?"

"Fine," I said. I knew what Lucky really wanted to know—whether I'd told Jake the truth about why I'd left the military. Since I didn't want to disappoint him with the truth, I added, "Jake and I drank some homemade ale he made. It tasted like jet fuel. I overdid it so I slept on the couch. I sent you some texts but they kept coming back as failed because of the reception."

Lucky glanced at his phone and began looking at my messages. His smile widened with every one that he read. I remembered how frantic I'd felt when I'd realized there was no way to let him know I was spending the night with my brother. Lucky was already so on edge about me leaving him...

The reminder had me focusing on the road instead of the man next to me. I followed Lucky's directions out of town and down a quiet winding road until he pointed to a packed-dirt pull-off.

"Come on," he said. "Do you still have any of those water bottles in the back?" He began rooting around in the back seat until he came up with an old beach towel and a couple of water bottles. "Perfect."

I followed him along a narrow trail through the woods until we came to a wide stream rushing with clear water. "This is nice. How come more people aren't here?"

Lucky turned back to me. "There's a huge waterfall about two miles farther down with a bigger swimming hole at the bottom. Everyone goes there instead. This one never has anyone in it. It's small, but private."

He turned back around and reached over his shoulder to pull at his T-shirt, yanking it over his head and revealing the flawless skin of his back. As he followed the riverbank to an area where it widened and deepened into a swimming hole, he continued pulling off articles of clothing.

I almost tripped over every obstacle in my path since I couldn't take my eyes off the free strip show.

"What are you doing?" I asked.

He turned back toward me after arriving at a large boulder and setting his clothes down. "Skinny dipping. With you."

Lucky shucked off his boxer briefs and turned back toward the water, showing me the pale skin of his luscious ass below the darker tan line of his lower back. Good god.

I looked around frantically, wondering if anyone could see him from any vantage point. When I realized no one was around, I wondered if I could fuck him right here in the woods. My dick was way too hard to undress without becoming a spectacle.

"Lucky," I croaked.

He stepped into the water before turning to face me. His flaccid cock and heavy sac hung between his muscular thighs. The neatly trimmed patch of dark curls above it made me wonder if he ever thought of me when he pulled out his clippers.

"Take off your clothes, old man," he teased. "It's just us boys out here."

I pulled off my shirt and tossed it on top of his clothes on the rock. "Don't forget old men know how to spank naughty boys," I warned, stalking closer.

His laugh was light and open. He looked so damned carefree and at home here in the woods near his home. I watched as he navigated the slippery rocks out to the center of the stream before making his way closer to the deeper swimming area. He was a natural.

As I finished removing the last of my clothes, I watched him swan dive off a rock into the dark blue depths of the swimming hole, his nude body catching the dappled sunlight as it arced through the air.

I raced to the edge of the water to make sure he hadn't hit his head or gotten tangled in any debris. But his head popped up right away, revealing a wide grin full of white teeth.

"Come on in, the water's great!"

I strode in without questioning him and screeched to the heavens the minute the frigid water reached my balls.

"Fuck!"

His laughter almost made it worth it. I turned to make my way out of the ice bath, but Lucky grabbed my wrist and yanked me all the way in. I splashed down next to him, completely submerging myself in the glacial runoff.

"Jesus," I sputtered when I came up for air. "Do you hate me? This is horrible."

He continued to laugh as he grabbed me and wrapped his lithe body around mine. My hands automatically went to his sexy ass and held on.

I leaned in and kissed his purple lips. "You're frozen," I murmured against his mouth.

"Warm me up," he said back.

We made out in the water, making our way over to a submerged rock at the edge so we had something to sit on. By the time we finished feeling each other up, we were more used to the awful temperature of the water and able to swim around to warm up even more. We teased and splashed and flirted for who knew how long until I realized Lucky's phone was ringing.

"I think your phone is ringing." It was muffled under all the clothes, but it seemed like the third or fourth time I'd heard the same sound.

He shrugged and ignored it until it happened again. We both made our way out of the water and shared the towel to dry off enough to get dressed again. Once Lucky had his shorts back on, he pulled his phone from the pocket and frowned at it. Suddenly, the phone was shaking in his hand as he tried to dial.

"It's Bennett," he said, putting the phone to his ear. "Five missed calls."

I finished putting my shoes on and moved to help Lucky do the same as he began talking to his father. By the time he got off the call, we were halfway back to the truck Lucky was practically running by then.

"Lucky, what is it?" I asked as I grabbed his arm to keep him from tumbling over a large log.

His voice was shaky as he said, "It's Xander. He got called in on a search for a missing child early this morning. How the hell didn't I know that was happening? I could have helped."

I could tell there was more to the story, so I took Lucky's hand in mine and led him back to the truck. I unlocked it and opened the passenger door for him. "Did they find the kid?"

Lucky's hand carded through his damp hair repeatedly. "Yes. But he fell into a sinkhole and can't get out. It's near some snowmelt runoff and the water is making the whole area even more unstable. Xander rappelled down to the little boy but then the tree he was anchored to fell over, cutting off easy access to drop another rope. We're not sure how injured Xander is from the fall since he's a stubborn asshole. Bennett's beside himself with worry. I've never heard him that scared, Zach," Lucky admitted. The near terror in Lucky's voice was proof that his father wasn't the only one who was scared. I closed my fingers around Lucky's.

"He'll be okay, baby," I said.

Lucky nodded but it was clearly forced.

When I started the truck and pulled onto the road, Lucky stared out the window. He was tapping his foot incessantly. "I can't," he finally said.

"Can't what?" I asked as Lucky began tapping at his phone before holding it up to his ear.

"Bennett wants me to go home but I can't just sit there waiting to hear something." Lucky's whole body tensed when his call went through. "Chaska, shit, I'm glad I caught you. Can you—" He paused while listening to the man on the other end. "Fuck! Why...? Never mind, congratulations. I can... No, no. I have a pilot. I just need a helicopter with the right equipment."

He listened some more, pointing with a long index finger when I needed to turn onto a different road. I had no idea where we were heading, but I knew better than to argue with him during an emergency involving his family.

"Chas, he's a licensed SAR pilot, longline certified, and... shit. Chas, dude, he's an instructor. He's *my* instructor." The man on the other end continued to speak, presumably to argue with Lucky about why he couldn't lend us whatever helicopter Lucky was asking about. Lucky cut him off when he whispered, "Chas, it's my dad. He's trapped in Foxfire Gulch. We both know how long it will take a SAR team to get here from Denver. Xander doesn't have that kind of time." Lucky's voice cracked with his last sentence. I reached across the console and wrapped my fingers around Lucky's free hand. He kept his eyes downcast but his hold on my hand bordered on painful.

"Thanks, man, I owe you," Lucky said softly before disconnecting the call. He barely paused before dialing again.

"Dad, I'm headed to Chaska's. Zach and I are going to get Xander using one of his helicopters, okay? Just hang tight."

I could hear Bennett's shouted tone through the phone, but Lucky cut him off. "Dad, there's no time to explain but I can do this. You need to trust me." His voice was suddenly steady and firm. "I'm certified in airborne search and rescue. So is Zach. We're going to get him back. I promise you."

He hung up while Bennett was still shouting on the other end, and I wasn't clear on whether Lucky had ended the call to protect himself from Bennett's strong emotions or to focus on the task at hand. Either way, I needed him to know I had his back.

"Who's Chaska and can I trust his bird?"

Lucky turned to me and let out a breath. "Yes. Turn right here and pull into the gravel parking area. Chas is the closest thing to a search and rescue pilot we have. He normally runs short flights to Denver for charter and medical emergencies, but when anyone goes missing, he'll take the chopper up and search from the air."

"Then why do you need a pilot?" I pulled into the spot he'd directed me to and hopped out of the truck.

Lucky turned to walk backwards toward a small building next to a helipad. "Because last night his daughter gave birth to their first grandchild and he went out and got shitfaced. Are you going to help me or not, Zach?! Fuck, I don't have my jump bag."

Before Lucky could take another step, I quickened my stride and grabbed his arm. "Listen to me and listen good," I said in a no-nonsense voice. Lucky's body was shaking violently but he kept his mouth shut as his eyes met mine.

"Xander is going to be okay, do you hear me? I know you're scared for him, but you need to put that away right now and focus on the job at hand because fear has no place up there." I pointed at the sky. "Now tell me what you need to do next."

Lucky pulled in a deep breath. "Get the equipment and check everything twice," he said. He pulled in another breath.

"Good, now go," I said. "I'm going to do my walkaround." I gave Lucky's fingers a squeeze and then followed him to the helipad and began inspecting the exterior of the bird while he ducked inside the building to check in with Chas. Thankfully, it was the same model as one I'd flown in the army and everything looked familiar. After checking it out, I made my way inside and introduced myself to the older man in charge and began asking questions about his maintenance protocol, insurance coverage, and rescue equipment. He asked for a copy of my license, and I emailed everything over to him from my phone.

It only took a few minutes, but by the time we were ready to load up, Lucky was bouncing nervously on his feet.

"Deep breath," I reminded him. "Remember that these procedures are in place for a reason."

"I know that! Fuck, Zach. Just do it. Stop talking about it." He threw himself into the back of the helicopter and began organizing equipment.

I didn't blame him for his anger and frustration, but it was something I'd need to make sure was completely gone by the time he hooked on the line. There was nothing more dangerous for all involved than a distracted rescuer. Chas was on the radio with the park service, and I realized we needed an updated weather report before we headed out. Finally we were ready to lift off.

"Strap in," I called to Lucky through the radio. "Remember, you're not getting on that line without an emergency pack. When we land at the loading area, I want you to strap it on and make sure there's a handheld radio in it."

"Got it."

I already knew from a follow-up call to Bennett that Xander only had his phone with limited cell reception. So far, he'd only been able to get texts out. The rest of the search crew was about two hundred yards away, but they couldn't get any closer because of the soft, wet ground and the evaporite rock in that area.

We landed half a mile away in a clearing where some emergency vehicles had gotten as close as possible to the site. Bennett was there with several other men, including my brother.

"Jake's here," I told Lucky in case he didn't see him in the group. "He'll have a jump bag and all the medical kits." Thank god Jake was a doctor. If one of the victims was injured, Jake would be ready to treat them as soon as we pulled them out.

Once we landed, Bennett and Jake approached. Jake offered to help prep the longline when he realized what we were doing, but Bennett was quick to pull Lucky aside.

"You're not going up there," he shouted to Lucky over the noise of the rotors. "I know you've done some search and rescue, Lucky, but this is different. This is serious."

"I know," Lucky said while connecting the belly band and triple-checking the equipment. I took the opportunity to clip an extra harness onto the back of his equipment belt as well as a coil of rope he could use to make another one if needed.

"Lucky," Bennett pleaded. "You can't just insert yourself into this situation when the danger is—"

Lucky turned and put both hands on Bennett's shoulders, meeting his eyes. "Dad. I'm a certified longline rescuer. I've completed advanced training in airborne alpine rescue. I know it's hard for you to believe me, but I need you to trust me right now. I need to go now before the ground becomes even more unstable or we lose more access. But I swear to you, I *am* going to get him out of there."

Bennett's pale face was lax in disbelief as he continued to hang on to Lucky's arm with an iron grip. It was Jake who interceded. He put his hand on Bennett's shoulder. "Come on, B. Let's let them work. My brother knows what he's doing. This is what he did in the army."

Bennett spared Jake a glance but then he shook his head and I could see the terror in his eyes. Even if he'd managed to mentally process what Lucky had told him, he still knew the risks. He was essentially being asked to risk his son's life to save his husband's. It was an impossible choice.

"Dad," Lucky said gently. "You have to let me go."

"Can't," he croaked and then he was looking at Jake, then me. I could see the tears welling in his eyes. "Keep him safe!" he demanded.

I wanted to tell him that I'd give my own life before I let anything happen to Lucky but chose to nod instead. "I will," I promised.

Bennett shifted his eyes back to his son and I had no doubt he was finally seeing Lucky the man instead of Lucky the boy. He quickly snatched Lucky up into a death grip of a hug before releasing him and backing away so we could finish up. When it was time to go, I checked Lucky's connection to the line again and lifted his chin with my finger. "You've got this. *We* have this. Don't forget your training. I know it's going to be hard, but you need to think of this as any other rescue, okay?"

He nodded. "I can do this, Zach. I have to do this."

"I know, baby," I said softly, wanting to kiss him so fucking badly to make sure he knew he wasn't alone. But the best thing I could do for him was to get this bird in the air and rescue his father. "Let's go."

As I began to lift off, I tried my hardest not to notice Bennett's horrified face when he realized Lucky was being lifted into the air as external human cargo. I followed the coordinates the rescuers had called in and within moments, we could see the downed tree across part of a large open hole in the ground and the group of colorful rescuers standing a couple hundred feet away.

Slinging him down into that hole without a spotter wasn't going to be easy, but then again, real-life airborne rescue rarely was. As I steadied the line over the exposed hole in the ground, I listened to Lucky's descriptions in an effort to spot for himself.

We moved slowly, making sure not to tangle the line in the branches of the fallen tree as he moved past it. I felt sweat roll down my back into my pants as I worked to keep the helicopter as steady as possible.

"Hold!" Lucky called through my earpiece. It was much easier said than done. I could hear Lucky talking to Xander and the emotion in his voice made my jaw tighten. "Zach, he's hurt."

"Status of injuries," I requested so I could relay the information back to Jake. Why the fuck hadn't I insisted Jake ride with us? The extra couple of minutes could make a difference depending on the injuries.

Lucky paused and came back with a stronger voice. "Xander's injuries include: possible head injury, dislocated left shoulder, probably broken ribs, probable broken femur, and several minor lacerations to hands and face. The child is a six-year-old male suffering from suspected dehydration, exposure, and possible shock. Several scrapes and bruises, but no suspected broken bones."

"Strap in the child and let's get him out of here," I said. "The sooner we get the boy back to Jake, the sooner we can return for Xander."

I could hear him talking to the child as he presumably strapped him into a harness and connected him to himself and the line. He gave his emergency pack to Xander and called for me to begin the lift. I heard Xander tell his son he loved him and to be careful, but whatever Lucky said in response was lost on me because I was focused on the delicate process of lifting Lucky and his human cargo.

This time I went even more slowly, trying to keep the line as far away from the sharp branches of the tree as possible. Lucky had a good sense of direction as he called out instructions to me over comms. When they were finally free of the hole in the earth, I could see the rescuers jumping up and down in the distance to cheer us on.

Getting the little boy out was only half the battle. Trying to lift two grown men through the small opening would be even more challenging. I could only hope the weather stayed calm and clear.

We landed very carefully in the clearing and Jake immediately approached to take the child from Lucky. I noticed a pickup truck pull up at the edge of the clearing and a crying woman come racing out of it to meet the child. Chaska had mentioned the child's parents being at the rescue site, so I assumed it had taken them some time to get brought over here to meet up with the boy.

As soon as he was free of the victim, Lucky called for me to take off again. Bennett stood at the edge of the group with his hands in front of his mouth. He still looked terrified, and I didn't blame him. Head injuries were serious and time to treatment was critical. I'd learned that from Lucky during our training, so I knew he'd be conscious of it every second Xander was delayed from critical care.

Once we hovered over the sinkhole again I noticed a light mist on the windshield. I didn't mind the mist, but I hoped to hell it didn't bring any wind with it. One light gust could send Lucky swinging into those tree branches and tangle the line, endangering everyone involved.

"Hold!" Lucky shouted through my earpiece. He wasn't low enough yet to have reached Xander.

"What is it?" I asked.

"Pull up! Pull up!"

I didn't stop to question the command, I simply pulled the bird straight up just in time to see the motion of another tree falling at the edge of the sinkhole. Lucky must have noticed it coming loose from the soft ground.

Cold sweat poured off me as I realized how close he'd come to being hit or trapped by it. "Status," I demanded.

"Yeah. Clear. Fine. Fuck, that was close. Go again."

The image of that tree taking Lucky off the line kept replaying in my mind. If he hadn't noticed it because he'd been more focused below him on Xander's position instead of keeping an eagle eye on his surroundings...

"We need to reassess," I said.

"No. Go again. We're clear."

"It's protocol to reassess hazards, Lucky. We need to—"

For the first time since getting on the line, Lucky's voice broke in my ear.

"Zach, please. I have to get to him... please. He's my dad. The ground was shifting beneath him even as we spoke. We're running out of time."

"Zach! Zach, get him out of here!" I heard Xander call as his voice came through on the comms.

"No!" Lucky shouted. "Lower me, Zach. I can do this!"

The lump in my throat prevented me from responding right away as my conscience warred with itself. I knew Xander wanted me to do whatever it took to keep Lucky safe, even at the cost of his own life, but could I really let an innocent man die just to ensure Lucky lived? Xander was as biased as I was, if not more so. I leaned over to put my eyes on Lucky, nothing but a red jacket and white helmet hanging far below. My heart pounded in my chest, whatever part of it wasn't dangling from that fucking line, anyway.

"Zach..." Lucky said more softly over the comms. It was what I didn't hear that had me hyper-focused on him. There was no panic or desperation in his voice as he said just my name again. He sounded every bit the professional he was. And right now what he needed was his pilot to trust him and follow his commands so this rescue mission could be completed.

"Prepare to drop," I said through my teeth. "Let me know when ready."

CHAPTER 30

LUCKY

"Ready."

I breathed a sigh of relief that Zach wasn't aborting the mission. My father continued to call across the radio in a desperate effort to get Zach to change his mind.

"Dad," I said. I had to repeat myself three times before Xander finally fell silent. "Dad, I'm coming down, so I need you to keep the line clear. I need to be able to give Zach directions."

"Lucky," my father murmured. Despite the noise of the helicopter, I could hear how tired he sounded. I hadn't really had much chance to talk to him when I'd gone in to get the kid out and I doubted my father had really had a chance to process that it had been me on the rescue line at the time.

"Dad, I can see things from up here that you can't. I promise you, I can get us both out safely. I need you to trust me."

"Dropping," Zach interrupted quietly. It was a reminder that I needed to focus.

"I'll see you soon, Dad, okay?"

My father didn't answer, but I tried not to focus on what that could possibly mean.

Zach had much less room to work with this time, and I knew lowering me into the narrow open area without a spotter was like trying to thread a needle with a helicopter. When he finally got me down to where Xander lay in the mud below, I called for Zach to hold. The longline disappeared above me into the daylight, and I lost sight of the helicopter I was attached to.

"Dad," I called, stepping over to where he lay in a heap on the ground.

"Lucky?" he croaked, blinking his eyes open. Since he'd been talking to me only a few minutes earlier, he was clearly disoriented which only confirmed his probable head injury. We needed to get him to the hospital.

I checked his vitals as quickly as I could and explained what I was doing as I strapped him into the harness. Every time he yelped or winced in pain, I felt a tightening in my chest. If I tried using a Stokes litter, we'd never be able to get him out of here before another tree fell or more of the ground caved in.

"This is going to hurt like a bitch," I warned.

"Language," he said automatically.

I smiled and hooked him onto the line, holding him tightly and trying to keep his shoulder from being jostled. "I promise to put a dollar in the swear jar when we get home," I said.

"Your dad—your dad and I will be able to take that vacation now," Xander tried to joke.

"Something tells me that after this, Dad's not going to let you out of his sight or out of bed for a while."

"From your mouth to God's ears," Xander murmured tiredly.

"Dad, I need you to stay awake," I urged as I patted his face. When his eyes opened, I added, "And gross, by the way."

Xander managed a small laugh. The ground suddenly shifted beneath us.

"Lucky, it's going!" Zach called just as I snapped myself onto the line.

"Ready to lift!" I called through the comms in my helmet.

I wrapped my arms around my father as the earth around us seemed to disappear before our very eyes. It made it difficult to determine how high Zach had gotten us lifted. It seemed to take forever for us to clear the sinkhole, but once we were fully airborne again and heading back to where Jake and Bennett were waiting, I started to breathe easier.

Until I realized Xander had slipped into unconsciousness. *Airway, breathing, circulation.* I checked frantically for breath sounds and a pulse, finding both despite the difficulties of our position. I shouted to Zach to hurry up.

"He's non-responsive! Dad! Dad! Please wake up. Stay with me." Xander's eyes fluttered open. He looked so pale, but at least he was back with me. "Oh, fuck. Thank god. Don't do that to me. Stay with me. We're almost there."

Zach finally set us down carefully in the clearing where emergency vehicles and Bennett waited. As soon as we were safely on the ground, Jake and Bennett came running out to help, followed by medical first responders with a stretcher. Zach set the helicopter down and shut down the rotors so he could join us outside.

The first responders called out to Zach. "We're loading him up with you. Haven County Med is expecting him. Helipad in the northwest corner of the parking lot. They're already waiting to guide you in."

Zach hopped back in immediately and started up the rotors again. As soon as Jake and I got Xander loaded into the back and Bennett was hovering over him, I closed the bay door and hopped in the co-pilot's seat. "Let's go. I'll guide you there."

It was the longest twenty minutes of my life. Between telling Zach where to go and listening to Jake assess my father and communicate his condition to the hospital, there was no way to tune out Bennett's sobs as he begged Xander to keep his eyes open. I heard all the little stories Bennett told Xander to try and keep him awake—the kind of stories that seemed inconsequential but were the truest representation of a relationship. I wanted desperately to reach across the console

CHAPTER 31

ZACH

"Any news?" Oz and Ash, each holding a baby in their arms, were waiting to greet me when I stepped into Xander and Bennett's house and both uttered the same question at the same time.

"Xander's in surgery," I said. "That's the last I've heard. Jake called me just as I was leaving the hangar."

Both men looked crestfallen. "Yeah, he called us too," Ash said. "We were hoping you'd heard more."

I shook my head. "He did ask me to stop here and grab a change of clothes for Bennett, Lucky, and Xander."

Oz nodded and reached for a bag on a small table by the front door. "Here, we put some stuff together. Tell Bennett the babies are good." Oz lifted the baby in his arms a bit.

"Where's Aiden?" I asked as I reached for the bag. As tired as I was, I really just wanted to get back to the hospital to check on Lucky. I'd tried calling him only to discover he'd left his phone in my truck.

"He went to pick Xander's aunt Lolly up to take her to the hospital," Ash responded.

I nodded. "If I hear anything else, I'll call you," I said.

Oz leaned in to give me a half-hug. "Tell that brother of yours to come home to me as soon as he can," he said softly.

"I will," I assured him. I turned to go when an unfamiliar voice called out from behind me.

"Um, excuse me."

I turned and saw a young man standing awkwardly in the doorway leading to the kitchen. "Did you say you're going to the hospital?"

"Yeah," I said in confusion as I glanced at Oz and Ash.

"Zach, this is a friend of Lucky's from when they were kids."

The man stepped forward, hand extended. "Calvin, sir. But everyone calls me Cal these days."

I guessed the man to be about the same age as Lucky, possibly a little older. Although he was wearing a relatively sedate outfit, jeans and a white button-up shirt, the tattoos peeking out from beneath his clothes in various spots along with the small gauges in his ears made him seem out of place. His dark hair was shorn short and while he was on the tall side, he looked skinny.

"Cal and Lucky knew each other before Lucky came here to live with Bennett and Xander," Ash interjected. Something in the way he said the words was off and when I looked back at Cal, he'd dropped his eyes.

"Would it be too much trouble to get a ride with you?" Cal asked. "To the hospital, I mean."

"Cal got here about an hour ago," Oz said. "He's been... *eager* to see Lucky since he heard about the accident."

"I don't want to cause any problems," Cal interjected before I could speak. "And I..."—Cal began rifling through his pockets—"could probably pitch in for gas money." He pulled out a couple of dollars and some change. Color flooded his cheeks when he looked up at us. "I, uh—"

"It's fine," I interrupted. Although I had my suspicions about the guy, I didn't want to embarrass him. "We need to get going, though," I said to him.

"Yes, of course," Cal said. "Thank you, sir," he added as he reached down to grab a backpack off the floor.

"Zach," I said. "Call me Zach."

Cal nodded and hurried to follow me as I said my goodbyes to Oz and Ash and left the house. The guy kept to himself once we were in the truck. That fact should have made me happy but I soon found myself asking, "So how do you know Lucky?"

Cal actually jerked in his seat like he'd forgotten I was there. His frame was stiff as he shifted his gaze from the windshield to the passenger side window and back again.

"Um, we went to school together a long time ago."

"So you're from around here?" I asked.

Cal glanced at me, then shook his head. "No. It was back when he still lived in New York. Before B... I mean, Mr. Crawford, took him in."

I considered what Lucky had told me about his childhood. He hadn't exactly had an easy time of it as a kid. Something about the guy sitting next to me told me he hadn't either. It was the way in which he held himself. He was trying to appear relaxed but was failing miserably.

"So you know Bennett too," I prodded.

Cal lifted a hand to his mouth so he could chew on his fingernails. It was such an odd gesture for someone of his age. I wondered if he was even aware he was doing it.

"Yeah, B... Mr. Crawford ran this group to help poor kids. He brought a bunch of us out here to learn about nature and stuff."

"That sounds pretty cool," I responded.

Cal was silent for a long time. "It was," he finally said wistfully. Something about how Cal was holding himself made me decide to back off. We rode the rest of the way to the hospital in silence. After parking the truck, we made our way inside.

"They're in the surgery waiting room," I told Cal. The young man nodded and in his eagerness to see Lucky, presumably, ended up walking several feet ahead of me. When we got to the elevator, I hesitated.

"You coming?" Cal asked as he held the door with his hand.

"I'll take the stairs," I murmured. I'd never been a fan of enclosed spaces even before I'd left for the army. I was even less of one after the attack in the small room that had left my teammates dead.

I took the stairs two at a time despite the ache in my knee. I knew I wouldn't be able to embrace Lucky the way I wanted, but just seeing him and knowing he was hanging in there would be enough until I could get him alone.

It only took a few minutes to reach the floor I was looking for, but the scene I walked in on as I reached the waiting room was completely unexpected. Lucky was standing just outside the waiting room door like he'd been in the process of exiting the small room. I was so glad to see him that it took me a moment to notice what his eyes were practically glued to.

Calvin.

The young man had just stepped off the elevator and, like Lucky, was standing frozen in place. I couldn't see Lucky's expression, but there was no missing Cal's from my vantage point. He looked both horrified and relieved. He also looked like he couldn't move.

"Calvin?" Lucky said, clearly shocked.

Cal didn't move. He didn't speak. He just stood there like he was made of stone.

I couldn't say how long the pair just stood there like that, but Lucky was the first one to move. His pace was slow and uncertain as he closed the distance between himself and Cal, and I felt this odd need to step between the two men. Whoever Cal was to Lucky, friends wasn't the right term.

Because friends didn't hesitate to approach one another. They didn't look terrified.

"Calvin?" Lucky repeated as he got closer and something in Cal's stance finally changed. His shoulders dropped and the backpack he'd been holding hit the floor with a thud. Even from where I was standing, I could see Cal shaking.

"Calvin," Lucky said again, but this time his voice was entirely different. It was gentle and patient and full of understanding.

"I'm sorry," Cal croaked and then he began to cry. "I'm so sorry, Lucky," he repeated, covering his eyes with his hands.

I was still reeling from the one-eighty in Cal's behavior when Lucky closed the distance between them and, without hesitation, wrapped his arms around Cal. Cal let out a harsh sob, then he was clinging to Lucky.

I had no clue what to make of the scene or how to react to it. I hated that the first thing I felt was jealousy but there it was. I figured the sight of Lucky in any man's arms would probably always provoke that particular emotion for me.

"Hey, you made it," I heard my brother say. I forced myself to tear my eyes from the scene before me and looked at my brother who was stepping out of the waiting room. He was dressed in scrubs.

"Yeah, uh, how's Xander?" I asked.

"He's in recovery," Jake said with a smile. "The surgeons had to put a pin in his leg and one of his ribs perf'd his lung but they were able to fix everything. He'll have to be monitored for a concussion but there's no sign of a brain bleed. Bennett's with him now."

"That's good," I said. I was beyond relieved for Lucky. At the same time, I couldn't bring myself to look at my lover and the young man he clearly had some kind of past with.

"He looks different," Jake murmured. He was looking at Lucky and Cal who were *still* embracing. My fingers fisted on the handle of the bag of clothes.

"You know him?" I asked.

Jake nodded. "I met him briefly when Bennett brought a group of kids out from New York to get the 'real wilderness' experience. That's how he and Xander got back together. Xander was leading the group."

"And Cal?" I asked, trying to keep my voice neutral.

"He was a real thug," Jake said. "Treated Lucky like shit," he added. "No respect for anything, a bully toward most of the kids." Jake sighed. "He wasn't all bad, though. Bennett said Calvin was the reason he found out that Lucky's foster home wasn't safe. I guess something happened between him and Lucky too because Lucky was nursing a broken heart for quite a while after Cal left."

I froze at that. "Lucky was only fifteen on that trip, wasn't he?"

When my brother nodded, my stomach fell out. Lucky had told me he'd had his first kiss when he'd been fifteen. Which meant the person who'd likely given him that kiss was...

It was all I could do not to let out a howl of protest. Never in a million years would I have thought I'd come face to face with the person who had a piece of Lucky I'd never get to have. But to have had him right there in the truck next to me, to have him currently clinging to Lucky like he was never going to let him go...

"Zach," Jake said, interrupting the dark thoughts I was currently having about Cal.

"What?" I snapped.

Jake eyed me as he asked, "You okay?"

I nodded. "Fine," I bit out. "Here," I added as I shoved the bag of clothes at him. I turned on my heel without another word. I'd managed to make it ten steps before Jake caught up to me. He grabbed my arm and bodily dragged me into what appeared to be a supply closet.

"What are you doing?" he snapped. It was so uncharacteristic of my brother to express his anger that I was completely caught off guard.

"Nothing," I responded.

"Really, because it looks to me like you're walking out of here without even letting him know you're here."

"What—"

"Save it, Zach. I'm not stupid. I saw the way you were holding him on the helipad after we got here. Are you going to try and tell me that you were just comforting one of your students?"

I ground my teeth together. "He's practically family," I said. "I was just—"

"No you weren't," Jake interjected. "Saying you look at Lucky like he's family is like saying Oz and I share a bit of brotherly affection."

"I don't know what you're talking about," I said even as heat crawled up the back of my neck.

"I saw you on that hilltop with him just before you went after Xander and the kid. I *heard* you on the radio! And then the helipad... how stupid do you think I am, Zach?"

"He's an adult, Jake," I growled as I crossed my arms.

Jake looked at me like I'd grown two heads. "That's your response?" he asked in disbelief.

"Look, I know this makes it awkward for you and Xander—"

"I don't give a shit about me or Xander or Bennett," Jake spat. "I care about that young boy out there!" he added as he pointed toward the hallway. "That boy who's had feelings for you from the day he met you. That boy who grew into a man and never once looked at you with anything other than stars in his eyes. That *man* who has spent the last hour watching the waiting room door like a hawk because he was waiting for *you* to get here." Jake shook his head. "I thought it was just a crush those first few months, but I knew there was something there long before he was old enough to do anything about it."

"I never touched him, Jake. In fact, I—" I began before snapping my mouth shut.

"You what?"

My skin felt tight and itchy as I looked around the small, dark room. It felt like the walls were starting to close in on me. The only thing keeping me sane was the dim bulb above our heads. "I tried to discourage him. He was eighteen, so he thought..." My voice dropped out as I remembered the Christmas party where Lucky had laid all his feelings out for me to see.

"Jesus," Jake said as he shook his head. "You're what happened to him when he was eighteen. He changed right after Christmas... and you re-enlisted a couple of weeks later."

"Is there a question in there somewhere?" I asked dryly.

Jake studied me like I was a bug under a microscope. "Lucky eventually came back from it, but you didn't. What the hell happened over there, Zach?"

The light above my head flickered. It was all I could do to keep my voice even when I said, "Open the door, Jake."

"No, I'm sick of the 'I'm fine, Jake' routine. I want some answers, damn it."

Jake was holding the door shut with his hand and his foot, though

I knew it would be easy to dislodge both. But the last thing I wanted to do was forcibly move my brother.

"I served my country and I came home," I said simply. "And yes, I fucked Lucky because he wanted it and I had no reason to turn him down. I'm sorry if that hurts your sensibilities, Jake, but it was just two guys hooking up and having some fun—"

I wasn't at all surprised when Jake's fist connected with my jaw. I was actually surprised it had taken him so long to come after me for my crassness. I managed to stay upright, but Jake was no lightweight. My head spun as I tried to maintain my balance. Jake was panting as he stepped back. I wanted him to hit me again, but he only stood there and stared at me like I was a stranger.

The light above us chose that moment to give out, so I shoved past Jake and opened the door.

And came face to face with Lucky.

CHAPTER 32

LUCKY

I didn't bother driving back to my house because even without the phone finder app, I knew he wouldn't be there. I knew from Ash that Zach had gone there long enough to collect his things, but he hadn't told Ash or Oz what had happened at the hospital or where he was going. In fact, neither man had even noticed Zach return to the house and Ash had only seen him when he'd been striding toward his truck, bag in hand.

Which was probably the way Zach had wanted it. I'd already figured out he wasn't a fan of confrontation, especially if the circumstances had anything to do with him. But he was sure as shit getting a confrontation tonight.

I found him at a cheap motel about twenty miles north of Haven. His truck was one of only a few in the parking lot, so it was easy to find a spot for Aiden's rental car in front of the room.

I'd wanted to follow Zach out of the hospital the moment he'd stumbled out of the dark supply closet he'd been fighting with his brother in, but I'd been unwilling to leave until I'd had a chance to see Xander and make sure with my own eyes that he was okay. Luckily, fate had been on my side and there hadn't been any real need to rush after Zach. The extra time had also given me a lot of time to think.

And I had a shit ton to think about.

Between Cal's surprise arrival, the near miss with my father, and Zach's cruel admission that he'd only been using me for sex, my brain was pretty much at its max. There'd been a tiny part of me that had just wanted to let Zach go because confronting him served no purpose. But on the drive to the little truck stop town of Henryville, I'd come to accept something.

I didn't need to confront Zach for him or for us, but for me.

I climbed out of Aiden's car and strode to the motel room door that looked like it would fall off its hinges as soon as I knocked on the door. The hinges stayed put.

When Zach opened the door, he didn't seem at all surprised to see me. He looked like I felt.

Worn out.

Zach turned on his heel and disappeared into the room, leaving the door open. I followed him in, shutting the door behind me.

Simply put, the place was a dump.

"How'd you find me?" Zach asked. He was sitting on the edge of the bed, his back to me. There was an unopened bottle of whiskey sitting on the nightstand.

"You still have my phone. I used the Find My Phone app on my father's phone to locate it."

Zach reached into the pocket of the jacket he was wearing. He pulled out my phone and studied it for a moment, then reached for the bottle of whiskey. "Sorry you had to come all this way to get it," Zach murmured.

"I didn't come here for the phone. I only used it to find you."

Zach opened the bottle and took a swig of the brown liquid. "No more lessons, kid. You broke the rules."

"Don't need any more lessons," I said. "You've taught me more than enough. In and out of bed." I walked around the bed so I could see his face. "I am curious to know what rule you think I broke, though."

Zach stood, took another swig, then slowly approached me. A few weeks ago, the intimidating move would have had me quaking with fear and excitement. Admittedly there was some excitement because unfortunately there was just no turning off my body's desire for Zach. But I wasn't in the least bit afraid of the man.

"No boyfriends or husbands, current or past," Zach said.

"Calvin," I said with a nod of my head.

"He's the one, right? The first kiss?"

"He is."

I didn't miss the slight tic in Zach's jaw. He took another drink from the bottle, then handed me the phone. "I guess rules are meant to be broken."

"Just like some rules are made up after the fact."

"I didn't—" Zach began, but I cut him off.

"Of course, rules don't mean shit if you don't actually enforce them." I tucked my phone in my pocket.

"I don't under—"

I held up my hand, effectively cutting Zach off again. I ticked off my fingers as I spoke.

"No kissing or sweet words; me having to watch and wait for your order to breathe after I've taken your cock down my throat; you'd come before me, maybe even more than once; on my back, on my knees, or on my stomach for as long and as hard and as fast as you want it." I dropped my hand and stepped closer to Zach so my front was practically pressed up against his. "You've kissed me so many times I have no hope of counting. And I don't know what world you live in, but endearments like baby and sweetheart are, in fact, sweet. You've shoved your gorgeous cock down my throat but go ahead and try to deny that *I'm* in control when that happens. And you've never once made me hold off on my pleasure while you take yours. In fact, I think there've been plenty of times where you've made *me* come more than once before you came."

I stroked my fingers down Zach's sternum. "Oh wait, there was more though. Yeah, that's right, you made sure to explain how we wouldn't be spending the night together and that there wouldn't be a repeat." I paused until I was sure Zach was watching my every move. "I think we both know how those rules turned out. But interestingly enough, there wasn't a thing in there about past and present boyfriends."

Zach's jaw hardened. He lifted the bottle to take another drink, but I intercepted it. I stepped away from him and set it on the table in the room.

"All those rules are supposed to keep the people you're with from developing feelings for you, but I think it's the opposite. I think they're meant to protect you, to keep you from ending up with another Mitch." I turned around and for the first time since I'd stepped into the room, my resolve faltered.

"I only wanted to be with you, Zach. That's all," I admitted. "Pretty stupid, huh?" I felt tears prick the backs of my eyes. "I knew telling you I loved you wouldn't be enough. I had to show you. That asshole said the words to you all the time, I bet. So they don't mean anything. I was so sure you'd feel it every time I touched you. That you'd hear it in my voice and see it in my eyes. I thought if I just had enough time, I could undo what that *man* made you believe about yourself."

The tension in Zach's body was so tight, I was sure he'd shatter into a thousand pieces at any moment.

"What do you want, Lucky?" he asked, the words clipped.

"I wanted you to know that I would have fought for us, Zach. I would have kept our relationship under wraps for as long as you wanted, because I knew it wasn't the same as it was when I was with Davis or any of those other guys. You were never ashamed to be with me and despite what you told your brother, I know what we had wasn't just about sex for you. But you won't fight for us, will you? You trust me to do my job right, but you don't trust me with your heart, do you?"

I wasn't surprised when Zach didn't answer me. Nor was I surprised that he hadn't reacted in any kind of way. There was no emotion in his eyes whatsoever.

And that was how I knew I'd completely lost him.

"Call your brother," I said softly as I searched my pockets for my keys. "Luckily, he doesn't believe any of that bullshit about you using me for sex, but he deserves to know why you keep pushing *him* away."

I turned to go but when Zach softly called my name, my heart flip-flopped crazily in my chest.

"I owe you a kiss goodbye," Zach murmured.

It was all I could do not to lose it right there and then. I doubted Zach was trying to be cruel but whatever his reasoning, it was taking every bit of strength I had left to walk out of that room without begging the man to give me… *us*… another chance.

"New rule, Zach," I said. I couldn't bring myself to look at him as I walked toward the door. "Kiss me because you want to, not because you have to."

I paused at the door, hoping beyond hope that Zach would appear at my side or I'd feel the length of his body along my back, but when there was nothing but stale air, I hurriedly left the room without looking back. But not before the words I'd never been allowed to say out loud to Zach had slipped free.

"I love you, Zach."

It was a struggle to get in the car without falling apart after that. I saved that moment for when I was a good mile from the motel and I was able to find a deserted access road to pull into. As I let the tears coast down my face, I once again asked myself the same question that had been plaguing me from the moment I'd borrowed my uncle's car to go after the man who would always hold the biggest piece of my heart.

Why can't you just fight for us, Zach?

CHAPTER 33

ZACH

I was aware of Jake long before I saw him. It had always been that way, even when we'd been kids. People had always likened it to the sixth sense twins had, but I chalked it up to the fact that I'd spent most of my childhood with my big brother. And when I hadn't been with him, I'd known where he was. My parents had thought it was cute but it had become this strange sense of self-preservation for me. I hadn't had many friends when I'd been growing up, but Jake had been that one constant in my life who'd always been exactly what I'd needed. Friend, brother, parent, protector, earpiece... the list went on and on. When he'd been missing, it was like a part of me had been gone too. But in the past couple of years, I'd tuned out that connection.

So as I worked on the cabin being renovated, I wasn't really sure what kind of response I'd get when Jake reached me. But simply put, I'd had no place else to go. After leaving the hospital, my intent had been to just go... to put Lucky and Jake in my rearview mirror and move on.

But there'd been no place to move on to.

And truth be told, if I'd really wanted to escape, I could have done a lot better than stopping at the first crappy motel I'd found a mere twenty miles from Haven.

The plan had been to drink myself into a deep sleep and then try to deal with things in the morning, but then Lucky had shown up and blown those plans to hell. He had a way of doing that.

Everything he'd said had been spot on. I hadn't meant any of the shit I'd said to Jake about using Lucky for sex. I'd just wanted to escape my brother's questions because I'd been too afraid I might actually answer them with the truth.

I'd thought I'd have the strength to pick up and go the next morning, but when the motel manager had come the next day to remind me it was past checkout time, I'd thrown him enough cash for another night. The next day I'd done the same thing. We were closing in on a week now, and I still had all my things in that disgusting little room surrounded by pizza boxes and empty liquor bottles.

No answers had been forthcoming, though. Just like there'd been no desire to get in my truck and head north or east or south. I'd picked up my phone dozens and dozens of times with the intent of reaching out to Lucky, but I'd never hit send on any of the texts I'd created.

My body had finally decided it was time for my head to stop feeling sorry for itself this morning, and after what had to be the longest shower in the history of the world, I'd gotten in my truck and driven the only direction my brain would let me.

West.

Back to Haven.

Well, Haven adjacent anyway.

"Here," I heard Jake say, then he was tapping my shoulder with something. I glanced over and spied a coffee mug that said Don't Hate Me Because I'm Fabulous.

"It's not that weird tea crap Oz tried to make me drink the other morning, is it?" I asked as I carefully sniffed the top of the cup.

"Nah, it's the good stuff. Two creams, no sugar, right?"

I nodded and took a sip of the coffee. I couldn't help but remember the times Lucky had brought my coffee to the bedroom in the mornings during our last few days in Glacier.

"Did I wake you?" I asked as I held up the hammer I'd been using to nail down floorboards in Jake and Oz's rental cabin.

Jake shook his head. "Not me, but be warned that a certain fashion designer was making plans for his latest live model," my brother said with a small smile. "He's thinking about designing women's lingerie."

I chuckled and set the hammer down, then stood so I could lean against the makeshift workbench in the room.

"How's the…" Jake began as he motioned to his own face. He was pointing to the position of the bruise on my jaw, the one he'd given me.

I shrugged. "I'll survive," I said.

Jake sighed. I could see he was already frustrated with my lack of response.

"The light in that room we were in was flickering," I began.

Jake was clearly confused. "What, in the storeroom at the hospital?"

I nodded. "I knew it was going to go out, so I wanted to get out of there. But I also knew you weren't going to stop until you got some answers."

Jake hadn't moved since I'd begun talking. His entire frame tensed up when understanding dawned.

I shrugged. "It's not the dark on its own, though I'm not really a fan of that either. It's the combination of sudden light and loud sounds." I hesitated and took a sip of the coffee before adding, "Let's just say those storms we used to race outside to watch aren't really my thing anymore."

"When?" Jake asked. "When did it happen?"

"During my last deployment."

"Are you getting treatment?"

I shook my head. "No, but I know I need to look into it now. It's not going to go away on its own."

"Is that why you haven't been coming back to visit?"

"Among other things," I said with a nod.

"Lucky," Jake offered.

"I never touched him, Jake. Not until I ran into him again in Montana."

"But you wanted to."

I sighed and set the cup down on the workbench. "Not at first. He was a kid, for god's sake. But then he got older, and I found myself starting to feel things I shouldn't..."

"Is that why you re-enlisted?"

I returned to the section of flooring I'd been working on, since I needed to keep my hands busy. "There were a lot of reasons," I said.

Jake continued to lob questions my way, and I did my best to answer them. Before long, he was working on the floor next to me. It made it easier to tell him about the incident that had gotten me discharged from the army, the offer from Tag, and the encounters with Lucky. It was only when the topic of Mitch came up that I found myself shutting down. The idea of telling my big brother what I'd let Mitch do to me made me physically ill. But my brother was a smart man and instead of pushing me, he suggested a lunch break instead.

By the time the sun started to fall, we'd finished putting down the subfloor in the cabin next to Jake and Oz's. My brother's husband had kept himself scarce, claiming to be busy preparing for some kind of party the following day, so it was just me and Jake watching the sunset over the horizon from the porch steps, some of his homemade beer in hand.

"I don't deserve him," I finally blurted when Jake failed to bring up any mention of Lucky.

"I think he's the only one who gets to decide that," Jake responded.

"He's got his entire future ahead of him. He's young and smart and sweet and, and... and what the fuck would he want with an old, broken-down solider anyway?" I snapped.

"Yep, you're probably right."

"About which part?" I asked.

"The, uh, young part?" Jake suggested.

"I'm right that he's younger than me?"

Jake nodded firmly. "Yes, you are one hundred percent right. He's younger than you."

I snatched Jake's beer to see if he'd already drunk the whole thing. It was actually fuller than mine. I shoved it back at him. "In case you missed it, *brother*, I'm looking for some advice here."

Jake side-eyed me. "Are you seriously asking me, the man who almost lost the most amazing man on the planet, to tell you to buck up and not be a selfish idiot?"

"But you didn't lose him," I pointed out.

"Yeah, because he wouldn't let me go. Unlike me, Oz has his shit together. When he wants something, he goes after it. I'd say Lucky's the same. Just make sure you don't do something stupid like blowing him off when he decides to give you a second chance."

I flinched at that. Jake stopped mid-sip and looked at me. "You didn't," he said.

"I thought I was doing the right thing," I growled.

"But then you realized how foolish you were being and you at least texted or called him, right?"

I turned my head to glance at the cabin that we'd been working on. "You know, you could easily add a bedroom. Might make it easier to rent it out. If you need some help with it, I could maybe, you know…"

"Zach, why do you think Oz and I waited so long to renovate the damned thing? We already know who we want to live there."

I glanced at Jake and saw him looking at me pointedly.

I found myself smiling because I hadn't even considered that my brother might want me around after everything I'd put our family through. But staying in Haven after I'd so spectacularly driven Lucky out of my life… I stared at my beer and began shaking my head. "I don't—"

"Oz!" Jake called over his shoulder. Their ugly little hairless dog began barking just inside the door.

"What are you doing?" I asked.

"Calling for reinforcements," Jake said.

I laughed. "The old Jake wouldn't have had any problem convincing me to move in next door."

293

My brother looked at me like I'd grown a second head. "Seriously? That"—he pointed to the cabin—"will have your name on the deed inside of a week, I guarantee it."

"Then what are the reinforcements for—"

"Yeah?" Oz called. He had a piece of sparkly fabric in his hand. He automatically dropped down onto Jake's lap and stole a sip of his beer. "He agree to take it?" he asked.

"Pffft, as if there were ever any doubt," Jake responded.

Oz nodded his head like it was a ridiculous notion.

"Lucky stopped by to give this dolt a second chance and Genius here doesn't take him up on it *and* he doesn't call or text afterwards. Go."

With every word Jake spoke, Oz got more and more tense. When my brother was finished, Oz was shaking his head at me. He began clicking his tongue.

"Okay, yes, I fucked up," I said. I tapped my fingers on the beer bottle.

"Oh honey," was all Oz said right before a gleam entered his eyes and he began twining his fingers together like some old cartoon villain.

Oh, hell, this can't be good.

CHAPTER 34

LUCKY

I started off the Fourth of July with a stern talking-to.

At myself.

I was bound and determined to enjoy the day. After four days in the hospital and two on the sofa at home, Xander was thankfully well enough to join everyone for our annual holiday cookout. He'd have to spend the party propped up in a chair with his casted leg elevated, but at least he wasn't on strong pain meds anymore.

After showering and throwing on a pair of shorts and a red, white, and blue T-shirt, I hustled downstairs to help Bennett with the babies. Lola was happily mashing cereal into her face while Danny's entire face lit up as I entered the room.

"Wuck!"

I stared at him as the room went silent around us. Bennett put his hand over his mouth and looked over at Xander who was sitting at the table between the babies with his cast on a stool under the table.

"Did he just...?" Xander asked with a grin.

"First word!" Bennett whooped.

I scooped Danny up from his high chair and grinned at him, feeling the first moment of lightness I'd felt in a week. "That's me, little bro. Lucky. Say it again. Luck-eee."

Bennett scrambled in the junk drawer. "Where's a pencil? I need to write this down. What day is it? Oh, duh. What time is it? Where are the pencils? Why don't we ever have any pencils in here and how many measuring tapes does one house need?"

Xander smiled big and winked at me. "Score one for big brother. I've spent months repeating Dada, Dada, *Dada*, and the first word out of his mouth is Wuck."

I laughed and snuggled the sticky monster against my chest. "Good, smart boy. Takes after me. Isn't that right? Such a smart boy."

"Why thank you," Oz said, breezing in the back door with a white, pink, and turquoise scarf floating behind him from its loose knot at his neck. "But, honey, I am a leeeetle older than you. So, really, it's *you* taking after *me*."

Jake entered behind him rolling his eyes. He held a suspiciously familiar shape under one arm. I noticed our dog Bear's tail thump in the corner of the room despite his continued snores.

"Wuck!" Danny called to Jake, reaching his arms out with a squeal for the ugly mutt the man carried. "Wuck!"

I rolled my eyes and dumped the kid in Xander's lap. "So much for that. I'm equivalent to the family lint ball."

"Hey!" Oz said. "You take that back. Darla is on vacation, so Boo's salon visits are a smidge overdue. It's not our fault."

Jake handed me the skinny little thing before I had a chance to put my defenses up.

"Ew," I said before putting Boo on the floor. Bear's tail thumped faster, betraying his false chill. As soon as Boo pranced over to the big black beast, Bear swiped one giant lick up the side of Boo's face, making the hair disaster even more dire. Boo didn't seem to mind, spinning once, twice, and then settling underneath Bear's chin for a morning nap.

Jake ruffled my hair. "How you doing, kid?"

I shot a glance behind him in the hopes that maybe Zach had come with him. He hadn't. The knot that had been in my chest from the moment I'd walked out of Zach's shitty motel room tightened even more. I wondered how that was even possible.

"Oh, uh, fine." I was enjoying the day. This was me, enjoying the damned day. "Did you bring your bathing suits?"

We always spent a good portion of the day floating on silly cartoon rafts in the lake behind the house before it was time to light up the grill for burgers and hot dogs.

Oz's forehead crinkled with a frown. "Aunt Lolly said we skinny dip on odd years."

"For real?" Cal asked from behind me. He entered the kitchen still looking half-asleep.

"Not for real," Bennett said. "Want some coffee?" Despite the fact that my fathers weren't Calvin's biggest fans, considering the way he'd treated me when we'd both been kids, they'd welcomed him into our home when it'd been clear that he had no place to go. The Calvin who'd shown up unexpectedly in Haven a week earlier was a far cry from the bully I'd thought myself in love with so long ago.

"Yeah, thanks. That'd be great." Cal glanced at me with a soft smile. "You sleep okay on that couch again? I told you I can share or I can take the couch. I feel bad kicking you out of your own room. Don't wanna overstay my welcome either."

Xander glanced at me with an encouraging smile. Cal had been nothing but polite and sweet the entire week, helping with the babies and cleaning up in the kitchen while Xander recuperated. I had to admit, he'd been a godsend.

It was clear he was no longer the insensitive kid I'd known in New York. He'd been the last person I'd expected to see at the hospital the night Xander had gotten hurt. I'd been impatiently waiting for Zach to arrive, so I hadn't had any kind of defenses up when the boy who'd been my first kiss had appeared in the hallway. It'd been something in the way he'd held himself that had told me something was seriously wrong and while he had yet to confirm that or explain what he was doing in Haven, when I'd hugged him that night, he'd sobbed uncontrollably in my arms while whispering the same word over and over into my ear.

Sorry.

"You're fine," I said with a smile. "I've enjoyed the company. It's been kinda fun showing you around Haven. You gave me a good excuse to get out and see everyone and remind them about the party."

And it was true. Entertaining Calvin had at least given me something to distract myself from pining over Zach. And Cal really had been good company. This new version of him was, quite frankly, everything I *should* want in a boyfriend. He was even more handsome than he'd been in high school. He listened when I spoke and always made sure I was comfortable wherever we went. He was the first person to jump up to do a chore when one needed doing. And most of all, he wasn't shy about wanting me, though he'd been careful about expressing his interest in me when we were around people he didn't know.

The corners of his lips turned up in a shy smile as he reached over to squeeze my arm. "I've enjoyed the company too. You know that."

Xander noticed the interaction and winked at me. It was such a corny dad move, I almost rolled my eyes at him. Instead, I cleared my throat and stepped closer to Bennett. "Can I get you some, um, breakfast or something?" I asked Cal.

"I can get it," he said, moving up behind me and brushing against my back as he reached for the fridge door. There was a tiny part of me that kind of wished the spark that should have been there was. Or that my breath quickened anytime he came into a room. I even lingered a moment by the fridge to see if maybe those little offshoots of electricity just needed time to catch up.

Until I caught my dads exchanging amused glances.

Great. All I needed was the two of them matchmaking me right now.

I waited until Cal was halfway through doctoring his coffee before I grabbed the keys to Xander's SUV off the hook by the door. "I'm going to pick up Lolly and those guys. Be back in a bit."

Cal turned around. "Oh. Let me come with you. I can keep you company."

I smiled at him and waved my hand. As much as I enjoyed meeting the new and improved Cal, I needed some time to myself. I supposed it was for grieving or something. Bottom line was that keeping the fake smile plastered to my lips was no easy task. "No need. Be back before you're done with breakfast."

Bennett leaned in to wipe Lola's mouth with a wet cloth. "When you get back, we should already be setting up down by the lake. I told everyone to come earlier this year because of the nap schedules and stuff."

As soon as I was out the door, I blew out a breath and relished the time alone. After Xander had been released from the hospital, he and Bennett had sat me down to ask about the longline rescue stuff. I'd finally told them the truth about not spending my summers at Yellowstone as a tour guide. I'd admitted to becoming trained as a paramedic as well as my ultimate desire to be an alpine search and rescue expert. They'd been understandably upset, but they'd felt much more betrayed by the secret than the decision itself.

"Lucky," Xander had said, "Of course we worry about you. Of course we want you to choose a career where you aren't dangling from a freaking rope over a mountaintop. But—"

Bennett had reached over and squeezed his hand. "But if you hadn't… the three of us wouldn't be sitting here together right now," he'd said softly with a grateful smile. "We're so proud of you."

I'd burst into tears. We'd spent a long time talking. I'd explained how it had started with a simple EMT class and then escalated to more search and rescue technique classes and eventually paramedic training. By the time we finished talking, they'd been clear as a bell.

They wanted me to be happy.

I ran fingers through my hair as I pulled the SUV out of the driveway.

Happy.

The one thing I hadn't told them about was Zach, and that was mostly because I still felt a sense of loyalty to him to keep the relationship we'd had a secret. I had no doubt Xander and Bennett would have eventually come around to the idea of me dating a man who was considerably older than myself, but with Zach's defection, it was a moot point. I thought of Zach and the absolute dead end he presented in my life. I'd been a fool to ever think I could change him or expect him to change for me. That was elementary level bullshit, the kind of thing teen bloggers even warned against in those silly quizzes Minna always made me take.

Top Ten Mistakes Everyone Makes with Their First Crushes.

I laughed out loud. "Number one, expecting him to change."

The song "Truth Hurts" came on the radio, and my laugh cut off as soon as I recognized the beat.

"Number two," I whispered to myself, "he's just not that into you."

Before I slipped into a complete pity party, I reached for the channel dial and spun it away from the stupid Lizzo song. Today was about celebration. I was going to enjoy the day.

Even if it fucking killed me.

I squinted at something in the middle of the road in front of the Haven Hotel.

"Oh for god's sake," I muttered, rolling down the window. "Aunt Lolly, what are you doing?"

She stopped and stared at me. The two dozen balloons she held in one hand bobbed and weaved in the morning sunshine while her other hand held a leash tied to a goat.

"Surprise! Happy Fourth!" Her grin was contagious, and I was thankful she was at least fully dressed. She wore a flowy yellow sundress that reached almost all the way down to her purple flip-flops. "I brought us some meat for the grill."

I blinked at her and then the goat by her side. "No."

She looked at her boyfriend, Steve, in confusion before turning back to me. "But I told Xander I'd bring the main course."

I stared at the goat whose white fur looked as soft as clouds. "Aunt Lolly..."

Steve shifted and I realized he was carrying a large cardboard box with *All-Beef Patties* stamped on the side.

I looked back at the goat. "What... what are we eating, exactly?"

Lolly looked even more confused. "Well, I'm having a veggie burger, but I brought an assortment."

Steve's mother, Wanda, pushed her way out the hotel's front door.

"There you are. I couldn't find you anywhere. I told you to wear a bright color today so I could find you."

I looked back at Lolly's bright yellow dress and the twenty-plus metallic silver star balloons in her hand, but decided against saying anything.

"Let's get going," I said instead, pulling over to the side of the street so I wouldn't block traffic.

"Who's that?" Wanda asked loudly enough for people in Idaho to hear.

"THAT'S LUCKY, MOM," Steve said.

"What's lucky?" she asked.

"HE'S LUCKY," Lolly shouted, pointing at me.

The older woman narrowed her eyes at me. "How so? Is that some kind of innuendo?"

Steve laughed and shook his head, stepping toward the back of the SUV. I shifted the SUV into park before hopping out to help him. Once we loaded the box into the back, Lolly tried stuffing the balloons in. As soon as she got about half of them in, they'd start escaping out my open window and she'd have to start all over again. When we finally had all the burgers, all the balloons, Steve, and his mom loaded into the vehicle, we were left with Aunt Lolly and one fluffy goat.

I put my hands on my hips and looked at Lolly.

"It can sit in my lap," she said hesitantly.

"Tie her to the bumper," Steve suggested, nodding toward Lolly with a straight face. "She can walk."

I looked back at Aunt Lolly. "I think you need a new boyfriend," I whispered before realizing he was referring to the goat.

"WHAT DID HE SAY?" Wanda asked from somewhere behind the balloons.

"The goat!" Steve said. "Tie the goat to the bumper."

"Hey dude!" someone said from across the street. "You know you've got a flat tire, right?"

And that was how we came to arrive terribly late to the party on a tiny spare tire with a fluffy but surprisingly foul-smelling goat sitting on my great-aunt's lap, and silver metallic balloons trailing tendrils of curly ribbon hanging out of the windows.

Bennett's face was one giant "O" shape of surprise, Xander's maniacal smile made me wonder if he'd gone back on the good pills, and Oz's tiny American flag thong bathing suit looked downright tame, all things considered.

"We're here," I said, dropping the keys on the ground and heading straight for the nearest cooler of beer. I didn't care if I wasn't technically old enough to drink. I'd aged ten years since I'd left there that morning.

As soon as I passed through the crowd of friends, family, and townsfolk and plucked a cold bottle of beer out of the cooler, I twisted off the top and took a long swig. Cal walked up with a big smile. "Aww," he said, reaching to pull me in his arms. "You look like you could use more than a beer. How about a hug?"

I laughed and clutched him back. "You have no idea. Next time I'm taking you up on the offer to come with me."

As he held me tightly for a few beats, I spotted Zach's truck parked at an odd angle in our driveway.

As if I'd summoned the man, he appeared in front of me a moment later. "Hey," he said. I was still processing the fact that he was there, in front of me. My stupid heart leapt into my stupid throat as I drank in the sight of him. "I need to talk to you," he blurted.

No *how are you*, no *I've missed you*, just another demand. The old me would have jumped at the opportunity, not caring about the delivery system. But I'd spent the better part of a week reliving that moment in his motel room where I'd said *everything* and he'd said nothing. I'd once again laid my soul open to him and he'd done nothing but dismiss me as if I were nothing but an annoying bug to be squashed under his foot. In that time he hadn't bothered to call or text. But *now* he wanted to talk?

"I don't think so," I murmured. I turned away from him with the intent of seeking out the safety of my house.

"Lucky!" Zach bit out, clearly frustrated. Cal had moved off to the side and several people milling around us were discreetly trying to watch the show as they sipped their drinks.

I stopped and turned, then made my way back to him. "You really want to do this here?" I asked angrily. "It's a small town, Zach. You sneeze and people at the hardware store say 'God bless you.' I said what I needed to say to you and you had every chance to respond." I lowered my voice and added, "Don't worry, I didn't tell a single soul about us, so you're in the clear. Walk away. It's what you're good at." I sighed when I considered the harshness of my jab. "Just go, Zach. I'll make sure people only thought you were drunk or something."

I turned on my heel so I could make my escape before bursting into tears but came to a dead stop when I heard a familiar voice behind me shout, "Lucky Reed!"

I turned to see Zach climbing on top of one of the picnic tables nearby.

"What the hell?" I said to no one in particular.

"Lucky," he continued, loudly enough for the entire world to hear him. "I have something to say to you."

I turned around, looking at everyone who'd gathered for my family's annual Fourth of July party. Everyone had stopped what they were doing to stare at the gruff Army Ranger standing above them on the table.

But the Ranger was only looking at me.

The sun shone down on him like a warm spotlight, illuminating the overgrowth of stubble and the bags under his eyes. I resisted the urge to go to him and wrap my arms around him.

But it wasn't my place. He'd made that clear.

"Lucky," he said again, this time his voice cracking. He cleared his throat. "A few years ago I told you I was sick of you always being right there. I..." He looked around as if realizing just how many people were there to witness my humiliation.

My face burned as I remembered the night of the Christmas party when I'd thrown myself at him. I felt Cal shift forward as if to say something, but I held out my hand to stop him. If anyone was going to defend me, it was me.

But before I could say anything, Zach continued.

"I lied to you," he said, meeting my eyes again. They were so full of anguish and sorrow, I thought my heart would fall right out of my chest. "I was never, ever sick of you being right there. From the moment we met, you brought this light into my life that I thought had been burned out forever. I wanted what you were offering me that night. I wanted it so damn bad."

He rubbed his hands over his face before looking at me again. "Fuck, I don't know how to do this," he admitted. Then he looked around at all the people, noticed the kids and said, "Sorry kids, don't say bad words because it's... bad."

I felt my heart explode when Zach looked at me helplessly. I found myself walking toward him, not really noticing as people parted like the Red Sea for me. When I went to step up onto the picnic table, Zach reached a hand down to help me.

"You're doing pretty good," I said with a wet laugh. "I'll put money in the swear jar for you."

Zach laughed and relaxed considerably. He was holding one of my hands in his while he used the other to cup my cheek. "I've missed you so much," he said softly.

"Me too," I agreed with a nod. The people around us faded to the background as Zach caressed my face.

"Lucky, sweetheart, you're the best thing that's ever happened to me, and I've been so stupid. So selfish. I took the gift of your love, of your patience and I... I don't deserve you," he said softly. "But I want you so much. So much." He took a deep breath and stood up straighter, reaching back to pull something out of his back pocket. When he brought his hand back around, he dangled something green above his head.

Someone said, "Is that mistletoe?" and someone else asked, "Where the hell did he get mistletoe in July?"

I stepped closer, wondering if all of this was really happening.

"Lucky," he continued. "I love you. So much." He dropped his eyes briefly and studied his shoes. "I *do* trust you. With my heart, with my soul, with every part of me." He raised his eyes. "I'm sorry if I ever made you doubt that. I will always fight for us. If you still want—"

"I do," I cut in and pushed into his arms. When I pulled him down for a kiss, he came easily and then his mouth was on mine.

Zach put his arms around me so he could give me a proper kiss. The kind that left me breathless by the time he released me. He tipped his forehead against mine. "I love you," he whispered.

"Love you," I returned, my voice cracking a little as I tried to blink back tears. A commotion coming from around the table soon got our attention.

"Mom! Mom, what are you doing?" I heard Lolly's boyfriend exclaim. She was halfway up on the picnic table with us.

"WHAT?" she yelled to her son. The man and Aunt Lolly went to grab the woman before she could hurt herself.

"WHAT ARE YOU DOING?" he repeated. "THEY'RE MAKING UP!"

"I'M GETTING IN LINE. THE BIG ONE HAS MISTLETOE!"

"WANDA, THE MISTLETOE IS SO HE CAN KISS LUCKY. *ONLY* LUCKY!"

Wanda looked beyond disappointed as she allowed Aunt Lolly and her son to help her down to the ground.

"Hold that thought, baby," Zach said, then he gave me a quick kiss. I then watched my delicious Army Ranger hero climb off the table, hold the mistletoe over his head, and give Wanda a peck on her cheek before handing the mistletoe to her with a grin.

Several old ladies as well as a few younger ones were crowding the table and yelling things like, "Me next!" and "Get in line!" I began laughing as Wanda cradled the mistletoe protectively against her chest and told the women around her to "get in line."

"Uh, Lucky," Zach said as he eyed the growing crowd.

"Welcome to Haven, Zach," I said with a chuckle.

"Help me," he implored as he gripped my hand.

I opened my mouth to tell the crowd to keep their lips to themselves when I spotted my fathers standing near the grill. Well, Bennett was standing while Xander was sitting, but neither man looked too pleased.

"Um, okay, so here's the thing," I said to Zach. "It's either them," I explained as I motioned to the rambunctious crowd waiting to kiss him. "Or it's them." I nodded in the direction of my parents. Zach tensed and then looked back and forth between the crowd and the parental units. Then he looked at me.

"Got any Chapstick?"

CHAPTER 35

ZACH

"You okay there, son?" Bennett asked me for the second time in less than five minutes.

I instantly stilled in my seat and nodded my head. "Yes…"

Hell, was I supposed to call him Sir? Or Mr. Reed? Jesus, the man was my age.

"I'm fine," I finished lamely as I glanced at Lucky. Despite the grilling I knew was coming, I couldn't help but smile as I took in his heated cheeks and bright eyes when his gaze met mine. We were holding hands beneath the kitchen table.

I snapped to attention when Xander cleared his throat but I didn't release Lucky's hand. I didn't care if his fathers knew what we were doing beneath the table—I'd be damned if I let go of Lucky after only just getting him back.

I found myself looking at Lucky again. He was mine. Really mine. I still couldn't believe he'd given me a second chance.

But despite the chaos of what had transpired after my very public admission, I'd still been forced to face the music when Xander and Bennett had caught my attention and had both jerked their heads in the direction of the house. I hadn't hesitated to take Lucky's hand when I'd followed them, but much of the self-confidence I'd tried to build up as we'd walked had started to fail me the second we'd sat down at the kitchen table. I'd felt like the proverbial kid getting caught with his hand in the cookie jar, but when I'd forced myself to try and release Lucky's hand, he'd been the one unwilling to let go. That, in itself, had been the boost I'd needed.

Still, I was facing off against two men I respected the hell out of. And I sure as shit didn't want to have a strained relationship with my boyfriend's parents...

I sucked in a breath.

Oh god, I had a boyfriend.

Beautiful, sweet, strong, selfless Lucky was my *boyfriend*.

I was thirty-something and for the first time I could say I was in a real relationship. Not the toxic, one-sided kind, but the real deal.

"For god's sake," Bennett muttered. I realized I'd gotten sidetracked again and was staring at Lucky like a heartsick fool.

"Okay, clearly you have it bad for our son," Xander said as he covered his husband's hand with his own. "So we'll keep this simple." He ticked off his fingers as he spoke. "First off, when did all this start?" he asked, his eyes narrowing. "And second, what makes you think you deserve someone as amazing as our boy?"

"Dad," Lucky began, but I silenced him with a quick squeeze of my hand. The things Xander and Bennett needed to hear were things they needed to hear from *me*.

I understood the first question. They wanted to make sure I hadn't acted inappropriately with their underage son all those years ago when we'd first met. "Nothing happened until this summer," I clarified. "But I'll admit that things started to change for me a few years ago when I started to see Lucky as less of a kid and more of a man." I found myself watching Lucky as I spoke. "It scared me," I admitted. "Not because of you guys or Jake or any of that, but because..."

"Because why?" Bennett asked softly.

"Because no one ever wanted me just for me before," I admitted. "But I knew he did. I know he still does," I murmured.

Lucky nodded slightly as he held my gaze. I found myself pulling our joined hands out from beneath the table. I pressed my lips against his knuckles. "And as for your second question about deserving him..." I fell silent for a moment as I studied the man next to me. "I might not deserve him today or tomorrow, but I promise you, I will be worthy of him someday. Even if it takes the rest of my life to prove it, I'll never let him regret loving me."

Lucky's eyes looked wet as he let out this soft laugh and then he was leaning in to brush his mouth over mine. Not surprisingly, my heart began pounding harder in my chest when he told me once again that he loved me.

When we separated, Lucky looked at his fathers. "I'm sorry I kept something else secret—"

"I asked Lucky not to—" I began to say, but then Lucky softly said my name and when I looked at him, he shook his head. I nodded and fell silent. As much as I hated the idea of Lucky taking the blame for my behavior, I knew there were things his fathers needed to hear from *him* too.

"I knew when I first met Zach all those years ago that he was it for me." He looked at Bennett. "Just like you and Dad knew when you were kids."

Xander and Bennett shared a glance and then their fingers laced together, much like mine and Lucky's.

"But never in a million years did I think I'd live up to my name... that I'd get lucky twice," he whispered. "First with you guys making me part of a family I'd always dreamed about"—Lucky's eyes shifted to me—"and second with bringing my soulmate back into my life when I was sure I'd lost him for good." Lucky squeezed my hand but moved his eyes to his dads. "I had the courage to take a chance on Zach because I watched you two take that chance with each other when fate brought you together again. And just like you, I finally found the place I was always meant to be."

I forgot all about Xander and Bennett as something inside of me that had been knotted up for so much of my life finally seemed to loosen and then give way altogether. In its place was a sense of peace that I hadn't felt for a really long time, and all I could do was sit there and stare at Lucky as I tried to process the new sensation. My ears only perked up when I heard Bennett say the word "rules."

"Until there's a ring on his finger, it's separate bedrooms when you come to visit—"

"What?" Lucky exclaimed while Xander said, "Babe, seriously? That is some heteronormative bullshit. You worried about unwanted pregnancy?"

I found myself sitting back in my seat as Bennett, Xander, and Lucky began negotiating all the ground rules Bennett was insisting on. I figured I'd let my man handle this particular argument, because I'd already learned one really important thing from Lucky about rules.

They were meant to be broken.

EPILOGUE

ZACH

Minna's eyes narrowed at me as she shoved a cardboard box into my arms. "Don't hurt him."

I nodded and chose not to point out that she'd said some variation of that at least a dozen times since July. "Yes, ma'am. Where do you want this one?"

"It's Leah's sex toys; shove it in the closet in our bedroom for now." She turned back to head outside for another load as I stared at her back and tried to forget the words that had just come out of her mouth.

Familiar laughter came from the back of the small rental house. "Your face," Lucky said with a snort. "I wish I had my phone to get a picture."

"Mpfh." I double-timed it back to the ladies' bedroom and dumped the box in the closet with a little prayer I'd never see it again.

When I walked back out to the living room muttering about how I'd never imagined myself living with a bunch of college students again, I spotted Lucky leaning over to get some cold bottles of water out of a cooler on the floor. His sweat-dampened T-shirt rode up, exposing the dimples over his ass. Dimples I'd pressed my tongue into early that morning at the hotel in Billings. I could still taste his sweet skin on my tongue.

I reached down to adjust myself as he stood and offered me one of the waters.

"Why are you looking at me like you want to eat me?" he asked with a crooked grin.

"I want to eat you," I admitted with a straight face before downing half of the water.

"Gross," Minna said, moving past me with a full trash bag in her arms. "I think we need to set some ground rules about sex in the house."

I put the cap back on the bottle and pointed it at her. "Says the woman who literally tried to do something called the Sexy Spider in the back of my truck last night."

She tossed the bag down and lifted her hands in defense. "Hey, that wasn't the house. And Leah was all sleepy and shit. How was I supposed to resist her?"

"Mpfh." I huffed again, reaching for Lucky. "Maybe we should try the Sexy Spider later. Christen our room the Minna and Leah way."

Leah walked in with a giant pizza box. "You have two hundred percent too few vaginas for that move. But we could show you the Bottle Rocket if you want. I learned it from my high school boyfriend. We'd need some extra batteries though."

Min's eyes heated. "Ohh, the Bottle Rocket…"

"No," I snapped, pointing the bottle at her again and pulling Lucky against my front so I could feel that sweet skin of his lower back. "We're not doing this." I leaned in and took a sniff of Lucky's sweaty neck before running my tongue up his throat to taste the salt there.

Lucky's entire body shuddered against me. "Maybe… maybe they know some stuff… that… that we…" My kisses and nibbles distracted him enough that by the time I nosed my way down into the neckband of his T-shirt, he was asking, "Wha—?"

"Bedroom," I said. "Now."

Before he could answer, I threw him over my shoulder and strode back toward the door to our room. The girls hooted and hollered before Leah called out a reminder that Tag and his wife were expected soon to take us out to dinner.

"Tell them we'll meet them at the restaurant," I called over my shoulder.

"But I thought you were going to talk to him about a full-time job," Min said with a laugh.

"He already got it," Lucky called back. "Dinner's just to celebrate Montana's newest SAR expert."

I swatted him on the butt before squeezing it. He had the best ass.

"One day that's going to be you, you know," I reminded him. After kicking the bedroom door closed behind us, I set him down and put my hands on his shoulders. "One more year."

His face was open and bright, completely devoid of stress. It was enough to bring back the bubbly feeling I always felt around him.

"One more year until we help Chaska expand, you mean," he said.

I ran my fingers through his sun-streaked hair. We'd spent hours hiking and exploring around the mountains near Haven before it had been time to return to Missoula for Lucky's senior year.

"Or retire. His other daughter just told him she's pregnant. Pretty soon, the man's going to be too busy babysitting grandkids to fly his bird." I leaned in and kissed his full lips. "Haven's Helos," I said against his mouth. "What do you think?"

Lucky kissed me again, deeper. He took his time teasing me with his tongue until I'd forgotten what we'd been talking about.

"We have all year to decide," he said. "In the meantime, I need to take a shower if we're meeting your boss and his wife for dinner."

He tried to pull away to head to the shower, but I held him tight. "You know he's going to offer you as much part-time work as you want as long as we're still here in Missoula, right?"

Lucky's face softened. "Will it mean I get to work with you?"

"Sometimes. But it won't be as steady as working for the ambulance service was," I reminded him.

"But I'll get to rescue people from a helicopter." His grin grew wider. "With my hot pilot boyfriend."

I felt my face heat up. "You're the hot boyfriend," I muttered. "I'm the—"

Lucky leaned in and kissed the self-deprecating words right out of my mouth. "None of that broken Army Ranger bullshit. That's the past. This right here?" he asked, looking around at the combination of our things stacked around the bedroom. My old combat boots tumbled out of an open box onto the stuff sack holding Lucky's favorite two-man tent—a tent I planned to make plenty of memories in with him. He looked back at me. "This is our future."

"Okay, let's go shower," I grumbled since I knew if we didn't, I'd never get us out of there.

Lucky leaned into me, his eyes on the bed.

"Can we... can we do something first?" he asked. His arms were around my waist and he had his head pressed to my shoulder.

"I think we can multi-task in the shower," I suggested before I leaned down and kissed him. Lucky smiled against my mouth but kissed me back anyway.

"No, I was... I was wondering if we could just lie down for a few minutes."

There was a softness in his voice that told me his request had some kind of meaning for him.

I took his hand and led him to the bed. Once we were lying on the covers, Lucky put his arm around my waist and laid his head on my chest. He was uncharacteristically quiet but there was such a look of contentment on his face that I didn't dare disturb him. I followed his gaze and saw he was looking at our pile of outdoor gear that we'd stashed in the corner. Light filtered across the bed and cast soft shadows all around us as the sun began to fall.

"I dreamed this," Lucky said after a long pause, then he snuggled deeper into me.

"When?" I asked in surprise.

But Lucky just shook his head and murmured, "Doesn't matter. I'm just so glad it came true." He sounded so relieved that I found myself dropping a kiss to his temple.

A sense of absolute rightness went through me as I ran my fingers through Lucky's soft hair. We ended up lying there for several moments, and I was seriously considering sending Tag a message that we weren't going to make it, but Lucky chose that moment to shift his weight so his upper body was still sprawled over mine and he was looking me in the eye.

"Everything okay?" I asked as I pushed a stray lock of hair from his temple.

His smile was soft and serene.

"It's perfect," he responded. He turned his head and whispered those same words again. I glanced one last time around the room, our room, before letting my eyes close as Lucky's weight surrounded me like the softest of blankets.

He was absolutely right.

It was perfect.

AFTERWORD

Dear Reader,

We hope you enjoyed Lucky and Zach's story! If you've missed Book 1, please go back and check out *Lost and Found* to read how Bennett and Xander found their second chance and wound up pulling Lucky along for the ride.

As independent authors, we are always grateful for feedback so if you have the time and desire, please leave a review, good or bad, so we can continue to find out what our readers like and don't like. You can also send us feedback via email at skllbooks@gmail.com

Find more information about Sloane Kennedy at www.SloaneKennedy.com and more information about Lucy Lennox at www.LucyLennox.com.

Crossover Books with Lucy Lennox

Made Mine: A Protectors/Made Marian Crossover (M/M)

The following titles are available in audiobook format with more on the way:

Locked in Silence

Sanctuary Found

The Truth Within

Absolution

Salvation

Retribution

Logan's Need

Redeeming Rafe

Saving Ren

Freeing Zane

Forsaken

Vengeance

Finding Home

Finding Trust

Finding Peace

Four Ever

Lost and Found

Safe and Sound

Body and Soul

Made Mine

ALSO BY LUCY LENNOX

Made Marian Series:

Borrowing Blue

Taming Teddy

Jumping Jude

Grounding Griffin

Moving Maverick

Delivering Dante

A Very Marian Christmas

Made Marian Shorts

Made Mine - Crossover with Sloane Kennedy's Protectors series

Hay: A Made Marian Short

Made Marian Mixtape

Forever Wilde Series:

Facing West

Felix and the Prince

Wilde Fire

Hudson's Luck

Flirt: A Forever Wilde Short

His Saint

Wilde Love

King Me

Twist of Fate Series (with Sloane Kennedy):

Lost and Found

Safe and Sound

Body and Soul

Above and Beyond

After Oscar Series (with Molly Maddox):

IRL: In Real Life

LOL: Laugh Out Loud

Standalones:

Hot Ride (short story)

Inn Love (novella)

Free Short Stories available at www.LucyLennox.com.

Also be sure to check out audio versions here.

Made in United States
Cleveland, OH
12 April 2025